NOT IN MY FATHER'S FOOTSTEPS

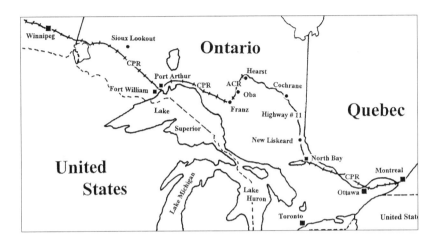

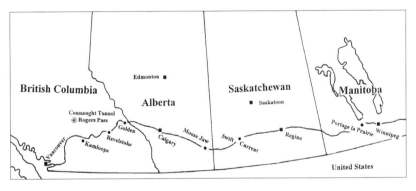

MARTY AND TAUNO'S JOURNEY

SPAIN

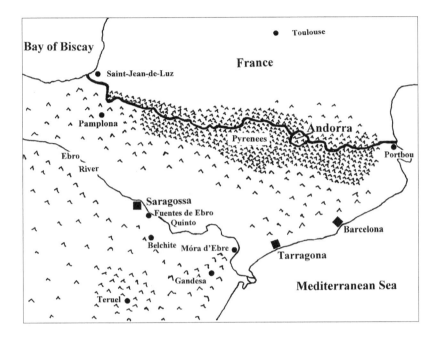

THE PYRENEES AND EBRO RIVER BASIN

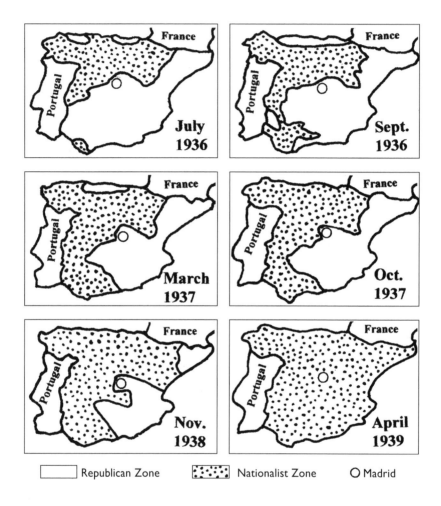

Republican Zone	Nationalist Zone	O Madrid

SPANISH CIVIL WAR 1936–1939

NOT IN
MY FATHER'S
FOOTSTEPS

A NOVEL

TERRENCE RUNDLE WEST

GSPH

GENERAL STORE PUBLISHING HOUSE
499 O'Brien Road, Box 415
Renfrew, Ontario, Canada K7V 4A6
Telephone 1.613.432.7697 or 1.800.465.6072
www.gsph.com

ISBN 978-1-926962-25-2

Copyright © 2011 Terrence Rundle West

Cover design: Virginia West
Book design and compostion: Magdalene Carson
Printed by Custom Printers of Renfrew Ltd., Renfrew, Ontario
Printed and bound in Canada

Library and Archives Canada Cataloguing in Publication
West, Terrence Rundle
Not in my father's footsteps / Terrence Rundle West.
ISBN 978-1-926962-25-2
I. Title.
PS8645.E78N68 2011   C813'.6   C2011-906299-2

In memory of my parents, Harvey and Gertrude,
whose quiet generosity during the Great Depression
kept families together and children from going hungry.

Acknowledgements

JUST AS IT TAKES A VILLAGE TO RAISE A CHILD, so it takes a host of friends and family to complete a novel. I am extremely grateful to Ernie Bies, Frank Pellow, Eliane Herz-Fischler, my sister Grace West, my daughter Virginia West, and my loving wife, Peggy, for their encouragement and insightful suggestions, and for ploughing through drafts one and two. My thanks, also, to the linguists behind this publication: Fred Leroux, who once again corrected my French; Rosita Del Rio, for the Spanish; Lucie Poliquin and her friend in Madrid, Spain, Maria Gloria Andrade, who provided the Basque; Stanley Anchel and Lila Nathans, for their assistance with the Yiddish and the Yiddish-English sentence structure; and Fran and Tom McSwiggan, for providing choice Irish expressions.

I'm indebted, as well, to several people who advised me along the way: Jules Paivio, Spanish Civil War vet, who invited me into his home and shared his experiences in that terrible conflict; Drs. Joseph Kozar and Andrew Samis, who steered me through the medical situations that arise in the story; Henriette (Chevrier) Jones for her explanation of hospital culture in the 1930s; Phillip Teitlebaum, who gave me a glimpse of the life of a Jewish boy in the Montreal of the 1930s; Roger Herz-Fischler, who counselled me on Jewish practices; Antonio Cazorla-Sanchez, Associate Professor of History at Trent University, who steered me to information on the war tours to Nationalist Spain conducted during the Civil War; Bill Waiser of the Department of History, University of Saskatchewan, and author of *All Hell Can't Stop Us*, the definitive account of the On-to-Ottawa Trek, for his advice and comments; Don Banks and Anne Siska for information on hobo jungles in North Bay and Port Arthur. Lastly, I wish to thank Susan Code McDougall, my patient, wise editor, who counselled me on where to expand, where to retreat, and how to get the most out of a scene.

Preface

WHEN I SET OUT TO WRITE THIS NOVEL, my intention was to set it around two Canadians caught up in the Spanish Civil War (1936–39). This, I reasoned, would permit me to explore the role played by Canadians in that conflict. But the more I got into the research, the greater my compulsion to understand the forces that had compelled over 1,500 of my countrymen to risk life and limb to combat fascism in a foreign land. And risk their lives they did—more than 400 never made it home, and those who managed to return were shunned by the government. So why did they go? In order to get to the root of this, I was compelled to take the research back as far as 1933. As a consequence, only the last third of the story takes place in Spain. One thing did not change, however—the bulk of the secondary characters, as well as all the events they encounter in Canada and Spain, remain historically accurate. Only the primary characters are fictitious.

Those interested in exploring in greater depth the events in this book may want to consult the bibliography, maps, and tables found at the back.

PART ONE

Montreal, Quebec
March 1939

Chapter One

—————

March 1939
Montreal

"ONE TO GO," ALICE MOUTHED to Rita as they finished the last bed on the ward and headed for room 691, the semi-private with the mysterious patient. The girls were careful not to run, lest Sister Yolande spy them from her perch at the nursing station and tack on more duties. It'd been a shift from hell. Twelve hours of bedpan steaming, patient washing, and bed carbolizing. And all under the watchful eye of the meanest supervisor in L'Hôtel-Dieu de Montréal. But at last, with Sister glued to her stool at the far end of the ward, they might be able to cut a few corners; maybe even get to sit down to dinner with their first-year classmates for a change.

Ordinarily there'd be two patients in room 691, but "John Doe's" mean streak had necessitated the evacuation of his roommate. He'd been there two weeks, but they still knew no more about him than when he came in. The girls' best guess put him down to a wannabe soldier, which, judging from the grenades he'd launched—plates, cutlery, catheter—could be close to the mark. Not that it was all bad; he'd calmed down lately and wasn't incontinent like many of the old gaffers on the ward.

The Franciscan priest looked up as the girls swished their blue-cotton uniforms into the room. "Evening, Father," they said in unison, nodding their snowy caps and trying to hide their annoyance. The priest sat slouched in a chair at the end of John Doe's bed, wiping his cataract-plagued eyes with a dirty handkerchief. Visions of shortcuts began to evaporate. There'd be no skipping the sponge bath or bed change tonight, unless they could distract him. Why couldn't he be on his knees in the chapel, or down in the staff room soaking up the news out of Europe with the other off-duty workers? These were exciting times. The Third Reich was flexing its muscles. Germany was blaming the Czechs for unspeakable atrocities and was in the process of soaking up Bohemia and other places no one had ever heard of. Normally, few would care about Hitler taking over Czechoslovakia, but the broadcasts claimed he was hungry for more. The Brits and French were getting antsy, and Canada, once again, seemed ready to give its customary, "Aye, ready, aye," response to the Mother Country. It was beginning to look like the Great War all over again.

In view of all the drama on the world stage, what could "mystery man" possibly have for the priest that could trump that? Sure, once they'd found him a bed big enough to fit his tall frame, the screaming meemies had stopped long enough to let them cut his blond hair and shave him. He was even beginning to look almost attractive, especially with the sores on his face healing. Once, when he'd been sleeping, Alice had gone so far as admitting that, with some meat on him, she might be up to smuggling him into the residence for a while. But other than the wild eyes and the occasional tantrum, there was still no communication. Nor visitors, save the good Father. For all Rita knew, he could be a German. Maybe even a spy. Perhaps the poor old cleric was a secret government operative sent to keep tabs on him. Rita smiled inwardly. Fantasizing passed the time, even though it was nonsense, because John Doe, in spite of his youth, had been admitted in the same condition as the other burnt-out winos—running sores, bleeding gums, protruding ribs, repugnant odour, and socks so fused to his feet that they had to be removed in the OR. No, there was no Nazi intelligence ring for the aging Franciscan to unravel here, just a conversion in the offing; perhaps a last notch on his belt.

Rita wagged a finger at John Doe. "No funny business," she mumbled. "It's been a long shift." Together the young nurses swung the patient's legs over the edge of the bed and worked him onto the chair. In his emaciated state, one of them could have handled him alone, but having seen his violent side, they were taking no risks. Kicking a chamber pot on the floor had been bad enough; plastering the crucifix on the wall with rice pudding made him certifiable. It had been days since the last outburst, but the lingering hint of chloroxylenol from the Dettol, splashed around in cleanups, still bit into the tear ducts. Today, if he made one false move, they'd be on him, like Joe Louis on Max Schmeling.

The priest's effectiveness was beginning to trouble the girls. In most Catholic hospitals, having a cleric about soothed uncooperative patients. But this one's presence seemed to coincide with John Doe's outbursts. Alice wondered if she had detected a cause and effect.

"The radio's set up for the news in the staff room, Father," Rita said. "Wouldn't you like to get the latest out of Europe?"

The priest clenched his teeth. "It's all bad."

Alice moved around to the far side of the bed, her large backside blocking the cleric's view. "What do you get out of these visits, Father?" she asked. "It's not as if he talks or anything." The girls made eye contact. Decision time. Both linen and patient were passable; no visible stains. If they could keep the good Father occupied, they might get away with some minor sheet-tucking and pillow-fluffing.

"Wrong," the priest replied, stretching his legs in front of him and folding his hands in his lap. "He comes to life when I recite the rosary. I see it on his face."

Alice rolled her eyes, then like a baseball catcher signalling the pitcher, moved her hands at her waist. Rita nodded. A minor straightening was the call. They'd be dining with their classmates tonight.

"Could be anger," Alice said. "You sure he's even Catholic?"

"Has he eaten today?" the priest asked.

The girls bobbed to each other across the bed as they snapped the wrinkles out of the sheets. "Didn't notice," Rita replied. "No food on the walls. That much I know."

The priest stared at the patient, as if expecting confirmation, but John Doe's eyes were locked onto the crucifix. "Maybe with strength he'll find his tongue," he said.

"And probably cut us up when he does," Alice replied, helping Rita get him back into bed. "Some people are born ingrates." She began humming "Red River Valley." Doe raised his eyebrows.

"Oh, look!" Rita said. "Maybe he's a cowboy. He seems to know that one."

Alice stopped the music. "Figures," she said, chuckling in a low voice. "It's an old hobo song. Bet he picked it up in some jungle near a railway track."

The priest shook his head, frowning and glancing at the door, as if wishing them on their way. The student nurses folded the top sheet under John Doe's chin. They had begun their escape when they were stopped by a mucousy cough, followed by a Humphrey Bogart whisper. "That song," he said, "the words I know have nothing to do with cowboys and everything to do with a valley called Jarama."

The cleric leapt to his feet. The student nurses turned at the door. John Doe hacked up phlegm, which he spat into the enamel bowl at his side. "My God!" Rita exclaimed. "It speaks! Maybe now we'll find out.—"

The priest's hand came up for silence. His eyes locked onto John Doe. The patient swiped at the spittle on his chin and wiped it on the bedclothes. "Ever been to Spain, priest?" he groaned.

A beatific smile spread across the priest's face. "What? No!" he stammered. "Never been there myself. But Father Blouin now, from the seminary, he served in Barcelona as a young man and he says—"

"You priests killed it."

The cleric's smile collapsed. "Killed what? Barcelona? You're confused. I've seen pictures of it in the *Messager St. Antoine*. It came through a bit of a bad spot, there, but still looked pretty good to me. That cathedral, what's it called?" He glanced up at the crucifix above the patient's head for assistance.

"La Sagrada Familia," John Doe snorted, struggling to pull himself up to a sitting position.

"Yes, that's the one . . . you've seen it? Incredible. Right?"

Doe's eyes rolled. "Too much stone to burn."

Excitedly, the priest approached, fumbling for words, as if terrified of a relapse into silence. "It's an uplifting story. They've been building it for forty years, you know, and it's still only partly completed, which isn't surprising given the civil war, but Father Blouin says that with common sense finally restored in Madrid, they'll be moving on it again, probably pretty soon, even if the costs are out of this earth because—"

"Mother of God!" Doe cut in. "Is that all you black robes think about? Money and the state of your property?" The priest dabbed at his eyes to hide a scowl. He turned, shooing the girls from the room with a flick of the hand. Doe continued. "How about a prayer for Spain and the vulgar crimes committed in her name?"

Father clasped his hands in front of him, his head bobbing slowly. "If you're referring to the viler transgressions of the civil war, I'm aware of them, and, yes, they say it was very bad. Not only did the Bolsheviks shoot priests, but," he turned to see that the nurses were gone, "nuns were despoiled and young girls forced into prostitution."

John Doe stared at him for a second then looked away. "Jesus Christ," he moaned, "you don't know shit."

The Franciscan stiffened as he exchanged his handkerchief for a rosary. "I admit, some of the details are fuzzy, but," his chin came up, "I am acquainted, albeit in general terms, with the horrors endured by the Church and all God-fearing Spaniards in that ghastly conflict."

"And exactly where would you have gleaned this insight, Father? That publication for clerics, *Messager St. Antoine*? Missives from the pope? One of Adrien Arcand's rags, perhaps?"

A hint of colour found its way to Latendresse's cheeks. "Other sources, too," he replied. "A series of articles come to mind. They appeared in the papers a couple of years back—accounts by a young Montrealer travelling with Franco's troops. Unfortunately, he disappeared; supposedly swallowed up by the Republicans. But, while he was still writing, he set the record straight on what was going on over there, I'll tell you."

John Doe's laugh might have echoed off the walls, if not for the protesting lungs that turned it into a coughing fit. "Those articles," he said, when he'd regained control, "you might want to cross-reference them."

The Franciscan glared at him. "You're entitled to your point of view, young man, and I to mine."

"Oh, I get it. Can't accept the word of a drunk, eh?"

"*Au contraire*. I trust anybody who gives me a convincing argument. 'Course, that requires civil conversation, a concept that appears to elude you."

"Convincing argument, my ass. I've yet to meet a priest who's a good listener. Why would you be an exception? You say conversation; I hear monologue."

The priest plunked himself on the chair beside the bed, absentmindedly wrapping the beads around his fist. "You surprise me, young man. For two weeks, I've watched you, but never figured you for a church-hater. Question is, why?"

"No, Father. The question is, why did you waste fourteen days praying over me? There must be other patients more willing to lap up the mumbo jumbo."

The priest stared at him for a long second. "No one's spiritual health goes unattended in this hospital," he responded flatly. "But the men in this wing are older and, frankly, goners. You've got your life in front of you." He leaned forward and proffered the hint of a smile. "I'll admit, though, the instant they brought you in, I figured you'd be a challenge."

"I bet."

The smile receded. "Don't you want to get back on your feet? Become a contributing member of society? Reconnect with family, perhaps?" John Doe shook his head. "There must be something I can do for you."

"Sparing me the intrusion will suffice. And no, I don't want to contribute to this society. Frankly, it sickens me."

Father sat back. "Sorry to hear that. I was hoping I'd be able to lend assistance."

"That's bullshit. Plain old curiosity has kept you hanging around. You and those young nurses. I take in every word. I'm the Hôtel-Dieu enigma. You're all dying to know what loathsome sin—greed, murder, sex—lies at the root of my downfall." He winked at the priest. "Titillated by the possibilities, aren't you?"

The Franciscan caressed the rosary with the palm of his other hand. "You're an alcoholic. You've been delusional. Maybe still are."

Doe came up on his elbows. "I *was* delusional when I went to Spain. Now I see crystal clear."

"You may think so, but—"

"Tell me, Father," Doe interrupted, "is it possible for a priest to concede that a Church, so wrong on Spain, might just be responsible for my present state?"

The priest kissed his rosary before replying. "I daresay you've seen some terrible things, my boy, but time and trauma do strange things to the imagination. Past wrongs, however slight, grow in magnitude. Become uncontrollable demons."

John Doe fell back on his pillows. "*Merde!*"

Father pursed his lips. "Which isn't to say that Mother Church never makes mistakes. Priests are human. If it makes any difference, I'd already concluded that the Church was somehow implicated in your problem."

"And just how had you arrived at that?"

The priest squared his shoulders. "From the *jugum Christi* you were wearing under your shirt the day they brought you in." The patient frowned. The cleric leaned forward. "The scapular. The Yoke of Christ."

Doe bolted up. "You have it?"

" 'Course it was in bad shape. But I recognized it immediately. What puzzles me is how a man in your condition came to be wearing such a holy symbol. Are you a member of a religious order? Defrocked, perhaps?"

"Not on your life!"

"I didn't think so. These days few young clerics can be bothered with the chaffing and incessant straightening of the scapular."

"You get used to it."

"Which brings us back to why you'd have a scapular. Perhaps you stole it and wear it as some sort of sick joke. Is it possible you lifted it from the dead body of a Spanish priest? Say, as a trophy?"

An orderly entered carrying a tray. When he left, Father rose and cut the meat on the plate. He then straightened the pillows so the patient could sit up. When it looked like he was about to feed him, John Doe grabbed the fork and speared a piece of food. "Where's the scapular now?"

"Cleaned and safe at the seminary."

"Have you told anyone?" The priest shook his head. John Doe pushed the food around carefully in his mouth to avoid the cankers. He chewed then swallowed with effort. "Scapulars aren't that unusual," he said.

"Ones with cardinal markings are."

"Am I getting it back?"

"Depends."

"I came by it honestly."

"It'll take more than that."

John Doe put the fork down. His eyes wandered to the crucifix on the wall. "If we were to talk, it wouldn't be under that cross dangling up there."

Latendresse rose and removed it, smiling at the shadowed imprint left behind on the beige wall. His eyes then flicked momentarily to the portrait over the bed, a picture the patient had yet to notice. In it, a radiant, haloed, but troubled Jesus, clothed in fluttering white robes, ascended into heaven. The priest smiled, extending his hand. "Father Latendresse," he said. "Pierre, if you prefer."

The patient hesitated before accepting. "Dollard," he replied.

"Doll-aard . . . ?" Latendresse responded, stretching out the last syllable as he fished for a second name.

"Just Dollard for now."

The priest nodded, his gaze falling on the battered glasses case on the bedside table. It had lain there untouched for days. His hand went out to pick it up, but something in Dollard's face made him stop. The fabric on the case had been ripped and worn down to the metal. To one side of the centre was a small hole, large enough to insert a little finger. Latendresse shuddered.

PART TWO

Montreal, Quebec, 1933

Chapter Two

Saturday, May 20, 1933
Montreal

"SO, DOLLARD, HAVE YOU DECIDED?" Yvon shouted from the back seat.

Dollard clutched the wheel with his huge hands, wondering if his friend had somehow read his mind and knew he was scheming for a way to steer the guys into something tamer than their usual Saturday-night, sin-bin fix. With Shannon now in his life, he had good reason for avoiding the whores that tended to top these outings. Not that a little nooky wouldn't hit the spot, but if he was going to wean himself from the fleshpots, he had to start sometime. However, his problem was twofold: how to find the strength and save face at the same time. Treat it like a test, he'd told himself, the way an alcoholic puts whisky in his path for the satisfaction of overcoming the urge.

"Decided what?" Dollard replied, looking at Yvon in the rear-view mirror. He flicked his high beams at an oncoming car that had failed to dim.

"Your Classics dissertation, stupid. Have you picked a topic?"

Dollard relaxed inwardly. Their turn off Côte Ste. Catherine onto Laurier loomed ahead. He raced for it, revving the engine and slamming the car into third gear without using the clutch. It was a trick he'd learned from the movies. "Think I'll be doing it on Epicurus," he said. The car went into the turn, fishtailing as the lower gear engaged. In the passenger's seat, Big André's arm found the dashboard. In the rear, Marcel and Yvon gripped the strap above the doors. Abe, stuck in the middle, planted both hands on the back of the front seat. The sound of screeching rubber echoed off storefronts as they rounded the corner. An older couple on the sidewalk leapt for the protection of a doorway. The boys howled at the reaction.

Marcel rolled down the window. "What's that brown stuff running down your leg?" he shouted to the couple as they sped by.

Dollard grinned. In the rear-view mirror, he could see the man shaking his fist. "Watch this," he said, braking hard. The car slid to a halt. Heads twisted to catch the man's reaction. Another knee slapper. The missus had grabbed her husband's arm and was propelling him up the street. Dollard sped up, suddenly remembering he was driving the company car with *L'imprimerie Desjardins* emblazoned on the front doors.

He hoped the old fogies hadn't noticed. The last thing he needed was another angry call to his old man's printing company. Why couldn't one of the others drive for a change? Why was it always left to him? Yvon, André, and Marcel were all good Outremont stock. Depression or not, their fathers had cars. Even Abe Agulnic's dad had one—a huge Packard with a chauffeur. People in the Square Mile had money, too. Lots of it. Too bad most of them were English. Abe was all right, though. Hebe or not, he spoke good French.

"I can't believe you're stupid enough to do Epicurus again," Yvon persisted, when they'd slowed. "Father Fortier checks up on his students, and the university's already got you on probation. Ten will get you twenty he'll be asking Father Grenier what you did last term. Then you'll be up the creek."

Dollard blew air through his lips. "Not a chance. We're talking hockey coach Grenier here. For him, the playoffs against Laval are more important than some inane Classics topic. Besides, I'm sick of that place. Time to join the world. Get a job. Do something meaningful."

Beside him, André sneered. "Dreaming again, Desjardins. There's a depression on, or haven't you heard? Best you could hope for is a job in one of your dad's printing shops."

Dollard pretended to gag. "*Crisse*! How depressing. It's all coming to me now," he chanted in his best bogeyman tone. "I see a black and white tiled room with a pedestal sink and rows and rows of printer fluid in jars. And there I am, D. Desjardins, aging lithographer, staring out over endless trays of typeset." He slapped his forehead with his hand.

"And your fingers are gnarled and stained," Abe joined in.

Dollard was about to say, "Just like a Jewish banker," but caught himself. " 'Course I'm not alone," he responded. "I'm on a bench with a bunch of other losers, probably you guys, and we're all dressed in white shirts and wearing metal armbands and little green visors." His jaw waggled in a throaty shudder.

Big André chortled. "Your old man would be happy," he said.

"You got that right. Three generations of Desjardins in the printing business. A dream come true. Shit! I think I'm going to puke."

Marcel leaned forward, flicking the back of Dollard's ear with a finger. "You forgot to mention l'abbé Groulx and Adrien Arcand hanging over your shoulder as you set type for *Le Miroir* or *Le Chameau*, or whatever they call their rags these days."

Dollard's chin came up. "It's *Le Patriote* this season. But the flavour hasn't changed." His voice went deep to mimic Arcand, his father's friend and most important customer. "Down with booze, broads, jazz, movies, the English, and those dirty, funny-hatted, money-grubbing, bagel-eating, communist—" André delivered a sharp elbow to his ribs. Dollard shot a glance at Abe in the rear-view mirror. André pulled a flask from the inner pocket of his sports jacket. The others stared straight ahead, swigging from the flask as it made the rounds.

Dollard knew his slip had killed the mood for the moment and was sorry, but they'd all made the same error at one time or other, so there was no need to be uppity. Besides, Abe was used to it. Jews had to be, otherwise they'd have up and left Montreal long ago. He smiled inwardly. His parents would kill him if they knew he was keeping company with a Yid. But having Abe around added spice, like going to bootleggers and peep shows, or playing Barbotte with the gamblers on Cypress Street. Besides, Abe wasn't what you'd call a real Semite. He was an Uptown Jew. Not at all like those Lowertown refugees with their push-carts, ringlets, and cold-water flats.

They were on St. Laurent now and headed south. Dollard wasn't surprised that the boys had shut up. Travelling through the heart of the ghetto seemed to be giving legs to his comment about Jews. That was all right with him. The silence was just what he needed to spring the suggestion he'd been working on. He cleared his throat. "Why don't we make it Connie's Inn tonight?"

The boys moaned. Beside him, André stiffened. "You're joking? Right?"

"Why not? You guys got something against jazz?"

André turned to stare at him. "Come on, Desjardins, it's flesh we're after. We can do Connie's tomorrow night." From the back seat came shouts of agreement. André pressed on. "Toots Henderson flashing her black tits at the Gayety Theatre's what we agreed on, wasn't it?"

Dollard shrugged. "That's what we did last time and the time before that. How about setting our sights a bit higher?"

"Jazz is going to do that?" André said.

"Damn right. It's good for the soul; puts you in the spirit of another man's culture. You can learn things."

André's face screwed up as he studied Dollard. "Jesus Christ, Desjardins! You been reading your catechism or something?" The boys in the back laughed.

"Piss off!"

As usual, the Gayety Theatre didn't disappoint. Foot-tapping patrons filled ashtrays as they leered through the haze at the new batch of black girls from the States parading their assets. B-girls chatted up the patrons, prodding them to order expensive cocktails. Harassed, scantily clad barmaids raced about with trayfuls of fresh drinks to plunk down, too busy to clear tables. As the evening wore on, the gin went down, and the noise went up. The boys stuck to beer but drank heavily. Within a couple of hours, their pedestal table had morphed into a forest of empty quart bottles. Dollard paced himself, but tried to hide it. A ruckus broke out nearby. The boys turned. A patron must have groped a waitress. Two bouncers were half dragging, half carrying him to the door.

André sized up the enforcers as they hustled the offender away. He leaned into Dollard. "You and I could take those assholes," he slurred.

Dollard ducked his head. "For Christ's sake, keep it down. No way are you getting me into a fight. I'm finished with that crap." Instantly, he regretted his tone. He smiled, but it was too late.

André rocked back and forth as he struggled to focus. "Wassa matter with you?" He waved his hand a few inches from Dollard's face. "All night you've been off on a cloud." Dollard leaned back in his chair. The other boys shut up, all ears. "Know what I think? That little Irish gold digger's got you pussy-whipped."

Dollard shook a fist at him. "You foul-mouthed son-of-a-bitch. One more crack like that and . . ."

André raised his hands. "Easy, man, easy," he said. Dollard took a long swallow of beer. The others did the same. "Christ, Desjardins, she does have her hooks into you, doesn't she? Do you realize what you're playing with? Bring that girl home, and your old man'll have you out on your ass in a wink." Dollard looked away, but André pressed on. "And who'd blame him? Guy's got a right to be pissed with a son going gaga over a girl barely up from the Griff." He leaned forward. "She's not one of us, Dollard, and never can be."

"So? Neither's Abe."

"You got the hots for him, too?" André cackled. "Wouldn't surprise me. You've been acting queer enough lately."

The boys laughed. Dollard jumped up, knocking over his chair. A bouncer made a beeline for the table. André struggled to his feet. "It's all right. It's all right," he repeated to the bouncer.

Dollard righted his chair and ordered another round of Black Horse. The bouncer hovered a few tables away. "Stay out of my affairs, André.

You don't hear me talking about your problems."

"Like what?"

"Drinking, for one." He hoped the other guys might pick up on their friend's weakness, but no one took the bait. André flinched, but let it slide.

"Fine. Dump on me if it makes you feel better, but it doesn't change a thing." He reached over, hiccupped, and put a hand on Dollard's shoulder, blinking to focus. "Here's what I figure. Friend to friend, okay? She's not putting out and you're frustrated. Solution?" Dollard stared at the Belgian stallion on his Black Horse beer bottle, but made no effort to interrupt. "Take her up to the cottage and plank her good and proper."

Dollard glared at him as he knew he should, but it was a solution he'd thought about himself. "Jesus Christ, you can be crude," he said.

André flopped back in his chair. "Do it and you'll discover she's just another girl; probably nice, but no better than any of ours and definitely not worth kissing away a fortune for." He stopped, his head swaying as he let the wisdom of his counsel sink in. "Got it?"

"If you guys knew her, you—"

"Sure, sure," André slurred, "introduce us sometime. In the meantime, we all get laid tonight, *as planned*. And that includes you, Desjardins. Soon as Toots finishes her act, we're off to Ontario Street." Grins blossomed around the table. Dollard examined his shoes. André poked him on the shoulder. "Think of it this way, Desjardins. If Little Miss Right is so special, aren't you saving her virtue by shagging the odd whore? Sort of doing it for her sake."

Dollard tipped his head to the ceiling as he polished off his beer. André had a point. Sating the hunger in his gut might be in her best interest. He tried to picture Shannon in his mind, but the image was no competition for the large breasts on the girl he'd last tasted, the one he'd dubbed, "Throaty Laugh." He shook his head. "Throaty" wouldn't go away. From the stage came a fanfare of music. The room fell silent. Toots was about to entertain.

As semi-regulars to 312 Ontario Street, the bouncer waved them into the lounge, where the girls leapt out of their chairs and began pawing them. Throaty was nowhere in sight. Disappointment washed over Dollard. That she was with someone else, probably some old guy, gave him the shivers. To his surprise, the urge to do it with anyone else wasn't there.

One by one, his friends made their selections and disappeared up the stairs. Dollard remained behind, wishing it were willpower and not happenstance holding him to his resolve to stay chaste. Two options presented themselves: wait for the others to return, and claim he'd finished fast, or take one of the girls upstairs just to talk. He was leaning toward waiting, when a waif appeared across the room. Dollard stopped short as she locked her Orphan-Annie eyes onto his. It crossed his mind that "Daddy Warbucks" might have left her behind while he tended to personal affairs upstairs with Throaty. She couldn't be working. Flustered by the swelling between his legs, he tried to break eye contact. She kept coming toward him. By the time she reached him, he knew for certain what she was all about, but his addled brain was in revolt. Decency championed rejection. The erection shilled for the opposite. His breathing grew shallow as she stopped in front of him. He opened his mouth, but closed it just as quickly. She put her small hand in his and turned for the stairs. His feet followed. Half way up they ran into Throaty coming down. She slowed and cast a disapproving eye. Dollard wasn't sure if it was for him, or the child stealing her regular.

By the time they entered the room, Dollard had rallied enough to trust his voice. It occurred to him to ask her age, but he feared the answer. "Where are you from?" he stammered instead. She ignored the question, moving to the washstand and pouring water from the pitcher into the large porcelain bowl. He watched her struggle with the heavy vessel and drop it back onto the stand with a thud. With her eyes no longer on him, he took her in. The frail arms and tiny frame were those of his little sister. Shame overcame him. Here was a youngster to be taken out for ice cream or given a go on the merry-go-round. Instead, there she stood lathering up a washcloth and motioning for him to get his pants off so she could wash his penis.

"What's your name?" he whispered.

"Desirée."

"Not that, your real name?"

She motioned him forward impatiently. He didn't budge. "Why is that important?" she said, finally.

"What are you doing here?" he mumbled. "Maybe this isn't such a good idea."

A look of terror swept over her. She threw the washcloth into the basin, dropped her robe, and lay down on the bed. The pose she struck was supposed to be alluring. Dollard looked, but didn't budge. His member faded. Tears welled up in her eyes. "Just because you don't do me," she stammered, "you still have to pay."

He picked up her robe, walked to the bed, and draped it over her. "Desirée. We don't have to do anything. I'll still pay."

"I'll get into trouble if they find out downstairs."

"No one has to know."

"You won't say anything? Promise?"

He seated himself on the bed. She sat up and pulled her legs into her body. "So, tell me," he said, "where are you from?"

"Trois Rivières."

"How the hell did you wind up here?"

She picked at a toenail. "Father lost his job at the mill and . . ." she began to sob. Dollard pulled her close and rocked her. She nestled in. For a long period, neither spoke. Suddenly, she stiffened, her head craning for a glimpse of the Big Ben on the bedside table. "Your time's almost up," she whispered.

Dollard reached for his wallet. "I'll pay for another . . . trip."

At the end of his second half hour, she reached for her robe. He looked away as she put it on. "Do they search you to see if you're holding anything back on them?" he asked. She nodded. "If I gave you some money, do you have a hiding place? It would be for your family." He handed over the last of his allowance—twenty-six dollars. She stared at it, eyes growing like she'd just unwrapped her first Christmas doll.

At the door, she tried to kiss him, but he turned and buzzed her on the cheek. "Do something for me," he said. "Don't come down until I leave with my friends."

"Will I see you again?" she asked.

Dollard shook his head. "No. I can't. I'm engaged." She tried to smile. A pang of guilt for the white lie washed through him. He wasn't engaged, but he'd just made a decision; by this time tomorrow he intended to be.

Out in the car, conversation was sparse. Not unusual, considering the waning effects of the alcohol and the solemn mood, bordering on remorse, that usually followed whorehouse rutting. This was the time in the evening that troubled Dollard most, because this was the time André could turn ugly at the slightest provocation.

Dollard drove Abe home first then turned north for Outremont. The silence in the car was a blessing. Revulsion, guilt, anger, and loathing swirled inside him. Revulsion and guilt for the unpardonable sin he'd almost committed; anger for a society that turned a blind eye to children forced into prostitution; loathing for the privileged upbringing that sheltered him from reality. One hour with Desirée had opened his eyes more than three years at university. She'd put a face to the tough times most people were experiencing. If there was comfort, it was in the thought that in a life of self-gratification, he might at last have done something honourable. Perhaps it was a start. If so, where would it take him? So far he'd failed to stand up to his father, break with his filthy habits, or work up the courage to marry the girl he loved. But if he did marry Shannon, was André right? Would he be disowned? If he was, how would they survive? His Classics education hardly equipped him to put bread on the table—not in these troubled economic times.

They were on St. Urbain approaching Duluth when three young men stepped onto the road. Lost in thought and still woozy from the beer, Dollard had failed to see the stop sign. "Look out!" Yvon screamed from the back. Dollard hit the brakes and the car squealed to a halt. For an instant, no one moved, until one of the pedestrians slapped the hood with the palm of his hand. "Asshole!" he shouted in English.

Instantly, André was out of the car. Dollard gasped. Two of the boys were wearing yarmulkes. "Fucking Yid!" André shouted.

"What did you call us?" The boys turned and began walking off at a hurried clip.

André caught up, kicking one of them in the backside. "Piss off back to Poland, you useless pieces of shit."

The biggest turned and swung. André ducked and caught him with a haymaker to the plexus. The boy went down like a poleaxed ox, clutching his stomach. His friends turned, kicking and screaming, but even without the help of Yvon and Marcel, who'd sprung from the car for a piece of the action, it was a mismatch. Dollard shot through the intersection and parked, but by the time he reached the melee it was over. An eerie stillness filled the air, punctuated by heavy panting and moans from the downed boys. André spat on them.

Dollard looked around. A spectator was hurrying up the street. "For Christ's sake, get back in the car," he yelled, pushing his friends in the direction of the company sedan. He was about to jump in himself when he caught a glimpse of the intruder approaching from the rear. Dollard watched him squint at the licence plate before reaching into his pocket and extracting what appeared to be a pistol. In six leaps, Dollard was on him, but the intruder raised his hands, exposing a glasses case.

Dollard pulled up short, as he sized him up. He was a bookworm type who couldn't have topped more than 140. Easy pickings for the six-foot, 180-pound hockey player. Still the man stood his ground, fumbling to extract his glasses. Behind them, the boys limped away, abandoning their Samaritan.

"Put on those glasses and I'll—"

"What? Beat me up like you did those boys?" Dollard was surprised by the intruder's French.

"You heard me! Put them away!"

"Sure, soon's as I get your licence number," he replied, unfolding the wire stems.

Dollard stepped closer, blocking his line of view. From across the intersection came the sound of car doors opening, the others getting out. "Stay in the car," Dollard ordered. The intruder stepped sideways, but at the same instant Dollard brought his hand down knocking the glasses to the sidewalk. "What the hell's the matter with you? Leave!" The intruder bent for the glasses. Dollard moved to block him, his foot coming down hard on the glasses. Dollard stepped back. Both men looked down.

"You've smashed my glasses. Jesus! Finals are coming up."

For a second, the two men sized each other up. "I'm sorry," Dollard said, finally, reaching for his wallet. When he saw it was empty, he shrugged and ran for the car.

<hr/>

Noon, Sunday, May 21, 1933
Montreal

DOLLARD'S HAND FOUND SHANNON'S as they exited the church and squinted into the noonday sun. An outsider might guess their smiles were for the white-frocked altar boys struggling with the heavy front doors. But an outsider would be wrong; their smiles were for each other. Out on the gravel pathway, parishioners basked in the spring sunshine, everyone seeming to talk at once. The men nodded and jested as they tugged at tweed caps. Wives raised their hands above their kerchiefs to shield their eyes as they spoke. Dollard held his fedora tight at his waist, lest people notice that it was a Borsilino and far beyond the reach of his fellow worshippers. His smile broadened at the aroma of incense clinging to the clothes and hair around him; a cleansing fragrance that would follow people down the walkway, out onto the street, and into kitchens and parlours. Kids darted back and forth through the crowd. They churned up gravel as they brushed past adults and sneaked up on friends. Grey-faced mothers, shoulders stooped, brows lined from the burden of making ends meet, barked commands in singsong voices to keep their broods in check. Dollard struggled to pick up snippets of conversation as they passed, desperate to improve his English for Shannon, but hampered by the musical lilt to the banter—brogue, she called it.

He could see why she was proud of her upstart Irish parish and their new church. Of course it lacked the towering steeples, or thundering bells, of his. Still, with its Celtic cross above the rough-cut stone walls, and its curious medieval tower, it wasn't without its charm. He wondered if she knew the full story of how Saint-Viateur parishioners, his family included, had petitioned the bishop to keep the Irish from crossing the line into French-Catholic Outremont. One day it would have to come out, along with a myriad other matters afflicting his conscience.

Had he been exiting his own church, he would have been banging people on the back and exchanging barbs with friends in loud shouts. Around him, people would have been cracking up at his jokes, as if they mattered. But in Shannon's presence, erhe felt no need to bellow. With her, he was a different person—comfortable, considerate, content. It was enough to be beside her, savouring her words, feeling the movement of her body as they strolled. He wished his mother could see him at these moments. But that would be awkward. Soon, maybe, when the right time came, he would find the courage to bring his girl home.

"Don't look so nervous," she said. "They won't eat you." She exchanged smiles with Father O'Rourke, who gestured to Dollard with his chin and popped his eyebrows up and down, *à la* Groucho Marx. Dollard considered answering her, but bit his tongue, fearful that on hearing broken English her neighbours would turn and stare. Slowly they worked their way toward the street.

On the sidewalk, Shannon dropped his hand, sliding her arm up his, pulling him in closer, nodding to neighbours as they moved. Heads turned. A few faces brightened, mostly mothers, chins bobbing in envious approval. His eyes swept the crowd for her folks, but he'd only ever seen them from a distance and couldn't quite remember what they looked like. They knew he and Shannon were walking out on Sundays, which put them giant strides ahead of his folks. She was anxious to take him home, but only when he had steeled himself to return the compliment. Until then, she'd keep the relationship to holding hands, the odd squeeze, and a few serious kisses on special occasions. Lately, the special occasions seemed to have multiplied.

"I like the smell of Lifebuoy on a man," she said.

For an instant, he stiffened, wondering if somehow she'd surmised his need to scrub himself clean this morning. He'd been in the tub so long his sister had been banging on the door. "Cleanliness is close to godliness," he said, quoting his mother on one of her sober days.

"I don't suppose you told your parents you'd be attending St. Raphael's this morning?" she asked, lowering her voice as they picked up the pace. They were heading for Côte Ste. Catherine and an early spring picnic in Mount Royal Park. The congregation began to thin. Shannon's smile sagged at the slow shake of his head.

He coughed into a fist. "Would've created problems. I thought it best to attend an early mass with them at Saint-Viateur. No awkward questions that way."

She quickened her pace in silence. Dollard attempted to match her gait, but she slowed suddenly, throwing him off. "Commendable that you'd go twice in one day," she said flatly, "but sooner or later you're going to have to show more—"

"I wanted to tell them," he interrupted, "but today's a bad day." Shannon tipped her head and glanced at him, waiting for an explanation. "The cardinal's just back from Italy and was serving mass. 'E'll be coming to our place for dinner tonight. The last thing I need is *Papa* discussing my love life with 'im."

Her head bobbed up in exaggerated nods. "Typical, the cardinal would favour a French church over ours. Couldn't be seen mingling with the Irish, now, could we?"

"'E's sure to ask questions about 'is 'omily, so I 'ad to attend." He steered her onto Courcelette, where he'd parked the car.

"We did kick the plague, you know."

He bent down to unlock the door. "What are you talking about?"

"Us. The Irish. We're no longer contagious."

"It's not like that," he countered weakly, opening the door and turning. "'Ow about driving the rest of the way," he suggested, hopefully.

"And miss a healthy walk?" she replied, smiling.

Her change of humour relaxed him. "Or even better, we could go up to the Laurentians and still be back in time for dinner. You've never been to our cottage, and no one would be there."

She eyed him for a second then touched his arm. "I'd like that,

Dollard. Someday . . . when you get things straightened out with your folks."

He nodded and reached into the back seat, exchanging his fedora for a cap and extracting a picnic basket. Until he stood up to his father and brought her home, the car and all the things he longed to shower her with—horse races, chicken in a basket at the Lido, jazz at the Terminal, dances at Normandie Roof, the family chalet at Ste.-Agathe—would be off limits. It couldn't go on.

"I feel guilty about this," Shannon said, staring at the food in her hand; an *hors d'oeuvre* he called it. They were on a blanket on the east side of Mount Royal Park, backs against a tree. But they weren't alone. The long-awaited spring sun had sucked citizens from their tenements and cold-water flats. Down the slope in front of them lay a panorama of flying kites, strollers at the Cartier Monument, and ballplayers on Fletcher's Field. Even some of the park's nocturnal residents were up and stirring, although a few late risers still lay buried under the mounds of cardboard and newspaper they called home. "They remind me of fresh graves," Shannon had remarked on a previous outing.

"You feel guilty about the food every week, Shannon. Come on. A picnic lunch is the only thing you let me treat you to."

She tipped her head onto his shoulder. "Oh, Dollard, I can be such a drag."

His face screwed up. "Drag?"

She smiled. "It means a . . . pain in the backside, a tiresome do-gooder."

"Ohhh! I get it, an *emmerdeuse*." This time they both laughed.

She bit into the food and brightened. "My goodness! This *is* good. What am I eating?"

Dollard scrambled to his knees and began preparing more. "The crackers are called Ritz, and the stuff I'm spreading on top is *pâté de foie gras*."

She bit into the second offering. "Kinda like head cheese, only better," she said.

He nodded. "It's a paste made from goose liver. Very rare these days."

"Your mother won't miss it?"

He blew air through his lips. "Not a chance. She rarely sets foot in the kitchen." He flopped onto his back and grabbed her bare foot. "I've got a confession," he said, tickling her toes.

She squirmed. "My, my! Dollard Desjardins opening up. This *is* progress."

"The lunch," he said, screwing his eyes shut tight. "I didn't make it myself." When he opened them her brow had wrinkled. "Cook did. She knows all about us."

"And she's all right with it?"

"Why not? You're Catholic. That's good enough for 'er. Not like my parents."

She accepted a ham sandwich, frowning at the absence of crusts before biting into it, then washed it down with a swallow of Orange Crush. "I suppose this is a bad time to bring them up again? Your parents, I mean."

He shrugged as he gazed off toward Fletcher's Field. Someone was rounding the bases, and the crowd was cheering. They were too far away to make out any words, but he guessed they'd be Yiddish. Why couldn't his family be happy with her? It wasn't like he was bringing home a Jew.

She faced him on her knees and smoothed her skirt. "Your family's free to believe what they want, Dollard. They have a right to their opinions about the Irish. But you're twenty-two now; old enough to make your own decisions. Living up to your father's expectations is tearing you apart."

His hand hovered over the sandwich tin, but he drew it back, crossing his arms. "I know."

She leaned forward, taking his hands in hers. "Go with your own plans. Become that journalist, even if your dad insists it's to be the printing business for you."

Dollard swallowed. "He's got this thing about reporters. Calls them nomads. Says it's a profession of drunks, blasphemers, and divorcees. Atheists, too. Maybe 'e's right . . . about the split marriage part, I mean. They're away from 'ome a lot, you know. Can't be easy."

"What marriage is?" she replied. "You have to work at it. My uncle's a seaman, but my aunt's still with him."

He straightened his shoulders. "Shannon?" he said, in a low voice. She held his gaze. "Could you ever live with a reporter?"

She nodded coyly. "I know one I might be able to stand."

He got to his knees and faced her. They held hands at arm's length, like kids forming a bridge. "The one you 'ave in mind—think 'e could be a good one?"

She bit her bottom lip in mock contemplation. "He's got the makings."

Dollard felt his pulse quicken. "This fellow, 'e is tall, blond, and broad-shouldered, perchance? A Classics student at the Université de Montréal?" She nodded. "Would 'e be better off ditching the Classics for journalism courses? I mean, Latin and Greek doesn't get the news reported, does it?" He placed his hands on her waist and drew her closer. He expected she'd tilt her forehead onto his, to thwart a kiss in such a public place, but she moved forward on her knees. Their bodies locked.

"Mightn't it be better . . . for this student . . . to switch to that school in Paris he's always talking about? The one that teaches reporting?"

"*Bonne idée*," he whispered, inhaling her breath. " 'Course 'e'd need a woman to 'elp 'im on 'is way. Like a nurse, say." Her chest rose and fell against his. He tightened his grip.

She straightened, placed a hand on both sides of his face and, like a gypsy reading a crystal ball, stared deeply into his eyes. "I know one of those, too," she sighed, placing her mouth on his.

7:00 p.m., Sunday, May 21, 1933
Montreal

DOLLARD HUSTLED INTO THE KITCHEN, plunked the picnic hamper onto the counter, then scurried over to the mirror beside the dumb waiter. It crossed his mind that Cook, Mme. Plante, might ask him how lunch had gone. He cast her a furtive glance in the mirror. She wore a faint smile as she adjusted the heat under a pot. Since childhood, she'd been the woman he'd brought his cuts and bruises to. "Am I late, Cook?" he asked, staring at the swinging door leading to the dining room. He pulled a black comb and a small tube of hair cream from the inner pocket of his sports jacket.

She wiped her hands on her apron. "What do you think? It's after seven o'clock. They're just finishing soup."

"*Mama*'ll forgive me."

"It's not your mother you have to worry about," she replied, wincing at the cream he combed through his hair.

"I can handle *Papa*."

Her shoulders bounced as she stirred the pot. "That'll be the day," she chuckled. "Carrying on like a Hollywood playboy doesn't mean you've got what it takes to stand up to him."

"Hey! I'm no youngster," he protested, spreading his legs like a gunslinger as he brought the comb to his scalp. She watched in amusement as the hair fused into thick cables running straight back from the brow, making him look like a European count. When he was satisfied, he pocketed the comb, patted his head with both palms, and wiped his hands on a tea towel.

"The usual freeloaders in attendance, I suppose?" he asked, straightening his tie and checking for signs of lipstick.

Cook frowned as she snatched the tea towel away. "Only if you call His Eminence, Cardinal Villeneuve, l'abbé Groulx, and Monsieur Arcand freeloaders," she replied sharply, dropping the towel into a hamper.

Dollard rolled his eyes. "Torture!" he said, pretending to choke himself. "Two clerics and a patriot."

She returned to her stirring. "Better mind your p's and q's in there young man, or you'll be eating in the kitchen for the rest of the week."

"I'd prefer that."

The new serving girl came in from the dining room, balancing Great-grandmother's soup tureen on a tray. Dollard moved to help, closing his hands on hers and walking her and the heavy load to the counter. Cook watched from the corner of her eye, her jaw tightening. With the prized crockery safely delivered, the girl disengaged and shifted closer to Madame. A year ago, he might have sized her up, testing her for future consideration. New help usually arrived in the form of undernourished, working-class girls from homes with empty pantries. Often they filled out nicely in the Desjardins kitchen and were willing to show their gratitude to the good-looking son of the house. Today, the thought hardly entered his head. The dreamy afternoon he'd just had with Shannon trumped inclination. Still the impulse to tease was irresistible, if only to get a rise from Cook.

"And what's your name?" he asked, chuckling at the cheeks now pulsating like the neon sign outside the Gayety Theatre. The girl slipped behind Cook, who glared at him, chin down.

"Doll . . . ard," she growled.

He winked at her. "Just trying to be friendly with the new help," he said.

"Don't pay him any attention," Cook said, checking the consistency of the sauce she was working on. "He's a boy in a man's body. In the old days, I'd've turned him over my knee."

Dollard bowed deeply to the blushing servant. "Wish I could stay and chat," he said, in a deep theatrical voice, "but this actor has a role to play. Beyond yonder door await my fellow thespians." He rose on his toes, raised his right arm with the palm down, and goose-stepped toward the dining room. Behind him, he caught the warning tone in Cook's voice as she spoke to the girl.

Conversation stopped as Dollard entered the room. This was not going to be easy. It seldom was. The secret was to reply in simple terms to prying questions about his love life, school, religious obligations, and just about everything else he didn't care to share. A half-hour earlier, as he walked Shannon home, he'd described the invariable Sunday dinner scene awaiting him: Father at the head of the table, firm-jawed about Dollard's shortcomings—his shallow friends, mediocre school results, lack of interest in the printing business. Mother at the opposite end, bare-shouldered and silent, fingering her pearl necklace. Guests in their usual places—Cardinal Villeneuve and l'abbé Groulx to Father's left, separated by his sixteen-year-old sister Yvette; Adrien Arcand and twelve-year-old Marie to his father's right, with the son in between.

Dollard approached his mother, bending to kiss her on the cheek. She put down her wine and smiled up at him. "Where have you been?" she whispered, the smile never leaving her lips. "Your father's fit to be tied." He nodded to the guests and was about to take his place when the cardinal, in a move befitting a lord, raised his hand to the latecomer. Humbly, Dollard approached, longing just this once to give the hand a lumberjack's pump, but kissed the ring, as expected. "How was Rome, Your Eminence?" He felt the eyes upon him as he rounded the table, rumpled Marie's hair, and took his place.

Conversation resumed. The cardinal was expressing Rome's jubilation with the charismatic leaders now emerging in Europe. The men nodded excitedly. Dollard inhaled deeply. "Mussolini and Salazar show great promise," his eminence continued. "The crosses are up again in the schools, the clerics are back in charge of education, and Mother Church is playing her historic role in the governance of the state."

Arcand tipped his wine in salute. "Good to hear we're making progress."

The smile then left Villeneuve's face, as he sat back, folding his arms. "Then there's the matter of the republican governments in France and Spain. Both are in a moral slide—France with its new anti-clerical laws and Spain having banished the Jesuits. Even Mexico has declared war on the Church. Did you know that they now only permit one Catholic priest for every 50,000 souls?" He reached for a bread roll, shaking his head sadly. "No doubt about it, we have our work cut out for us." Dollard longed to ask the cardinal exactly what work that might be, but bit his tongue.

Arcand leaned forward. "This man, Hitler, seems to have the communists on the run."

A murmur of approval made the rounds of the table. Groulx frowned. "There's something about that man that bothers me. He's Catholic, but has few words for the church. And have you seen his eyes?"

"With all due respect, Lionel," Arcand replied, "he's giving the Germans the kind of leadership we could use here." He tapped the table with a finger for effect.

In spite of his determination to remain aloof, Dollard discovered himself listening. It seemed the Old World was opening doors to intoxicating possibilities—fascism, socialism, communism, anarchism—each in need of dissection and explanation. He knew just the journalist for the job and was about to risk a question when Marie elbowed him in the ribs.

"The movie," she asked in a low voice, "was it as good as they say?" He winced at her bad timing. The word movie had coincided with a lull in the conversation. Chins came up. Marie went beet red and bowed her head. "Sorry," she mumbled under her breath.

L'abbé Groulx looked at Dollard over the top of his glasses. "Seems to me we discussed movies at this table a couple of weeks back," he said, sipping his wine. "Didn't we decide they were a blight on the moral health? People see Greta Garbo and John Barrymore kissing and touching in public and take it for acceptable behaviour. And if that's permissible, why not run around in scanty clothes, flirt with strangers, cheat on your spouse, divorce, and skip church." He shook his head sadly. "Don't get me wrong, in the proper hands, movies can be a wonderful influence. But Hollywood, and the example it sets—hedonism, nihilism, liberalism—are a cancer on the Quebec race."

Dollard slumped. Another lecture. Last week's diatribe attacked the licentious contents of magazines, such as, *True Confessions*, *Ballyhoo*, and *Film Fun*. He cleared his throat. "There was nothing else to do," he responded. "So, a friend and I took in *Duck Soup* with the Marx Brothers. An innocent film. Lots of laughs." Hurriedly, he selected a name should they query the friend's identity.

"Innocent?" Groulx responded. "And you believe that?" He bit into a bread roll.

Dollard stared at l'abbé, hoping a smile would follow. "With all due respect, sir, how could a film about a nincompoop named Rufus T. Firefly, leader of a non-existent country named Freedonia, who declares war on a neighbouring state for no reason whatsoever, possibly harm anyone?"

L'abbé's eyes scrolled heavenward as he raised his thick linen napkin to his lips. For a happy instant, Dollard believed the subject closed, until Arcand rushed to fill the void. "I've read about *Duck Soup*, and I know it to be a thinly veiled attack on Italy, Portugal, and Germany. You've a lot to learn about Hollywood, young man, *and* the Jews who control it." He turned to Monsieur Desjardins. "I know we don't discuss *those* people at this table, Emmanuel, but perhaps you'd permit me to make this one point?"

The host smiled, but shook his head. "Save it, Adrien. We men can hash it out over cognac after dinner."

Dollard caught the impatience in his father's voice. He knew it had nothing to do with Arcand's choice of subject and everything to do with a son who refused to take life seriously. He groaned inwardly, thinking of his friends who'd soon be listening to that new, black, jazz band from Chicago at Chinese Paradise. There'd be no slipping out to join them tonight.

The Pequegnat clock on the study wall showed nine o'clock. Dollard moaned inwardly. The evening promised to be another *tête-à-tête* with the stonefaces and their anti-everything crusade.

"So, tell me, young man," the cardinal asked, swirling his cognac in the snifter as he sized him up. Dollard braced himself. "What's happening to our Royals these days? Haven't seen a ball game since I left for Rome."

Dollard tried not to show his relief as he gulped a mouthful of cognac. "We thought we were going to lose them," he answered, smarting from the firey liquid burning down his throat, "but Charlie Trudeau stepped up to the plate with twenty-five thousand bucks. He put in lights at Delorimier Stadium, too. Promises to be a good season."

Arcand nodded. "What with that Englishman Holt and the Jews controlling the city, it's nice to see one of *our* own coming forward for a change." He turned to the cardinal. "Guess the Yids keep a low profile in Italy these days, eh?"

Villeneuve positioned his cigar a foot above the ashtray and tapped it with a forefinger. A grey bomb drifted down, exploding among the cigarette butts below. "I wouldn't refer to them in quite those terms, but it's a fact that Mussolini has things under control." He smiled. Everyone laughed. Dollard, too, although he wasn't sure why it was so funny.

"They do make a lot of noise," Arcand pressed, "Il Duce steps on the Jew bitch's tail in Italy, and we hear the barking all the way over here." He tilted his head back, attempting to blow circles with the smoke, but wound up coughing instead.

"Be nice, Adrien," Groulx scolded. "It's the Lord's day. Besides, we don't want to shock the youngster in our midst."

Dollard felt the blood drain from his face. Was he still the child they once shooed from the room to tell their off-colour jokes? An overwhelming urge to shock surged through his gut. Desirée, that would do it. Or better still, tell them he was marrying an Irish woman of humble means.

Arcand turned to Monsieur Desjardins. "Isn't it time the boy learned the facts of life, Emmanuel? He'll be graduating next year and going to work in your shop. Anyone handling my publications had better know which way is up in this world."

Monsieur Desjardins tapped a pointed toe at an imaginary obstacle on the floor. Dollard held his breath. From the unease in the room, he wondered if he was about to be inducted into some secret sect. He'd heard tales of an arcane society, called La Patente, dedicated to the protection of all that devout Quebecers held dear. His father's head came up with a nod.

Arcand turned back to Dollard. "You lead a good life, young man—beer, cars, girls." Dollard opened his mouth to respond, but Arcand talked over him. "It's time you started paying attention to some of the publications that pass through your father's shop." He leaned forward. "Take my latest article in *Le Patriote*, for example, 'Drinkers of Blood.' Have you read it?"

Dollard felt an urge to loosen his collar. He screwed up his face in feigned contemplation. "Haven't had much time for outside reading," he replied. "What with my big dissertation on Epicurus coming up before the—"

"If you had," Arcand interrupted, "you'd know how the Jews murdered 40,000 Christians in Russia, in less than four years. There was ritual blood-drinking, too."

Groulx turned away. Dollard frowned, trying to remember what André had said once about something called the Protocols of the Elders of Zion. Abe had gotten uptight, but they'd laughed it off and gone on with their Saturday night prowl. Dollard wished he'd paid more attention. "Isn't that something that happened a long time ago?" he suggested.

Arcand shook his head. "Doesn't matter; the Jewish conspiracy progresses in a continuum. When you've covered the news as long as I have, you learn to read between the lines. Take those guys Leopold and Loeb who murdered that boy Franks in the United States a few years back. What do you think of the names?"

Dollard repeated them in his mind a couple of times. "Jewish?" he ventured.

Arcand nodded. "Two Jews working for the cause. Which should be a warning. With 50,000 of them in Montreal, we have to be vigilant. Who knows what they're up to? If they had their way, there'd be a casino atop Mount Royal instead of a cross and the name would be changed to Mount Sinai."

Dollard glanced at the others and swallowed. There'd been brief sorties in this direction in the past, but they'd always pulled back in deference to him. Arcand seemed to be the designated spokesman. Where was he going with this? Was this about Abe? Sure, the Jews were hardly favourites in Montreal—scratch any Englishman or Frenchman and you'd soon discover that. But were they really up to what he was hearing?

"Nothing far-fetched in what I'm saying," Arcand continued, placing a hand on Dollard's shoulder. "Jews are chameleons. It's not the ones shuffling down the street collecting rags you have to watch out for. It's the ones who dress and speak like us. On this side of the ocean, people haven't figured it out yet, but Mussolini and Hitler know what's going on. It's up to the educated classes to sound the alarm. Anti-Jewish leagues have sprung up around the globe. Don't you think it's time we had one here?"

Dollard brought his eyes up from the rug. "The people in those leagues, are they . . . fascists?"

"Don't be afraid of the word," Arcand replied.

Dollard felt the blood drain from his face. Those Jews on St. Laurent, the ones with their trinkets and scrap metal, had he missed something?

Were they decoys, lulling Gentiles with their backward ways while others masquerading as locals undermined them? And of the 50,000, how many had gone underground? He reached for the cognac. "They say they're communists, too," he said, hesitantly.

Arcand smiled. "You've got it. Scratch any ism—bolshevism, socialism, liberalism—and you'll find a Jew."

Dollard looked to the men, but they seemed occupied with other matters: his father relighting his cigar; the cardinal twirling the globe on the desk with an index finger extended, ready to prod some unexpected country to action; Groulx frowning at the bookshelves as if forbidden copies of Zola, Rousseau, or Anatole France might jump out and assault him.

"Fact is, Dollard," Arcand continued, "our world is under threat, and each man Jack of us must decide what's to be done about it. If it isn't communists like Marx, Lenin, and Trotsky—all Jews, by the way—stealing from hard-working men of vision like your father, it's socialists, like Caballero in Spain or Blum in France—another Jew—who steal from the productive to squander on the unskilled and lazy."

He stopped and waited for a reaction. Dollard searched for something intelligent to add. "But here . . . in this country . . . we're holding tight with democracy. Right?"

Arcand shook his head. "Democracy is fine as far as it goes, but putting the individual ahead of society leads to selfishness and greed. We," his hand drew a circle to include the men in the room, "feel that corporatism serves us best." He smiled at the puzzled look on Dollard's face. "It's a form of government that works for the greater good of the greater number, while looking out for their morals at the same time. You see, corporatism makes it possible for business, labour, and church to form an inviolable bond with government. Everybody co-operates, everybody benefits; labour is adequately rewarded, and business profits flow unhindered by work stoppages. Spiritual necessities are attended to as well."

Dollard bobbed his head in approval, praying there'd be no questions, even though he had a myriad of his own. He tipped his head to the floor and adopted a contemplative air. Corporatism? Best to find out more. As for the Jews, it was understandable that Mussolini and Hitler would want to lay down the law. What wasn't clear was how to go about cleansing Montreal. One thing was certain, he felt good about the warm feeling this talk had generated in his gut. There was a delicious closeness in the room. He wondered what he could do to aid the cause. He looked up to catch his father's gaze. Monsieur Desjardins had contributed nothing to the conversation, but from his expression hadn't missed a word. He looked at his boy, and, for a moment, father and son were alone. Monsieur Desjardins smiled and raised his glass. Dollard walked to his father's side.

L'abbé turned to the cardinal, clearing his throat. "Your excellency, have you seen Emmanuel's latest addition to his electric train collection?"

Villeneuve's eyes widened. "Haven't had the pleasure," he replied.

"You're in for a treat," Groulx continued. "He's built a model of the marshalling yards at Lévis across from Quebec. It's a complete replica, right down to buildings, landscape, and vegetation." He turned to his host. "How'd you do that, Emmanuel?"

Dollard watched his father's eyes grow wide as milk caps as he began explaining his use of plywood, dowelling, cardboard, screening, plaster of Paris, and something called Air Fern that he'd picked up in New York City.

"*Pour l'amour du ciel*, Emmanuel," Groulx said, "take him downstairs and show him."

Monsieur Desjardins reached into a cupboard and handed out Pennsylvania Central train caps. "We'll make up a freight train for Rivière du Loup," he beamed. The guests donned their caps and headed for the stairs. "I'll need two engineers and a yardmaster to work the switches. Volunteers?"

Groulx held up his hand. "Dollard and I have something to discuss," he said. "We'll be along in a few minutes."

Dollard picked at a hangnail as he watched Groulx from the corner of his eye. Groulx topped up the glasses. What lecture this time? Horse races? Drinking? Saturday-night crawls? Shannon? How did priests get to know so much? Even with 900,000 souls in the city, Montreal was still a hamlet. A train whistle echoed up from the basement, followed by laughter.

L'abbé looked like a man with a lot on his mind. "You were hanging onto Arcand's every word just now," he said, studying the globe on Monsieur Desjardins' expansive oak desk and giving it a spin. Dollard nodded. The earth made several squeaky revolutions before slowing to a halt. Western Europe popped up. Groulx stared down at it before raising his eyes. "Best learn to cross-reference your sources before jumping to conclusions."

Dollard frowned. "Sir?"

"Arcand," l'abbé began, his fingers working their way up and down the buttons on his frock like they were keys on a piano, "means well, but is long on hyperbole. Don't get too close." Dollard's brow furrowed in puzzlement. "On the Jewish thing, for instance, he fancies himself out front, with the province close on his heels. From where I sit, he's getting lip service, but little commitment. You've got too good a future to go down with a man the people might turn on one day."

Dollard buried his nose in his brandy snifter to hide the clash of emotions he was sure were visible on his face. That he wasn't on the carpet for his personal life was a relief, but just when he was getting a handle on Quebec and the Jews—even establishing a position of his own—here was Groulx, raising doubts.

"With all due respect, isn't he getting tons of commitment? We've heard him at the table expounding on the $18,000 Prime Minister Bennett paid him to get Conservatives elected to Ottawa. Then there's the 50,000 people who've signed up for his Ordre patriotique des goglus. And aren't you a regular contributor to his newspapers?"

Groulx tipped his face to the ceiling and steepled his fingers. "Let's put our thinking caps on for a minute, young man. Go back to 1837."

Dollard braced himself, suppressing an urge to bite off the ragged hangnail plaguing his thumb. He plumbed his memory for what significant event could have taken place almost a hundred years ago.

"Then it was *Les Patriotes* rebelling against the English-dominated government." Dollard nodded in silence. "Know why they failed?" More silence. "Because the people weren't ready for Papineau. He was too far out front of the pack. He moved too soon." Groulx's eyes came off the stained-glass light fixture on the ceiling and locked onto Dollard. "In his haste, he not only ruined a lot of people, but set nationalism back a century."

Dollard held his gaze. "And you think Arcand could damage the cause by acting too soon?" He wasn't sure what, exactly, the "cause" entailed, but the word was out and it sounded right.

Groulx pointed a finger at him. "*Voilà*," he said, "you've made the connection. I'm impressed." For a long moment, priest and parishioner stared off in thought. Another burst of laughter filtered up from the basement.

"So, how does one go about muffling him?" Dollard asked, finally.

Groulx pushed away from the desk, shaking his head. "We wouldn't want to shut him up, just slow him down. The cause, as you call it, needs his fire. But he has to alter course—less anti-Semitism, more French Canada. And he has to work on coordinating with other movements, such as St. Jean-Baptistes, Jeune-Canada, and *Achat chez nous*. With a united front, it would be just a matter of . . ." He stopped and stared intently at Dollard. "You understand this is a confidential conversation, don't you? I mean, we're just two academics knocking around ideas, here."

Dollard nodded, feeling a sudden urge to square his shoulders. Even as a university student in a country where less than one percent of the population finished high school, he'd never thought of himself as an academic. But here was the renowned l'abbé Groulx talking to *him*, as if they were two intellectuals of equal standing.

Dollard inhaled. "Can I take it from your articles that you really do hold with him on the Jews?"

L'abbé's jaw dropped and he placed a hand on his breast in a quizzical pose. "Anti-Semitic articles? *Moi*?"

"Yes . . . in . . . *Le Goglu* and *Le Chameau*," Dollard replied, thankful the timbre in his voice was holding.

"And you're certain it was me and not, say, one Jacques Brassier, or Lambert Clossé?"

Dollard felt a hot flash invade his cheeks. "But they're both you . . . sir . . . aren't they?"

"Perhaps," Groulx smiled.

"I see," Dollard said, stealing a peek at his hangnail. "It wouldn't do for a man in your position to be sucked under if Arcand's ship founders."

Groulx stared at Dollard over the top of his steel-rimmed glasses. "I'll admit that anonymity has its advantages, but it's not my own hide I'm looking out for. It's for the greater good. If Arcand should be torpedoed, it's important that some of us are left to fight on."

"Then I am correct? You did publish those articles?"

L'abbé began to pace in front of the desk. "Let's put it this way. Were I to appear before the judge of judges," he directed a finger heavenward, "I'd plead guilty with an explanation."

Dollard drained his brandy then, staring in horror at the glass he'd emptied so quickly in l'abbé's presence, slid it under his chair.

Groulx cleared his throat. "Arcand needs encouragement, and, yes, I have intimated that Jews might not exactly be a blessing for Quebec."

He clasped his hands behind his back as he continued to pace. "I may even have suggested that Hitler could be on the right track." He turned at the wall and retraced his steps. "But consider my intervention as a little white lie for the good of our race." Dollard watched him reach the window, sniff at his father's prize orchids, and reverse course again. "You see, we've always been a simple nation—Catholic, French, agrarian. Now we're not so sure. Urbanism, modernism, consumerism, materialism, liberalism, and hedonism all have us muddled. We've lost our way."

"So the Jews *are* responsible? Like Arcand says."

The priest's jawline tightened. "Maybe, maybe not, but that's not the point. You see, Adrien's onto something more important than putting a few Jew noses out of joint. Whether they're responsible or not, they personify the ills that have befallen us." Groulx gave the globe another twirl as he passed the desk. "Sure, advocating their expulsion may be a hopeless dream, but it's a rallying point. It focuses attention on *our* plight and it puts *us* one step closer to regaining *our* pure state."

"So, it's really about galvanizing our people around a common cause?" Dollard ventured.

Groulx reached the inner wall of the study and stared for a second at the painting of Grandfather Desjardins' first print shop. "The difference, my dear Dollard, is that he believes the rhetoric." He pivoted with a military snap. "Don't get me wrong, there are no Jews on my Christmas card list. They'd take over the university if they could. The English at McGill have good reason to place quotas on them."

"So, how do you advocate getting them out of Montreal?"

Groulx stopped suddenly and pulled a chair over in front of Dollard. "I don't believe for a second we'll ever be rid of all the Jews and foreigners, but we might be able to stem the contamination by convincing a few to stick to their own districts—English in Westmount, Italians in Jean Talon, Irish in St. Anne, Jews around St. Laurent."

At the mention of the Irish, Dollard reached for his snifter. Without missing a beat, l'abbé took the empty glass to the bar, speaking over his shoulder as he moved. "It's in the mixing of cultures that our ways get debased. You don't notice it at first, but it doesn't take long for a cherished custom or institution to slip away. And when it begins, it's the deluge. Take that beautiful meal your mother served tonight. Where do you suppose the food came from?"

Dollard shrugged, trying to remember the names on the delivery vans that came regularly up their lane.

"By my best guess," Groulx continued, handing back the glass, "I'd say, Harrison Bakeries, Guaranteed Pure Milk, Kellenberger's Meat Mart, and Steinberg's grocery store. See anything wrong with that?" Dollard nodded. "That's why we have to get behind the *Achat chez nous* programme and buy from our own. Why should Eaton's, Ogilvy's, and Mappin's get all the business? What about our stores?"

Names of his favourite restaurants and bars began scrolling through Dollard's head. Few were French. He swallowed.

"And it's not just the loss of business," l'abbé continued. "Our stores find themselves having to compete by staying open Sundays and forcing clerks and shoppers to skip mass. They expect the workers to learn English, too, which only leads to intermarriage and dropping birth rates. And that, my friend, will be the beginning of the end for the French-Catholic race in North America."

Dollard shook his head. "Not if I can help it," he said, his voice betraying the gamut of emotions that ran through him, from fear to defiance.

Groulx turned and faced him straight on. "I'd like to see you involved in the struggle for our national symbols—a flag, French on the money, the right to declare St. Jean-Baptiste Day our own national holiday."

"Wouldn't I have to sign up with Arcand to do those things?"

Groulx shook his head. "Try Jeune-Canada. You'll feel at home there. Their rallies are something to behold. I'm their guest speaker next week at le Gesù auditorium on Bleury. They're quite the intellectuals. Do you know Laurendeau?"

PART THREE
Montreal, April 1939

Chapter Three

April 1939
Montreal

A WEARINESS ENVELOPED DOLLARD as he pulled back the curtain of his second-floor window. He watched Latendresse exit the house and turn onto the sidewalk. The caregiver neither looked back nor waved. Not surprising. In the face of Dollard's ingratitude, the man had reason to be frustrated, even suspicious. The priest couldn't seem to get it through his head that all he wanted was to be left alone. Father Pierre certainly had been kind enough—springing him from the hospital, providing him with room and board when far too many still slept on the streets. All for such little reward. The place selected for his convalescence, the only single-family structure on a dismal east-end street, was the home of Latendresse's widowed sister-in-law. For the time being, though, it was home. Temporarily, he hoped.

Dollard flushed as he watched Father Pierre disappear down the street. There'd been no talk of restitution, but Dollard resolved to make it right when he could; soon, when he'd managed to balance the load he was carrying. Certainly, it was time to start treating the priest with the civility he deserved. The man meant well. Caring for a dyspeptic ingrate who chain-smoked his way through the days while staring into space had to be a burden. Dollard's excuse for rarely going out was anything but convincing. He said he didn't savour being recognized. Hollow; *Le Devoir* had never published his picture alongside his byline from Spain, and the chances of bumping into an Outremont neighbour among the tenements off Hochelaga were remote at best. Even if it did happen, so what? It would be like running into an acquaintance in a whore-house—look straight ahead and keep going.

Dollard returned to the bed and sat down, elbows on his knees, fingers running through his hair. He reached for his cigarettes, examining the blue lettering on the orange-beige package: "Buckingham Fine Cut," he read aloud, "Philip Morris & Co." Like everything he now enjoyed, the cigarettes were courtesy of Pierre, but why an American product? Why not Macdonald's, made right here in Montreal and employing hundreds of east-end girls? Was this, in a tiny way, Father Latendresse showing that he did not subscribe to l'abbé Groulx's *Achat chez nous*?

He smiled. But the grin faded with the inevitable vision of Marty. Not only had Marty's family been adversely affected by *Achat chez nous*, but one of girls he talked about, Riva, worked for Macdonald Tobacco.

Feeling his pulse quicken and the moving picture in his head about to resume, he lay back on the bed. In the months this film had plagued him, he'd learned to lower the sound, even make the image fade, but shutting it off completely still eluded him. All it took was the right mood, smell, accent, or sudden noise to get it going again. Each time it resumed he could never tell which scene might play. This time he was at the firepit, with flames licking at the cauldron above it. He could hear bubbling. Something was cooking. Lamb stew, perhaps. But in spite of his hunger pains, he wasn't focused on the food. All he could see were two photographs tossed into the fire. Each bore the face of a young woman. One was Riva, the other Connie, the two women from Marty's past. He wanted to reach out and pluck them from the blaze, but something held him back. The girl's images curled up and turned to ash. Gunshots ring out, yet he can't take his eyes away from the fire. He knows whom the shots are for, but he doesn't look up. The scene fades to black.

Dollard sat up on the bed and wiped his brow with a forearm. There'd been a time when the confessional would have helped rid him of these scenes, but those days were lost. Still, if the healing powers of the Church were gone, Marty's parents were not. If he could bring himself to see them, explain what happened to their son, perhaps the movie would end once and for all. He'd tried before, even getting as far as their doorstep. It was time to try again.

Dollard's head was awash with memories as he began the long, steady climb up St. Laurent into the Jewish quarter. How many times had he screamed up and down this very street in the company sedan, caring naught for the accusatory stares. The stalls, carts, and hawkers were still there, although not as many ringlets and funny hats as he remembered. Today, seeing them through Marty's eyes, it was a homecoming. Even the names were familiar: Schubert Baths, Yiddish Folk Schule, Warshaw's Fruit, Moe's Smokes, Kellenberger Meats.

Kellenberger! He felt suddenly woozy. The butcher shop had come up faster than anticipated, catching him by surprise. Now there it was, looking just as Marty had described it. A horse and wagon plodded in front of him, momentarily obscuring his view. For a second, he focused on the nag and its cargo of granite slabs that would some day find their way to a graveyard, he presumed. What about Marty, rotting in a hole somewhere in Spain? No stone would ever mark his last resting place. Now Dollard was standing within feet of his parents' store, rehearsing in his mind for the hundredth time the words to explain how their son had taken him under his wing, changed the way he saw the world, and saved him from a firing squad—twice. That would be the easy part. What had haunted him since 2:35 a.m., April 15, 1938, was the role he'd played in their son's execution.

When the wagon had passed, Dollard lifted his eyes to the apartment above the store, wondering which window would have been Marty's bedroom. He noted with satisfaction that his heart rate was steady—above normal, yes, but not in the stratosphere. The time had come. Swallowing, he pushed off, moving quickly, fearful of a resolve that was already crumbling by mid-street.

Momentum and a few extra strides found him panting, yet inside the shop door and fingering the metal glasses case in his pocket. Above him, tiny bells announced his entrance. As his eyes adjusted to the dimness, he made out two men in flat caps hovering over a warped butcher's block. Marty's brothers, he thought. Their eyes lingered on him for a second then fell back to the carcass they were working on. In taking stock, his first reaction was astonishment. He'd at least expected a lighted candelabra, a ram horn or two on the walls, maybe even the word "Kosher" plastered on a sign overhead. Instead, he found little to distinguish this establishment from the Outremont shop his mother sent Cook to. Sure, there'd been that small, strange-looking container to the right of the entrance with the plaque in what had to be either Hebrew or Yiddish. But everything else—enamelled white interior, sawdust on the floor, charity box next to the cash, sausages hanging from hooks, cuts of meat in glass cases—was standard Montreal. Only the calendars behind the cash register seemed different. They lacked the usual hockey, hunting, or fishing themes, opting instead for scenes from the Holy Land—a wall in front of which bearded men stood praying, a photo of an ancient tower, and a narrow street in an old city, probably Jerusalem.

A middle-aged woman, glasses on the end of her nose, sat perched on a stool near the cash, clutching a newspaper. The double chin and shawl said it all—Marty's mother. Dollard could feel his resolve ebbing away, the need for a drink growing. *I'm not ready for this,* he thought, but, as he turned, an older version of Marty exited the walk-in icebox. He stopped. On his shoulder, he balanced a meat-laden tray. For a second, he swayed under the weight, as he felt with his foot for the thick, wooden door him. He kicked it, causing it to close with a heavy, muffled click.

Mr. Kellenberger caught Dollard's eye. "What can we do for you today?" he asked.

Dollard's mouth opened, but no sound escaped. He shifted his weight while Mr. Kellenberger deposited the tray on a white table and placed his hands on his hips. Mrs. Kellenberger lowered her paper, to take in the customer's dishevelled state and mismatched clothes. The couple glanced at each other then back at Dollard. Marty's father tried again, this time in French. "*Que voulez-vous acheter?*"

Dollard coughed into his fist. "'Ow are you fixed for . . . liver?" He flushed. Why had he picked liver? The only meat he detested. Was it because he'd grown up believing that liver was the way to a Jew's heart? Or was it a subliminal need to explain to these people that because of inaction on his part, their son would not be coming home. That instead he lay like chopped liver in Catalonia's terra rosa soil.

"How much?" Mr. Kellenberger asked as he reached into the cooler.

"Three pounds." Dollard answered, then groaned aloud. Mr. Kellenberger stopped. One of the boys at the block whispered to the other, then both looked up. Dollard plunged his hands into his pockets in search of the money he suddenly realized wasn't there. "Excuse me . . . sir. I seem to 'ave left my wallet in the car. I'll get it . . . be right back."

Dollard caught the smile on the brothers' faces as he broke for the door. "What kinda car would that be?" one of them shouted. "Desoto, Buick, Bugatti?" Their laughter tore into him as he made his escape.

PART FOUR

Montreal, 1933–34

Chapter Four

Saturday, June 3, 1933
Montreal

"SAY YOU'LL COME TO THE MEETING, Marty," Riva coaxed, walking backward in front of him as they sauntered west along Mont Royal Avenue toward St. Laurent. They'd left the YMHA dance early, the floor being crowded, the atmosphere sticky, and the room noisy. Not that leaving was Marty's idea; the congestion and bumping that pushed them together like tango dancers in a Bogart movie had him in an amorous mood. He'd hoped for the same effect on her. Apparently not. Instead, she'd suggested that a dose of cool breeze coming up from the St. Lawrence was in order.

The weather had been unseasonably muggy, so much so that the spring of 1933 was going to be remembered for its humidity. Stupidity, too, Riva had just announced, a remark Marty had no intention of pursuing.

Even at ten o'clock, the street was still alive—boys flowing in pods daring each other to approach girls coming the other way; families sitting on balconies and wrought-iron stairs, exchanging mock insults with neighbours; hand-holding lovers strolling to the strains of "Stormy Weather," drifting from the windows of tenants rich enough to afford a radio and pay the radio tax.

Martin Kellenberger and Riva Lilovsky were not holding hands. In her controlled moments, like now, Riva insisted it wasn't prudent, not with their futures dragging them in different directions—she back to the Russia her parents had fled before the communists had transformed it into workers' paradise; he back to the medical books at the Université de Montréal.

"So, you going to come to the meeting, or what?" she persisted.

Marty shook his head. "Cripes! Haven't I told you a hundred times, politics doesn't interest me."

"Chicken!" she mocked, flapping her arms and giving her best city-girl rendition of a hen laying an egg. Two boys playing with yo-yos on the curb stopped to stare.

"Take your mother. She goes for that stuff."

"Sure," Riva replied, pivoting to walk beside him, "*Mame* at the

Young Communist League meeting; wouldn't stand out at all." She reached over and began tickling him under the chin.

Marty grinned. "She's crazy enough to go," he said, raising a shoulder to deflect her. They stepped apart to let a couple pass between them. The boy was straightening his tie, the girl had her lipstick out. A pang of envy seized Marty in the lower gut. These were supposed to be their best years. Why was there seldom room for anything but talk and the odd peck? He came to a decision. If her mother was still out playing pinochle when he got her home, he was going to press for more.

"*Mame*'d go all right," Riva replied, placing her arm in his. He brightened. "Never passes up a chance to hear Fred Rose. But it's you who needs it." She did a little hop-skip, falling into step with him. "Come on. What do you say?"

"I'd say you've forgotten Section 98."

She hunched her shoulders and growled in frustration. "With you constantly bringing it up, how could I?"

"So?"

"So, just because it outlaws every association to the left of Mussolini shouldn't stop us from following our consciences."

Marty shook his head. "One of these days, Riva Lilovsky, they'll catch you thumbtacking union posters to telephone poles and it'll be bye-bye soft job at Macdonald Tobacco and hello Bordeaux Jail."

"*Ish kabibble!*" she moaned. "You really are gutless, aren't you?"

He stopped to face her. "Prudent, Riva. When your family's in retail, you don't wear politics on your sleeve. And you sure as hell don't risk being shut down by the police." They resumed walking.

"Prudent schmudent. It's your family who's in business, not you. Cripes, students are supposed to be consumed by the great enigmas — religion, politics, the meaning of life. If you're this stuffy at twenty-two, what'll you be like at fifty?"

"Guess you'll never find out, will you? What with you dedicating your life to Joe Stalin and his five-year cure for Russia's ills, I'd say your hopes of ever —" He stopped short. In the dim light, someone had called his name.

"Hey, young Kellenberger," the voice repeated. Marty and Riva turned to see a hand waving from a crowded stairway. "The poster outside your old man's butcher shop says he keeps a finger on the scale when he serves us. That true?" People on both sides of the street laughed.

Marty sighed. "No, Mr. Selick, it's not."

"Just joshing ya," Selick replied.

For a few steps, neither spoke. "Your father still losing business over that *Achat chez nous* crap?" Riva asked.

"It'll pass," Marty replied. He felt her stiffen and instantly regretted his choice of words. Hopes for an amorous end to the evening took another hit.

" 'It'll pass,' " she mimicked. "God, you can be pathetic! A handful of xenophobes declares war on your father's butcher shop and you, helpless Yid from the *shtetl*, just sit there minding your own onions until it blows over. Those laws you keep reminding me of, they're there for you, too, you know."

He hesitated, not sure how much to tell her. He'd tried contacting the police once and it had amounted to nothing. A month earlier, he'd witnessed three Jewish boys being beaten up on St. Urbain. Against his father's advice, he'd gone to the police with a licence number, but four weeks had passed, and still no action. His father had been right. Nothing was going to happen. All he had to show for the episode was a pair of crushed lenses and a bitter taste in his mouth. To make it worse, he'd seen the guy at the university, but hadn't told Riva for fear of badgering.

"Face it, Riva, some laws aren't meant for us. Trying to use them only makes things worse."

"Wrong! It's playing dead that makes things worse—whets the anti-Semite appetite. Maybe it's hard to prove it's discrimination when they deny us membership in their clubs, but hounding your *fater* at the shop has got to be indictable."

Marty sighed. "Could we give it a pass, Riva? Just for tonight?"

"Right, so you can go on hiding in the reeds." She shook her head. "Don't you have a breaking point, Martin Kellenberger?"

"I'm a realist. Every time we push back, nothing happens."

"So, what's there to lose?"

"A great deal! Get your nose out of that communist drivel for a while and you'll see that a lot of people around here wouldn't mind seeing us stuffed onto steamers and shipped back to the Old Country." He stared at her. " 'Course, that won't bother Riva Lilovsky and her old lady, because they're going back on their own."

"I hate a quitter," she mumbled, upping her pace and putting distance between them.

For a while, he walked behind her, knowing that by the end of the block she'd have cooled down. At least she hadn't denounced him for a *farreter*, right here on the street with all these ears tuned in. If she had, it would be everywhere by noon tomorrow: Marty Kellenberger, the butcher's son, traitor to his people. *Tate*'s regulars would come in to cluck. Some might even take their business elsewhere; just like many of the French ones were doing, thanks to the posters. What was wrong with considering his own future, distancing himself from the *Yiddiskayt* around him? Was it so bad to be just a tiny bit selfish? Most Jews his age knew what they were after; they wanted to blend in, move out, and up. Normal people called it progress, but in Riva's book, you advanced by butting heads.

"Be reasonable, Riva," he said at the stoplight. "I'm two years away from graduation. I can't be seen plastering posters on poles and running off to communist meetings. The university would kick me out, and Uncle Max would stop bankrolling my tuition."

"People die for their beliefs," she said coldly.

"It's not that I'm yellow, if that's what you're saying! And I'm not blind to all that anti-Semitic garbage, either. It's at the university, too, you know. Scrawled messages—'*Les crimes du bolchévisme sont les crimes juifs; le seul ennemi de la civilisation chrétienne c'est le Juif; les Juifs ne sont pas desirés ici.*' I hate that stuff, but not enough to let it ruin my chance at a medical degree. Besides, most of the *goyim* students in my department think it's nuts, too."

Riva frowned. "How come you never mentioned this before?"

"It comes and it goes," he shrugged. "Lately, a small group called Jeune-Canada has taken to marching around campus like Mussolini's black shirts. Some of the Jewish boys have been harassed. I'm lucky. My French is good. I fit in. And my name works in my favour, too; Kellenberger sounds German. The guys in my class are decent chaps. They've taken to calling me Kelly, like I was Irish or something."

He expected an outburst. Instead she took his arm. At Mrs. Steinberg's grocery store, they turned onto St. Laurent, strolling past Lipinsky's, where he'd had a tooth pulled, Agulnic Men's Wear, which supplied his Uncle Max's tailor-made suits, the *cheder* he'd been sent to after school to study Hebrew and the Talmud, and past Harry's Miscellaneous, which supplied street urchins with buttons, combs, pencils, shoelaces, and needles to hawk to passersby. He took a deep breath. "Why do you have to go away, Riva?"

"Because I owe it to *Mame*. Because with *Tate* gone, we only have each other. Because I'm dying to see what's really happening over there.

The reports are fantastic, if you'd only listen."

He selected his words carefully before replying. "But can you believe them? I mean . . . they say Stalin and that Lavrenti Beria guy have blood on their hands."

"*Mame* says it's all anticommunist propaganda."

When they stepped off the Main, Marty moved in closer. He liked this part of the walk. Light standards were spaced farther apart and cast long shadows. For a few blocks, his mind drifted into more pleasant thoughts, but the shouts and animated conversation that greeted them as they turned into her alley blew them away. So did the lingering odour of evening meals—a mélange of chicken fat, gefilte fish, and fried potato latkes. The neighbours were not abed, so the instant Marty and Riva made their appearance the noise died, and twenty-eight pairs of mischievous eyes peered down.

"Chin up," Riva whispered, dropping his hand.

He gulped at the gauntlet they'd have to run. She lived in a four-storied, U-shaped structure that ran down both sides of the alley before joining at the bottom. Every floor came with balconies, and every balcony was full on this warm, spring evening. Marty felt like a player on a stage. Recognizing a face, calling out a name, would ease the fright, but the ambient glow from the odd twenty-five-watt bulb slanting through windows was not enough for him to make out any features.

"Hello, dears," a raspy voice called. He slumped, recognizing the cigarette-enhanced tones of Mrs. Lilovsky. "Riva's fellow's a medical student at the university," she announced, with just enough braggadocio in her voice to annoy the gallery. "He's taken her dancing."

"My, my . . . *dawnsing with a doctor*," someone jeered. The gallery came alive. "You'll kick him where it hurts, eh, Riva, if he tries for one of them physical exams?" That earned a howl. "Watch out for probes with mysterious objects, young lady," came a rejoinder from the third floor. More taunts showered down as they crossed the alley. Riva smirked. Marty winced. When they hit the stairs, the cheers, cackles, and catcalls died off and the gallery returned to other preoccupations—knitting, rolling cigarettes, telling off-coloured jokes, talking over each other.

"Don't listen to them," Mrs. Lilovsky advised as they met at the door. "They don't mean any harm. Laughs are hard to come by these days."

Riva motioned him to a chair at the table and headed for the toilet. Boyfriend and mother exchanged smiles, interrupted by a hissing-splashing sound that filtered through the thin bathroom wall. Marty's imagination went into overdrive. Mrs. Lilovsky scurried to the kitchen to bang the kettle and run the tap. She began humming a Guy Lombardo tune. "We'll have tea," she announced.

Marty nodded and looked off in a vain attempt to be alone with the intimate picture of Riva engaged in the act of making water. His breath grew shallow. Greyness drifted across his vision. Juices gnawed at his stomach. He felt a rising panic, terror that Mrs. Lilovsky might ask him to stand up and reach for the cookies on the top shelf. Nervously, he removed his new glasses and placed them in the metal carrying case.

"Best thing about that rally at the Mount Royal arena last week," Mrs. Lilovsky announced when Riva had returned to the table, "was how it had folks speaking up for the Jews in Germany. About time."

If Mrs. Lilovsky had wanted to pour cold water on Marty she couldn't have picked a better topic. "Yeah, impressive," he offered weakly, his fantasies gone as he felt Riva's eyes burning into him.

"How would you know?" she blurted out. "You didn't bother to attend."

He swallowed. "I read about it."

Riva turned to her mother. "Most important rally in years and guess who's too busy studying to take part?"

"I had an exam."

She ignored him. "All-star cast on the platform—Rabbi Rosenberg, Dr. Abramowitz, Mayor Rinfrit, politicians from Ottawa and Quebec, even Protestant ministers. The whole kit and kaboodle, but, oh, no, our boy is too preoccupied to take the time to consider our cousins in Europe."

The kettle screamed and Mrs. Lilovsky got up to make tea. She returned with the pot in one hand and three magazines in the other. "Have a look at these," she said to Marty.

Reluctantly, Marty put his glasses back on and glanced at the publications. His first instinct was to wonder about Mrs. Lilovsky's priorities. So much precious cash allocated to periodicals and so little to clothing and shelter. The thought faded as he took in the front covers. One extolled the glories of the revolution. It featured glowing proletarian faces sweating happily under the hammer and sickle and surrounded by a boundless harvest. He smiled inwardly at the clumsy propaganda. The second wasn't as easy to dismiss. It showed long-faced evacuees—men, women, and children—on a street surrounded by piles of clothing and furniture that appeared to have been thrown from the windows. A crowd had gathered to taunt them. Some carried placards that read, "*Juden Raus.*" Immediately, his mind shot to the signs outside his father's shop. But it was the third cover that caused him to sit up. Under the banner, "No Escape! Even in Death," were six photos of defaced Jewish gravestones, each taken in a different European country.

Riva plunked a small tin of Carnation milk onto the table. "Guess they thought it would blow over, too, eh?" she said, pointing her chin at the gravestones.

Marty raised his cup to his lips. "All right, all right," he shrugged, "maybe I should have gone to that rally, but it's too late now."

Riva pulled her chair in closer. "Not for the counter-rally set for a week Thursday at le Gesù auditorium."

Marty winced as he took a sip of scalding hot tea. Did nothing escape her? Jeune-Canada signs announcing the event had been plastered around the university, but how would it have come to her attention at Macdonald Tobacco? The rally promised to be a grudge affair put on by budding fascists and was potentially dangerous. He looked across at her. "Don't even think about it," he said.

"Why not?"

"Because your French isn't good enough."

"But yours is. And I understand enough to get the gist."

"You only understand enough to get it wrong. Besides, you'd never be able to keep your mouth shut."

"I'll only speak to you and in French. Promise."

"Your Byelorussian accent would give you away in a flash."

"So?"

"So, they beat up some Jewish boys outside of the YMHA last month for no reason at all. What do you think they'd do to the likes of us wandering in?"

"I'm willing to take the chance if you are," she replied, holding his gaze.

"No, Riva, you're willing to have me take that chance," he argued, jabbing his chest with a thumb. "If there's trouble it'll be me who gets pummelled." He looked pleadingly at her mother. "Please tell her she's crazy." Mrs. Lilovsky looked down and began refilling the cups. Marty slumped in his chair, scouring his brain for a way out that would somehow prove he wasn't yellow. "You know it's on a Friday night . . . *Shabbat.*"

Riva blew air through her mouth. "Since when has that ever bothered you? Besides, I'm sure any rabbi would forgive us under the circumstances." She cocked her head and waited for an answer.

He took another swallow of the still hot tea. "I might go," he said at last, "but I have conditions." She nodded eagerly. "You're to dress goyish, and under no circumstances, no matter how worked up you get, are you to breathe a word."

Riva raced around the table and kissed him on the lips. He sighed. This was as good as it was going to get tonight. At the door, Mrs. Lilovsky handed him two books — *The Coming Struggle for Power*, by John Strachey, and *Moscow Dialogues*, by Julius Hecker. He made a mental note to glance at them for Riva's sake, and to keep them out of sight at home. His mother would be furious.

As usual, Mrs. Lilovsky got in the last word. "In the Soviet Union, anti-Semitism is against the law," she shouted over Riva's shoulder as the door closed. "Did you know that?"

Thursday, June 15, 1933
Montreal

"WHAT ARE YOU SHAKING YOUR HEAD AT?" Riva smirked, as they left her alley to head for the Main. "You're the one who told me to dress Gentile for the rally."

Marty took her hand, twirling her in a pirouette for closer inspection. He took his time looking at her, drinking in every contour. He wondered who'd loaned her the clothes, but knew better than to ask. He was so used to Riva, the sensible proletarian, armoured in thick-soled shoes and the blue-grey pinafore with the tight collar, that the bourgeoisie garb left him confused. Tonight her shoes were a soft white leather with a delicate strap across the top that matched her ankle socks. The skirt, also white but with large red polka dots, was long and cut in the loose-fitting style favoured by most girls he knew, but made from a gauzy cotton that spoke of a bolder, less inhibited pedigree. It swished with each step she took, clinging momentarily to her thighs and hips as she moved. Her white blouse came with short sleeves, but even so, she'd rolled them up showing more skin than he was used to. Gone, too, was the high collar, replaced by a v-neck that plunged a good three inches toward her bosom.

"It's just that . . ." he stammered.

"What?"

"The objective was to be inconspicuous. You look so . . . pretty . . . every eye will be on you." A surge of pink flickered across her cheek. She feigned a frown.

"Don't talk nonsense," she scolded. "I'll blend in perfectly with those French girls. I've seen how they dress at the university."

"Never noticed, myself," he said, biting his lip as he watched her from the corner of his eye.

She cuffed him on the shoulder with the back of her hand. "Liar!"

"Why, Miss Lilovsky, do I detect a hint of jealousy?"

"You wish," she answered, taking his hand and squeezing it.

They turned onto St. Laurent and began the long descent toward le Gesù theatre on Bleury. The clanging streetcar coming up behind caused Marty to consider springing for tickets, but he knew she'd object to the expense. Besides, the evening promised to be a difficult one, and arriving early was not on the agenda. Getting there late and leaving early was more likely to ensure an evening of no mishaps. That is, if he could keep Riva from shooting her mouth off. "Those shoes you're wearing," he said, leaning over to check them once again.

Riva sighed with mock impatience as she raised her skirt several inches. "Was one ogle not enough?"

He took in the delicate ankles and slender calves disappearing under the skirt. "Can you run in them?"

She dropped her skirt, the smile, too. "I have no intention of running anywhere."

"If the evening turns ugly, we may have to get out of there fast."

"Come on!"

"I'm serious, Riva. These Jeune-Canada types take this stuff to heart. The way they see it, they let us into Montreal, then we turned around and sided with the English."

She gave him a sideways glance. "They've been doing a number on you at the U. de M., haven't they?"

"Don't be ridiculous. It's just that sometimes it pays to walk in the other guy's shoes."

"So, what are you going to tell me next? That Judaism is a threat to Catholicism?"

"Depends on your perspective."

She threw her head back. "Baloney!" she spat.

He wished for once she could get past the righteous indignation and see the bigger picture. He'd already explained the theme for tonight's topic—Jews, Communism, and Commerce—but she didn't seem to get it. He had a bad feeling.

On Bleury Street, they found themselves caught up in the flow heading for the auditorium. Six young men talking in boisterous tones overtook them, bumping Marty slightly as they passed. Riva opened her mouth to protest, but he squeezed her arm and she let it go. There was a defiant air about their laughter and loudness. He longed to be home, nose in his anatomy text.

Entering the hall, he relaxed. The gathering was filling up fast, with only a few rows at the back still vacant. He smiled to himself as he picked two seats close to the aisle and near the door. Within minutes, all the chairs were taken. Still, people kept pouring in, lining the walls and entrance. Like a *brasserie* on payday, smoke and a high-pitched excitement filled the air as voices rose and fell. Everybody seemed to be talking, nobody listening. That the crowd was young and energetic worried him—a weapon in the wrong hands.

Riva glanced at the packed room and leaned over, cupping her hands around his ear. "When Jews gather in numbers like this, the fire marshal shuts them down."

Marty nodded, but made no reply for fear of being overheard. Beside them, a young man signalled to a friend two rows up. "Know what this is?" he shouted, drawing an imaginary dollar sign in the air. "It's how a Jew makes an 's.'" Several people laughed.

"What'd he say?" Riva demanded. Marty shrugged. "No, come on," she insisted. "I heard the word *Juif*."

"He told a joke."

"About us?"

"We tell priest-nun jokes, don't we?"

"Yeah, but—"

She was interrupted by the audience rising to its feet as the evening's speakers filed onto the stage. A short, slender priest wearing a black-buttoned cassock and the mate to Marty's glasses approached the lectern, and the crowd fell silent. The cleric prayed for divine guidance.

"The guy in the dress with the cauliflower ears and a brush cut," Riva whispered, as they sat down, "who's he?"

Marty glanced at the people closest to them, but they were too mesmerized by the man at the podium to have overheard. "L'abbé Groulx," he whispered into her ear. "Father confessor to this group and a prof at the U. de M."

"Who're the others?" The man ahead of them must have sensed the English cadence because he cranked his head in their direction before turning his attention back to Groulx. Marty answered as quietly as he could.

"Jeune-Canada leaders. Big wheels on campus. The tall skinny guy with the lip hair is André Laurendeau. To his right are Dansereau, Manseau, and Dagenais."

She looked at him in surprise. "For an apolitical, you know a lot."

He shrugged. "They're regular soap-boxers at the university."

"What about the Smooth Joe with the armband?" Riva asked, pointing to the aisle. "Is he one of them, too?"

"If he's wearing an armband he's probably security."

"Wow," Riva whispered, "Check the blond hair on him. That's what I call a dish."

"Shush." Marty replied, turning his head to look at the guard. Instantly, he brought his hand up to shield his face.

"What's the matter?" Riva chuckled. "You owe him money, or something?"

Marty shook his head.

"But you know him?"

"Seen him on campus," he shrugged. "He's on the hockey team, I think."

"You should take me to more games," she laughed.

Marty might have answered if not for the blond who was now working his way up the aisle, checking the crowd as he moved. At last, he disappeared from view, only to mount the stage where he took a seat next to the exit. Marty relaxed, shifting his attention to l'abbé Groulx.

The cleric was true to form. Marty found himself sitting on his hands, praying Riva's French wouldn't be up to understanding the rapid-fire harangue. But Groulx surprised. Within minutes, after taking a mild shot at new Canadians, he accepted an award from the historical society and sat down. He'd said nothing whatsoever about the Jews.

Riva gestured to the adoring crowd around them. "What did he say that was so magnificent?"

Marty breathed easier. She hadn't understood a word. They just might get out of here in one piece after all. "It's not what he said they're applauding. It's who he is and what he stands for."

"Which is?" Marty ignored her, concentrating instead on the lip hair approaching the microphone.

Laurendeau spoke in a conversational, yet rapid, tone that seemed to lull Riva. In his well-rehearsed speech, he blamed immigrants for congregating in ghettos, driving local merchants into bankruptcy. Riva, sensing a rising discontent ripple through the crowd, leaned forward, questioning with her chin.

"Tell you later," he whispered, more at ease than ever by the turn of events. He'd come fearing that in the face of Hitler's forty-fourth birthday, and Herman Goering's friendly talks with the pope, anti-Semite hysteria would be the order of the night; so far, the speakers were pulling their punches. Better still, he detected a schism between the nationalists, who were hosting the evening, and the politicians, who were taking a beating from the podium. Here was proof that Riva's hysterical "to the barricades" philosophy was inappropriate, and his father's "keep your head down until it goes away" more fitting.

When Dansereau took the podium, Marty's pulse, however, revved back into high gear. To add to his discomfort, Dansereau's slow delivery and Parisian-like accent made his speech almost intelligible to an Englishman. Riva began to squirm. "Jews do not deserve equal status," he boomed to loud hurrahs. Marty stiffened, fearful of the volcano beside him.

He didn't have long to wait. When Dansereau's, "*Les Juifs doivent rester à leur place*," ricocheted off the walls, it was too much for Riva. "This is bullshit!" she responded in a voice that carried several rows. Heads twisted, people stood, Marty felt the blood draining from his face.

An older man directly behind them leaned forward. "Better get her out of here," he advised.

At the podium, Dansereau stopped speaking, straining to interpret the commotion at the back of the hall. The blond hockey player was up and moving. Marty pulled Riva to her feet, but with the scrum gathering around them, escape was proving difficult. Tongues lashed out, answered by Riva's sharp retorts and Marty's troubled silence. To his surprise, however, his mind remained clear. He placed a hand on each side of Riva's face, holding her steady and drawing her in until they were nose to nose.

"Riva!" he demanded. "Get a hold of yourself!"

When she stopped squirming, he relaxed his grip and tucked her in behind him. The crowd hesitated, waiting for a spark. He glared at them, daring them to strike. Marty felt a hand tighten around the back of his neck. It was the blond hockey player, surrounded by a retinue of marshals. They stumbled toward the exit, the crowd parting like the Red Sea. A roar of boos filled the air, punctuated by Dansereau's repeated calls for order.

Popping through the doors into the cool night air, Marty felt like he'd walked into his father's meat refrigerator.

"Bar the door!" the hockey player ordered, releasing his grip on Marty and pushing him forward. "We don't need spectators."

Marty turned, glaring. "Going to pound the piss out of us like you did those young boys on St. Urbain?"

The blond blinked. "You?" he responded in English.

"Yes, me, you friggin' asshole."

"I didn't do that."

"Yeah, right. They just fell bleeding onto the sidewalk by themselves."

"You didn't see what 'appened."

"I saw what I saw. Those boys were Jews. You beat the bejesus out of them and got away with it. But you won't always have the law on your side. One of these days the tables will turn and—"

"Get you gone!" the blond screamed, shoving Marty with both hands, "before I let some of the lads 'ave a go at you." He stood with his arms out, holding back two guards who had turned their attention from the door to the argument on the street.

Riva tugged at Marty, but he shrugged her off. "That how you operate?" he yelled to the blond. "Get others to do your dirty work while you watch?"

"*Decampez*! Go! These lads 'ave their dander up. I can't 'old them back much longer."

"You owe me a pair of glasses, you prick."

"Piss off!"

"What was that all about?" Riva asked when they'd reached Ste. Catherine and slowed to catch their breath.

"Not now, Riva."

"Did you hear that guy?" she asked. "'Get you gone? Dander? Lads?' Sounded like he'd just swallowed a Dickens novel."

"Maybe he's got an Irish mother, or something," Marty muttered.

"Come to think of it, he kinda let us off easy, didn't he? Could be beating people up's not his forte."

"Or he doesn't like doing it in front of an audience."

Chapter Five

6:15 a.m., Friday, April 14, 1934
Montreal

MARTY SWITCHED OFF THE GOOSENECK LAMP. Electricity was money and *Tate* was having a hard enough time without wasting it. The dawn light filtered through the gauze curtains. For a moment, he allowed his eyes to adjust before pulling the book in closer. By the shadows in the alley, he guessed the time to be after 6:15, but wouldn't risk waking the house by walking to the kitchen to check. In thirty minutes, his folks would be up: *Tate* tip-toeing downstairs to check on the butcher shop; *Mame* to wake the household by running taps and banging pots on the stove.

He didn't have to turn around to know his two younger brothers in the double bed across from his cot would be curled under the covers to cut the light. How they must hate this predawn study ritual. Still, other than rolling about, they seldom complained; Marty was the student in a family that prized academics. Soon he'd be a learned man with the letters M.D. after his name. Not quite rabbi status in the eyes of the folks, but close enough to warrant sacrifice from every member of the family. For Marty, it was both gift and burden.

He raised his head from the text, surprised to hear his mother's slippers shuffling over the linoleum toward the bedroom. The door opened a crack. "The Lilovsky girl is here," she announced in a stage whisper.

"She has a name, *Mame*," Marty replied, grabbing his pants from the chair. "I hope you asked her in."

"Why'd she be coming here this early in the morning?"

"Ah, *Mame*," he moaned, "you've gone and left her in the hall, haven't you?" He brushed by, making a mental note to set her down for a good talk. It was one thing to disapprove of the Lilovskys' politics and secular lifestyle, another to be downright rude.

"Riva," he said, opening the door.

"Let's walk," she replied looking over his shoulder. Mrs. Kellenberger stood behind her son with her hands on her hips, her hair up and her lip down. Riva leaned closer to Marty. "What I've got to say is best heard in private." She nodded to Mrs. Kellenberger as Marty raced to the bedroom to finish dressing. Both women eyed each other awkwardly through the doorway. Neither spoke.

"You have a paper to work on, no?" Mrs. Kellenberger asked when he returned.

Marty rolled his eyes as he tucked in his shirt. "Come on, *Mame*, it's well in hand." He closed the door and caught up to Riva, who'd already started down the hall. They walked in single file, careful to avoid the milk bottles.

"What's up?" he asked, slowing when they hit the street and praying the words "Russia," "visa," and "imminent departure" were not about to cross her lips. The threat had been hanging for so long with no followup he'd almost allowed himself to believe it would never happen.

"Keep moving," she responded, taking his arm and propelling him south on St. Laurent. He frowned as they sped up. She cleared her throat. "Do you know a man at the university by the name of Rabinovitch? He's in Medicine."

"Yeah," Marty nodded, "Sam. He's a year ahead of me. First in his class. Interning at the moment. Not sure where."

"Notre-Dame Hospital, that's where," she replied, "but not for long."

They'd only covered a block, but already he could feel the dampness working its way under his collar and across his chest. He lifted his chin to do up the top button on his jacket, puzzled as to why she would know where Rabinovitch had been placed. He waited, knowing better than to press. Couldn't she just give him the whole shot for a change, instead of sifting through the facts? It occurred to him how much she was like his mother, but he wouldn't dare go there. Finally, he could contain himself no longer. "What's going on?"

She took a deep breath. "Did you know that Jewish doctors aren't fit to administer to Gentiles?"

He looked straight ahead. "Don't be ridiculous."

"Tell that to your colleagues."

He took a deep breath. "What're you talking about?"

"Midnight, last night; Notre-Dame Hospital. A bunch of Gentile interns ganged up on Rabinovitch, laid down their stethoscopes, and walked out. Apparently, with a Jew in the house, your medical friends refuse to practise."

"How do you know all this?"

"Neighbour was rushed to Notre-Dame last night. His wife told us."

Marty ran a hand through his hair. "Strike!" he mumbled, looking off. A wave of numbness hit him, followed by an overwhelming urge to retrace his steps, climb back into his obstetrics text, and shut out the world. "Has it made the papers?" he asked, finally.

She shrugged, grabbing his hand and breaking into a trot. "We're about to find out," she replied, reaching for the front door of Moe's Smoke Shop.

At the newspaper rack, Riva scanned the English papers, Marty the French. Moe frowned suspiciously from his stool at the front counter. "No mention in the *Gazette* or the *Star*," Riva announced.

Marty returned *La Presse* to the rack and cracked open *Le Devoir*. "Here it is." He began reading aloud. "*Les internes manifestent contre un collègue juif.*" Thoughts of disappearing into his books dimmed as words and phrases reminiscent of an Old-World pogrom jumped off the page: "overdue lesson . . . social leeches . . . usurpers of jobs that belong to our grads." As he read and translated his voice grew louder and sharper, bouncing off the walls like the announcer at Bluebonnets Race Track. Customers turned to stare.

"Christ," Marty groaned when he'd finished. "They're pretty sure of themselves. They've allowed their names to be printed." He held the paper at arm's length, so that Riva could see the fourteen names listed on the page. "I know half these guys."

Riva shook her head. "I've been warning you."

He slapped the paper against the rack, as if to knock sense into his striking classmates.

"Hey!" Moe hollered from his perch. "The deal is you *pay* for the paper then you get to tear it apart. *Kapish*?"

Marty marched to the counter, rummaging in his pockets for a coin. Riva reached around him with a nickel. Outside, they stood shoulder to shoulder in the middle of the sidewalk, studying the article and ignoring the logjam they were creating. Suddenly, Marty scrunched the paper into a ball and launched it at the trash barrel beside Moe's step. It missed and rolled back at him. He kicked it wildly. A pedestrian jumped back cursing, as the paper ball arced into the air and disappeared under a truck.

He turned on his heels, striking south, with Riva scurrying behind. "Where you off to?"

"You better get to work, Riva," he responded without turning.

She matched him stride for stride for a full block before speaking again. "You going to the hospital?" He shook his head. "Where, then?"

"The university. Dean Turbide's office."

"What for? The strike's at Notre-Dame." Marty ignored her.

Riva grabbed his arm and pulled him to a halt. "I love it that you're finally on the trolley, but what are you intending to do?"

He stared back at her and shrugged, wanting her help, but afraid of it at the same time.

"Please tell me you're not about to kiss Turbide's ass, or beg for permission to help Rabinovitch."

"I've got to find out what's going on."

"Then what?"

He broke eye contact, staring at the horde of young girls heading for work at the textile factories. "Then I guess I'll figure out what to do next."

Riva's brow furrowed. "Already you're making a tactical error," she said. "Turbide's the enemy. Never approach an adversary without a plan of action."

"Turbide? The enemy? Get real!"

"I know what I'm talking about, Marty. Ask yourself, what does Riva do in her spare time?"

He hesitated as the crowd flowed around them. "Stir up shit, according to my mother."

She grimaced, but let it go. "Fight for other people's rights. That's why I know how to play the game."

"Come on, Riva! This is not one of your union matters."

"Really? It's got all the markings: man denied right to work, discrimination in the workplace."

He bristled, wondering if she was exaggerating for effect. Flared nostrils answered that question. "You're jumping to conclusions," he replied, gruffly, "which is why I have to talk to Turbide before going off half-cocked."

She stepped back, bumping into a sad-faced girl of no more than fourteen. The youngster appeared to have been poured into her mother's house dress and sent off to labour in a Peel Street sweatshop. The girl apologized in French. Riva ignored her. "Don't get uppity, Martin Kellenberger. Mark my words: Turbide'll turn out to be just another pacifier bent on sweeping this whole affair under the rug. You'll see, Rabinovitch will be thrown to the wolves to avoid publicity."

Marty held up both hands in a gesture of appeasement. "Listen, I know you have more experience in this sort of thing, but I do have a conscience as well as a brain. If it turns out as bad as you say, I won't let this affair slide. But talking to Turbide has to come first. I trust him. After I hear him out, I'll know better what to do."

"All right, Marty," she nodded. "That's not bad. I'll help where I can."

He turned, expecting her to leave, but she stuck with him, taking his arm. "Hadn't you better get to work?" he asked. "If you don't show up soon you could lose your job. There are thousands ready to take your place."

"So?"

"So, with no money, you'll never get your old lady back to Russia."

Riva waved a hand dismissively in the air. "Truth is, I'm finished at Macdonald Tobacco."

"You got fired?"

She shook her head. "Something better came up."

Under other circumstances, the "something better" would have triggered warning bells, but it was comforting to know she wasn't abandoning him, so he held his tongue. After several steps, he coughed into his fist. "If I'm wrong, and Turbide turns out to be what you suspect, how would you recommend proceeding?"

She leaned into him as they moved. "Well, for starters, you have to put yourself in the shoes of the dean and the hospital admin. How do you think they're feeling right now?"

He scratched his head. "Angry, I'd say. Maybe embarrassed."

Riva blew air through her lips. "Worse, Marty . . . exposed . . . shown up as incompetents." She seemed amused by his frown. "They've lost control, so, they're thinking, screw Sam Rabinovitch, we've got to save face, here." Her head bobbed up and down to punctuate the validity of her theory. "You watch, they'll be scheming to pack him off to some English hospital in the dead of night."

"Don't be too sure," Marty replied. "I know Dean Turbide. He's a bulldog. I suspect he's furious over the insult and the insubordination. If I'm right, he'll be digging his heels in to support Sam."

"Let's hope so, Marty. But just in case, why not approach him assuming the worst. That way, at least you go in prepared." She patted his arm. "For starters, you've got to convince him that abandoning Sam is opening a Pandora's box. Make him believe that with Sam's supporters mobilizing, the peace and quiet they all covet will be impossible."

Marty stared at her. "Supporters? Mobilization? What are you talking about?"

Riva smiled. "This is the part I'm good at—getting people to mount the barricades. All we have to do is crank them up."

"To do what?"

She raised her arms. "March, sign petitions, and take part in some of those Ghandi-like sit-ins. In short, 'stir up shit,' to quote your mother, and grab headlines. When you create a stink, the press comes to you. That gives you power."

"Power?"

"Yes, power to define the issues; brand the strikers as selfish little hypocrites who play the race card to feather their own nests."

"What nests?"

"Wake up, Marty. They want the best jobs for themselves. They're terrified of having to compete with Jewish doctors. Solution? Lock them out, even if it means withholding medical services from sick patients."

"You believe that?"

"Marty, if we put the right twist on it, Turbide and the hospitals will be spitting the strikers out like last week's pea soup."

He swallowed at the intensity and excitement in her tone. She moved with her jaw set and her feet coming down hard, like she was descending Mount Arafat with Sam's name on the sacred tablets. He'd seen the look in pictures—Christians staring down lions, Russian peasants storming the Winter Palace. A shiver worked its way up his spine.

"All those things you talk about," he said, "the marches, protests, and stuff; sounds to me like they come at a high price."

She smiled. "Don't worry about the money."

"It's my future I'm thinking about."

They stayed with the flow of people going southward. For a block, neither spoke. Marty took in the sad faces around them: mothers clutching children in doorways with their hands stretched out; young men in clothes wrinkled and soiled by sleeping on the ground; glum women trudging to the factories. These were the people Riva had at heart. He prayed she wouldn't drag her communist friends into the Rabinovitch affair.

At the steps of the medical school, they stopped, and Riva touched his arm. "Remember," she said, "it's important that Turbide and his cohorts at the hospital believe we're capable of raising a stink."

"You want me to go in there and scare the hell out him?" He noticed her fists tighten.

"*Gevalt geshreeyeh*! What do you think we've been talking about? That part's crucial." She looked over his shoulder. "I'll wait out here. I couldn't stand to see you lose your nerve."

"No, come with me. But let me do the talking. You're not to say one word."

11:30 a.m., Friday, April 14, 1934

DOLLARD RUSHED INTO THE HALLWAY and stopped. "Monsieur Arcand, *quelle surprise*," he said, motioning to his friends, Marcel and Yvon, to keep going. "What brings you to the university this morning of all mornings?" Around them, the corridor was filling with students, shouting and slapping backs.

"I wanted to catch you before lunch."

Dollard frowned, but tried not to show it. Since l'abbé Groulx's warning about Arcand's extreme politics, he'd kept his distance, confining himself to a few polite remarks at Sunday evening dinners, but avoiding direct conversation over cigars and cognac. He accepted the proffered hand, and, for a second, he and Arcand stood toe-to-toe, like dance partners. Dollard flushed as he saw his friends grinning down the hall. "Go on ahead without me," he shouted. "I'll catch up."

"All right," Marcel yelled back. "We'll be at the Snake Pit Lounge, and don't forget, we're making an afternoon of it."

Dollard looked at Arcand sheepishly and winced. "You caught me at a bad time. You see, Father Fortier's off to Rome a bit early and we just finished our last Philosophy class. A bunch of us are going out to, kind of, celebrate."

Arcand gave him a knowing smile. "Won't take a minute," he replied. "How about a coffee?"

The smell of sausages and burnt toast greeted them in the cafeteria. Students sat scattered about in little groups, some talking, some poring over notes, a few still playing cards, as if finals weren't around the corner. Arcand paid for the coffee then nodded at an empty table away from anyone else. Dollard glanced at the clock on the wall and waited while the family friend measured out three spoonfuls of sugar like it was gold, methodically depositing each into his cup. When he was done, he smiled, then began stirring, slowly and rhythmically. "Heard the news?" he asked at last, "about that Jewish student, Rabinovitch?" Dollard nodded. "What's the buzz on campus?"

Dollard's eyes were fastened on the spoon in the cup. The clinking was getting to him. "Bit of a stew in the Med school, they say, but not much happening in this building." Arcand looked disappointed. "Fact is, sir, most are focused on exams. Only the showoffs pretend they're not." He gestured toward the card players.

At last, Arcand stopped stirring and raised the cup to his lips. "This could be the story of the year," he said, smiling. "I see an opportunity here for you, young man."

Dollard looked up. "Opportunity?"

"If I've read things right," Arcand said, setting the cup carefully back on its saucer, "I'd say your heart's more in journalism than managing the family business." Dollard blew on his coffee, but held his tongue. "Fact is," Arcand continued, "*Le Patriote* needs an insider on this story—a man on campus. I figure with your Jeune-Canada connections, nobody'd bat an eye if you nosed around a bit. You know," he winked, "scared up the facts and worked on a few angles. That kind of stuff."

Dollard, feeling the scalding hot coffee on his lips, tried not to react to either the burn or the news. "You know how Father feels about reporters. He'd kill me. Maybe you, too." He took another sip, more carefully this time.

Arcand leaned forward. "Does he have to know? The way I see it, you'd get the behind-the-scenes information, write it up, then pass it on to me. If your articles pass muster, I'd print them as they are, under a *nom de plume*, of course. If they don't quite meet my standards, I'd touch them up a bit. Be a great experience for you."

"What are you looking for?"

"The effect the strike's having on campus. You know, what the student body thinks, names of any troublemakers who might come to the fore. That sort of thing. Analysis, too, of course," he hastened to add. "Look for themes. If you've got a nose, and I suspect you have, you'll find lots. I've read some of your articles in the school paper. Good stuff. Flair. Your bit last year on the rally at le Gesù was masterful."

Dollard winced. He'd been forced into that article and hated himself for it ever since. "Suppose I uncover information that doesn't quite fit your . . . turn of mind?" he asked. "Say, I find the strikers' motives are more about long-term security than conviction? Do I get to report that?"

"If that's the way you see it, but like I say, I'm the gatekeeper. I decide what goes into *Le Patriote* and what doesn't." He sat back in his chair, palming his cup in both hands like it was a chalice, a superior smile creasing his face. "It's good you've got standards. Just remember, sometimes there's a higher calling in journalism than merely reporting the facts."

"I don't get it." Dollard frowned.

"A paper's duty is to see that a public good comes out of every event."

"Regardless?"

Arcand sat up. "Take this strike, for instance. Sure there'll be opportunism—on *both* sides. The Jews will milk it for publicity, and maybe a few of our boys will see it as an opportunity to secure their own futures. But that's not the main issue. What's important here is the message."

"Which is?"

"Immigrants have to learn that they're only welcome if they know their place—that we'll all be better off when they understand the limits."

Dollard stared into his cup, wanting to lash back, but finding no solid ground to stand on. Why was this position so troubling from Arcand, but acceptable from Groulx? "So it's fine to manipulate the news if it suits a cause?" he said, with an edge to his voice. "Is that what you're saying?"

Arcand dipped his head. "I support interpretive journalism that betters society." His jaw tightened. "You've a lot to learn, Dollard. Eventually, you'll discover that all papers tailor the news to fit their views."

"With all due respect, sir, I've noticed that mostly in your papers."

"Take *La Presse*, for instance," Arcand replied, ignoring the hit. "Read it and you'd think Tachereau's Liberals sit with the celestial hosts. Meanwhile, down the street, *Le Devoir* paints horns on him."

"But don't you agree that—"

"It's your choice," Arcand interrupted, rising to his feet. "Do you want this job or not?"

Dollard looked up. "I'll do it," he answered.

Arcand's smile broadened. "Welcome to the world of journalism," he said, extending a hand across the table. "By the way, if you come upon any interesting Jewish types, I'm to know immediately, especially if they're big names. I'll see that the information gets to Dean Turbide. The small fish you can pass on to your cohorts at Jeune-Canada." He winked. "Some of them know how to handle the Bolshies."

11:45 a.m., Friday, April 14, 1934

RIVA STORMED PAST THE DEAN'S SECRETARY and out into the hall, her teeth clamped so tightly it would take a rib spreader to pry them apart. "Royal screw-up!" she hissed, as bells rang and students poured through classroom doors into the corridor. "Where the hell was your brain back there?"

Marty stared at her, frightened by the vein bulging from her temple. "I thought it went rather well," he replied.

"*Oy vey*," she groaned, ignoring the students who were clustered about. "You were supposed to be firm. Make him sweat. Remember?"

"Why are you getting so worked up, Riva? The man was perfectly reasonable."

"Open your eyes. He's a cunning asshole. First he kept us cooling our heels for more than four hours, then he played you, tested you for resolution. And guess what? He didn't find any." She began mimicking Turbide's franglais: " 'So, *Monsieur* Kellenberger, you are, *comment dit-on*, contemplating *action de la part de Monsieur* Rabinovitch?' To which you reply, 'Oh, well, only as a last resort, *sir*, it's not the kind of thing I'm very good at, blah, blah, blah, ha, ha.' Christ almighty!"

"For God sakes, Riva, getta grip." He raised his hands in a calming motion and ushered her into an empty classroom. "We were both there," he said, when he closed the door. "He doesn't want the strikers to win any more than we do."

"What he wants is the road with the fewest potholes. And you just showed him which one that'll be."

Marty scowled. "There you go again, imagining things. Know what I think? You're disappointed because you didn't get a confrontation. Turbide's taking the high road and it pisses you off."

She folded her arms. From the next room came the sound of footsteps and laughter. She took a deep breath then swallowed. "All right," she said, "let's start again. When we first went in, how did he appear to you?"

"I don't know. Nervous, I guess."

"Right, because we show up out of nowhere and all of a sudden he realizes that Sam Rabinovitch has comrades. But five minutes of you fumbling like a freshman and he's relaxing. Guess why?"

The "freshman" barb stung. "Listen here, Riva," he said, deciding not to play her game. "You've had your say, now it's my turn. Maybe I'm not very good at this kinda stuff. Guess I'm like *Tate* — confrontation turns my stomach. But what I saw in that room was a man ready to —"

"If you don't learn to fight," she interrupted, "you'll be eating shit all your life. Just like your father."

He felt his fists tighten at his sides. "Oh, I get it," he snapped. "I should be more like your old man?" She took a step back. "He was some fighter, wasn't he? And what did it get him? A bullet in the head courtesy of the czar's secret police." He went over to the windows and stood peering through the glass, breathing hard. Outside, a workman on a ladder was lowering a storm window to a helper. The ladder must have shifted, because the window slipped, crashing to the ground in an explosion of crystal shards, followed by curses and accusations. He heard Riva moving, but refused to turn. If she left him, he'd find his own way. Maybe his parents were right. He was too dependent on her. A second later he felt her breath on his neck and her arms encircling him from behind.

"Sorry, Marty. I'm used to instant action. Bred in the bone, I guess."

He turned to face her and sighed. "Worst part is, you weren't far off the mark. I did botch it, didn't I? I meant to talk tough, but couldn't bring myself to play the hypocrite."

"Hypocrite?"

"Come on, Riva, all those scary tactics you brag about, that's just rhetoric, right?"

She shook her head slowly. "Play it right, and you and I can put together an army of demonstrators that'll rock the daylights out of these strikers."

He watched the sparkle return to her eyes. "Please tell me the demonstrators you refer to won't be from the Young Communist League?"

"Why not? At least they know how to put feet to fire."

Marty slapped both hands on the top of his head. "*Fey*! Just what I need, me leading the Red Menace at the barricades. You any idea how long I'd last at this university pulling a stunt like that?"

"At least you'd have a clear conscience."

"Right, and end up spending the rest of my life working for my uncle at the textile plant."

<hr>

1:20 p.m., Sunday, April 16, 1934

AS A STAGING GROUND for a demonstration, St. Louis Square was too small. Marty could see that now. Already it was filling up and they were still forty minutes away from kickoff. The plan was to gather here then head down St. Denis to the university. He swallowed hard as he hopped onto the dais and steadied himself. To call it a dais, Riva's word, was to overstate the reality of planks laid over orange crates—it was as shaky as the rally they were trying to pull off. It had all seemed so heady twenty-four hours earlier when he and Riva, plus Mrs. Lilovsky and a handful of her union cohorts, had plastered the inner city with notices. Marty had fought to make the hospital the target of the march, but lost.

He knew he should be gratified by the crowd pouring into the square, but their politics, as evidenced by the placards and chants, shilled for myriad organizations and philosophies. To Marty's horror, the bulk of them appeared to have turned out for the wrong demonstration. Signs advised denizens to "Support the Young Communist League," "Make Trotsky Your Cause," "Grow with the Marxist-Leninists," "Vote Socialist," "Destroy Capitalism," and "Crush Fascism." Precious few bothered to mention the cause they were gathering for—Dr. Samuel Rabinovitch. Augmenting this explosive cocktail was the way disparate factions had clustered in groups and were screaming epithets at the competition. War could break out at any second. The noise was so great that spectators on the balconies surrounding the square had covered their ears with their hands. To add to his woes, rain threatened. He wondered how a downpour might affect the demonstration. With luck, it would drive everyone home and he could go back to his books.

Marty felt his heart rate rise as he stared out from the dais. Forty minutes to kickoff. If they didn't get underway soon, the lid was sure to blow off. He searched the crowd for signs of Riva. "Attention, please. Attention, please," he shouted into the blow horn, "would Miss Riva Lilovsky please report to the platform."

The noise dipped slightly, but only momentarily. While Riva failed to show, what he did see, to his dismay, was his father fighting his way to the dais, his face screwed up in anger.

"Stupid raised in Canada!" he boomed from three feet out. "What have you got yourself into, you? Come home, Martin. Now!"

Marty took a deep breath and raised his hands. "Take it easy, *Tateh*. It's all under control."

"This you take for control?"

"Why are you here?"

"To warn you. The police came to our shop. *Mame* fainted. Customers are talking."

"What'd they want?"

"You. 'Tell your son,' they said, 'break one law and it's Bordeaux Jail.'" He raised his eyes. "My son. Prison."

"Relax, *Tateh*. We have the right to assemble. We're breaking no laws."

"You crazy? This is Montreal. Here, police make laws."

"I don't have time for this now, *Tateh*. Trust me. In this country—"
Marty felt a hand on his shoulder and jumped. Turning, he found himself

staring past a scraggly beard into the hollow eyes of a common vagrant. The man wasn't alone. He'd come with an army of down-and-outers, each sporting the same uniform of mismatched clothes, matted hair, and leathered skin. Marty struggled not to recoil. *There but for the grace of God*, he thought, sniffing for the stench of booze and urine. To his surprise, he found none. Mr. Kellenberger stepped back, mouth agape. Marty held his ground. "What on earth do you want?" he asked the vagrant.

"You the guy with the vouchers?" he asked in a faraway voice.

"Vouchers?" Marty replied, his lip curling.

"We was told there'd be free food at the union hall if we joined ya."

"You know Sam Rabinovitch?"

"Who?"

"Rabinovitch. He's the one we're—"

"I've got your vouchers," a voice said from behind.

"Riva," Marty said, turning. "Thank God."

Mr. Kellenberger's face screwed up at the sight of her. "Socialist bloodsucker!" he muttered. "You're ruining my boy's future."

Riva flinched but turned from Mr. Kellenberger to the vagrant and began counting out vouchers. "Come to the Auditorium Union Hall after the rally," she said. "We'll be expecting you." The man nodded and signalled the others to move off to the sides.

"Wait!" Marty yelled. "Escort my father out of here, would you?" The man nodded and his group spread out, forming a pocket for Mr. Kellenberger, who hesitated, a look of horror on his face. "Don't worry, *Tateh*. It'll be all right. We know what we're doing." He watched his father disappear into the crowd before turning back to Riva. "What the hell *are* we doing? And where did you pick up those hoboes?"

Riva ignored the question. "This event is coming off better than we'd dreamed," she said, rubbing her hands. "And those 'hoboes' are neighbours. They live in Mount Royal Park under cardboard and newspaper."

"They have no idea what this is all about, Riva."

"Maybe they've never heard of Sam Rabinovitch, but they know injustice."

"Whatever." Marty shrugged. He ran his hands through his hair. "Riva, we've got problems. No way can we wait for two o'clock. There are too many factions. Battles are about to erupt all over the square. They're more interested in their own campaigns than ours."

Riva looked out, a huge smile spreading over her face. "Perfect," she said.

"You crazy? These guys will break every window from here to Ste. Catherine Street and we'll be held responsible. You know what they do to organizers, don't you?"

The first drops of rain hit the platform. "Calm down," Riva said. "This group is never going to leave St. Louis Square."

Marty frowned to hide his relief. "I don't get it," he said.

"Today is just step one. We've achieved our objective."

"Which was?"

"We've proven to the press that we can draw a crowd. They'll take us seriously now. If we march there'll be a confrontation with the police. By cancelling, we show our human side." She gave him her best smile. "Know what you're going to have as soon as we dismiss this bunch?"

"For God's sake, Riva, not twenty questions."

"Reporters crawling all over you. It'll be in all the papers tomorrow. Radio, too."

"Oh, great!" he moaned.

"So, let's get it going. I'll introduce you to the crowd. Be brief. Strike a reasoned, responsible tone. Stress the principles we're fighting for. When you've finished, dismiss the crowd and we'll go home."

"You're nuts. I'm no orator. Even if I was, do you actually believe a few soft words will convince this rabble to leave? You can't crank them up and dismiss them with a snap of the fingers."

"Good Lord, Marty, you should attend more rallies." She gestured to the crowd. "This is calm. Nobody's cranked them up. Today, they're too caught up in their own squabbles to join our campaign. We've given them an hour to scream at each other. They'll go away happy."

"I don't believe it."

"I'm telling you, they're not out for blood today. Next week, if things don't start breaking for us, we can turn up the pressure."

"Next week? What the hell have you got up your—"

She raised her hands. "Just announce that if the Rabinovitch affair isn't resolved by Tuesday, there's to be a serious march, and this time we'll be pulling out all the stops."

"What's that supposed to mean?"

The drops had turned into a light rain. She took the blow horn from him and walked to the front of the stage. "Ready?" she asked, looking back.

He gazed out into the crowd, praying his father was out of earshot, praying the assembled throng of malcontents and mischief-makers would leave on command, praying this nonsense would soon pass. How had things ever gotten this far? He'd never be ready for something like this, he thought.

7:00 p.m., Sunday, April 16, 1934

MARTY TOOK HIS PLACE AT THE TABLE in full knowledge as to why the family had been summoned on such short notice—they'd gathered to rescue boy academic from a fatal attack of altruism. They were all here—*Mame, Tateh,* older brothers and their wives, his younger siblings. He hoped he wasn't too tired to put up a good defence.

If someone had asked him how much time had lapsed since he and Riva had first met with the dean, he might have said a month. In fact, it had been a mere fifty-six hours. In that short time, they'd cranked out crates of literature, organized and cancelled a rally, and garnered more publicity than he'd thought humanly possible—radio stations were quoting him on the half-hour, and newspapers were publishing his picture alongside that of Dr. Rabinovitch. So far, press coverage had been kind to the cause, but not to Marty's hopes for a gentle exit. His suggestion to the press, that protests would continue should the authorities not resolve the strike in Rabinovitch's favour, had been twisted into ominous headlines: "Demonstrators Hang Tough," "Public Disorder Inevitable," and "Medical Department Faces Keel Hauling." Alarm bells were ringing in the Kellenberger household. Vaunted son was self-destructing, and they all knew who was behind it.

They weren't alone in their anxiety. Dean Turbide had called Marty in early Sunday morning to read the Riot Act. The meeting had been short. The dean, registrar at his side, cautioned him on his future in medicine should he push too hard.

"I don't believe this," Marty said to his hushed family. "One of our doctors gets sacked and the Kellenbergers play the three monkeys—eyes, ears, and mouths taped shut."

Mr. Kellenberger raised a hand to silence the sudden uproar. "You take Rabinovitch for the first Jew to get picked on ever? You think you can come in here and lecture me about persecution? Old World pogroms this family survived. Why? Because we knew when it was to act and when it was to shut up. Sure, sure, easy, bending never is. But to be a Jew is to be a martyr. Those who fail to endure the bad never live long enough to enjoy the good."

Marty slumped, overcome with weariness. He considered giving up and going to bed, but that, too, would be bending. He chewed on his thoughts for a moment as he considered a response. "I understand, *Tateh*, but this is not Byelorussia. Here, we have a chance. But only if we take a stand."

"It's that Lilovsky girl," Mrs. Kellenberger interjected. "With nonsense she's filled his head."

Marty winced as he searched for a rejoinder, but seeing his father's finger in the air, he opted to tackle his soup instead.

"You're all by yourself on this, I tell you. Keep it up and it will be bye-bye doctor. That scruffy rabble around you yesterday, you think they'll be picking you up when on your face you fall?"

"How can you say I'm alone, *Tateh*? There's only one paper in this whole city backing the strikers and that's *Le Devoir*. Can't you see? For once, we Jews have allies."

Mr. Kellenberger produced a newspaper from under his chair and began slowly unfolding it. Marty recognized the glint in his father's eye. "So, Mr. Smartypants," the elder Kellenberger began, "tell your *tateh*, if it's so good, how come other hospitals are joining the strike?" He ran his finger along the paper: "Sainte-Justine, la Miséricorde, Hôtel-Dieu, and Saint-Jean-de-Dieu—they're all going out. Soon, turning on you and Samuel Rabinovitch will be the whole city."

"Or, come to its senses," Marty shot back. He glanced quickly from his father to the rest of the family, searching for support. None was forthcoming. They might be family, but he was all alone on this one.

"Bah! You think a goy will stand by a Jewish doctor when his kid needs patching up at emergency? Let it go, Martin. Listen to your *tateh* when he tells you it's better to be a dog in peacetime than a soldier in war."

"Oh, I get it. Like a good Jew, I'm to pretend nothing's happened?" His raised voice bounced off the walls and shot back at him. He'd been trying to keep it down, but the buzz, frustration, and fatigue were getting to him.

Mr. Kellenberger stiffened, but held his tone. "What I want is for my son to use the brain God gave him. What's the good of getting kicked out of school when all Rabinovitch needs to do is move quietly to an English hospital? Eh? If you fight a wave it overpowers, but let it roll over you and it will pass."

"Enough with the proverbs already!" Marty shouted, slamming his fist on the table and knocking over his water glass. His little sister began to cry.

Mrs. Kellenberger was opening her mouth to speak when they heard a throat clear at the end of the table. The family turned in surprise to the newest daughter-in-law, Miriam. Her eyes trained on her lap, she spoke softly. "I think you're very brave, Martin," she said. "But *Tateh's* right. To press on is to jeopardize your own prospects. Have you talked to Rabinovitch?"

Marty dropped his own gaze to the table. He stared at the water from the upset glass as it wicked its way across the tablecloth. "Tomorrow," he said softly. "I'm going to see him tomorrow. Rumour is he's holed up at Notre-Dame Hospital and is ready to concede. I hope not. If he is . . . then, maybe . . . I will, too."

"What!" Mrs. Kellenberger demanded. "You dished up all this *kaka* and you haven't even talked to him? What are you? Some kind of *meshugeneh*?"

"Enough, *Mame*," Mr. Kellenberger interrupted. "Martin was a little *fahklumpt* for a while. Now he sees his way. Pass the chicken."

The rest of the family relaxed as they dug into their food. Marty sighed, struggling with the thoughts warring inside him. Here sat his family and, whatever the issue—finding a new apartment, closing the Gentile branch of the butcher shop, raising money to send him to university—it was debated here. But there were rules: you could raise your voice, bully, and challenge, as long as you played every card in your hand and kept no secrets. Turbide had warned him that under no circumstances was he to contact Sam Rabinovitch. But he'd now told his family he would. How ironic it would be, he thought as he chewed, to see the striking interns pardoned and Martin Kellenberger thrown to the lions. He grimaced inwardly. No matter how he looked at it, he was a *schmuck*.

1:00 a.m., Monday, April 17, 1934

"GOOD GOD, KELLENBERGER! You scared the daylights out of me. How'd you get in here? It's one o'clock in the morning, for Chrissakes." Rabinovitch sat propped up in bed with a magazine. He glared out past the stubble on his chin at his unexpected guest. Marty had snuck in, squeezing the door shut behind him. A heavy smell filled the room—a mixture of stale air, old food, and rancid tobacco. He traced the odour to a pipe on the bedside table and a plate of cold gravy and french fries on the window sill. He wondered how long Rabinovitch had been cooped up in here. Pants and shirt were draped over a chair. Newspapers were strewn over the floor, one folded open at a photo of a svelte-looking Samuel Rabinovitch with a stethoscope around his neck. But the man on the bed reaching for his pipe showed none of the swagger of the man in the picture. No V for victory hovered over this head. Marty felt a knot forming in his stomach. He took a deep breath.

"Came in through the kitchen and up the back stairs; helps to know the hospital. A good source told me you were holed up here."

Rabinovitch began packing tobacco into his pipe. Marty had seen him do this before, but never so clumsily. Little bits fell onto the bed-clothes. "They've been talking about you, Kellenberger. And it ain't pretty. The word 'provocateur' keeps coming up."

Marty smiled, surprised at himself for taking the statement as a compliment. "I have a good coach. There's more to come. Tuesday. Something big. You'll be pleased." He looked for a reaction, but Sam had disappeared behind a screen of smoke. "That's why I'm here," he continued, "to get you to coordinate your statements with our next move."

Sam waved a hand at the cloud separating them. "I figured this wasn't a social call."

There was a raw Saturday-night drinker's edge to Rabinovitch's voice that disturbed Marty. The thought of a drink was suddenly appealing, but peering through the smoke he saw no evidence of alcohol and wasn't about to ask. Sam coughed into his fist. "Don't get the idea I don't appreciate your efforts, but there's something you should know." His eyes moved from Marty to the cross on the far wall. "It's over. Done. *Siz genig.*"

Marty reached for the metal pipes of the bed's footboard, hands tightening. "You can't quit, Sam. Not now. Not with all the press and politicians we've got coming on board. "Shit! By Tuesday, with the demonstration we're working on, we'll be getting national coverage."

Rabinovitch coughed then swung his legs over the side of the bed. "You're not making it any easier," he said.

"What are you talking about?"

"Figure it out, Kellenberger. You've got too many communists and wide-eyed radicals behind this. The press is sure to pick that up. It's the kiss of death."

"I admit, some of them may be from . . . peculiar persuasions, but they're not in control here. We've got people from all the parties and—"

Sam raised his hand to cut him off. "I'm sorry . . . but I said it's too late and I mean it. Fact is, I'm tuckered out. Ninety-six hours of meetings, interviews, finger-wagging, and threatening phone calls have me done in." He puffed on his pipe.

"What are you going to do?"

"Can't tell you. Sworn to secrecy."

"We can win, Sam. Hell, even the faculty's coming on board."

Sam arched his spine slowly, a hand supporting his lower back. "You've misread the faculty all along. They were behind me from the start. They never wanted the interns to win."

"They sat on their hands, did nothing."

"They kept their mouths shut because they figured the strike wouldn't last. And that's the way it looked, too, until you and your band showed up throwing *bupkes* at them. Now they can't give in without giving the appearance of siding with a bunch of pinkos." He shook his head. "You've pissed off a lot of people, Kellenberger."

Marty brushed a magazine off a chair and plopped down. "I don't get it. Why in all this chaos does it have to be you backing down?"

"Isn't it obvious? Seventy-five interns are out on strike, surgery and emergency have been shut down at five hospitals, and regular doctors have been pulling triple shifts. They've hit the wall." Marty groaned and slumped forward. "You all right, Kellenberger?" Sam asked.

"Bloody hell! For once in my life, I take a stand, just to discover that the guy I'm sticking my neck out for has weak knees. Has it occurred to you that you're not just fighting for yourself? For God's sake, if the neanderthals win it'll set us back decades."

"You're wrong about them, Kellenberger. They're not neanderthals, just a bunch of confused, frightened young doctors who've been sold a crock about segregation. One day they'll wake up with one heck of a conscience."

Marty moved to leave. "Someone will be waking up with a bad conscience, but it won't be them."

Sam attempted to laugh, but a cough interrupted. He walked to the sink in the corner and began adjusting the taps. "You might as well drop it," he said, as they squealed to life, "because it's all academic now."

"Jesus, Sam, at least tell me what you've agreed to."

Sam studied him for a moment, then shrugged. "Right. I owe you that much. Can you keep a secret from that girlfriend of yours?" Marty nodded. "My resignation from Notre-Dame Hospital was delivered an hour ago. The director and the dean are to convene a press conference first thing in the morning."

"*Feh*! On what terms?"

Rabinovitch splashed water on his face then reached for a towel. "Pretty well what you'd expect. I signed a statement about wanting to get on with caring for the sick and seeing emergency departments up and running again, which is all true. In return, I get my pick of English hospitals if I want. Truth is, I'll probably clear out of here and head for the States."

Marty gripped the door handle. "You've sold out," he mumbled.

Sam threw the towel in the sink. "Look, I hate to see those sons of bitches winning as much as you do. But they're not getting off scot-free. They'll be on probation. It'll be expulsion for anyone pulling a stunt like this again. Ever!"

"I see," Marty sneered. "It's all taken care of. The perpetrators go back to work and you slip away. Case closed; everybody's happy. With one exception, the insider who 'threw shit at them,' as you put it?" Rabinovitch looked away as Marty opened the door. "One thing's certain," Marty continued, his voice trailing off, "a head will roll. Guess we know whose that will be, don't we?"

<hr />

4:00 p.m., Tuesday, April 18, 1934

DOLLARD STORMED INTO ARCAND'S OFFICE. The journalist held up his hand. "Before you utter a word," he said, studying the scowl lines on Dollard's brow, "let me say this: I'm delighted with the work you did on the Rabinovitch assignment. With a little guidance, you'll make a class A reporter." He pointed Dollard to a chair. "So, what seems to be troubling you?"

"You emasculated my article," he said, glaring down at him. "I want it republished, exactly the way it was written."

"Ohhhh, so that's it," Arcand replied, placing his pencil on the desk. "Didn't I make it clear that a little editing might be in order?"

"What was printed bears no resemblance to what I handed in. I poured my soul into that report—skipped classes and even . . ." He bit his lip. He'd almost blurted out that he'd stood Shannon up and was in trouble for it.

Arcand shrugged. "Par for the course, my boy."

"I did everything you suggested and more. I interviewed Rabinovitch, the strikers, and Dean Turbide, not to mention as many hospital administrators as I could buttonhole."

"Commendable. Like I said, a fine job." He steepled his fingers together and looked up. "So, if I'm happy, and I'm the boss; what's your problem?"

"The bastardized product that got printed, that's what. In your version, Rabinovitch comes out a complete asshole and Turbide was backing the strikers from the start."

"Turbide's not complaining."

"It was a hatchet job."

"Fact is, your article was a tad one-sided. I had to give it . . . balance. Snip a bit here, add a bit there. You have a problem with editing?"

"Fine, delete a few metaphors, kill the odd adverb if you must, but you've no right to tamper with the guts. You reconstructed it to say things I never intended."

Arcand opened the silver cigarette case on his desk and popped a gasper between his lips. He picked up the lighter, flicking it several times before abandoning it for a match. His eyes never left Dollard. When the cigarette finally caught, he took a long drag. "Let's get something straight, here. I'm the editor," he said tapping his chest, "and you're," his finger swung to Dollard, "the reporter. You hand your article to me, and I edit it to reflect the bigger picture. That's how it works."

"Journalistic honesty be damned?"

Arcand released a long column of smoke. "Stop with the petulant child! We're not talking some minor university essay, here."

Dollard plunked into the chair in front of the desk and began rubbing his knees. "So, this is what reporting's all about, eh? Some sucker works his ass off, takes risks, so a know-it-all editor can butcher it?"

"You were hardly covering an anarchist revolt in Barcelona," Arcand chuckled.

"I brushed up against a few . . . questionable types." Arcand raised his eyebrows. Dollard continued. "At the rally in St. Louis Square."

"Really?" Arcand said, sitting up. "If there were so many 'questionable types,' as you put it, why so little mention in your report? A bit odd, don't you think?"

Dollard looked away. "Because, in the end, it all came to nothing. The 'Internationale' got sung, some broad introduced the speaker, who mumbled something about another rally set for the following Tuesday, and everyone went home."

"Why?"

"It started to pour, that's why."

"So, who was this speaker?"

Dollard examined his fingernails. "Some myopic klutz in wire-rimmed glasses. I think his name was Kellenberger."

"Didn't you interview him after? The other papers did."

"With the downpour and crush, he got away before I could get to him."

"Strange, it wasn't raining that hard in my part of the city." He watched Dollard swipe at some imaginary lint on his pants before continuing. "I'm puzzled. It looks to me like you skated away from him. How come?"

"I told you. I couldn't get close enough."

Arcand cocked his head. "You know him, don't you?"

"Don't be ridiculous; he's a Jew."

Arcand plunged his cigarette into a sea of butts in the ashtray, pounding out the fire and unleashing a wave of stale nicotine in the process. "All right, time for a little honesty, here. From my editor's chair, I see three flaws in your report: first, you failed to nail a principal player; second, you let personal feelings interfere with good judgment; third, you failed to comprehend the real motive behind Rabinovitch's refusal to walk away from the issue in the early stages."

Dollard glared at him. He was willing to concede on points one and two, but not on three. He'd unearthed enough to understand why a man of Rabinovitch's integrity would not roll over without a struggle.

"You misjudged Rabinovitch," Arcand continued, "mistook opportunism for altruism."

"What are you talking about?"

Arcand picked up a paperweight from his desk and explored the floral pattern in the glass. "With seventy-five interns and five hospitals against him, and more about to join, do you think he was ever going to win? 'Course not. He had no business being at Notre-Dame Hospital from the start and knew it. So what does the sly bugger do? In a bid for sympathy, he plays the discrimination card and winds up with a peachy position in an English hospital." Arcand returned the paperweight to the desk. "I've seen it all before. The Jew crowd's good at that. It wouldn't surprise me if they planned this whole thing from the start."

"Impossible!" Dollard replied. "Rabinovitch had a contract with the hospital. He's a trained doctor and top of his class."

"A doctor attempting to take the place of one of ours."

"That's not true! Dean Turbide told me there were more openings for interns than there were qualified people. That's why the Jew got hired at Notre-Dame. Every one of our guys who applied for an internship got one, too."

Arcand shook his head. "You miss the point. There should be more of our boys at med school, but the Jews keep grabbing all the places."

"I haven't encountered that many," Dollard frowned.

"No surprise there. You're studying the Classics. Jews don't go in for that kind of stuff. No money in it." He looked at the clock on the wall.

Dollard took the hint and got to his feet. He'd never thought much about what Jews did or did not choose to study. Abe Agulnic was the only one he knew and Abe was in law. Lots of money to be made there. Coincidence? He wondered if he could raise the subject with him without hurting his feelings.

At the door, Arcand stopped him with a question. "Be honest with me. Aside from this little . . . disappointment, did you have a good time?"

Dollard felt the blood rise to his cheeks. After his outburst, how could he tell Arcand that he'd floated through the past four days with scant regard for food, gambling, sex, or even the company of his best girl. He turned, surprised to see a grin on the editor's face.

"Don't bother answering," Arcand grinned. "It's written all over you." He reached for another cigarette. "You know, Desjardins, the two of us could have a good future. Of course, that would depend on whether or not you learn the cardinal rule of journalism."

Instinct screamed at Dollard not to bite, but curiosity got in the way. "Why do I get the feeling that this cardinal rule has nothing to do with reporting the facts?"

"Well, of course it does. That goes without saying. But it's deeper than that. It involves understanding the paper for which you're reporting and the philosophy to which it subscribes."

"What the hell's that supposed to mean?"

Arcand's smile broadened. "When you've figured it out come back and I might have another job for you."

Wednesday, April 19, 1934

Riva walked into One Minute Lunch and plunked herself down beside Marty at the counter. He signalled to the waiter, who moved to the coffee urn. Without speaking, they watched him pour the scalding black liquid into a mug and set it down in front of her.

"Sorry, Marty. Guess I wasn't much help to Sam, eh?" She grimaced as she sipped the bitter coffee. "Vladimir Ilyich would be disgusted with me."

"You may have been more successful than you thought, Riva."

"How do you figure?"

"Woke me up."

"Really?" She leaned over and rested her head on his shoulder. "You just saying that?"

"I like myself better this morning."

She shifted back to her stool. "At least now you'll be getting that assignment in. The one your mother's been harassing you about."

He nodded. "I'll be done by next week. Then it's off to Uncle Harvey's textile plant for the summer. That lab job at the university, though? The one they promised me. Looks like it's about to be terminated."

"How come?"

He swallowed, but didn't answer. "Good thing Uncle Harvey's expecting me at the plant."

Riva chuckled then burst out laughing, spewing coffee across the counter. "That'll put us both in textiles," she announced between gasps, "on opposite sides." The quizzical expression on his face brought on new spasms. "I start my new job next week," she sputtered. "It's with the Needle Workers Industrial Union."

Marty screwed up his face in mock horror. "We'll be enemies," he groaned, "me in the front office, you sneaking around out back trying to unionize my workers."

"*My* workers is it, already?" she shrieked. "*Oy veh*! What would you do if you caught me?"

"My duty, of course—call the cops, release the dogs, turn on the hoses." He saluted into the mirror across from the counter.

"You wouldn't!"

He leaned over, pecking her on the lips. When she returned it he slid off the stool and pulled her in close, kissing her passionately. "Marry me," he whispered.

She turned back to the counter, picking up her mug and holding it halfway to her lips. Their eyes locked in the mirror. "Not yet."

"Why?"

"You know the answer. *Mame*'s not well and she's still bent on Russia. I've got to get her there, if only to exorcize the obsession." She slid off the stool. "But when I get back . . ."

He stood. Again they kissed, her tongue sliding over his. "Hey, buddy, come up for air," a jokester yelled. When they disengaged there was clapping.

"Take me home," she whispered in his ear. "*Mame*'s gone for the day."

Chapter Six

———

July 14, 1934
Montreal

FOUR WEEKS AT THE TEXTILE PLANT had Marty counting his blessings—he had a job. Originally, it was supposed to be for the summer, but that was before the letter arrived from the university. As soon as he saw the letter-head he knew what it was all about. So did the family. The dean's choice of words—hiatus over expulsion—had a softer ring, but they meant the same. The verdict was that in view of insubordination and adverse publicity brought upon the university by the unbecoming conduct of one Martin Kellenberger, it would be in the best interests of both institution and student to part company for a period. They hadn't barred the door completely, but the message was clear. His mother pleaded for him to try McGill, but that was a non-starter—they already had their quota of Jews. Besides, he'd been turned down there before. His matriculation marks had not quite reached the requisite ten percent above the gentile average. With the exception of Uncle Harvey, who saw the potential in an employee "with something between the ears," the family saw him as a *shlemiel*. A dark cloud hung over the Kellenberger household, and Marty wondered what it would take to redeem himself and find a new place in the world.

Before the rally, life had been study, study, study. Now he found himself making choices, setting priorities, and outlining new courses of action. While the textile mill was not the job of his dreams, perhaps, it did provide him with a living and a chance to pay off university debts. In addition, he could set money aside for the day he got back into medicine. Already Uncle Harvey was singing the praises of his new employee. On the day Marty uncovered a double billing, he announced that at last he was backing the right Kellenberger. Throughout it all, Riva was a source of comfort and encouragement. If only she'd stop plying him for information about wages and conditions at the factory.

As Marty exited the factory gates he found Riva waiting. For a block, neither spoke. A month on the job and he still felt uncomfortable leaving the factory in the company of *real* workers. Even meeting their eyes was difficult, but he was beginning to understand why. He'd been parachuted into a manager's job, over the heads of long-standing employees, because he was the owner's nephew. His education set him apart, too. He tried to downplay his differences, but they still radiated like a beacon in the way he dressed, spoke, and tackled problems.

"They're afraid of me," he said in a low voice.

Riva tipped her head. "Of course! You're God Almighty. Snap a finger and they comply. Anything you want. Need extra work done? Fine. Gotta drop my salary to make ends meet? Okey-dokey. Want a little ass on the side? Right-o, Mr. Bossman."

He shook his head and frowned. "Where do you get that stuff, Riva?"

She took a deep breath. "Experience! Why do you think I quit Macdonald Tobacco?" She kept her eyes focused on the young girl ahead. "The foreman started pressing me. Son of a bitch had a wife and kids, but wouldn't stop pawing the girls. You know me. When it came to my turn, I fought back. Got sacked. No! Erase that. Fired."

Marty slowed. "Those other girls? The ones the foreman, you know, made demands on. You mean to tell me they just—"

She shrugged. "Look at these young things," she said, gesturing to the throng pouring out of the factory. "What are they? Fourteen? Sixteen? Eighteen? Put yourself in their shoes. Each is probably the sole wage earner in the family. If you knew there were ten people waiting to take your place, could you go home and tell the folks that you'd quit on principle—that the only family paycheque was history?"

"Guess I should try to learn more about the employees, eh?"

As they rounded a corner, Riva stopped. Ahead of them a cluster had formed around a worker. "Here's your first opportunity," she said.

"Looks private to me, Riva."

"Nonsense. They're talking shop." She egged him forward.

He took a deep breath and approached. Riva held back. "*Qu'est-ce qui se passe?*" He asked, clearing his throat. "What's wrong?" The crowd parted. At the centre, a girl had collapsed against a wall. She was sobbing, the others attempting to console her. Seeing Marty, she raised her arms, as if trying to shield herself, her shoulders shuddering with each gulped breath. Marty handed her a handkerchief and she dabbed her tears.

A tall, dark-haired girl with a prominent nose stepped forward. Her gingham dress and bobbed hair did nothing to distinguish her from any of the other employees, but there was something refreshing in her bearing as she faced him with her shoulders back, her chin thrust out, and her black eyes alive and searching. Marty guessed her to be his age. The girls waited for her to speak. The crowd grew. It occurred to him that she might be one of those reps from the Congress of Industrial Organizations, the ones his uncle had been trying to keep away from the plant. They and the International Ladies' Garment Workers had been hanging around the gates, attempting to sign up the employees. Uncle Harvey claimed they'd been making inroads with the cutters at other shops and, if not stopped, could wind up ruining the whole *shmata* trade.

"There is nothing you can do 'ere, Monsieur Kellenberger," she said.

The distressed girl opened her mouth to speak, but noting the shaking heads around her, closed it again.

Marty signalled the tall girl to follow him over to where Riva was standing. "You know my name," he said, crossing his arms.

"We all do."

"You'd tell me if the girl's trouble had something to do with the plant? Right?"

The tall girl looked off for a second. "What would that accomplish, Monsieur Kellenberger?"

"Because, if something's . . . amiss, I might be able to . . . do something." She smirked. He forced a smile and continued. "As they say, 'an unhappy workforce makes for an unproductive team.'" There was a long pause. Her smirk became a full grin.

"'Ave you ever been on the shop floor, Monsieur Kellenberger?"

"Of course. I had a tour when I joined—cutting room, sewing room, shipping, the whole works."

"With your uncle, as I recall," she said.

"Business takes me out there occasionally."

She hesitated. "Try doing it more often. You might find it an education." She turned to rejoin her friends.

Marty glanced awkwardly at Riva and then at the tall girl. "I'm not your enemy," he said to her back.

She glanced over her shoulder. For a second, he thought she was coming back, but instead she started speaking to the others in low tones. They looked at him as she spoke.

Marty wished he'd asked the girl her name. At least then he could find out where she worked, maybe stray into her section, talk to her some more. Stalking the building would achieve the same thing, but that meant coming face-to-face with a host of mysteries best left alone.

It was a couple of months before Marty ran into the tall girl again. The shop had just closed, and he and Riva were walking down St. Urbain when she rushed up from behind.

"May I 'ave a word, Monsieur Kellenberger?"

Marty stopped. It took a minute before he could place her. "Sorry, but I never did get your name," he said finally.

"Délorèse Laplante. They call me Dolly. Some of the girls are taking up a collection for Monique Dupont. We were wondering if you'd care to make a contribution."

Marty frowned. "Excuse me, who is she?"

"Monique. Remember? The girl on the street a while back, the one who was crying."

Marty nodded, careful not to look in Riva's direction. "I see. And what's this collection all about?"

"She 'as to quit. She's pregnant."

"Does the father have a job?"

"Yes! With you. He's Monique's boss in shipping."

"She's very young. Is this their first then?"

Dolly looked from Marty to Riva before answering. "For 'er, yes, for 'im, no. He 'as a wife and five children."

Marty felt Riva's hand tighten on his arm. "*Oy vey,*" she moaned. Marty pulled out his wallet and handed over a dollar bill. Dolly thanked him and left. Riva waited until she was out of range before speaking. "It all fits, doesn't it?" Marty shrugged, knowing exactly where she was going. "When we caught her bawling back then she'd probably just found out she'd been knocked up. Now she has to quit, before it starts showing. Goddamn men and their dicks! What are you going to do about it?"

He tugged at her arm, but her feet had put down roots in the sidewalk. "Be reasonable, Riva, over four hundred people work for us. We're not their nannies. We can't be butting in every time somebody—"

"Your foreman raped that girl," she interrupted, her voice rising.

"You don't know that. Maybe she led him on . . . for favours on the shop floor." He spoke in a stage whisper, hoping she'd take the hint.

"That asshole used his position to get into her pants."

"Keep it down, Riva." She clenched her fists, but resumed walking. "Even if it's true," he said after a moment, "what can anyone do about it now?"

"What *you* can do is tell your uncle. Have that bastard fired. Because, if you don't, I will."

"All right, all right," he replied. "But you stay away from Uncle Harvey. For everybody's good. In his books, you're the *shmendrik* who got me kicked out of school. I'll bring it up tomorrow."

She slowed. "Why not do it now? You could go back and . . ."

He locked his arm in hers, forcing her to keep moving. "Because it's not that simple. First, I'll have to look up this Monique Dupont, to find out what line and shift she works on and who might be her foreman — could be any of several guys. Then I'll have to find that girl Dolly to confirm the name. Even then, it's circumstantial. It's not uncommon for these girls to have a vendetta against their bosses, you know; they get themselves into trouble then single out some *shmuck* to pin the blame on."

Riva glared at him, but didn't speak.

"What?" he said. "It happens."

Marty picked lunch three days later to broach the subject. His uncle passed it off with a wave of the hand. "Come on, Marty," he replied, unscrewing the cup from his thermos and filling it with borscht. "Anytime you get men and women together, there's bound to be some hanky-panky. Boys will be boys."

"We're talking rape, Uncle Harvey."

"Rape-schmape! You know what Confucius says: 'Woman with skirt up run faster than man with pants down.'"

"This isn't his first. I've got it on good account that he's done this to at least four other girls."

Harvey jammed the cork back into the thermos. "Look! Some girls spread their legs for lots of guys. Then when they get caught, they've no idea who did it to them. It's like backing into a buzz saw and trying to figure out which tooth bit you. So what do they do? They put the finger on the one who can deliver the biggest payoff."

Marty held up four fingers. "Four others, Uncle Harvey. Count 'em. Four!"

"I don't give a shit how many. Tarnoffsky's got faults, but he's a good foreman; knows the *schmata* trade. Who do ya think loses if I sack him? He'd be hired in a flash by the competition around the corner."

"You could at least talk to him."

"Un-uh," Harvey replied, wiping his mouth with a handkerchief. "He'd just turn around and make life miserable for all the girls. Then guess what? Production plummets. No, siree. We got orders to fill."

Marty stiffened. "So, we do nothing?" He watched his uncle, examining the red smear from the borscht on the handkerchief and noting the resemblance to lipstick. Had he uncovered the source of Harvey's fondness for borscht? Was it a ruse to put Aunt Monica off the dalliances he was famous for? And were these encounters all society women from the Square Mile, or did some come from the shop floor? Were Tarnoffsky and Uncle Harvey two peas in a pod?

"Listen, my boy," Harvey said, shoving the handkerchief into a pocket, "we got bigger fish to fry." Marty bit into his apple and waited. "Your little *babushka* friend there, the one who meets you at the gates after work, will have to do without your charms today. You and I got a meeting at Minsky Dress and Bonnet on Bleury Street. Us 'n fifty other owners." He rubbed his hands. "Them goddamn unions think they've got us by the short and curlies. Well, they ain't the only ones who can organize. We've got a few surprises up our sleeves."

August 15, 1934

"STOP FIDGETING," RIVA WHISPERED, brushing Marty's ear with her lips. "You're doing the right thing." In theory, she was correct, but somehow the word "traitor" kept blinking in his head. Not that it should. This scheme, albeit risky to his personal future, had his full backing, or so he kept reminding himself.

They were huddled in a booth at the back of Mom's Café on Ste. Catherine. Across from them sat Dolly Laplante, looking suspicious, but confident. She had chosen to wear a wide-brimmed black hat that resembled the one Paraskeva Clark wore in her self-portrait hanging in the Musée des Beaux Arts. Riva loved that painting as much as the thin-faced, high-cheek-boned artist, whom she claimed for a fellow traveller. That Dolly had turned up looking like a dead ringer for Clark had won her Riva's instant affection.

Marty cleared his throat. "I'm about to stick my neck out here, Miss Laplante," he said. "Before I do, I need some honest answers. Everything you say will be treated in strict confidence." Dolly looked puzzled. "Are you a member of a union?"

Dolly hesitated then nodded slowly. "Yes . . . the Catholic Confederation of Labour. Aren't we all?"

"To your knowledge, has our shop been unionized by any other syndicate?"

Dolly looked from one to the other. "You can't expect me to answer that."

Marty examined his hands. "Look, we mean no harm. Trust me. I don't own the factory. I'm indentured labour, just like most of the girls. To be honest, I'm beginning to find my uncle hard to love."

"Easy to say, Monsieur Kellenberger, but 'e's still family, which makes the rest of us outsiders."

Marty took a deep breath. "If I were anti-union would my . . ." he pointed to Riva and struggled for the correct word to describe their relationship, wanting desperately to say fiancée, ". . . girl be working for the Needle Workers' Industrial Union?" He turned to Riva. "Show her your card."

Dolly inspected it closely. "Pretty easy to forge," she said, at last.

Riva sat back, crossing her arms. "Remember that girl, Monique Dupont? She finally got money, food, and a visit by a doctor, didn't she?" Dolly's eyebrow arched imperceptibly. Riva lowered her voice. "It came from NWIU."

"You arranged that?"

Riva nodded. "We pressured the union into it. In return, Monique gave us an earful on things happening on the shop floor."

"What did she tell you?"

"How the pay seldom gets above five bucks for a seventy-hour work week; how two and three girls are forced to punch the same card to avoid minimum wage laws; how overcrowding and bad lighting lead to accidents on machinery that have no safeguards; how maimed workers are fired without compensation."

Dolly's face remained expressionless. She crossed her arms. "Pretty standard in the industry, n'est-ce pas, Mlle. Lilovsky?"

"You think it's acceptable for workers to get lung disease from foul, dusty air, or collapse from heat stroke in summer? You're good with girls stuffing their panties with rags to avoid asking for pee breaks?" Dolly cradled her cup while she looked away. "Wouldn't you love to do something about it?" Riva pressed.

"This is either a set-up or a test," Dolly responded at last. "You didn't bring me 'ere to tell me what I already know. With you," she pointed to Riva, "I feel comfortable, but with you," the finger moved to Marty, "I 'ave fear. You are front office. What is your angle?"

As the waitress was writing up the bill for the couple behind, Marty cleaned his glasses on his shirt, wishing she'd hurry. Dolly seemed to appreciate the delay. At last, with the sound of retreating footsteps, he resumed. "I'm concerned that our factory's a powder keg."

"*Mon Dieu*," Riva mumbled, "they all are."

Marty ignored her. "And it's getting worse. On your side, to complain is to get fired and to organize is to get beaten. My side keeps tightening the screws. I see the lid blowing off, like it did in Russia, and when it does everybody loses — you, me, Uncle Harvey, all the workers."

Dolly set her cup down hard. "Are you suggesting the workers back off?"

"No!" Marty replied, checking over his shoulder. "It's in everybody's interest that you take on the owners. Just don't pound them into the ground when you win. Changes can be made that are good for both sides."

"Suppose the workers were to get the upper 'and. Aren't you worried that after being treated like *merde* for so long they'd explode?"

Marty nodded. "They'll need to be restrained. Destroying equipment and stock would only chase the textile trade away — to Toronto or New York or Timbuktu."

Dolly leaned in. "Let me get this right; you want me to become a *recruteur* for the union?"

Riva nodded. "With a union comes discipline," she answered, "discipline to lay down tools in a reasonable and controlled manner."

Dolly sat back down and folded her arms. "Unionizing is slow and dangerous. Organizers get their 'eads split open. New recruits wind up blacklisted. And it doesn't matter that unions are legal; members still get 'arassed by the cops and denounced from the pulpit."

"Nobody's saying it'd be easy," Riva said, placing a hand on Marty's shoulder, "but we have Mr. Front Office in our corner. Listen to his proposal."

Marty sucked air through his teeth in an attempt to tame the flutter in his breast. The same intoxicating feeling that had enveloped him during the Rabinovitch affair had returned. Riva pushed in closer. "Between my uncle and Riva," he began, "I have a window on both camps. As I see it, the workers have the numbers, but no organization. Management, on the other hand, has the law and police, plus a regiment of goons at their disposal."

"Big odds," Dolly said.

"On the surface, yes," Marty replied, "but not insurmountable. If I were to feed you information about management's plans, you'd be able to keep one jump ahead. I could point out the traps, so you'd know when to push and when to back off. The owners can't be everywhere at once. They don't have a war chest big enough for that."

Dolly pushed her cup away and swept the table clean of imaginary crumbs. "Why 'ave you come to me with this? Lots of girls at the factory are more into unions than me."

"Perhaps," Marty replied, "but I've checked the records. You're the only one whose family isn't dependent on your paycheque."

"You picked me because I am expendable?"

"We picked you because you're a natural leader. The others look up to you."

She pulled her cup back in and began running her finger around the rim. "Sounds like you've got *un petit dossier* on me while I know nothing about you."

"Ask."

Looking from one to the other she lowered her eyes. "Politics? Are you communists? Because I am not."

"I am," Riva said.

Dolly nodded and turned to Marty. "And you? You seem to be *un avocat* for revolution. Where will you stand if it comes? With the proletariat or *la bourgeoisie*?" Riva turned to Marty. "Good question," she said.

Marty bit his lip. Both women waited. "I'll say this much, the communists don't have a monopoly on fighting injustice."

The first few days were the most difficult. Sitting behind his desk, Marty polished his glasses on the quarter-hour, jumped at unexpected movements, and laughed too hard at people's jokes. A thousand times he told himself all this was ultimately in his uncle's best interest; however, by the end of the first week, with Harvey betraying no signs of suspicion, he began to pry. It paid off. Meanwhile, Uncle Harvey was having a rip-roaring time plotting against the Bolshies. There was a new purpose to his day—a union needed trampling, upstarts put in their place. Surprisingly, flabby Harvey had another side—he was a brilliant strategist. But he also liked to brag, and his nephew was all ears.

As for the triumvirate—Marty, Riva, Dolly—they met regularly in the back booth at Mom's Café, plotting. In the process, Riva and Dolly had become as thick as thieves. There were moments when Marty felt left out, but events were moving too quickly to stew about it.

By late August, the brass at NWIU had tried a few revolving strikes around the city. Harvey Dress's turn was bound to be coming up soon. But there was a problem—theirs was the least unionized in the garment district, so the three conspirators would have to pick up the pace. And they'd also have to work around the thugs Uncle Harvey had hired to prowl the plant during working hours. The girls took on the task of signing up members, making sure that Marty—for his own good—knew none of the details. He went about his work with a permanent flutter in his stomach, expecting something to break at any minute.

Marty was in the office when it came. The instant the whir and whine of machinery began to fade he leapt to his feet. Why would someone have cut the power at 9:15 on a Monday morning? It certainly wasn't Uncle Harvey's doing, as he was away at a meeting. He ran to the window overlooking the floor to see strangers rounding up the foremen and corralling them in a corner. Wide-eyed workers shuffled about nervously, while a man in a tweed jacket with a bullhorn jumped onto a table, kicking a pile of fabric onto the floor. At that instant, the secretary in the next room screamed and the door to the office crashed open. Before he could protest, Marty found himself being frogmarched down the corridor and into the shop. As he stumbled along, he managed to stuff his glasses into their metal carrying case for safety. Around him, a phalanx of angry men propelled him toward the foremen, now barricaded in the far corner.

"Brothers and sisters," Tweed Jacket announced. "The Needle Workers Industrial Union has arrived. We're here to put an end to dangerous working conditions, stop penalty clauses, and raise wages. What would you say to twelve dollars and fifty cents a week?" He paused for a reaction. Beside Marty, three of the foremen broke free and began barking warnings at the workers. Union reaction was swift. Large men with thick necks surrounded the protestors, and the sound of fist on flesh carried across the shop floor, accompanied by grunts and moans. Someone applauded. It caught on, augmented by rising cheers. "There's power in the union," Tweed Jacket cried, raising his arms for quiet. "Sign on for your families. Sign on for progress. Sign on for solidarity. You've nothing to fear. Who's first?"

Nobody moved. Marty held his breath, fearful as to what could happen next. Then Dolly stepped forward, jumped onto a table, and signed with a flurry. Instantly, the room became a blur, as people rushed the clipboard bearers.

Marty might have cheered, too, if not for the disturbance at his feet. Instinctively, his hand went for his glasses. A foreman with a torn ear and broken teeth was trying to sit up. A few feet away, a second man lay unconscious on his back, his huge belly rising like a drumlin. He could have been someone's uncle taking a nap, but from the gurgling sounds, the man was drowning in his own vomit. Marty dropped to his knees, rolled him over, and began probing the mouth with his fingers. Once cleared, he turned to a third casualty, whose broken arm stuck out at a grotesque angle. The crowd stood back. The man's bowels had opened.

Calmly and efficiently, Marty tore up fabric and attended to the wounded. Workers swarmed around, but he paid them little attention, until he felt moisture seep through his clothes. The workers were spitting on him and the injured foremen. He began to take stock: these people hated management; he was his uncle's surrogate; law and order had been suspended. The crowd was on the verge of becoming a mob. He was fair game. A strange sensation enveloped him, more sadness than fear. Perhaps a beating was what he deserved. He'd set this chain of events in motion, betrayed his uncle, and, by his collusion, was responsible for the injuries to the foremen. He waited for the first blow as he went about his tasks. Then, from behind, came Dolly's familiar voice.

"Don't give management cause to sic the police on us," she pleaded in French. "We need our jobs. Sign up for the union then go back to your posts." Marty was too busy to track what happened next. He might have noted the sirens and shouts, followed by heavy union boots bolting for the exits. Someone got off a last message through the megaphone, about signing up at Auditorium Union Hall after hours. Mostly, he was preoccupied with his own troubled conscience. Up until now, improving the lot of his uncle's workers had been a game. But the knights and pawns had disappeared, replaced by puke, shit, and blood. He shook his head. If signing up members could go so wrong, what would a full strike bring?

September 4, 1934

"MAYBE YOU SHOULD THINK about meeting the union halfway, Uncle Harvey," Marty suggested from his desk.

His uncle glared at him. "Don't you utter that word in my presence. You say union, I hear cancer. Look what happened at Fortune Fabrics.

No sooner had the cutters been given some slack, than the pressers, drapers, and finishers wanted their pound of flesh. Then that chickenshit Dubinsky caved in."

Marty swivelled his oak armchair to face his uncle. "But Fortune Fabrics is getting their orders out on time. You said so yourself."

"Sure, they're keepin' the retailers happy, but how much do ya think they're makin'?" His index finger joined his thumb. "*Gornisht!*"

Marty was about to ask how he knew their competitor's bottom line, when a commotion erupted in the outer office. Heavy footsteps stomped over the secretary's loud protests. The door crashed open and three strangers strode in, studying the office like they were foreclosing on a farm. It didn't take an Einstein to know who they represented. Their leader, wearing a wide-brimmed fedora badly in need of blocking, pulled out a piece of paper and slapped it on Uncle Harvey's desk. "Our demands," he announced.

Harvey nodded. "All right," he said, "you've delivered them, now piss off."

Marty wasn't surprised by his uncle's calm reaction. In fact, Harvey'd been warning him for days to expect something like this. Plus, Riva had confirmed that Harvey Dress would soon be up for strike, although she'd not said when. Dolly, of course, had been fired and had joined Riva at NWIU. Marty was glad the waiting was over, but terrified the union men might know about his complicity and inadvertently expose him.

"You don't frighten me, you commie sons of bitches," Harvey sneered. "Mildred! Call the cops!" he shouted to the secretary.

The union spokesman smiled and cleared his throat. His two bodyguards stood behind him, legs apart, arms across their chests. "Seeing that you're not of a mind to invite us to sit and chat, I'll be brief," he said.

Harvey cut the end off a cigar and tapped it on the desk. "Take your time," he replied. "Our guys will be here in a few minutes. Nice fellows. You wouldn't want to miss them."

"Oh, we're not worried, Mr. Bigbucks," Fedora continued, "seeing that your phone is out of order."

Harvey reddened. "Just say what you came to say and get out. I got orders to fill; payrolls to make up."

Fedora frowned. "Siccing your goons on us won't help fill those orders," he said, "not if we're provoked into calling the workers out."

Harvey lit a match and smiled. He held the flame in front of his face, watching it flicker and catch. "Careful with the threats, *boychick*. My secretary's taking this down." Eyes turned to see Mildred scribbling furiously on a steno pad.

"Times are changing," Fedora sneered. "This is a union shop now. Co-operate and you'll do good business. Screw us around and your workers will get very unproductive."

"They'll starve," Harvey said, blowing smoke.

"They're starving now," the union man countered, checking his watch. "You've got two weeks to comply with our demands." He jerked his head to the door, and the intruders marched out, snatching the steno pad from Mildred on the way by.

Harvey crossed to the window overlooking the shop floor. "Poor suckers," he said, staring at the workers through the dust and fluff floating in the air, "they got no idea what they're bringin' down on themselves."

Marty nodded, disturbed by what he'd just witnessed, but not in the way he'd have anticipated. The Uncle Harvey facing down the union men was someone he hadn't seen before. Here was a man ready to fight for what belonged to him. Qualities hard to ignore. Qualities to be admired. Why couldn't he just be the fat prick underpaying his workers and forcing them to labour in dangerous conditions? Marty cleared his throat. "So, what's our next move?" he asked.

Harvey turned around, smiling. "As that American guy, the footballer, would say, 'the best defence is a good offence.' Hold onto your hat, Marty, my boy, 'cause we'll soon be pounding the bejeesus outta these bastards. The cavalry's just over the hill." He smacked his palm with a fist. "Truckloads of torpedoes arriving from the States next week. Up from Chicago. And these guys are veterans."

Marty turned away, feeling somewhat better. The uncle he needed to hate had just walked back onto the set.

<hr>

September 11, 1934

AS PREDICTED, THE GOONS ARRIVED, and shortly after, the revolving strikes began. So did the cat and mouse games. In preparation for Harvey Dress's turn, Marty had to draw up a list of one hundred employees to fire. To Riva's horror, he enlisted Dolly's help. He figured that she'd have a better idea which families could best afford to lose a paycheque. Harvey's plan was to fire twenty-five workers for every union action. The list was posted.

Harvey was a new man. Gone were the long faces, unending complaints, and lethargy. These days, he arrived early and left late. He even stopped seeing his bit on the side, although he spent time with her on the phone. He targeted selected workers, offering them sweetheart deals to side with him. He also saw to it that the owners cozied up to the clergy, who in turn railed against the strikers from their pulpits. The owners dubbed him "the general" and gave him a staff car. But the phoney war couldn't last forever. Marty was alone in the office when the call came in.

"Hello, Martin Kellenberger speaking."

"It's on," Riva whispered. "General strike."

"When?" he asked, lowering his voice.

"Tomorrow. Over a hundred shops." Marty drew a breath. "You still there?" she asked.

"Yeah," he replied, staring at the door, praying his uncle wasn't about to come through it. "Make sure nobody gets hurt."

"No promises."

"What am I supposed to do while all this is going on?"

"You could try talking sense to your uncle."

Marty's eyes hadn't left the door. "Sometimes he gives me suspicious looks. You're sure no one else at the union hall knows about me, eh? Just you, Dolly, and a couple of big wigs?"

"Look on the bright side, Marty. Now you won't have to fire any more people."

"You didn't answer my question."

"Gotta go."

Like all wars, the strike was expected to be short. It dragged on for four weeks. Marty spent much of it in the office, one ear tuned to the radio, the other to his uncle barking orders into the phone. Like a good commander, he spent long days hectoring the owners and urging the Catholic Confederation of Labour to infiltrate the picket lines.

By six o'clock on the first morning, strikers had flooded the factory gates singing, passing out pamphlets, and waving placards. Radio broadcasts estimated that 8,000 demonstrators clogged the streets between Bleury, Ste. Catherine, and Peel. Spirits were high. A few attempts were made to break into Harvey Dress to cut the electricity, but the goons beat them back.

By the end of the first week, the radio pundits were calling it a stalemate. As for Harvey, he was standing firm. He'd convinced the owners to concentrate the American enforcers around Harvey Dress so he could bring in scabs. But, to his surprise, a matching number of union strongmen mysteriously materialized to offset the advantage. A few heads were smashed and a few arrests were made, but with the press out in full force, both sides kept their rank and file in line. In the end, only a few scabs made it through the lines. Not enough to make a dint in Harvey's list of orders. In short, another draw.

Day eight caught the press napping. Union headquarters on Ontario Street were mysteriously ransacked; a strategic victory for the owners. Armed with the union's files, they began to blackball and blackmail. Marty combed through the files feverishly, praying that if his name was there, he would be the one to find it. To Harvey's frustration and Marty's relief, they found no source for the leaks.

Day nine saw cracks forming on the owners' side. A few shops wanted to settle. They agreed to $7 a week for non-specialized workers, rising to $12.50 after twenty-four months. Harvey ranted. Marty prayed for acceptance. The NWIU turned it down. Rank and file union members heaped scorn on their leaders for letting the increase slip away, but went along with it. The stalemate continued.

By day eleven, the lines were clearer, the trenches deeper. The owners revealed their plans to the press. "Sweat Shops to Move to Suburbs," headlines screamed. For the workers, West Island might as well have been San Francisco or Shanghai. Union brass saw it as an idle threat. More days passed, more orders went unfilled, and more workers fell on the mercy of relatives and friends. But the strike was becoming old news. Other stories crept onto the front pages: J. Edgar Hoover's men were hot on the heels of robber and murderer John Dillinger; Stromboli was spouting fire in Italy; quintuplets had been born in a shack in northern Ontario; Hitler was wrestling order from chaos in Germany. The clergy stood firm in the belief that collective ownership and workers' rights bred anarchy and that Salazar, Mussolini, and their ilk held the solution to social chaos. Meanwhile, in Quebec City, Premier Taschereau tended to more important matters. Owners grew frantic, the public weary, and strikers increasingly hungry.

Day thirty brought an armistice. A twenty-percent increase was offered across the board, which strikers latched onto like shipwrecked sailors. Nothing was put to paper. Marty and Dolly were relieved, Riva was placated, and Uncle Harvey was enraged.

October 3, 1934

A WEARY GROUP GATHERED AT MOM'S on that first Saturday after the strike. Fall was in the air, if any of them had cared to notice. In addition to the three regulars, a high-profile union lawyer had tagged along under the pretext of fêting the conspirators. When it came to public faces, only those of Cardinal Villeneuve and rising political star Maurice Duplessis graced the front pages more often than that of this union man. Sitting with him in a public place terrified Marty. They'd been so careful. Besides, it was time to breathe again, plan for the future, talk Riva out of Russia, and work on getting back to university.

Conversation was awkward in the union man's presence. "What'll it be?" he pressed. "I'm treating." No one answered. "Come on, it's a celebration."

Marty and Riva opted to share a banana split—five mountains of ice cream over banana and smothered in whipped cream and crushed pineapple. It came with a tiny bamboo umbrella. When every last bit had been scraped clean, they played rock-scissors-paper to see who got to take the umbrella home. Dolly had gone for the butterscotch sundae and was devouring it like it was her first meal in days.

Riva pushed the empty dish away with a sigh. "Come on guys, why so quiet?" she asked. "At least we got the promise of a twenty-percent increase, didn't we? Not that they'll honour it. What's your uncle going to do, Marty?"

"He says there's not a snowball's chance in hell he's actually going to—" Riva elbowed him in the ribs. Marty turned, wondering what gaffe he'd committed. Dolly cranked her head over her shoulder and gasped. There at the cash register, with a furred, peroxide blonde on his arm, stood Uncle Harvey. Marty's first impulse was to duck, but by the flush spreading across his uncle's jowelled face, it was too late. For a second, Harvey stood like a child caught licking the icing off the cake. But embarrassment for the blonde evaporated as he put two and two together. Harvey ordered the blonde to sit on a stool as he began marching back to their booth. "Ingrate!" he hissed. Marty held his gaze. "You sneaky little son of a bitch. I knew somebody on the inside was doing me in, but I never figured it for—"

"It's not like you think, Uncle Harvey."

"Flesh and blood. My own sister's boy. The one I bankrolled for university and gave a job to after his Trotskyite bitch got him thrown out." He pointed a finger directly at Marty's face. "And for thanks? A knife in the back!"

Like dominoes, quiet fell across the restaurant from booth to booth and heads turned. The union lawyer opened his mouth to speak, but Dolly shook her head. "You won't buy this, Uncle Harvey," Marty began, "but as God's my witness, I had your best interests at heart."

"You crapped in my face."

Marty swallowed, praying his voice wouldn't crack. "You were facing disaster. I saw it coming. You wouldn't listen."

"Bullshit!"

"You find a twenty-percent salary hike hard to swallow? That's peanuts. Try having your fabrics ruined, or your machines wrecked, or your shop torched, because that's where you were headed."

Harvey shook his head in disgust. "Garbage! Workers respect force. As long as they saw me standing strong, none of that was ever gonna happen. That's the way the real world works. But, you, you could never get that through your skull. You and your old man, two peas in a pod, both too chickenshit to stand up and fight. Like sewer rats, you prefer to skulk around in the shadows."

"That's enough, Uncle Harvey."

"When the Frenchies put the pressure on, did you fight? A Kellenberger? Don't be stupid. You stuck your head in a hole, shut down the *traif* branch of the business and trotted off to the synagogue to pray it'd all blow over. I would have helped your old man if he'd shown some guts. That's what families do. Stay loyal. Not sell each other out."

Marty felt his fists tighten. "Don't you dare talk to me about loyalty. Not with that bimbo up there at the counter. Who is she? An old school chum? Taking her home to meet the kids and Aunt Monica, are we?"

Marty saw the "f" word forming on his uncle's lips, but it never came. Instead he leaned over the table, his face inches from Marty's. "You dumb, little four-eyed turd," Harvey said in a low voice. "Smack dab in the middle of a depression you get yourself kicked out of university and fired from a good job. So, now that you've kissed your family off, what're you gonna do?"

"I'll manage."

"Really? Your old man can't afford another Kellenberger in the shop, so who's gonna hire you? The English won't because you're a Heeb, the Frenchies won't because you're English, and when I'm done spreading the word, no self-respecting Jew in this city will touch you with a ten-foot pole." He turned to the others. "See if little Miss Pinko here can help you out with that bit of baggage, *boychick*. Or your commie-lawyer friend. And don't forget that university loan you owe me. Get a job in this town and I'll garnishee every penny you bring in."

"Shove off, Harvey," Marty said. "Your whore up there looks impatient."

Harvey straightened to leave, then stopped, noticing Dolly for the first time. "You," he barked. "I know that face. You work for me?"

"Sadly," she replied, "I used to."

"Step on my property and you go to jail for trespassing. That goes for all of you."

PART FIVE
Riding the Rails, 1934–35

Chapter Seven

Autumn 1934
North Bay, Ontario

"WATCH YOUR STEP," the conductor called out, as he helped passengers exit the train at North Bay. While a few pressed coins into his hand before moving off, most didn't. When Marty's turn came, he looked straight ahead, refusing to give up his suitcase as he stepped down.

With each mile since leaving Montreal, the leather bag had assumed greater and greater importance. Along with a couple of photographs, it was a precious link to his family and their past. Although badly battered, his father had carried it from Grodno, Byelorussia, to Pier 21, Halifax, and then on to Montreal. Once again it was back in service, holding a few necessities for his own personal exodus.

Word had it there was work at the gold mines in Kirkland Lake, so to increase his chances he'd made some changes — Martin Kellenberger had become Marty Kelly, second-generation Irishman with antecedents out of Limerick, should anyone ask. Papers in his pocket proclaimed it so. It wasn't something he was proud of.

Ten-thirty on a Saturday night and the station platform was packed. Cries of recognition filled the air. Cheerful souls rushed to embrace, but Marty Kelly stood alone, wondering how to kill ten hours before making connections to Kirkland Lake in the morning. A hotel was out of the question. Instead, he figured on a little exploration to stretch his limbs before settling for a hard bench and a long night in the station waiting room. In the morning, when the Temiskaming and Northern Ontario wicket opened, he'd buy a ticket with his precious funds, for the final leg of his journey.

The people on the platform moved off. For several car lengths, Marty flowed with them, but as he closed in on the station he noticed that not everyone was in a gay mood. From under the eaves of the building, where the high platform lights cast long shadows, sunken eyes peered out from dirty faces. He swallowed. Not since the rally in St. Louis Square had he come face-to-face with such emaciated, defeated men. Head down, he quickened his step and reached for the station door.

"Whoa! Whoa!" a voice demanded. "Where do you think you're going?"

Marty looked up to see a TNO policeman barring the door. "The waiting room," he replied. "Want to check the schedule."

"Got a ticket?"

"Not yet. I was told the wicket was closed until morning."

The policeman's lips curled to a sneer. "Nice try," he said, pointing to the vagrants hugging the station wall. "See those guys?" Marty nodded. "They've all tried that. Once."

"But I have money."

"That's an old one, too. Flash a few bills you have no intention of spending, snuggle up in the waiting room for the night, then hop a freight in the morning."

"Hop a freight?"

"If you've got the dough, find yourself a hotel and come back at train time. There'll be no freebee digs on my watch." The constable sized him up. "I've seen the likes of you. Hobo-in-training. Probably headed for Kirkland expecting to find work. You won't and you'll be back, hanging around like the rest of them layabouts."

"Surely you don't think I'm like . . ." he lowered his voice, "them."

"Move on!"

From the direction of the wall, Marty detected a faint stirring. Hollow eyes burned in his direction. Instinctively, he transferred his wallet to a front pocket and pushed off, intent on rejoining the flow of passengers, now funnelling toward the street. He hustled to catch up, yearning for the warmth they'd shared on the train. He quickened his step, but the closer he got, the faster they evaporated—into carriages, up alleys, through welcoming doors. In ten minutes, he found himself alone on an empty street. For a while he sauntered, looking in store windows at goods he'd be able to afford once he found work in the mines. Why had the constable scoffed at the thought? Did he appear too frail? Too much the academic? Marty Kelly, Irish-Canadian, would change that—put colour in his cheeks, calluses on his hands, muscle on his bones.

A hotel came up, the Empire. He hesitated. One night? Could he afford it? A uniformed doorman stepped through a mahogany door onto the landing. With him came the aroma of roast beef and gravy. It tumbled down the steps, swirling around Marty, and invading his nostrils. His mind went to what remained of *Mame*'s cooking in his suitcase, wishing he'd been disciplined enough to stretch it out more. The doorman crossed his arms and shot him an accusatory glance. Marty pushed on. North Bay was locked up for the night.

With no one in sight, and his mind on food, treating himself to a bite seemed appropriate. Last piece of chicken or not, he'd eat it now and splurge on breakfast in the morning; maybe at the Chicago Café he'd passed earlier. Checking once again that the street was entirely his, he nestled his backside onto the front step of a drug store. He was about to take a bite when he picked up the sound of heavy footsteps approaching from the side street. Shoving the chicken back into his pocket he lunged for his suitcase. He was barely on his feet when two policemen rounded the corner.

"Hold on, there!" one of them ordered.

"Good evening, officers," he replied, turning.

"Identification," the chubbier one demanded. Marty extracted papers from his wallet. The officer tipped them to the streetlight for examination. "Irish, eh?" Marty nodded. "You're scrawnier than the Irishmen we grow in these parts." His partner laughed. "Money?" Marty spread open his wallet exposing several bills, mostly ones and twos. The policeman nodded. "You can't hang around here like a common vagrant."

"I'll be on the train for Kirkland in the morning. Be a waste to rent a room for so short a time."

The officer looked at him suspiciously. "There's a YMCA couple of blocks down. If we catch you out after midnight, we'll be running you in."

Marty resumed walking, a plan taking shape in his head. "The lake," he said, half aloud to himself. "Why not spend the night along the shore, away from prying eyes?" He began retracing his steps, but as the railway tracks came into view he noticed pockets of light flickering in the distance beyond the marshalling yards. His chin fell. "Bonfires," he mumbled, "hoboes." Visions of the angry eyes at the station came flooding back. Quickly, he changed his direction from west to south, parallel to the tracks and down Main Street.

After several blocks, at the point where the tracks forked, he spied a dark patch in the direction of the lake which he took for a wooded area. Cautiously he approached, cocking an ear for the telltale signs of vagrants or police. In the distance, brakemen wagged lamps to engineers, linking up cars to a chorus of brakes and banging metal. Finally, sucking air, he sprinted across the tracks, his suitcase slapping against his leg. Hopping over the last rail, he slid down the embankment and lay still, listening. Before him lay the shelter of the woods. Behind him, a yard-locomotive closed in. He pushed off. In the darkness, a branch caught him on the cheek, sending his glasses careening through the air. He lunged into the blackness, catching them by some miracle and stuffing them into their metal case. His panic eased, only to re-emerge with the smell of smoke and the sounds of muffled conversation. Stopping dead, he tried to locate the source over his pounding heart.

The first shaft of light flickering through the trees brought relief—it spoke of human contact and warmth. He hesitated. Would these men welcome him? Were they as dangerous as they looked, or just down on their luck, like himself? For several minutes, he peered through the bushes, arms wrapped around himself to keep warm, ears cocked to the crackle of the blaze. The flame beckoned; he wavered, but the bitter tones and derisive laughter held him back. Finally, he pulled his collar up and backed off. The voices faded and were replaced by the sound of lapping water. He came to a huge willow tree and stopped. To the west, moonlight flooded across the still lake, while farther up, the glow from several bonfires flickered along the shore. Exhausted, he leaned against the willow and slid to the ground. The dampness cut into him, but he welcomed it. It would keep him awake and vigilant. There'd be ample time for sleep on the train.

He had no idea of the time, save that it was still dark, when voices woke him. Scarcely breathing he sat up, staring at five forms pilfering his suitcase. A sixth man held a torch. "Well, looky here," one of them exclaimed, holding up soap and shaving gear. Others were pulling on clothes—his clothes—over the ones they already wore. Marty crawled back to the willow, trying hard to disappear under its hanging branches.

"Cor, blimey!" the tall man in the greatcoat announced, examining an object in his hand. "Know what we got ourselves here, boys?" The others stared, puzzled by what appeared to be some form of bizarre headgear. Marty swallowed as he recognized his father's yarmulke, brought from Poland to the new land. "We got ourselves here a genuine Jew boy." Activity at the suitcase intensified.

"Jews got money," an Irish voice boomed, as they turned toward him. Marty considered proclaiming his new-found ancestry, but thought better of it. "Where's your wallet, kike?"

Through a hail of oaths, Marty sprang for the darkness, but a foot shot out sending him sprawling. Kicks and punches rained down on him. He groaned as a blow caught him between the legs. After that, it was a free-for-all, ending only when blackness cloaked his consciousness.

When he finally came to, he tried to open his eyes, but, with the bright sun so painful, opted instead to keep them closed while he licked his swollen lips and checked his teeth for injuries with his tongue. He might have drifted off again if not for the voice.

"Welcome back to the land of the living, Mr. Kelly," it said.

Marty moved his head carefully to see who else might be there, before realizing that he was the Mr. Kelly in question. He cracked open his eyes. A young, barrel-chested man of about his age, with high cheekbones and fair hair, was sitting on a log in front of a dead fire pit. "How do you know my name?"

"That was easy," the man replied, holding up Marty's wallet.

"Thieving bastard!" Marty groaned.

"Whoa! Don't blame me, old boy," the man protested. "I picked it up on the trail. Heard the ruckus in the night and decided to check it out come morning."

Marty tried to sit up. "Got to get to the station," he mumbled. "Ticket wicket'll be open."

The stranger laughed. "Unless you've stashed moola in a safe place, I don't think there'll be much ticket-buying today."

"Think I'm stupid enough to leave it in my wallet?"

The stranger shook his head. "My guess is you put it in your sock." Marty craned his neck to take in his feet. Bare toes stared back at him.

"How long do you think it would take for a hobo to check there?" Marty fingered the dried blood on his face. "Bastards!" he said.

"Try to see it as some kinda welfare, Mr. Kelly. They've got no money or food. Then you come along—the only Good Samaritan in the neighbourhood." The stranger rose to examine the contents of Marty's suitcase strewn on the ground. Marty watched him move, envying his thick red-and-black-checked Mackinaw and dark wool pants. "They were actually quite restrained," the stranger said.

"How do you mean?"

The young man poked at the contents. "I see socks, underwear, sweater, a glasses case, toothbrush, and a book on . . ." he leaned forward and picked it up, "medicine. Then there's the greatcoat I spread over you."

Marty cringed, noticing the coat for the first time. "Filthy rag isn't mine. Mine's a khaki and grey down-filled parka. If I catch some asshole in it, I'll kill the son of a bitch."

"Easy now, Mr. Kelly. I'm not saying what happened is right, but those boys are desperate. Maybe in their shoes, we would be, too."

"What are you, an apologist for hoboes?"

The stranger laughed. "Just saying, we all do things we wish we hadn't. Take that guy with your parka, for instance; maybe he'll remember one day what he's done and hang his head. And even if you ran into him, say, coming out of one of your Catholic confession boxes in a state of grace, would you still be up to pounding him out?"

Marty pushed himself to a sitting position, ignoring the pain it caused. "Confession box?" he exclaimed, then cursed under his breath.

The stranger straightened. "You are Catholic, aren't you? That's what your ID says."

"Yeah, sure. Caught me off guard . . . idea of coming upon some prick in my parka outside of a church." The stranger smiled. Marty tried, but it hurt too much. He wondered where this man was from. There was an accent he couldn't place—the Ws and Ths were not spot on. "You Catholic, too?" Marty said.

"Hell, no, I'm Finn with a little Swedish thrown in, which makes me Lutheran. Turns out there weren't enough of us where I grew up to warrant a minister, so we opted for the United Church. Got nothing against you guys, though."

This time Marty managed a smile. "What's your name?"

"Tauno Jaakkola," the stranger replied, reaching out his hand.

"What are you doing in here?" Marty asked.

"I could ask you the same."

"You look too savvy to be caught in a place like this."

Tauno laughed. "Not my first night in a jungle." In the distance came the sound of trains on the move—shuddering, chuffing, whistling. "Me, I'm just another castoff who's broke, homeless, and out of work. That and being single makes me a lazy bum. If I were married, now, that would make me a fella going through a rough patch and deserving of government assistance."

"You think they pick on single guys?"

"Don't they? Stop long enough in some town to catch your breath, and it's a lockup, or a labour camp in some remote hole." He kicked at a rusted sardine tin. "The men who beat you up, the country's chock-a-block with them. Have you seen their eyes? Empty. Those chaps are like the wind, blowing back and forth from coast to coast, searching, searching, never finding. No hope." He shook his head.

Marty began the seemingly difficult task of getting to his feet by rising to one knee and sliding his back upwards against the willow. Tauno took a hesitant step toward him, then stopped. Marty swayed before catching his balance. He began running his fingers up and down his legs. "Nothing broken below," he announced, rotating his head slowly in huge circles like a sprinter limbering up for a race. He slid his fingers across his ribs, inhaling sharply at the sore spots.

"You a doctor, or something?" Tauno asked.

"Almost. It's a long story." He gasped as he pressed on a particularly sensitive rib then relaxed. "Bruises. That's all. I'll be all right."

Tauno returned to his log. For several minutes, neither spoke. Marty tried a few hesitant steps. His new acquaintance seemed lost in thought. Finally, Tauno broke the silence. "You got plans?" he asked.

"I was told I might find work in Kirkland Lake, gold being the only commodity that hasn't gone sour."

Tauno laughed. "Waste of time. They only take miners with experience. Besides, you hardly look . . ."

"Fit?" Marty interrupted.

"I was going to say husky enough. Working underground is tough. You should try for something softer than the stopes."

"Like what?"

"Can you carry things?"

"You got a job in mind?"

Tauno shrugged. "The possibility of," he replied in a voice that suggested he was only at the considering stage, "but it would be temporary." He stared at Marty, taking in the weeping cuts and the purplish-yellow bruises that marked his face.

Marty tried to push his chest out. Other than carry a few quarters of beef in his father's butcher shop, he'd never done any real physical work. He couldn't recall the last time he'd actually been out of breath, or built up a sweat. Still, there was nothing he needed more at the moment than a partner with street smarts. He began blurting out what he thought were his best assets. "I'm one year off my medical certificate. I can mend cuts, bruises, and set broken limbs. Maybe I could sell my services at back doors for bed and board."

Tauno's eyebrows went up. "Handy skills for what I have in mind. We could partner up for a bit? You and me. On a trial basis," he added hastily. "I'm lucky at hitchhiking. You'll be fine because you still look presentable—or you will when your face heals. I know the rails, too, and the jungles, and how to handle the men. I'm also pretty good at the scavenge. With me around, you won't get knocked about like last night."

"Deal," Marty replied.

"Swell. Here's what I'm proposing. I know a guy who sells fresh produce to grocery stores. Red's Greens he calls his business. He makes a run up the Ferguson Highway from southern Ontario every Monday. That's tomorrow. Red's first customer's in Temagami. After that, he keeps going until the truck's empty, usually Haileybury or New Liskeard, sometimes Timmins. The guy's got back problems, likes help. There's a big hill on the upper side of North Bay. We'll flag him down there. He drives a 1931 REO Speedwagon. Red. Can't miss it."

"He pays?"

Tauno shook his head. "Transport, a few loose greens, and you get to sleep in the truck—that's about it. The important thing is to get out of this town."

"Where're we headed?"

Tauno looked surprised. "This time of year? Vancouver. Right after a stopover in Hearst."

"Hearst?"

"My aunt Onja lives there. She helped raise me. We'll hitchhike in and hang around a week or two. Kinda fatten up for the migration. Can't stay long, though, winter's coming. Running west on an open train in a prairie blizzard is no picnic."

While Marty knew towns like Hearst existed, it was still a revelation. The gravel highway leading into it—a thin, 400-mile ribbon that crossed the Canadian Shield, the flat Lesser Claybelt, and the Great Claybelt, equally flat—sliced through primeval forest all the way. When it hit Hearst, it stopped. End of the line for automobiles. Ditto refugees from southern Ontario, Quebec, and a dozen European countries. Walled in by dense coniferous forest, the people had learned to pull together, or so Tauno claimed. This was New Ontario and, stuck in the wilderness as they were, survival hinged on putting aside Old World squabbles. From the false-fronted buildings and tire-rutted streets to the wooden sidewalks and boarding houses, it was a frontier town in every respect, where lumberjacks mingled with townsfolk, and the churches competed with bootleggers and prostitutes on weekends.

Marty took an instant liking to Hearst and to Aunt Onja. She was everything Tauno said she'd be. One look at the boys' gaunt cheeks and she dropped a log into the cookstove. For two days, Marty didn't budge from her warm kitchen. He was too young to remember the Old Country, but Onja's place spoke to him of his birthplace, Byelorussia. It had something to do with the aroma of cardamom from the coffee bread, rag rugs on the floor, a curtain over the passageway to the living room, and the knick-knacks from Helsinki and Rovaniemi. On day three, she marched them off to replenish the cupboard.

While at the store, Tauno was introducing Marty around when a train whistle blew. Nothing exceptional there, until a townsman came flying in with the news that the railrodders were coming. The announcement shocked the store into action. Tauno's face exploded in a wide grin; he knew what was about to happen.

By the time the horde from the train reached the store, the front door had been propped open and blocked by a heavy counter. The employees, like sailors preparing for a broadside, were at their stations — the proprietor to the door, girls to the counter, and men to the cellar for the hobo staples of sardines, beans, hardtack, and coffee. At Tauno's prodding, the two friends pitched in.

"What gives?" Marty asked, struggling up the stairs under two cases of Fray Bentos Corned Beef.

Tauno laughed. "When the first gang came off a freight train and swarmed the town a few years ago, owners like Mr. Chalykoff here were delighted with the trade. But when the train pulled out they found themselves staring at bare shelves; for every item sold, ten had been pilfered. After that, they went to the barricade system. Now railrodders don't get in. They show their money, order, and wait for the goods to be delivered." Tauno placed his case of Carnation condensed milk on the floor and knelt to open it for a dark-eyed salesgirl with Marcelled hair who'd been giving him the eye.

"Don't the men resent it?" Marty asked, depositing the Fray Bentos.

Tauno lowered his voice. "Does a bear shit in the woods? You betcha they do. You'll find out soon enough; when we're on the outside looking in."

Marty peered out the window. This was no sedate breadline outside the Salvation Army in Montreal. The men had scrummed up, elbows flying, tongues flashing. Those at the back kept looking across the field to the hissing locomotive under the water tower. He wondered if there might be a fight. "How come the police haven't shown up?" he asked.

Tauno shrugged. "There's only one cop and he's probably off somewhere. Wouldn't be the first time he wasn't around when the shit hit the fan. Just ask the merchant across the street. Couple of years ago, when he was mayor, there was no welfare, so a bunch of unemployed bushmen and farmers took it in their heads to break into his store. They figured if they helped themselves, the government would reimburse him; sort of forced welfare, you might say."

"Sounds fair to me."

"Yeah, well, the merchant was having none of it. He fired off two wires: One pleading to the government in Toronto for financial assistance and the other to the RCMP in Cochrane for protection. Then he laid a gun on the counter and pushed it up to the window."

"Sounds like the Montreal textile str—" Marty began, but stopped dead. So far his new friend hadn't queried him on his reason for hitting the road. Too much detail now, on how an Irish-Canadian came to be working in the front office of a Jewish business, would only lead to embarrassing speculation.

Tauno waited for Marty to complete his sentence. When he didn't, he continued. "Sure enough, two hundred hungry men come marching up through the mucky streets." The girl who'd set Tauno's knees trembling interrupted his story. They were low on tomato soup. Would he fetch a couple of cases from the basement?

Marty followed him to the stairs. "Well? What happened?" he asked.

"They're low on soup."

"No, to the storekeeper?"

"Oh, the strikers showed up all determined-like, but the gun gave them pause. Especially the married guys with kids. They were milling around undecided when the skies opened, so they broke into the theatre around the corner to hold a meeting out of the rain. Meanwhile, the merchant-mayor, who's expecting no help from anybody, gets a wire from Toronto saying the government'll provide the financing he's asked for. Great news; especially since it was the first welfare of its type in Ontario. So, off he goes to the theatre to announce it. It's only when he gets there that he really starts shitting bricks. They're singing the 'Internationale.' The 'Communist Internationale,' for Christ's sake. Right here in this hick town."

At the bottom of the stairs, Tauno began searching for tomato soup. Marty hung back, waiting for the story to continue. "And?" he prodded.

Tauno handed him a case and picked one up himself. "That's it. There is no *and*. It's just interesting, that's all. The merchant stood his ground, and by the time the RCMP constable came riding in on a railway speeder, it was all over."

"Proving?"

"Jeez, I dunno . . . proving it pays to hang tough, I guess. Or that you never know who might pop up to help when you're in a tight corner and you show some guts."

"Sounds like a fairy tale to me."

"Holy cripes, Marty. Action beats sitting around with your finger up your arse, don't it?"

"Most times it just makes things worse in the end."

At the top of the stairs, Tauno shifted the case of tomato soup to his shoulder and turned. "What the hell are you talking about, 'makes things worse'? You didn't lift a finger with those bums in North Bay, but you still got beat up, didn't ya?"

"Think what they might have done if I had."

"Yeah, well, maybe they might have backed off and you'd still have that damned down-filled parka you keep bitching about."

"Or maybe I'd be dead."

Tauno dropped his case on the pile behind the counter and turned to Marty. "Look," he said, lowering his voice, "we're going out on the road in a few days. Guys out there are like dogs. They can sniff fear. They'll know right away whether you've got the guts to stand up for yourself, or if you're just some fancypants to be pushed around. You better make up your mind right now. If we're a team, it means covering each other's backs. I'll keep my end of the bargain, but the first hint that it's not working the other way, and I'm cuttin' loose."

<hr />

Autumn 1934
On the Rails

"I DON'T FEEL RIGHT ABOUT THIS," Marty muttered, as they approached the ticket wicket.

Tauno shrugged. "Think I do? Look, we didn't ask Aunt Onja for the money, did we?"

"No, but she thinks we have job prospects in Winnipeg and wants us riding inside the train—not on top of it. Doesn't seem right, turning around and buying tickets only as far as . . . what's that place again?"

"Franz."

"Wherever the hell that is."

"Look, I feel like a turd, but we gotta think practical. Franz is one hundred miles down the line and Vancouver two thousand. By pocketing the difference in fares, we just might have enough cash to make it all the way without too much scrounging."

"Yeah, but, she's sure to find out, isn't she? Hearst is small; what's to prevent the ticket agent from stopping your aunt on the street and asking why her nephew would be buying a one-way ticket to Franz?"

Tauno shook his head. "Never happen. The guy's French and my aunt is Finn. You think they talk?"

Marty shuddered about what lay ahead. Boarding a moving train was hazardous. Even seasoned railrodders lost limbs and lives. Not that he'd expected a return ticket to better times, but at least Aunt Onja's gift meant safe passage as far as Winnipeg. Now that was about to evaporate. He squinted at the map of Canada on the waiting-room wall. "Where's this Franz, anyway?"

"South, on the Algoma Central."

"But Vancouver's west."

Tauno motioned him out of the ticket line and directed him to a vacant bench in the corner. "Look, I shoulda come clean with it earlier, but you're such a worrywart. We can't go directly west on the CNR, because that takes us to Sioux Lookout and that's Pock-faced Henderson's territory. He's one bull you don't tangle with. Guys have gone in there and disappeared. The lucky ones just get robbed, beaten, and sent packing on foot to the next town, ninety miles down the line."

"How do you know all this?"

"Because I made it through there two years ago by the skin of my teeth. By going south, we can pick up a CPR freight heading for the Lakehead. That way we avoid Sioux Lookout altogether."

"What if the freights don't slow down enough at Franz?"

"I'm pretty sure they will."

"Pretty sure?"

"We're gonna find out soon's we buy our tickets. Come on."

"And just how do we go about that? Ask the agent?"

"You'll see. Don't get yourself in a lather."

Out on the platform, they tucked their tickets away and headed down the tracks in the direction of the freight shed. En route, they stopped to watch the cattle in the corral. The steers had been watered and fed and were being herded back onto the cars for the final leg to the slaughterhouses in southern Ontario. After a few minutes, they continued walking. Just beyond the freight shed, Tauno led the way across the tracks toward the woods.

"Oh, no," Marty said, holding back, "I'm not going in there."

"You're the guy who asked whether freight trains highball it through Franz, aren't you?" Tauno said, pointing to the jungle. "Well, the answer's in there."

They stepped over the last track and followed what seemed to be the most travelled path into the shrubs. To Marty's eye, there was nothing to distinguish this jungle from the one in North Bay. His breathing grew shallow as he took in the piles of empty goof bottles, rusty tin cans, and dead campfires. Here and there, flies swarmed around little clumps of human feces. Tauno's pace quickened. Marty followed him into a clearing. A dozen men stirred. Only one got up.

"What can we do fer youse guys today?" asked the lanky guy with a careful smile.

Tauno reached into his pocket and pulled out a pack of Sweet Caps. "Got a few tailor-mades for the guy with info on freight trains out of Franz."

Lanky eyed the cigarettes, trying not to show interest. "Goin' which way?" he asked.

"West."

The hobo scratched his head and sat back down, motioning for Marty and Tauno to join him. "Three a day," he said. "If you ride the ACR down from here, though, you miss the first one and hafta wait eight hours. The good side is that all the trains gotta stop there to take on water."

"Cinderdicks?"

"Sometimes, but usually only the ones what rides in on the trains. Gotta watch 'em though, 'cause those fellers drag a jail with 'em at the back of the train." He laughed. "You see a caboose with bars on the windows, you don't come runnin' outta the bush. Got it?"

Tauno nodded and handed him two cigarettes. They seemed to loosen Lanky's tongue. "Best place to board is on t'other side of Franz, after she's watered up and picking up steam."

Tauno nodded slowly and handed him two more. "Any danger spots along the way?" he asked.

Lanky stroked his scruffy beard. "Nothin' to give ya the heebie-jeebies. Keep an eye out for the bulls in White River is all. After that, it's clear sailing all the way inta Fort William."

"And there?"

"Well, now, youse boys best be on your toes in that town, by golly. They's got railway cops and Mounties pourin' over trains like ants on molasses. Best to jump down before ya hits the marshalling yards. Be careful 'bout it, though. Swinging off into a signal light is a sure career-ender." Tauno gave him two more cigarettes.

"What about outbound for the west?"

Lanky sat back on his hands, sucking air through his teeth. "She's a toughie if you don't know the ropes. Safest is to git yourself over to t'other side of Port Arthur and wait there. The cops'll be checking as the train moves out, but they always start at the engine and work back. The trick is to hop on up front after they've done their sweep. They won't come back up, 'cause by then, the train's goin' too fast." He glanced at the cigarette package; Tauno fingered the remaining cigarettes. " 'Course, the hard part's boardin'. Not easy, 'cause you gotta be farther out of town, and by then, the speed can be pretty considerable. A fast man can do it, though. And once you're on, it's clear sailing into Winnipeg."

Tauno handed over the rest of the cigarettes. "Anything else?"

"Yeah," Lanky laughed, opening the package to store all his earnings. "Don't board the wrong train and wind up in Sioux Lookout."

Tauno got to his feet and the two men shook hands. Marty gritted his teeth when his turn came, but was surprised by the hobo's grip — hard as the iron rails the man stole rides on. A faint smile crossed Lanky's lips as he sized up the scrawny Montrealer. "Youse boys take care now."

They nodded and left. "Cripes," Marty said when they were out of earshot, "was that worth a whole pack of cigarettes?"

While it was dark and drizzly when they boarded the 6:20 a.m. train, the elements suited Marty's mood. In preparation, they'd acquired what Tauno assured him were necessities for the road — blackened clothes, goggles, bandanas, railway caps, rainwear, food, salt, cutlery, tin plates. He'd left his father's old suitcase behind at Aunt Onja's, in favour of a musty packsack. Best of all for Tauno, his aunt had insisted he take his late uncle's boots. Marty was envious. Made of leather to the knee and with toe and heel cleats, they were perfect for hopping trains.

However, neither the "new" clothes nor Tauno's coaching had stemmed the terror eroding away at Marty's confidence — too many paralyzing what ifs. What if he didn't have the mental and physical strength to hop onto a moving freight? What if they were forced to share with other railrodders? What if they wound up in Sioux Lookout? That their train travelled at the speed of a goose walking overland was all right with him. Even so, the one hundred miles to Franz, squealing through forgettable backwaters like Mead, Horsey, and Oba, passed by in a wink. By 10:30, they were nursing coffee in the café across from the station, trying to figure out how to spend the day there without cutting into their cash. Outside fell a grey curtain of drizzle.

"Oh, oh!" Tauno said, "looks like somebody's about to get the bum's rush."

Marty looked around to see a burly cook in a white apron and hob-nailed boots reading the Riot Act to the only other patrons in the room. The waitress was standing back, smirking.

"That sugar jar was full when you guys came in," the cook said. "You owe me twenty cents. Pay up and get out."

The men grumbled, but slammed the money on the table as they headed for the door. Marty turned back to the window, feeling more at ease now that they'd gone. Behind him, he could hear the cook and waitress conferring in low voices. Heavy boots approached.

"Our turn," Tauno whispered.

"You guys gonna sip that coffee all day, or are you gonna order?"

"We're thinking about it," Tauno replied. "Give us a few more minutes."

"Un-uh. Decide now."

Tauno looked up at him. "Just the bill, then, I guess."

Outside, they sauntered past the water tower, heading west. As he walked, Marty could swear eyes were peeking out at him from the bush. A half mile down the line they crossed the ditch for the shelter of a huge spruce tree. To their delight, it was more or less dry. Tauno rolled himself in his greatcoat and went to sleep. Marty sat wide-eyed with his back to the tree staring out into the drizzle. After what seemed an eternity, darkness began to fall. Marty's head had hardly bobbed to his chin when he heard a whistle and the braking of cars to the east. Tauno stirred, rose to pee, and sat back down. At the water tower, the train came to a stop in a loud release of steam. Tauno opened the thermos and hauled out sandwiches. Marty looked anxiously at the hissing engine in the distance.

"Relax and eat," Tauno said. "It's going to be a long night." When they'd finished he packed the thermos and looked directly at Marty. "Let's go over this one more time," he said. "We don't come out of the bush until the engine has gone by. Keep your pack tight on your back, so not to throw you off balance as you move. Run just a little slower than the train. That way, when a ladder comes drifting by, you reach up, latch onto it with one hand, take a couple a steps to get your balance, and swing up. You'll see; it's as easy as falling off a log. Just make sure your second hand comes to rest on the same rung as the first and you get a solid footing on the bottom rung. Got it?"

Marty nodded with a confidence he did not feel after each instruction. "What if the train's going too fast?"

"No chance. Loaded freights take a long time to build up speed. Piece of cake. Just remember not to look at the wheels. They're mesmerizing. They pull you in."

In the distance, two toots pierced the air in a cloud of black smoke. Seconds later, the engine lurched forward, tightening the slack on the couplings and snapping the train into motion in a series of mini-thunderclaps. Marty's eyes were glued to the headlight as it grew larger. Behind it, black shadows emerged from the bushes, scooting through the bulrushes in the ditch and up onto the stony roadbed.

As the engine passed them, the two friends sprinted for the tracks. "Shit!" Tauno hollered, over his shoulder. "Must be empty. She's got more speed than I figured on."

Marty hardly heard. Running up the embankment his eyes had come level with a giant wheel. He remembered he was to latch onto something, but with the wheel clicking on steel and the gravel caving under foot, his mind had gone to mush. When he finally did pry his eyes off, it was to see Tauno, swinging up onto the boxcar ahead and the train pulling away. The space between them grew. He ran harder. From atop the car, dark forms hollered for him to grab the ladder coming into reach. It was too late. Tauno disappeared. New voices screamed instructions. Another ladder came up, the train moving faster than before. He lurched for it. Contact. But only his hands. His feet flailed for purchase on the bottom rung, but the swaying, speeding train had his body floating away from the car, like a tethered balloon in a windstorm. The clicking beneath him grew louder and faster. His arms ached. He felt his strength ebbing away. He saw the ground and was about to embrace it when a calloused grip locked onto his hand and pulled him up. For a long moment, he hugged the ladder, gulping air. When he finally found the nerve to look up, it was into the smiling face of Lanky.

Lanky turned out to be worth a carload of cigarettes. On top of the train, he showed Marty how to hold on and position himself. After a few miles, Tauno made his way back to join them, and they put on their goggles and bandanas. At Amyot, where the train stopped to take on more water, they climbed down and found an unsealed car with a dozen or so occupants. He couldn't see their faces in the dark, but images of the transients in North Bay burned brightly in his mind. They found a vacant corner away from the pack. Tauno was soon asleep.

Twelve hours later they hit the ground running in Fort William, cleared the yards without mishap, and found themselves ambling in single file down a sooty street. Marty kept an eye open for his down jacket, but wasn't sure what he'd do if he saw it. They paraded in silence, heads tipped like tired horses plodding across a dusty plain. Rumblings, like distant thunder, were the only sound to break the silence. Marty was surprised by the noise, even more so when he realized it came from his own stomach. A wet fog drifted in off Lake Superior. He buttoned his greatcoat to the top, still unsure of their destination but too exhausted to care.

Lanky broke the silence. "If youse boys got no plans," he said, "yer welcome to jungle up with us for a bit. Our reserved ticket west's not good until Monday morning." He laughed at his own joke.

Tauno's head came up. "That's two days from now. Is that the first train outta here?"

"Nope," Lanky replied, pursing his lips. "I reckon it to be 'bout the seventh. But it's a big one and hard to police."

In spite of himself, Marty shook his head in admiration. "You got a timetable or something?"

"Sonny, when a feller's been hoppin' freights for as long as me, he gets to know. Been in and outta all nine provinces more times than I got fingers."

"You've seen the whole country?"

"Don't know 'bout that. Towns and cities, they's all alike from the tracks—same sooty smoke; same 'Help Not Wanted' signs."

Marty glanced at the blackened faces behind him. "Am I correct in believing this whole column's heading for the same jungle?"

Lanky looked down at him. "Yer a book-learned feller, ain'tcha?" he laughed, "Am I correct in believing," he mimicked. "Yes, Book Boy, ya'd be indeed . . . unerring in that 'superition.'" Around them, the hoboes chuckled. Marty cringed, praying the nickname wouldn't stick. Lanky put his arm around him. "No need to sweat, Book Boy, you'll find yer feet."

To Marty's surprise, he no longer flinched at the hobo's touch. There was something comforting in Lanky's presence. As for the rest of the rabble, he resolved to still keep his distance.

Finally, after a long hike to what was apparently the Port Arthur side, the column cut through the yard of a boarded-up factory. Ahead lay an expanse of bulrushes and swamp grass. Beyond that was a grain elevator with Pool No. 6 printed on the side. As they moved farther into the labyrinth of trails, they passed through several clusters of men lounging about on flattened grass. Tauno referred to these patches as moose yards. At long last, they came to a stream where they stripped to the waist and, in spite of the frigid water, began splashing away the soot. Some lowered their pants in search of lice and began flicking the little white grains at their buddies. Lanky put his lips to the water and took a long drink.

Marty tugged at his arm. "For God's sake, man, don't drink that stuff."

Lanky shrugged. "I bin doin' it in these parts nigh on five years and I'm still kicking."

Marty shook his head at Tauno. "We'll be boiling ours," he said.

"Whatever suits ya, Book Boy. Yer free, white, and twenty-one, but firewood ain't easy to come by in these here marshes."

On the second day, Marty discovered another reason for the weekend layover. "What's cooking?" he asked Lanky and his fellow legionnaires as they brushed off their clothes and slicked down their hair.

"Us'ns always gets slicked up fer Sunday dinner," Lanky replied, trying to flatten his beard with the palm of his hand. "Ya comin'? Be an education."

"You got a lead on some food?"

"Kinda." He winked at the others. "Tell ya what, Book Boy. Since you rookies shared your grub with me last night, I'm fer teachin' ya a few mooching skills."

A red light flickered briefly in Marty's head, but was extinguished by Tauno's nod. "Why not?" he found himself saying. "Beats hanging around here."

An hour later, the small band was moving through town. The only people out were families hustling to church. Sweat beaded on Marty's forehead, in spite of the near-freezing temperature. He noticed how the locals averted their eyes and positioned themselves to protect their families from the unwashed. The more optimistic of his band proffered good-mornings. Most people ignored them. The angry ones cursed under their breath.

A modestly attired young woman crossed the street to avoid them. "Get a loada the sweet patootie," someone said. Marty thought it was

Jack. He was getting to know their names. "Think she puts out?"

"Too scrawny for my liking," Gimp answered. "Looks a bit dry, too."

"Youse gotta have the right technique is all."

"Talk's cheap, Jack. You haven't touched a woman since your last bath in '29. Closest you get is peeking through windows, and I note you're pretty fond of that."

"Hey, can I help it if inside folks leave their blinds up? At least I'm not dead below the belt like some I knows."

Marty was beginning to wish he'd taken his chances and stayed back at the jungle, when he heard the strains of a brass band. Was this to be the promised Sunday repast? The music grew louder, joined now by the drone of off-key voices rising and falling in a haunting cadence. He caught something about saints gathering at a river. "Never noticed no saints at our river," Jack quipped. No one laughed.

As they drew abreast of an open door, Lanky slowed, "Matthew-Mark-Luke-and-John sandwiches anyone?" he asked in a loud voice. Only groans answered and everyone kept going, to Marty's relief.

"Damn sky pilots," Jack groused.

Marty still wasn't sure of their destination, but six blocks later it appeared they had arrived. In front of them stood a warehouse-turned-soup kitchen. A lineup snaked down the street. Thirty minutes of shuffling found them halfway to the door.

"Should have made a reservation," Tauno quipped.

Marty smiled, but his mind was on the two guards moving up and down the line, taking the measure of each man, even challenging a few. Instinctively, the men lowered their eyes. When they got to Marty and Tauno, they slowed, but kept on going.

"Watch for slivers," Tauno cautioned after they'd finally got their meal and had sat down on a rough-sawn bench. Marty gave only half a mind to the advice, more intent on making out what floated in his bowl. Poor lighting didn't help.

"Just swallow fast and hope for the best," Tauno advised, grimly.

"Crawlies I can take," Jack smiled, "it's the saltpetre what gives me the heebie-jeebies; interferes with me sex life."

Marty put his spoon down and looked at Lanky, who was shaking his head. "Don't pay him no heed. Wouldn't put it past 'em at the God box back there, but not here." After several minutes of slurping, Marty got to his feet. "Where ya goin'?" Lanky asked.

"For more coffee."

"Forget it. Ya has ta phoney up fer that."

Marty considered asking for an explanation, but hunger won out over curiosity, so he bit his tongue and sat back down.

Ten minutes later they were on the street again, rounding the corner, and heading back to the lineup. En route, the men exchanged coats and hats. Marty cast a quizzical eye at Tauno.

"They're phoneying up," his friend replied, "getting back in line in different clothes to fool the guards."

Lanky spoke up. "Best you guys don't try this. Not yet. Give it a couple of weeks. They'd spot ya now, you're still looking too respectable."

Tauno stared at him. "You'd waste another hour for that stuff?"

"It's food, ain't it?" Lanky replied with a shrug. " 'Sides, nothin' else to do."

"Guess we'll just wander for a tad," Tauno said.

Lanky scratched his beard. "Ya might wantta try some door-to-door mooching. Youse'd be good at it. Pick a nice house, walk to the door, and knock kinda gentle-like. When they answer, tell 'em you'll work for food. Use yer butter-wouldn't-melt-in-yer-mouth voice and go alone. Any more'n one a us guys scares the beejesus outta folks. And best make sure yer at least eight blocks from any track or highway."

"We'll think about it," Tauno said, turning.

When they were out of hearing range, Marty leaned into him. "We're not that desperate, are we?"

Tauno looked at him. "Didn't I see a restaurant with a twenty-five-cent breakfast on the way in?" Marty nodded. "What say we splurge?"

After bacon and eggs and real coffee, they wandered the waterfront all the way over to Fort William and back. It felt good to move with a full belly. They studied the grain elevators and marvelled at the lakers getting in one last run before freeze-up. It was late afternoon when they got back to the jungle. Lanky and friends had yet to return. Marty stiffened. New tenants had taken up residence nearby and were helping themselves to the bits of wood they'd scavenged the night before.

Marty thought of the distance they'd had to go to find burnables, but wasn't about to protest. Tauno had different ideas. "Hey!" he yelled. "Fetch your own."

The largest hobo, a man with broad shoulders and curly black hair, gave him a push. "Piss off."

"You can take 'em, Phil!" someone yelled, as the men began to circle.

Tauno regained his balance and was lunging for his opponent when Marty stepped in. "My friend's mistaken," he said. "We used up all our wood last night. Guess this must be yours after all."

Phil smirked and resumed loading up. The others looked disappointed. "Maybe them's got other stuff what don't belong to 'em?" someone suggested.

"Worth considering," Phil replied.

Marty noticed one man with a dirty rag over his eye, held in place by a broken shoelace. A mucousy rivulet had formed a caked delta along the shoreline of his beard. "You should have that looked at," Marty said.

"Don't burden him with wild hopes," Phil replied. Eye Patch looked at Marty with less hostility than before.

"We'd better get out of here," Marty said, after the others were gone.

"Not on your life," Tauno replied. "I'm getting a fire going for tea with the wood they left. If you want to go, you're on your own. It's your decision. I warned you before. You can't cave in and hope to survive when you're on the road."

For several minutes, Marty stood around making up his mind, while Tauno got the water boiling. It was only when the tea was made that he squatted beside his friend. "Don't ever do that again," Tauno said. "There comes a time when you have to—" He was interrupted by movement in the reeds. Both men looked up to see Eye Patch coming back, with Phil a few yards behind. "What did ya mean 'bout having my eye checked?" Eye Patch asked in a whiney, childish voice.

Marty was on his feet, bag in hand. "Cripes, isn't it obvious?" he asked.

"From the way ya spoke, sounded like ya might know somethin', is all."

"You need to see a doctor."

Eye Patch hesitated. Phil spoke up. "Gus's my brother," he said, "and he's kinda simple. Docs always wanna throw him in the nuthouse. Besides, they're just as likely to turn a hose on people like us."

Marty put his bag down. "Let me take a look." Phil hesitated, then motioned Gus to the cast-off sofa that had made its way into the bulrushes. "Don't put him on that verminous thing," Marty said, pointing to a wooden crate instead. "Sit him over there and get that filthy rag off his eye." He turned to Tauno. "Give me some of that boiled water." He opened his pack and withdrew a cloth bag from which he selected salt, tweezers, salve, sterile dressing, a package of needles, cotton balls, boric acid powder, and a small stainless-steel container—all of which he laid out on top of the bag. Marty sucked in air at the sight of the suppurating eye, but hid it from Gus, whose good eye swung back and forth from Marty to his brother. Tauno handed Marty the Sunlight soap, then poured water over his friend's lathered hands. Marty shook them dry.

Gus turned to his brother. "What's gonna happen, Phil?" he asked in a nervous voice.

"Nothing to worry about, Gus," Marty said, filling the stainless-steel container with boiling water, then dropping the needles in. He turned, holding up a cotton ball. "I'll just wet one of these and bathe your eye to get rid of the crust that's glued it shut. When we get it open, we'll know what has to be done."

"Will it hurt?"

"Tell me how this happened, Gus."

"Got a cinder in it a few weeks back," Phil answered for his brother. "I couldn't get it out and the fool kept rubbing it."

When he'd finished his examination, Marty approached Phil. The others appeared and crowded around. "All right, here's the deal," he announced. "He's got a corneal ulcer from an imbedded cinder. If not treated he could lose the eye. If I can get it out, I can treat it with boric acid and eye baths, but I really don't have the right equipment. It's risky. I could scar the eye. What do you want to do?"

"I'd be obliged if ya got it out, Doc," Phil said.

Marty nodded. "It'll be painful. You and Tauno are going to have to hold him while I try to get under it with the needle and flick it up."

Marty was just finishing up when a familiar voice shot across the clearing. "What the hell you up to, Book Boy?"

"A little repair job on Gus, here," Marty replied, embarrassed by the relief he felt at the sight of Lanky and the others.

Lanky looked at the clean gauze on the patient's face. "Holy she. . .it," he said, "ain't that just a dilly. Book Boy's a doc." He held out his hand like he was greeting him for the first time. "What's your real name, son? And your pal's, too?"

"Marty Kelly, and my friend here is Tauno Jaakkola."

He put one arm around Marty and the other around Tauno. "Boys," he announced, "like ya to meet two railroddin' buds a mine, Tauno and Doc Kelly."

By sun-up the next day, the ill and infirm were scampering out of the bulrushes like lemmings to a cliff. In no time, Marty was swamped and feeling like Albert Schweitzer. Cuts, sprains, minor fractures, leg ulcers, trench foot, boils, and beaver fever he could deal with. Serious ailments, like pneumonia, tuberculosis, dysentery, and scurvy—products of campfires, stoves in closed boxcars, cinders from belching engines, damp ground, sleep deprivation, wet clothing, and poor diet—were beyond his control, except to give advice. Around noon, Marty called Lanky and Phil over for a talk.

"Look," he said, "this can't go on. Except for a few drops of iodine, I'm plumb out of supplies."

"Then start chargin'," Lanky said. "Yeah, sure, they're broke, but there's more ways to payin' than cash. Make 'em bring ya stuff ya needs, before ya repairs 'em. Just tell 'em straight up: Want that cut fixed? Bring bandages. Want that broken arm set? Bring cloth for a sling. Get the picture?"

"They'd have no idea what's entailed, or where to get it."

"So, you tell 'em, that's all. Just don't ask any questions when they shows up with the stuff."

Marty stared at him. "All very nice, Lanky, but our freight train pulls out in six hours."

Lanky scratched his beard. "What's the hurry? Us'ns got nowheres ta go. One place's same as t'other. I'll explain it to the boys and we'll stay with ya. We'll catch a train tomorrow, or the day after, or next week." He leaned in and lowered his voice. "Look, Doc, this is the first time someone's done something fer these fellers, perhaps in years. And you've gone at it without makin' 'em feel like pieces of shit. Gawd, ya can't be turnin' yer back on 'em now."

"I've been watching," Phil said in a low, resinous voice. "You're a self-satisfied little bastard, but inside I see a good man." Marty blinked. "Stick with Lanky," Phil continued, "he's onto something. And don't worry about the men getting hold of supplies. In real life, I was a geologist. All the mining companies keep emergency kits on hand. That goes for highway crews, Forestry Branch workers, and railway gangs. The guys will know how to get their hands on it. And if they come up short, you and your friend can always appeal to the churches. One whiff that you're doing humanitarian work and they'll be falling all over themselves." He hoisted his packsack, turned, and walked away in the direction of the tracks. His group scurried after him.

Marty watched Phil go, wishing he'd chatted him up the night before, made contact, heard his story. He'd put all these men down for lazy tramps. But Phil had had a life. Maybe Lanky, too. What about the others? He looked into the faces around the clearing, trying to see beyond the dirt, the scruff, and the baked skin.

In return for Lanky's promise to get them to Vancouver, Marty and Tauno stayed on in Port Arthur. Two days stretched into a week. On the seventh day, it came to a stormy end when a foot of snow fell on the jungle. The hobo circus pulled out, and true to his word, Lanky shepherded his group, Marty and Tauno included, into a boxcar on the west side of town. They rubbed their hands in glee at their good fortune. The car came with horses and two feet of straw. The merry band cleared a corner of horse stalls and went to sleep. Twenty hours later they opened the door and saw Winnipeg. It was still snowing.

"Listen," Lanky said. "It ain't usually healthy ta hang out in a boxcar in a big city, but this here train's headin' for Alberta with livestock aboard. It won't be here long. I'm guessin' the chances a gettin' caught's dang small. What say we risk it?" The men nodded, and Lanky slid the door closed. "But youse gotta stay awake and listen for voices, and there's to be no goin' out to shit or pee."

For the next three hours, Marty listened so hard his ears hurt. At long last, the train chugged to life, but just as it did, shouts and screams came from several cars up. Lanky slid the door open a crack. Nine heads jockied to peer out. A few cars up, a band of hoboes had jumped four goons. The policemen were down and bleeding in the snow, as muffled cheers echoed from the other cars. "Dumb bastards," Lanky moaned. Marty was trying to figure out which side he was referring to when the brawlers lunged for the open door as it came by. Instinctively, he stepped back to allow them access. Lanky was having none of it. "Don't let 'em on," he hollered, catching the first man with a boot to the jaw. The surprised hobo tumbled backward, careening across the snow onto the adjacent tracks, his pals racing alongside the moving train as they pleaded to be let on. Lanky stomped on their fingers until they fell off.

"What the hell was that all about?" Tauno accused, when the door finally slid shut.

"Savin' our own skins, that's what. Them idiots pounded the piss outta them cops. If they got away on this train, every copper in the province'll be waitin' fer us down the line. Ya better pray them other cars were smart enough to shut 'em out. I'm warning yas right now, if this train slows up sudden-like, get ready to jump and run like hell. After that beatin', no cop's gonna show us no mercy."

Marty sank back in the straw, listening to the wheels. After an hour on full alert, he suddenly realized they were travelling at an abnormally high speed. "How come so fast?" he asked in a worried tone.

"Don't know," Lanky replied, "but I don't like it. Could be we's just making up time. Or could be they don't want no one jumpin' off 'til they's ready for us. We'll soon find out. We can't be far outta Portage."

Marty watched him open the door and peer out. Snow and cold night air blasted in, swirling up a mini-hurricane of chaff and horse bedding. "Portage coming up," he announced.

The words were scarcely out when there was an explosion of steel on steel and banging cars. Loose objects and bodies shot forward under the panicked, tethered horses. When the train screeched to a halt, Marty found himself enmeshed in a tangle of limbs and kits. For a moment, stillness reigned, only to be broken by the crackle of straw catching fire around an upset stove and the rumble of the boxcar door sliding open. Feet, fists, and elbows pounded Marty as his travelling companions struggled to flee. There was a rush for the door as a blinding wall of light shot into the car.

"Bath time for bums," a voice called out in laughter as the water hoses were turned on the car. Marty gasped at the scene: wild-eyed horses rearing; a wounded beast on its back, legs flailing; downed men scrambling to keep clear from the crazed animals; freezing water spraying everything and everyone.

By sheer luck, Marty found himself with Tauno, Lanky, and a handful of others, flattened against the door-side wall, clutching his glasses case. It was only when the hose shifted that they made their rush. The first five out fell under a hail of truncheons. The next four, Marty and Tauno included, were blown under the car by the hoses, but managed to scramble out the other side and flee into the dark. That their belongings were back on the train was of no consequence. What mattered now was escape. Marty looked about for Lanky, but he was gone. He and Tauno were alone.

It didn't take long to realize that survival depended on movement; increasingly difficult in clothes frozen stiff. Boots turned into snow-ploughs, but they kept going. Sometime during the night they crossed over a serpent-shaped stream they thought might be the Assiniboine River. Ahead lay an open field and a lane with a darkened building at the end. "Golf course," Tauno mumbled. "That'll be the clubhouse. I say we break in. We can be dry and gone by morning."

Marty didn't answer. Instead he cut an angle straight for the nearest window, Tauno at his heels. He knew if he hesitated he'd reconsider, so he kept moving, bringing his elbow up and driving it through the glass. Their eyes met. For a long second, they stood frozen in their tracks, ears tuned for a reaction. Nothing. Hearts thumping, they cleared away the shards and crawled through. Hurriedly, they lurched from room to room, checking lockers and closets for something, anything, dry to put on.

"Shit-a-goddamn," Tauno cursed. "No heat, no food, no clothes . . . nothing! Damn place has been stripped clean for the winter."

Marty forged ahead. "Hold on," he said, struggling to tame the shivering as he tugged at a door. "This one's locked."

Tauno shot over. "Must be the pro shop." He began kicking at the door with his heavy leather boot. When it flew open they burst into giggles. Even in the darkness they could make out the racks of clothing. Shrieking, they threw them into a huge pile, then dove in, pulling off their wet garments and substituting them for dry. They lay there, under a mound of sweaters and jackets, sucking on frozen chocolate bars found in a drawer.

Marty awakened to Tauno's boot tapping him in the ribs. "It's getting light. Gotta get clean of here. We'll tromp around a bit until the restaurants open."

Marty looked at him. "Restaurant? That's the first place the police will look. And us with all this golf stuff on."

Tauno shrugged. "Maybe we'll get lucky. Find an owner who won't turn us in. How much cash we got left?" he asked, when they were back on the road into town.

"Less than five bucks," Marty replied. "Can't see it lasting us to Vancouver." He touched his face. Nine days without a shave. He was pondering the advantages of a beard in winter when a man and a young boy came out of a house.

"Excuse me," Tauno said, "you wouldn't have anything left over from breakfast, would you, sir? It's been two days since we've—" The father yanked on his son's arm and kept moving.

"Thank you," Tauno said to his back. "Just thought I'd ask."

"Get a job," the man mumbled over his shoulder.

Heads down, they continued walking. "Worth a try," Tauno mumbled.

Marty shrugged as they tromped around a corner and into the path of a middle-aged woman coming toward them. She stopped dead, her hand flying to her mouth. Marty winced and had begun crossing to the other side when she spoke.

"When did you boys last eat?" she asked.

They looked at each other. "Day before yesterday."

"Come with me."

They followed her into a modest home.

"We're not after handouts," Marty found himself saying. "We'll work for food."

She looked at them. "Come to think of it, I do have a few things need doing. Storm windows for one. If my son were here, he would have had them on by now."

"That him?" Marty asked, pointing to a photograph of a boy who appeared to be caddying for an older gentleman. The man wore a golf sweater identical to the one he and Tauno now had on. The lady stared at their clothing, then looked away.

"That's my Jim caddying a few blocks over. It was taken five years ago when his dad was alive and times were better. He's out there somewhere, riding the rails, just like you boys." She turned to Tauno. "You gave me a start out there on the street. He looks a lot like you." She smiled sadly. "Now then," she said, dropping a log into the cookstove and sliding the kettle over, "it won't be fancy, but how does porridge and toast sound? And those outer clothes of yours should be hung up near the stove. How did they get so wet?"

Marty opened his mouth to answer, but stopped when she raised her hand. "No, don't tell me. I can guess. I can't bear to think of what they put you fellows through sometimes. Come to think of it, you might fit into some of my boy's clothes," she winked. "Mighten be a bad idea to cover the ones you're wearing." Marty felt his face go hot. "We'll look into that later. Would you like to freshen up after you eat? I could put water on for a bath."

Chapter Eight

November 17, 1934
Vancouver

MARTY OPENED HIS EYES, body swaying in time with the rocking boxcar. The train was slowing, and the sound of the wheels getting louder, as if they had entered a narrow canyon. Beside him, Tauno was stuffing his coat into his bag.

"We made it," Tauno said, smiling. "Vancouver."

Somebody slid the door open just enough to slip out, and a wave of damp air rushed in. Marty jumped to his feet, as others gathered around the open door, preparing to make their exit. He brushed the shavings from his greatcoat and approached, hoping for a glimpse of the Pacific, but all he could see was a row of flatcars and unending lines of rolling stock. Here and there, puffs of smoke rose from yard engines as they culled boxcars and put trains together. The marshalling yard seemed to go on forever. He tried to calculate from their speed where they would come to rest, wondering if he still had the strength to outrun the bulls across such an expanse of tracks. Food had been scarce since Portage.

Marty winced as the first boy leapt out of the moving freight train, his legs struggling to keep up with the upper part of his body. It was an unequal contest. After a few feet, the lad was down and rolling in a ball across the cinders and ties into the wheel of the nearest stationary car. "Shit!" somebody said, as they coasted past his limp form.

A minute later, the next man made his exit. This time the results were better. Then, they were all leaping out. Marty hit the ground a second after Tauno, running on cramped legs parallel to the moving train. Instinctively, he scanned the canyon. No police in sight, but in the distance he could hear shouts and barking. There had been no goodbyes.

Marty ducked under cars and over tracks, trying to keep up to Tauno. Too stiff to crouch low enough to keep his packsack from banging on the underside of the rolling stock, he tore it from his shoulder and began dragging it. The bag left a zig-zag trail in the cinders. Shit. The barking was growing louder. Finally, across several rows of empty tracks, he spied a high fence and the inevitable barbed wire. Tauno had already reached it and was running alongside, kicking it as he ran. The shouts behind intensified; a posse of police and yard bulls had spotted them and were closing in. Suddenly, the wire gave way to Tauno's kicks. Someone else had cut their way through here. An instant later, they found themselves wheezing their way down a street lined with warehouses. Around the first corner, they ducked into a doorway and sank to the ground. The sounds of pursuit faded away.

"Welcome to Vancouver," Tauno said, panting. "Cause for celebration." He reached into his pack for the box of crackers pilfered from a store in Kamloops.

"Where's that ocean you promised?" Marty gasped. "All I see are sheds."

"It's there," Tauno replied, "a couple of miles across town. 'Course, it's not really ocean 'til the other side of Vancouver Island."

They dusted themselves off and began walking.

"How far to this friend of yours?"

Tauno shrugged. "'Bout an hour. Depends if I got my bearings right."

"Will he be there?" Another shrug.

After several blocks, they came to a park where a game was in progress. They stopped to watch. Two teams of teenaged boys appeared to be trying to get a ball across a goal line. Marty and Tauno approached the sidelines where families had gathered to cheer them on. "What the hell kinda game's that?" Tauno asked.

"Rugby," Marty replied. "They play it on Fletcher's Field back home. The object is to . . ." He halted in mid-sentence, noticing that those closest to them had stopped cheering and were stepping away. It was infectious. In seconds, their whole side of the field had fallen silent. Marty glanced about for the cause, then realized that all eyes were on them. Instinctively, he ran his fingers through his hair and brushed at his rumpled clothing. Bewilderment turned to humiliation. He noticed that the spectators on the other side of the field appeared to be like them—hoboes who'd wandered in off the tracks. He was about to suggest joining them when his eye fell on a small band of hard-looking types in their midst—the very sort he'd learned to avoid.

Tauno didn't seem to have noticed anything, his attention focused on the game. "Jesus wept," he said, "this is one bone-crunching sport."

"Let's get out of here," Marty urged, tugging on his friend's sleeve.

Tauno pulled his arm away. "Ouch! That's got to hurt," he said, gazing at the tangle of limbs at centre field. A whistle blew. One by one the boys got up. All except one. A man raced to the boy and got him to his feet. Marty noticed that one arm was dangling at an odd angle.

"Dislocated shoulder," Marty observed.

The referee cupped his hands. "Is there a doctor in the crowd?" he shouted. People looked at each other, but no one moved. Instinctively, Marty stepped forward. Tauno followed him. A low murmur worked its way through the assemblage of parents.

"Go away!" the injured boy's father hissed.

Marty faced him. "Don't be fooled by appearances, sir. Even doctors aren't immune to hard times."

"Don't you dare touch my boy."

Marty shrugged. "Your call. But I advise haste. It's important to get the arm back in the socket as quickly as possible. The longer the wait, the greater the pain and the greater the chances of lasting damage." The father hesitated, so Marty pressed on. "I do this a lot. Itinerants keep falling off trains. I'm free, too." The father looked at the referee, then at his son, before finally nodding assent. Tauno held the boy while Marty snapped the arm back in place. It was over in an instant. Marty and Tauno collected their bags and left.

It was a couple of blocks before Tauno broke the silence. "That father sure was one ungrateful son of a bitch."

"Did you notice how they shunned us?"

"Two pieces of shit off the manure wagon. Rubes, that's us."

"How do you get used to it?"

"Comes with practice, I guess."

Marty was stewing on this when a hand grabbed him by the neck and spun him around.

"You," said the man, "are coming with us."

"Can't," Marty gasped, looking to Tauno whose arms had been pinned by another attacker. "My friend and I have an appointment."

"It's just been cancelled."

"What do you want?"

"You'll see. We have a job for you." He began propelling Marty toward a side street. "Take a powder," he shouted to Tauno who was struggling to break free.

"We're a team," Tauno hollered back.

"That's right," Marty stammered, "I'm useless without him."

The man frowned, looking at Tauno. "You'd better not be shitting me," he said.

Twenty minutes later found them approaching a four-storeyed flophouse with unhappy faces peering out through broken windows. Marty and Tauno tried not to make eye contact as they were led up two flights to a back room where a mattress with a man lay on the floor. A battered, jaundiced face peered up at them. Over him stood a slender man in tweed trousers who seemed to be in charge.

Tweed Trousers looked at Marty. "You a doctor, like they say?" Marty nodded. "Then fix my friend."

Marty looked down at the injured man. "I don't have to examine him to tell you he needs a hospital."

"Not going to happen."

Marty was about to ask why, when he caught Tauno's slight shake of the head. "All my equipment was lost on the rails. There's really little I can do."

"Examine him!"

Marty raised his hands. "All right, all right," he said as he kneeled to gently move the injured man from the fetal position onto his back. His face was a patchwork of cuts and bruises that formed a purple highway running under his shirt. Marty unbuttoned it. "I need a knife," he said. No one moved. "To cut to away the pants," he explained impatiently. He heard a click as a switchblade came into view.

"No funny business," Tweed Trousers ordered.

Marty ignored the festering cuts, instead concentrating on the deep bruising of the flanks, the swollen testicles, and the edema above the pubic bone. He took his time, before rising to his feet.

"The cuts are superficial," he said. Tweed Trousers frowned. "Uh, shallow, not deep. Still, they need cleaning before serious infection takes hold. As for the ribs, it appears they're only dislocated, not broken. The worry is the kidneys. Tell me, after your friend here fell into the rock crusher, or whatever, was he able to pee normally for a while?"

"I think so," Tweed Trousers replied.

"Then did the piss get bloodier and bloodier until it stopped coming altogether?"

"Yeah, that's about it."

"Then I'd say internal blood clots from the kidneys are plugging the urethra."

"The what?"

"The urethra. The tube that drains the piss from the bladder."

"Is that bad? Can you do something?"

"Bad? Yes. If the bladder bursts, it's game over. But with the right equipment it could be flushed out."

"This flushing-out business. What would you need?"

"A hospital."

"Out of the question. I told you that already."

Marty crossed his arms and sighed. "To get your man right would take a rubber catheter, a couple of large syringes, morphine, several basins to boil water, and loads of disinfectant."

"That stuff found in a drugstore?"

Marty scratched his head. "I suppose. But it would cost an arm and a leg."

Tweed Trousers broke into a grin. "Not the way we shop." He pulled paper and a pencil from his pocket and thrust them at Marty. "Write out what you need." Marty looked puzzled. "The boys'll fill the order, and you," he said, turning to Tauno, "are goin' with 'em. You got a bandana?"

December 16, 1934
Vancouver

"I CAN'T TAKE MUCH MORE," Marty said. "We've got to break out of this." They'd sought shelter from the driving winter rain in the CPR station and were weighing their options. The clanging heat from the radiators in the cavernous waiting room was a welcome respite. "Four weeks living with hoodlums has me a nervous wreck."

Tauno smiled as he looked over the crush of people hurrying through the station. "Hey, it could be worse. You're popular. You make the lame walk and the blind see. We haven't eaten like this since we left Aunt Onja's. With heads to bandage and ribs to bind, you should be happy. Meanwhile, I'm the guy that got taken on that first drugstore robbery. Good thing, too. They almost botched it; couldn't pronounce half the stuff on the list."

"They're sadistic brutes preying on unfortunates. And we live off them in infested digs. We're nothing better than indentured labour."

"You think the guys wandering the streets, or those strikers on picket duty we keep running into, have it any better? I've been there, and I'm telling you, our firetrap with its hoods, whores, and drunks beats cardboard castles in the park."

"Even with eight of us crammed into one bedroom?"

"You bet. We're way ahead of the guys we rode in with."

Marty scowled. "Bet there are no bedbugs or cockroaches in card-board boxes."

"Count your blessings, Buster. We've got shelter from the rain and a mattress to share. Not to mention a toilet that usually works. It beats crapping in an alley, or pissing out a window."

"Okay," Marty grumbled. "You don't have to draw me a picture."

For several minutes, they sat in silence soaking up the heat, hidden from the police by passengers coming off the noon train. But the crowd was thinning. In a few minutes, they'd be exposed. "Damn it, Tauno, we said we were going to look for work when we got here. Instead we're little better than tramps."

"Work? Don't be stupid. It's winter and this is Vancouver. The town's full of us guys. Unemployed flotsam and jetsam, the paper calls us. You don't really expect there to be any jobs, do you?"

"Then let's go back East."

"To do what? Freeze?"

"You're forgetting the other alternative."

Tauno raised his hands. "Don't even go there."

Marty noticed two CPR policemen on the far side of the room. "Why? The work camps can't be that bad."

"Twenty friggin' cents a day to be stuck in a walled compound in the bush with soldiers guarding you? No thanks."

"They're not soldiers. They're Great War vets. At least it'd be hon-est work. Here, it's just a matter of time before we get sent up."

Tauno smirked. "Jail mightn't be too bad. Lots of guys get them-selves locked up every winter."

The policemen headed toward them. "Why not give the work camps a try," Marty urged, buttoning his greatcoat, "say, just until spring? Maybe things'll be better by then."

Tauno shook his head as they braced themselves against the rain and headed up Seymour. Two blocks into the downtown district, Marty nudged his friend onto Dunsmuir. At number 412, they stopped, star-ring at the plaque that read Employment Service of Canada, Relief Camp Headquarters. "This is crazy," Tauno groaned.

"Got any better ideas? There's no harm in inquiring."

"It's a trap. Like joining a monastery. They lock the doors, put you in funny clothes, and you never go home."

"Make that dry, *warm* clothes," Marty corrected.

Tauno swiped at the rain dripping off his nose with his sleeve. "They work you like slaves."

Marty held the door open for his friend. "Think of the food and lodging."

"You make it sound like a country inn," Tauno shot back.

They entered a rotunda, to the right of which sat a desk and a grey-haired commissionaire reading a magazine.

Marty cleared his throat. "We're here to inquire about Relief Camp?"

The functionary dropped his magazine on the desk and leaned back in his swivel chair. For a long moment, he took them in, a sneer forming on his lips. "What makes you think we'd want the likes of you?"

"Asshole," Tauno said under his breath.

Marty sucked in air, not daring to look at his friend. "Because we're unemployed and willing to work," he replied.

"So say they all, 'til they're handed a pick and shovel."

Marty could feel Tauno stirring beside him. "We'd like a chance . . . sir." Tauno coughed, letting him know the "sir" thing was overstepping it.

The functionary continued to stare them down. Finally, he reached into a drawer and threw papers across the desk. "If you can read and write," he said, "fill these out." He raised a finger. "Lie and there'll be consequences—jail, fines." He leaned forward, the leer expanding. "Deportation if you aren't a British subject and never petitioned for citizenship."

By Tauno's foot shuffling, Marty knew he'd need containing, but his thoughts had leapt to his own precarious toehold in Canada. Could they find out about his Byelorussian-Jewish origins? "You'll get nothing but honest answers," he managed to say in a firm tone. Tauno bit his tongue.

The government man nodded slowly. "Acceptance to a labour camp is a privilege, not a right," he cautioned. "We don't take cripples, criminals, commies, homos, or troublemakers." He waited for a reaction, but the boys looked straight ahead. "And you better not be carrying union cards, or any other sort of social disease, either."

December 24, 1934
Vancouver

"YOU AND YOUR DUMB IDEAS," Marty grumbled, leaning against the wall. He'd positioned himself as far away as he could from the tables at the front of the auditorium.

Tauno leaned into him. "Nothin's held so much promise in months."

Marty glanced around the union hall. There was excitement in the air, but seriousness, too. A steady stream of men flowed in and out. Nervousness showed on the faces of those entering; expectation on those leaving. After an hour of shuffling and griping, Marty knew their turn would soon come.

This was Tauno's doing. The Women's Labour League of Vancouver was bent on ensuring all transients a happy Christmas. With sons and brothers lost on the rails in search of work, they reasoned it was their duty. And it wasn't enough just to put on a big meal. No, they'd arranged for billets in good Christian homes. Tauno had jumped at the chance and signed them up. Marty was terrified. Partly because to be caught in a union hall—they were to report to a labour camp near Revelstoke in a week—could get them sacked before they'd started, but mostly because of the risk of being unmasked. What did he know about Christianity? What if his hosts asked questions about Christmas and its characters, or expected him to know the words to prayers or hymns? Outside of "Jingle Bells," he was hopeless. Had the two of them been able to go to a home together he might have felt better, but Tauno, ever the solicitous friend, had told the nice lady at the sign-up desk that his chum was Catholic, while he himself was Lutheran.

Tauno nudged him in the ribs. "Think of it," he said. "Couple of nights away from Fleabag Hotel, not to mention bath, clean sheets, and turkey with all the trimmings." Marty might have responded if not for the lady at the microphone calling for a Mr. T. Jaakkola. Heads turned. Tauno pumped his friend's hand. "See you after Christmas," he said, striding to the table at the front of the hall. "Plum pudding, here I come."

Marty watched him leave with an austere-looking man in a blocked fedora and a crisp suit. He felt a sense of relief. With Tauno out of the way, he could wiggle out of the trap.

He began counting under his breath. When he hit a hundred, he'd slide out a side door. At sixty-three, the lady was blowing into the microphone, at sixty-eight the name Martin Kelly echoed off the walls. Impulse screamed for him to run, but curiosity trumped common sense. He'd just peek at the party who'd drawn his name, then sneak away.

Hiding behind a group of men, he snatched a look at the desk below the stage. There, wearing an expectant smile, stood a stout, dimpled woman in her Sunday best. Clutching a large black purse, she wore a black hat with a veil drawn down to her eyebrows, and a black fur jacket. Motherly eyes sparkled from behind rimless glasses. She looked back and forth in expectation, her excitement gradually giving way to disappointment with each passing second. Beside her, the lady at the mic shrugged, before calling for Martin Kelly a second time.

The lump in Marty's throat was not supposed to be there. Nor were the tears that welled in his eyes. Here was a woman who cared enough to invite a stranger into her home at this the most personal of seasons. Involuntarily, he approached the woman, her face lighting up as she extended her hand. He started to speak, but a sob broke through instead. "Thank you," he finally managed.

"Mrs. McMeekin," the woman responded, taking his hand like he was a long-lost relative. The dam in Marty burst, as the loneliness of the past months broke through. Mrs. McMeekin closed the gap between them, placing an arm gently around his shoulders. "There, there, Mr. Kelly, we'll give you a Christmas to remember. You'll think you'd never been forced to leave home." She took his arm in hers and moved toward the door. Marty fixed his eyes on the floor, relieved that Tauno wasn't there to witness his performance.

A block from the Union Hall, Mrs. McMeekin opened a car door for him. "My husband was to come, but he's a doctor and got called away at the last moment. Now I'm glad he did. It gives us a chance to get to know one another, don't you think?" She pointed the car south on Granville, into an area she called Shaughnessy, which he guessed from her car and clothing would be swanky. He began to sweat. How long would it be before he was found out?

Mrs. McMeekin started chatting, but didn't pry. Marty, searching for his voice, interjected where appropriate with monosyllabic responses. "You don't have to talk until you're good and ready," she said. "What shall I call you? Martin? Kelly?"

"Marty."

She nodded. "Righto, then, Marty, you just ignore my prattling. Dick, that's my husband, thinks I can be nosy. He's probably right, but what the heck, if one never asks, one never gets to know, does one?"

Marty cleared his throat. "I can understand wanting to know about a person coming into your home. Not too many would do what you're doing. I can't thank you enough."

She took her attention off the road for an instant and flashed him a smile. "I can see you're a boy with manners," she replied.

That was the last exchange for several blocks, which somehow didn't seem to matter. From the corner of his eye, Marty noticed Mrs. McMeekin begin to relax. "What type of medicine does your husband practise?" he asked at last.

"Delivers babies; cares for children."

Marty nodded. "Pediatrics," he responded, placing a hand on the dashboard as she braked for a light.

With the car stopped, Mrs. McMeekin shot him a look, her mouth slightly ajar. "You know something about medicine?" she asked. He nodded. "Oh, my goodness! Won't Dick be pleased." The light changed; she started up. "I'll be honest. He wasn't excited about having a . . . guest for Christmas. Now he'll be over the moon." The car lurched from first to second gear. "Poor Dick. He so wanted a son to join him in his practice, but I've given him nothing but daughters. Four, actually. The oldest is a nurse, but it's not the same, is it?"

She slowed the car as they turned onto a residential street. Marty's eyes widened. He hadn't seen homes like this since Outremont. "I understand about a father wanting sons to carry on in his footsteps," he said.

"Your father, too?"

He shrugged as he considered his answer. He felt drawn to Mrs. McMeekin, but it would be careless to come clean, explain that his father was a Jewish butcher of humble origin, that he himself had been kicked out of med school and banished from Montreal for siding with a band of illiterate workers. He swallowed the urge. "My brothers stuck with the family business," he responded. "I won't be following in my father's footsteps."

She waited for more, but nothing came. "Well, some of us have to branch out, explore new avenues." She patted his hand. The lump reappeared in his throat. He wished he'd opened up, but the moment was lost. She was slowing down, preparing to turn into a laneway.

Mrs. McMeekin was right about her husband. He was overjoyed when Marty told him he had one year left at med school, but was, at the moment, on indefinite leave. He pumped him on health practices in Quebec and conditions in hospitals back east. Marty plunged in, revelling in the opportunity to exchange views on topics from procedure to funding. He described operations he'd witnessed and teachers he'd found inspiring. They talked about that Montreal thoracic surgeon, Norman Bethune, who'd been pushing pneumothorax treatment at the Royal Vic. Dr.

McMeekin teased Marty about the rigours of internship he'd be facing someday, when his ship came in and he finally got back to school. Marty laughed, but his thoughts were on Rabinovitch. He couldn't see Sam ever looking back nostalgically on his experience.

At 4:30, Mrs. McMeekin called them into the kitchen for tea and sandwiches. She frowned good naturedly, as they continued to solve the nation's health problems. The two preteen girls snickered in the background. Their slightly older sister did her best to look bored. The eldest girl, Connie, was working at the hospital and wouldn't be back until evening. Marty hoped he wouldn't be awkward in her presence. Other than Riva, he hadn't left himself much time for girls.

Mrs. McMeekin cleared her throat. "If you two boys will just cut the shop talk for a second, I'll explain the Christmas routine to our guest." Dr. McMeekin winked at Marty and crossed his arms in an exaggerated attentive pose. His wife resumed. "We don't have a formal meal on Christmas Eve. Our tradition is to snack early, then dig into the baking after mass." The young girls licked their lips. Mrs. McMeekin leaned forward. "You will be joining us for church, won't you, Marty? It said Catholic on your application form."

Marty felt the blood draining from his face. He stared at his hands. "I'd like that," he stammered, "but . . . I don't have anything decent to wear."

"Not a problem," she replied, waving her hand. "Dick has a sports coat that'll look just smashing on you."

"That's very kind, Mrs. McMeekin, but the truth is I haven't . . ."

"Taken confession for a while?" she cut in. "Perfectly understandable. You've been on the road for goodness knows how long and unable to attend to religious duties. Not a problem. I'm sure the Lord will make an exception for one of His own as we celebrate the birth of our Saviour." She winked in a conspiratorial manner. "No need to mention any of this to the priest, of course."

He nodded assent, puzzled over the relationship between taking confession and attending mass, but let the subject drop lest he expose himself.

Marty held his breath as they entered the church. He felt like a swimmer diving into strange waters. *Just do what they do*, he reminded himself as the family paused inside the huge doors. His plan called for mimicking Dr. McMeekin, in case rituals for women differed from those for men.

Segregation of the congregation along gender lines would lighten his burden, but a quick glance up the aisle told him this was an integrated church.

The interior was just as he'd seen in the movies. Stained-glass windows portrayed scenes from the Bible. He wondered if he'd be able to identify any of the characters, or if they'd all be New Testament. At the front of the church, candles flared on either side of the altar. Above it hung a cross on which a man, obviously Jesus, was suspended. He wore a crown of thorns with blood trickling down the forehead and onto the torso. The word "kike" came to Marty's lips. He began to shiver.

When Dr. McMeekin pointed to a pew halfway up the aisle on the right, his wife dipped her fingers into a bowl of water mounted on a pillar, crossed herself, and struck out. The girls copied her movements, water and all. Marty hesitated then, plunging his fingers into the liquid, drew a cross in the air in front of himself and stepped aside, waiting for the doctor. To his relief, his host did exactly the same before placing a hand on Marty's back and ushering him up the aisle.

The sigh of relief at successfully jumping the first hurdle had scarcely left his lips when a new obstacle presented itself. Having selected a seat for her family, Mrs. McMeekin placed one hand on the end of the pew, made the sign of the cross again, and curtseyed—all in one dizzying, fluid motion. He studied the girls carefully, so he'd get it right, but they tricked him by abbreviating the action—they curtseyed, but didn't make the sign of the cross. Was this a prescribed signature of rank, or had they merely taken a shortcut? Was a man expected to curtsey? Should he bow instead? His turn came. He hesitated, half-bowed, half-curtseyed, then crossed himself quickly and swallowed. Dr. McMeekin replicated his action. Another victory, but from the sweat beading on his lip, mass was extracting its pound of flesh.

He was settling back in the pew, not daring to count his heartbeats, when the bench under the pew ahead was lowered and the family fell to their knees. Marty, last down, mimicked the pressed hands and bowed heads, holding the position until he detected movement beside him. A quick peek confirmed the family was sitting back. He followed suit.

For the rest of the service, he listened, learned, and discovered skills he didn't know he had. Barely ten minutes into mass, he made a life-saving discovery—his med school Latin had a new use. With the help of the missal, he could almost follow the service. Naturally, the responses weren't falling off his tongue, but getting the gist enabled him to concoct mumblings that were almost credible. Around him, no one flinched, least of all the girls, who were off in their own worlds as they intoned their responses. The word "hypocrite" nipped at his thoughts, but he pushed it away, focusing instead on sparing the McMeekins the humiliation of discovering they were harbouring an imposter. Even communion, the ritual he had feared most, failed to unmask him. When the time came, announced by bells, he copied the girls, accepting the host on his tongue, looking pious, and folding his hands in front of him on the march back to the pew.

The worst was over. He could accept the McMeekins' hospitality in good conscience, show them the respect they deserved. Chanting drifted down from the choir loft, mixed with the intoxicating scent of burning wax and incense. Marty found his eyes closing, his head tipping in prayer, his ego accepting a genuine need to communicate with God. Mrs. McMeekin was right; he had neglected his spiritual duties. His mind drifted to simpler days—*Shule*, and the rabbi who'd advised him that, "A great doctor works with an angel at his side." Marty had banished his angel and in turn been banished from medical school. He wondered if Christians made wishes at Christmas. If they did, he knew what his would be—a chance to finish his studies, settle down with Riva, and never move again.

By 9:30, they were back in the family living room with the tree alight, yuletide music playing on the radio, and the younger girls shaking presents. Mrs. McMeekin had just wheeled in the Christmas baking on the tea wagon, and Marty was about to explain a new procedure in anaesthesiology when the front door opened.

"Merry Christmas," a voice sang from the vestibule. The family rushed out. Marty held back, listening to the greetings and back pats, then rising at the approach of footsteps. Connie entered first, followed by her parents and the girls. He held out his hand, then dropped it. She did the same. Both blushed before finally shaking. The girls snickered, as they all resumed their places. Connie sat erect in her starched uniform, her slender legs set primly together and slightly aside. Marty stole glances at her. Her bangs and curls were done like Claudette Colbert's, whom she resembled, except for the nose, which hooked slightly to the right. He estimated that she was close to his five-seven, which made her taller than the great actress.

Dr. McMeekin cleared his throat. "Marty was just telling me about a new procedure that might interest you, Connie." She tipped her head.

Marty pried his eyes off her. "Pardon?"

"Anaesthesiology, Marty. You were about to explain—"

"Oh, that," Marty said, launching into a rushed explanation in a voice that was scarcely audible. Dr. and Mrs. McMeekin exchanged glances, as Connie asked a few polite questions then went upstairs to change.

Christmas Day for Marty started off like a long, heavy freight train. Over breakfast, he spun his wheels, rocked, and jerked. He kept glancing at the door, expecting a boyfriend to show up for Connie. The doorbell never rang. Then, as the day wore on, he got up speed. By mid-afternoon, they were all into a game of gin rummy with such ferocity that it was late into the evening before Mr. McMeekin called for a halt, suggesting they pick it up again in the morning. A heaviness took hold of Marty. His visit was scheduled to end Christmas night, but the McMeekins invited him to stay on. He accepted, wishing that Connie had put them up to it, then kicking himself for even thinking it. That she showed no sign of finding him interesting only made it worse. Why would she? His prospects were dismal, his situation worse. But when the time finally came for Dr. McMeekin to take him back to the Union Hall, she shook his hand and whispered, "You will come again, won't you? I'd like that."

February 1935
Labour Camp, B.C. Interior

MARTY WAS MARGINALLY CONTENTED. So far, labour camp hadn't been a disaster. Granted, they'd only been there a month, and, yes, isolation might take its toll in time. Still, with hot meals and a warm bunkhouse, he hoped they could stick it out until spring. The heavy snows weren't helping, he admitted, nor was the rising bitterness among the men. Many of them had spent the fall on strike in Vancouver against the very labour camps they'd been forced to return to. Their efforts had been futile—no increase in pay, no elected committees to handle complaints, no discontinuation of the infamous blacklists and unexplained expulsions. Their only gain had been free tobacco—placating to some, humiliating to most.

The rumour mill ran at full bore: somebody knew somebody who said a general strike was in the works; the great union man, Slim Evans, was coming to organize them; army guards were to be withdrawn; army guards were to be reinforced. The scuttlebutt was all over the map.

Then there was Marty's new problem, one Tauno swore he'd even exchange his high leather boots for. Connie had written six letters; Riva only two. He'd left Montreal certain of his feelings for her, but alone with his thoughts during the long winter nights, their future together looked dim. That her news was mostly about plans for Russia fanned his doubts.

More and more his mind dwelled on Connie. That she'd written at all was surprising. But six letters in four weeks had him awake in the wee small hours. Except for the farewell hug in full view of the family, there'd been absolutely no physical contact, but with each letter, he was astounded at how their interests coincided.

"These union guys are nuts," Tauno grumbled, fumbling with the buttons on his pants. "Their aim always exceeds their reach." Both men did their business in silence, watching the yellow piss eat caverns in the deep snow.

Marty looked over his shoulder to check that the guard was still hidden by the downed pine. "Guess the fifty cents an hour they're going after is a bit much, isn't it?"

"It's not just the money, it's the unemployment insurance and workers' compensation they're gunning for. What planet are these guys from, anyway?"

Marty shivered as he shook himself off and began the difficult task of buttoning up with numb fingers. Job finished, he pulled on his mitts. Tauno was puffing on a handmade fag, his eyes bulging. With the government now supplying free tobacco, they'd both tried their luck at rolling their own, but neither could get the hang of it. Somehow, they could never pack the tobacco tightly enough to keep the cigarette from going out. Even the Vogue paper refused to do the job. Marty had given up altogether. Tauno wasn't far off.

"The grapevine has it that the RCWU is planning another strike in April," Marty said. "You believe these guys have it in them to try again?"

"Why not?" Tauno replied between puffs. "Come spring, they'll be busting to get outta this joint. Sure, the last strike was a cock-up, but the people in Vancouver were good to them, so what've they got to lose? Question is, what do we do if it happens?"

Marty windmilled his arms to get the blood back to his hands. Their first few months together, Tauno had made the decisions. Lately, though, with Marty's flair for anticipating developments, that job had been slipping more and more to him. "I say go along. I'd rather be blackballed by the Relief Camp than the men. You okay with that?"

Tauno gave his roll-your-own one last try then flicked it away with his fingers. He watched it arc through the air then disappear into the snow before answering. "That's it, then. If they go, we go. Just don't you get us suckered into helping with the organizing. As long as we're rank and file, we only get our asses kicked when the strike fails. If we're leaders, it'll be jail."

They trudged back to their axes. The cutting was supposed to result in a road connecting Revelstoke to the Lower Mainland. At the pace work was progressing, Marty wondered if he would be alive to see it completed. "You know, Tauno, all this unemployment, civil unrest, and guys like us moving back and forth across the country can't go on forever." They reached for their tools and positioned themselves on either side of the downed tree. The guard gave them a dirty look. "Riva says the workers will win out in the end."

"Nonsense!"

Marty took a swing and stopped. "How you figure?"

"Because the cards are stacked against the little guy, that's why."

"They need workers to produce, don't they? Workers can lay down their tools."

Tauno pulled an emery stone from his pocket. "Good thing that Montreal girl's stingy with the letters," he said, rubbing the stone against the cutting edge of his axe. "The camp guards censor the mail, you know. Best you concentrate on the new love in your life."

"Connie and I are just friends," Marty shot back.

"Sure. Sure."

They fell into a rhythm, swinging at the tree limbs in silence, like carnies hammering pegs into the ground for the big tent. Behind them, other workers dragged branches to huge fires that sizzled, cracked, and flared up in resinous explosions. A whistle blew for the mid-morning break. With relief, they approached the fire, loosening the straps on their ear lugs and holding their hands out to soak up the heat.

Chapter Nine

"YOU SHOULDN'T ENCOURAGE ME," Shannon said, watching the ropes fly off the ship's deck and into the hands of the stevedores below. Winter 1935 had been a mild one, with ice on the St. Lawrence thin enough for the ships to break through by mid-April. The city, therefore, was in a festive mood and had come out to welcome the first Canadian Pacific liner of the year. Flags flew. Foghorns blared. On the quay, the crowd cheered the band.

Dollard wished she would see the logic. He put his arms around her from behind, pressing in close. "Why shouldn't I encourage you?" he said into her hair. "It's not 'opeless. It's what you've always wanted, to study nursing. But it's never going to 'appen unless you get those applications in."

"How can I, with rumours of layoffs at the fire department? You know they've started replacing non-French staff, don't you? Dad's worried."

"What's that got to do with you? Nursing schools provide room and board, don't they?" Behind them on the quay, a family spotted the party they were meeting and began to shout. "I've seen first-year girls at Hôtel-Dieu. They earn their keep, I'll tell you." He leaned over and smiled. She didn't return it.

"You make it sound simple, but it's not. I'm the oldest of seven. How can I quit the coal works if Dad's job is in jeopardy? Where else would he find work these days?"

Dollard stood stock still, his smile fading. He'd come today with a proposal worked out in his mind. Now was the time to get it out. "Supposing you 'ad . . . an allowance," he said.

She hesitated before responding. "Now where would I get—"

"From me," he replied. "My salary. I'm making enough working for my father to 'elp out."

"It wouldn't be right for a single girl to—"

"There's a solution to that."

She turned her head, searching for signs that he was joking, like on past occasions. "Oh, Dollard, you've no idea how tempting that is. But we've been through this. The time's not right. They don't accept married girls into training. And, if I'm like my mother, I'd be pregnant in a month and have to quit. You'd be stuck with a family and forced to work for your father forever."

"Maybe it wouldn't be that bad."

"What about the École Supérieure de Journalisme in Paris? You're not giving up on that, are you?"

He shrugged. "I could always quit Father's company and learn reporting on the job. That's 'ow most do it. Arcand says I've got natural talent."

She tipped her head up for a kiss. He responded hungrily, but one was all she allowed. "We have to be reasonable," she cautioned, pressing her cheek to his. "In all our time together, you still haven't introduced me to your parents. They still don't know anything about me, or journalism school, do they?"

He stiffened. This was not how he'd planned it. She was supposed to jump at his proposal, thus making it easier for him to get out his next bit of news. He took a deep breath. "There's something else they don't know." Shannon disengaged to make eye contact. "Arcand 'as another reporting job for me."

"Where?"

"Out West. There's a big labour dispute brewing in B.C. Apparently, those guys in the relief camps are at it again, demanding something for nothing. If it comes to a 'ead with the May Day parade in Vancouver, the whole city could be shutting down, docks and all. There's talk that the strike could spread east. I'm telling you, Shannon, the Red Menace is 'eading this way. There could be a revolution. *Dieu Merci*, Quebec's got a buffer."

"Buffer?"

"Yes. The Church, our laws, and, of course . . ." he almost said language, but bit his tongue.

"You'd be leaving, then?"

"Only for a few weeks."

"You haven't talked to your father about this, have you?"

He shook his head. "I will, tomorrow after dinner."

"What about your mother?"

"Shannon, *Papa* runs the show."

"Will you mention . . . us?"

He nodded. "I'll be telling them to get ready, because as soon as I return, you and I will be planning our wedding at St. Raphael's."

She threw her arms around him and kissed him. "I'm glad you're going to do this at last, Dollard," she said into his ear. "Promise me you'll be firm. This is our life."

Mme. Desjardins glanced down the table at her son. "*Le chat t'as mangé la langue?*" she asked, seemingly surprised by his unusual reserve.

Dollard looked up and smiled. Across from him, Arcand fiddled with his silver napkin ring. Next to him, l'abbé Groulx smiled. "Affairs of the heart, perhaps," he suggested. A chuckle rippled around the table.

Monsieur Desjardins ladled soup from the tureen, passing the bowls. "You could be right on that, Lionel. Apparently, our lad's Saturday outings with the boys have dried up. When I check the odometer on the company coupe Sunday mornings, there's hardly any mileage on it."

Dollard grinned as he searched for a rejoinder then pinched himself. His plan had been to hold his announcements until later, but with the wine flowing and his father in a good mood, a perfect opening had presented itself. He wished his sister Yvette, a strong ally in past family disputes, had not gone off with the Grey Nuns. At least Arcand would be lending support on the reporting job. He'd start with that.

"That trouble in western Canada we talked about last week . . ." A soup bowl came around. He accepted it from his younger sister and set it down. "It's liable to have an impact here in Quebec, isn't it?" The diners murmured, but didn't respond. "And it's important that we get accurate reports for a change, not that warmed-over, English-Canadian stuff they feed us from the *Gazette*? Right?" Heads nodded. "So, I'm going out there to report on it. For Monsieur Arcand's paper, *Le Patriote*."

Monsieur Desjardins' spoon stopped in mid-air. "I don't think so," he said quietly. "You have a job here."

A stillness settled over the table. Dollard pushed his bowl away and turned to his father. "I appreciate the opportunity to work in the family business, *Papa*, really. But I've been offered a chance to do what I've always wanted—report." He glanced at Arcand who seemed to have found something of interest to examine in his soup.

Monsieur Desjardins put his spoon down carefully and shot a look at Arcand. "Behind my back, Adrien?"

"*Voyons*, Emmanuel, he's a grown man. And he's got talent."

"It's not that I'm untried, *Papa*," Dollard continued. "That byline in *Le Patriote*, the one you seem to think is pretty good. That's me. Your son. I write those articles. But to grow as a reporter I need experience. It's important that I make this trip west. And that's not all. When I get back, I'd like to enroll in École Supérieure de Journalisme in Paris." He sat back and crossed his arms.

Monsieur Desjardins' eyes narrowed. "You know my views on

reporters: debauched alcoholics who spend their lives chasing stories and women and wind up in the drunk tank." He turned to the priest, his jaw tightening as he tried to keep his voice under control. "You knew about this, too, I suppose?"

The priest's hands came up in protest. "Not my doing, Emmanuel. Except . . . I've read the boy's stuff. He does have a gift. And the good Lord instructs us not to bury our talents."

Mme. Desjardins' hand went to her throat, as her husband's fist crashed to the table. Tiny waves rippled across the soup bowls. "This is my home. I will not tolerate conspiracies behind my back." His eyes swept the table for signs of any more insubordination.

Dollard stared above his father's head at Gagnon's *Wayward Cross*. He coughed into his fist. "You might as well hear it all. When I get back, I'm getting married."

Monsieur Desjardins stood up abruptly, shooting his chair back from the table. "Does this woman have a name? Have we been introduced? Who's her family?"

"She's a good Catholic girl."

"That's not what I asked!"

"She's the eldest daughter of a fireman. Her name is Shannon O'Driscoll; she works at the coal works and she is saving every penny she makes for nursing school."

"Does she speak our language?"

"Not yet, but she intends to learn."

Like a man at prayer, Monsieur Desjardins closed his eyes and dropped his head. "*Mon Dieu!* What have I done to deserve this?"

Shannon was excited by Dollard's unexpected visit to her home and so early on a Sunday evening. "What'd they say? What'd they say?" she pumped, when they were out on the street. Behind them on the sidewalk, her teasing brothers had fallen back, sensing something important in the wind. They'd seen this young Frenchman on her arm at church, but this was the first time he'd come to the apartment. Mr. O'Driscoll frowned from the upstairs window as they rounded the corner.

Dollard took both her hands in his. "I let 'em 'ave it with both barrels," he grinned, performing a little jig to the reel swirling in his head.

"I love you, Dollard Desjardins," she cried aloud. "And I want the world to know." He grabbed her arm and twirled her around. Smiling passersby gave them wide berth. "How'd they react? When am I going to meet them? What about journalism school?"

"Whoa, whoa," he laughed, "one question at a time." They abandoned the jig to stroll.

She checked over her shoulder. No familiar faces. The kids had gotten the message. She snuggled in closer. "Out with it, you big tease."

He inhaled deeply. "Well, first I told 'em I was going to Vancouver on a reporting job. Wow! You should 'ave seen the reaction. You'd think I'd just—"

"That was first? You told them that first?"

"Yes . . . to warm 'em up, get 'em primed for the main event." He felt her relax and continued. "Then, while *Papa* was doing the expected trashing of journalists, I dropped the main bomb: 'I'm getting married,' I said."

"And?"

"*Papa* banged the table, *Mama* spilt soup on 'er dress, and the guests, well, they—"

"Dollard! You're tormenting me. Skip the reaction. Right now it's results I want."

He quickened his step. "All right," he said, "it appears I'll be going to Vancouver after all. You know, for Arcand, to cover the labour troubles."

"What about us?"

Dollard kicked at a tin can on the sidewalk. Tiny bugs came pouring out, scurrying away in search of safer ground. "They want us to wait," he said at last, "until you've graduated."

"Oh," she responded, lifting her chin and staring down the street.

"What's wrong? That's what you wanted, wasn't it?"

"It's exactly what *I* wanted," she replied through her teeth.

"Then I don't get it," he said, baffled and annoyed at the same time. Hadn't he made progress, delivered the news at last? Why the sudden edge? It wasn't until she stopped and turned that he saw the tears.

"When we get married is *our* call," she said. "Not your parents', or mine. Don't you see, nothing's changed. They're still pulling the strings."

"That's crazy. My parents made a reasonable request. I told 'em 'ow much nursing school meant to you and 'ow important it was for your father not to lose his job." Shannon flinched. "What's wrong with that? You'd never ignore your parents. Why should I ignore mine?"

"Because yours are manipulating."

"They want what's best."

"For whom?"

He blinked. She pulled a handkerchief from her sleeve to dab at her eyes. Dollard felt his emotions pinballing from insult to anger to chagrin. How could she pass sentence on people she'd never met? Yes, his father was used to getting his way, but hadn't he allowed Yvette to join the Grey Nuns? Surely, in time, he'd allow his son to go his own way. Dollard wondered if he should be firm with Shannon, but there was something in her manner that screamed caution. She turned to leave. "Where are you going?"

"Home. To think."

He fell in behind. "But nothing's changed."

"Wrong! Everything's changed. My dad was right to be worried."

"About what?" They were closing in on her street. He tugged on her arm, lest they round the corner and into full view of the family. Shannon looked like she'd unearthed a horrible secret. His heart sank. He wondered if her father had found out about his visits to the brothel. "About what, Shannon?"

"All right, I'll spell it out. Dad said if Emmanuel Desjardins ever knew that we planned to marry after I graduated from nursing school and that my going away depended on him keeping his job, he'd be fired in a week."

"That's nonsense, Shannon."

"I hope so, Dollard, but it fits. Your father agreed to let you go to Vancouver. Could it be because he wants you out of the way while he gets my father fired?"

Dollard felt the blood drain from his face. "That's not fair. *Papa* may be tough, but 'e'd never do a thing like that."

"How do you know? Your father's an influential man with powerful friends. All those publications by Arcand and Groulx, and *Achat chez nous*, and Jeune-Canada, what do you think they're all about if not getting rid of anyone and anything that's not *pure laine*?"

Dollard tried to focus, baffled by the canyon that suddenly yawned between them. What was happening to the life he saw them sharing? "My family would never do anything to 'urt yours," he managed to get out.

Her shoulders sagged like she might cry, but she seemed to catch herself. "I hope so, Dollard. I hope so. Time will tell, won't it? My guess is you'll be gone a long time. They'll see to that. If my father's still working when you return, I'll beg your forgiveness." She looked into his eyes searchingly. "If he's been fired, you'll have to choose between me and your father."

Chapter Ten

―――――――

May 1935
Vancouver

"WHY WON'T YOU EVER LET ME show you around the hospital?" Connie asked Marty after her shift at Vancouver General. They were walking to the Snackery on Granville, her favourite spot. His, too, now, although it pained him that she always had to pay. He shrugged. "That's not an answer," she persisted. "I want to show you off, have you meet my colleagues. You said yourself you'd like to work there someday."

"I'd only embarrass you," he replied at last. She stopped to face him straight on, a quizzical look on her face. "Come on, Connie, look at me. I run around in wrinkled clothes, half the time I'm unshaven, and I only get a bath when I'm at your place. It's best your friends and co-workers don't know me. That way there's no risk of me running into them while I'm tin-panning for the union or marching."

"But we're not ashamed of those things, are we?"

" 'Course not, but I don't want them thinking, 'Poor Connie, how'd she ever get tied up with such riff-raff?' "

"Jeepers creepers, I don't care about that."

"There's something else, too." He looked away. "I'm host to an army of crawly travellers."

"That's not—"

"It's true and you know it. So does your family. Your little sister let the cat out of the bag last Sunday. I don't blame her. I put her out of her bed when I stay over and she winds up with lice."

Connie rolled her eyes. "Drat her hide. I'll wring her little neck."

"No, don't. I'm glad she came out with it. It's a wake-up call—time to face facts."

She pulled him into a doorway and hugged him. "It wasn't anything I wasn't aware of, Marty, and it doesn't bother me. Honest. Think I'd be with you if it did? I don't like the little critters, but they're temporary, and we're permanent. We are permanent, aren't we?"

He held her tightly, overwhelmed by his luck. He'd worried on returning to Vancouver two months before that her interest in him would have waned. Instead, she seemed to see beyond his current state and had encouraged him.

The contrast with Riva couldn't have been more striking. Where Riva had him constantly on guard, Connie was considerate and understanding. Time with her was soothing. In his mind's eye, he saw them together and contented, living the bourgeois life Riva despised. Still, there was the problem of his Jewishness. At first he'd held back telling her for fear it would drive her away. He knew better now, but still he held off, embarrassed by his own timidity. He also knew that the longer he waited, the harder it would get.

They resumed walking south. At the Snackery, she ordered the usual—fried mushrooms on toast to share and two chocolate malts. "So that explains why I've been initiating most of the smooching," she said, when the waitress had left.

"How can I ever set foot in your place again after that?"

She reached across the table for his hand. "It's not you, Marty, it's what's going on around us. What I don't get is why you refuse to leave that awful hotel the union has you in. Dad's sure he can get you a job at the hospital. Why not take him up on it?"

He held her gaze and half smiled. "Honest, I'd have jumped at the offer last Christmas, but I've come too far to turn back. When I first took to the rails, I saw all the guys around me as burnt-out winos. Kind of the way people see me nowadays."

"That's not true."

"But Port Arthur was an education. Most of the men aren't old, you know. They just look that way. Life has done that to them. Two months on the rails and I was just as 'old' as them—poor food and dysentery will do that. However, the more I got to know them, the more I saw how much they need someone to speak for them."

"But you have a future, Marty."

"I know, but shouldn't everyone? Slim Evans has a blueprint for change. Seventeen hundred of us followed him out of the camps to turn public opinion around. It wouldn't be right to walk away now." He squeezed her hand. "Can you see that, Connie?"

She nodded. "But do you have a chance?"

Marty shrugged. "If it was up to the locals, I'd say yes. But governments aren't budging, and our war chest is running out. The talk now is of taking the strike to Ottawa."

He saw the lines on her forehead deepen. "Would it be dangerous?" she asked. "How long would you be gone?" He shrugged again as the waitress set the food down in the middle of the table. Usually Connie only nibbled, saving most of the food for him, but tonight they both dug in.

"I know you, Martin Kelly, you'll get in so deep it'll bury you. Then I'll never see you again."

He leaned forward. "Don't talk nonsense, Connie. You're the best thing to ever come into my life. Wild horses couldn't keep me from you. I'll be back, soon's the strike is over and I settle some affairs in Montreal. Going to Ottawa with the union gets me almost there. My guess is we'd be leaving in the next week or so. That'd put me back here sometime in early August." Connie screwed up her face.

"And what will you do then?"

"Besides sweep you off your feet? Take your dad up on his offer at the hospital. With a job, I'll be able to put aside money to finish my studies."

"I can help there," she said.

They both smiled as they cleaned up the plate. Once done, Marty sat back. "You mentioned something about going to a movie?" he asked.

"Ah, trying to lure me back to the petting pantry, are we?"

He bounced his eyebrows like Groucho Marx. "Worked last time. I seem to remember going home plastered in lipstick."

"Got a movie in mind?"

"How about *Of Human Bondage*? I've heard good reviews."

"Too depressing," she answered. "*It Happened One Night* with Clark Gable and Claudette Colbert is playing at the Orpheus. They say it's pretty good. If we get a wiggle on we can still make it."

"And she's soooo good looking," he teased. "Just like someone else I know."

She dropped her head and laughed. "So you keep saying."

May 1935
Vancouver

DOLLARD LISTENED TO THE OPERATOR explaining that she had a collect call from Vancouver from a Mr. *Dez Sardines*. Would they accept the charges? Under other circumstances, he might have chuckled, but Arcand's secretary was hesitating and he feared she might hang up. At last, she made the connection and transferred the phone to her boss.

Adrien's rich baritone came on the line. "We accept Mr. *Dez Sardines'* call," he replied.

Dollard could hear laughter in the background. "It's Dollard. I'm ready with my first report."

"Fast work, you've only been there three days."

"Easy pickings. The town's jumping. Strikers everywhere—street corners, parks, libraries, department stores—anyplace that's free. Seems these guys have nothing better to do than sprawl against buildings and whistle at girls. When they tire of that, they line up for free food, or find other mischief to get into."

"Where are you now?"

"In a phone booth near the main library. Across the street, the strike bosses are lining the men up in columns and getting them ready to march. Add in spectators and cops, and there's got to be three, four thousand people here. Jeez, anything can happen."

"Language a problem?"

"Nah, my English is better than I thought. Besides, half of the strikers are foreigners. I listened to a Scotch union rep yesterday and nobody could understand what he was saying."

"They don't get upset with you taking notes?"

"I'm careful. I listen and write up later. I paid a guy ten bucks for his relief camp clothes. Now they think I'm one of them. It's perfect. 'Course, I had the rags deloused before putting them on. Say, you're going to reimburse me for extras like that, right?"

"Depends on whether *Le Devoir* buys your stories. Right now, we're a little hard up, which is why I'm giving the phone back to Lucille. She'll take your story in shorthand. Talk fast."

Vancouver – May 21, 1935. CITY ON THE BOIL: by Dollard Desjardins

If ever there was a town about to boil over, Vancouver would have to be it. The pressure here weighs on you the instant you step off the train. You see it in the haggard eyes and worried brows of decent folk as they scurry to their jobs. With 1,700 Relief Camp Workers' Union (RCWU) strikers roaming the streets by day and sleeping in alleys and flophouses by night, it's a miracle that responsible leaders like Mayor McGeer and Premier Duff Pattullo have been able to keep the lid on.

In civilized times when a mayor bans parades and demonstrations, the citizenry listens. Not this rabble.

They answer to one authority, and more and more it looks like that authority resides in Moscow.

Back in school, the nuns taught us to see God's hand in the wondrous transformation of nature—bud to flower, caterpillar to butterfly, ice to flowing river. But never could the good sisters have foreseen the grotesque mutation taking place in Vancouver. I'm referring here, dear reader, to the transformation of a labour union into an aggressive army. Yes! The RCWU has been whipped into a battalion, complete with divisions, squads, bellowing officers, and marching soldiers. They strut the streets like Kaiser Wilhelm's Stormtroopers. And the general of this hobo army is one Slim Evans, a man with communist credentials and a criminal record.

For close to two months, Vancouver has been on its knees, wondering when the Canadian Army will show up and praying for the union to run out of money and slink away. Their prayers may just have been answered. Rumour has it that the RCWU generals are considering taking this rag-tag army to the nation's capital.

Lest you be encouraged to celebrate, consider this: The West Coast's deliverance could be your worst nightmare. If these renegades actually head east, it'll be in a whirlwind. So the question is, will it blow itself out like an Alberta Clipper? Or will it come swooping off the prairie steppes like Attila the Hun's horsemen? Could this band of church-hating communists actually make it all the way to Ottawa? And, if the capital falls, what's next? Montreal? Quebec City? Is the infidel at the gates?

Dollard took a deep breath. "All right, Lucille, that's it. Put Arcand back on."

"Make it fast," Arcand said, when he picked up the phone. "Long distance costs."

"If Slim Evans takes his men east, I'm going to try to board with them."

"Now hold on, Dollard. Pull a stunt like that and your old man will have my ears for bookends. It's too dangerous."

"Dangerous? Most of these guys are skinny, pockmarked runts who'd blow away if you farted on them, and they survive the rails. Me, I'm in good shape. No way would I be falling off some train."

"It's being thrown off I'm worried about."

Dollard raised his voice over a chorus of cheers from across the street. "Bah! These guys don't scare me."

"Did you hear me, Dollard? Don't do it."

"Fine, I won't. But you've got to promise to reimburse me for the train ticket."

Arcand's voice dropped. "I'll pay."

Dollard laughed. "Look, they're on the move. Gotta go."

Dollard followed the march, sticking to the sidewalk, behind a wall of policemen. For blocks, the strikers snaked in long columns through the city core, turning down streets at random, snarling traffic. To his surprise, many people seemed amused by the spectacle of grown men demanding free food and lodging at the expense of the taxpayer. But the police were not enjoying the farce. Their faces reflected Dollard's concern, as did the shopkeepers, who were hastily barricading doors.

Several times the congo lines lunged for the sidewalk, as if ready to break through the thin blue line, but each time they retreated. Dollard had a hunch they'd eventually crash through, so he kept looking ahead to see what target might tempt them. When they turned off Seymour onto Hastings and the miniature Eiffel Tower atop Woodward's Department Store came into view, he had his answer. Racing ahead, he positioned himself at the main entrance. His guess was that the dozen or so policemen guarding the store would be no match for the strikers. He was right. The demonstrators veered suddenly, bowling the policemen over like pins. As they did, Dollard took a deep breath and stepped into the current. Instantly, he found himself on the tide flowing into Woodward's.

Inside, the crush was unbearable. Strikers plugged the aisles, bulldozing frightened employees and customers out of their way. Dollard bobbed along through Men's Wear, Furniture, and Appliances. In Lingerie, a few wiseacres picked up girdles and brassieres and began tugging them like they were slingshots. The men hooted, only to be ordered down by the strike marshals. Surprisingly, the strikers obeyed. Then, as quickly as they had entered, they burst onto the back street. Dollard frowned. Why was there so little looting or vandalism? Aside from a few upturned displays and a fight in Jewellery, a white sale caused more damage than had resulted from this.

Within an hour, Dollard was ready to file his second report.

Vancouver – May 24, 1935. STRIKERS HOLD CITY HOSTAGE: by Dollard Desjardins

An air of crisis hangs over Vancouver as rioting strikers tie up the downtown. Stressed to the breaking point, the local constabulary continues to display remarkable restraint in the face of unstinting provocation. Some officers have already paid a heavy price — after today, one of the lads in blue will be crippled for life.

It all began with 1,800 demonstrators charging off, four abreast, down Hastings, Granville and Georgia Streets. Just as the rally appeared to be nearing its end, and with nervous businessmen daring to sigh in relief, the hooligans broke formation, pushed the police aside, and swarmed into Woodward's Department Store. In the ensuing scuffle, displays were pushed over, property damaged and one policeman was rushed to hospital with a broken skull.

In short, a sordid mess. If there's a ray of hope to come out of today, it would have to be the no-nonsense response by local officials — Mayor McGeer finally read the Riot Act; police on horseback rounded up uncooperative unionists; demonstrators went to jail — all heady stuff and long overdue. Might one dare to assume that, at long last, a leaf has been borrowed from Italy's play book? Has Mussolini been whispering in McGeer's ear?

Arcand was delighted with the article. In fact, it made the late afternoon editions, almost as he'd dictated. Dollard relaxed. In haste, and against instinct, he'd placed first impressions ahead of fact-checking, yet his piece had been accepted. A lesson had been learned. In no time, he was filing at a rapid rate:

May 25, WHERE ARE THE FEDS?
May 27, HOPE GROWS, UNION SPLITS
May 29, UNION BATTALIONS ON THE MOVE

May 30, HOSTAGES TAKEN AT MAIN LIBRARY

Finally, on June 2, he fired off a short report with news as troubling to Easterners as it was calming to Vancouverites.

> *Vancouver – June 2, 1935.*
> ### *STRIKERS TO MARCH ON OTTAWA*
> *If you felt a strange breeze passing over you yesterday, one meteorologists could not explain, it was none other than the good citizens of Vancouver sighing collectively in relief. This city, held captive for months, will be liberated as of 10:10 tomorrow night. At that precise moment, strikers begin boarding eastbound freights for a new destination — Ottawa. Never since the November 11, 1918, armistice, has an announcement been so welcomed locally. But look out Eastern Canada, HERE THEY COME!*

Chapter Eleven

June 3, 1935
Vancouver

UNDER OTHER CIRCUMSTANCES, Marty might have rolled his eyes at Tauno's tired joke about the travelling salesman, the farmer's daughter, and the speckled-assed cow. Instead, he was working on a smile that he hoped looked genuine. The ruse wasn't for Tauno, but for the nervous first-timers his friend was trying to put at ease—youngsters who'd been assigned to their division and were terrified at the prospect of nights atop a speeding, rocking train. There'd be no riding the cushions for this outfit. With the feds refusing to negotiate and the RCWU strike in free-fall, Slim Evans and Co. had decided to gamble; if Ottawa refused to come to the mountains, then the mountains would go to Ottawa. In short, a thousand angry men were heading to the nation's capital to give the prime minister a piece of their mind. Marty and Tauno had guffawed at first, convinced the idea would fizzle and die. Surprisingly, it had caught on. "On-to-Ottawa" became the rallying cry.

Now, here they were, lining up at the CPR tracks off Gore Street and readying to board the 10:10 Seaboard Freight. Across town at the CNR yard, a group of similar size was preparing to do the same. At thirty men per boxcar, it was going to be tight. Marty and Tauno's unit, Division One, was allocated the first six cars behind the engine. Speculation was that the numbers would grow as disgruntled unemployed joined from centres along the way—Kamloops, Calgary, Medicine Hat, Regina, Winnipeg, Port Arthur, North Bay. Ottawa was in for it, and they had only to thank the Right Honourable R.B. "Bloody" Bennett.

Marty wished his friend would stop dragging out the joke so he could get the boys lined up properly. Two months ago he'd hated all the marching around to barked orders, but had gradually come over to the idea. If this campaign were to work, there had to be discipline. The freight yard teemed with people. For every striker, a half-dozen Vancouverites had shown up to see them off—brother unionists, CCFers, communists, clergymen, curiosity seekers, the Mothers to Save Our Youth League.

Around Tauno, the youngsters kicked the ground as they half listened. Mercifully, the joke was coming to an end. Marty was readying himself for the punch line when he heard his name being called. He looked up to see fingers pointing in his direction. The throng parted, and the division marshal emerged escorting Dr. and Mrs. McMeekin.

"We've been searching for an hour," Mrs. McMeekin said, hugging him.

"Ever see such a crush?" Marty responded. "You'd think we were off to the Somme."

An awkward silence set in. Dr. McMeekin shifted his weight, looking at the men awaiting the order to climb atop the boxcars. Marty followed his gaze across the dimly lit rail yard, wondering how they saw his comrades.

Strange how they had become comrades; trains, relief camps, sitdowns, and shared deprivation had done that. They were a scruffy lot. They peeked out from under wide-brimmed fedoras and cloth caps and squirmed against a backdrop of soot-stained sheds streaked white by decades of gull droppings. Ironically, the relief camp issue that many wore—khaki sweaters, black Mackinaws, heavy boots, and thick, grey trousers—was suited for the trip. Those without it had only themselves to blame—they'd sold their uniforms for the $10 they fetched on the street—enough for two weeks of high-end living. Now they would pay the price.

"Pity, Connie couldn't get out of her shift," Dr. McMeekin said. "Medicine, eh, you never know when you're going to be called."

Marty nodded. "We said our goodbyes over lunch."

An awkward silence set in. "My goodness," Mrs. McMeekin said, "these boys . . . they all look so thin. Vancouver hasn't been very kind, has it?"

Marty cleared his throat. "On the contrary. This city has responded to every tag day, silver collection, and tin-pan campaign we could muster, not to mention city welfare."

"Fifteen-cent vouchers don't go very far," she protested.

"Far enough at White Lunch," he countered, "and they were giving us two vouchers a day, not one. Then there was the music and rallies, even the odd free movie ticket. It's the province and the feds who've let us down, not you folks."

She smiled at him. "You were a bunch of rapscallions sometimes, weren't you? All those snake parades. Gave the merchants the willies, you did. Still, you were pretty well behaved." She turned to her husband. "Weren't they, Dad?" Dr. McMeekin nodded.

"Woodward's and Hudson Bay mightn't agree, Mrs. McMeekin," Marty replied with a grin.

"But May Day was something, wasn't it? All you young boys behaving yourself and not a policeman in sight."

Marty was comparing in his mind the reception accorded by Vancouver to what his home city might have handed out, when he heard forced laughter behind him. The long, drawn-out joke had finally come to an end. He relaxed, happy that Mrs. McMeekin hadn't heard the finale, with the farmer more worried about a lost cow than his daughter's virtue.

"Any chance of talking you out of this?" Dr. McMeekin asked, pointing to the boxcars.

Marty kicked at loose stones on the railway tie he was standing on. "Nothing I'd love more, sir, but the cause has got hold of me; can't rid myself of the idea that paying a man a fair wage for a good day's work beats locking him up. I used to see only the bad side — the bums, hoods, troublemakers, and freeloaders. Now all I see are eyes pleading for help."

Dr. McMeekin smiled. "Figured you'd say that," he said, "and I respect you for it, son. All of which doesn't make it any easier for some in our family to swallow, Mother and me included."

Marty reddened, his blush a mix of fear, guilt, and shame. Fear of an unknown future that might rob him of Connie; guilt and shame for his cowardice in not revealing who he really was. He fumbled for words, but was drowned out by parade-ground shouts rolling up and down the tracks. The men began buttoning jackets, pulling hats down snug, and tugging on gloves. Marty hugged his visitors as the column began to move to the ladder at the end of the boxcar. The McMeekins followed alongside.

"This is for you," Dr. McMeekin said, handing him a haversack. Marty marched forward with the others, unfastening the straps as he went. He gasped at the contents. The food, he might have expected, but the medical supplies were pure gold. "Look after the boys," Dr. McMeekin said, "and yourself." Tauno began helping the first-timers at the ladder. "And when this trek's finished, come back and we'll find work for you. You can stay with us." He winked. "Connie wouldn't have it any other way. And there's something else," McMeekin continued. "I've talked to my old friend Dr. Finklestein at Queen's University in Ontario." Marty's eyes widened at the name. "Get your credentials to him and he'll hold a place open for you in the fall. Don't fret the tuition, we've got it covered." Marty had reached the ladder and was pulling himself up, lips pursed to protest the generosity, but the doctor was ahead of him. "All I ask is that you consider practising with me for a couple of years after graduation."

Fighting the lump in his throat, Marty stepped onto the roof and began working his way to the front of the boxcar, settling into a spot between Tauno and a large lad with a small dog. The McMeekins continued following alongside on the ground. Under other circumstances, he might have shuddered at the number of men atop the car and the paucity of handholds, but his head was reeling with the future the McMeekins were proposing. It crossed his mind to jump down, go home with these people, and get started on the rest of his life. Then he looked around at the dishevelled, smelly lads who were now closer to him than any university mate had ever been. It was a tough school he found himself in. If this class were ever to graduate, it would only be by sticking together. Something new had entered his life—responsibility to something more than himself. He'd see this through and when he had, he'd be back. He promised.

Below him, the McMeekins waved. He waved back. "I love your daughter," he yelled. "I'll be back. Soon. And I'd be honoured to practise with you for as long as you'll have me." Dr. McMeekin jerked his thumb in the air in salute. The train lurched forward. The men cheered. Marty cupped his mouth with his hands. "Count on me."

Mrs. McMeekin blew a kiss. "Your room will be waiting," she shouted back. Down the car, a man with a squeezebox began to play. It was a cute ditty with a catchy refrain. Some of the men knew it and began singing. Marty listened, hoping to remember the words should he ever hear it again. On the third go, he joined in, chest swelling.

Hold the fort, for we are coming,
Union men! Be strong!
Side by side we battle onward,
Victory will come!

He looked back, but the McMeekins had been swallowed up by grey smoke. When he turned around, Tauno was smiling. He put on his goggles and mask and lay down, tipping his head into his forearm, and closing his eyes.

June 4, 1935

Kamloops, British Columbia

HOSTILE RECEPTION FOR STRIKERS
by D. Desjardins

Those 1,000 cheering roughnecks who clamoured atop the Seaboard Freight last night were a subdued lot as they rolled into chilly Kamloops this morning. A night of hurtling through the pitch black while clinging to a train will do that. If the objective was to pick up sympathizers along the way, then Kamloops is a crushing disappointment; thankfully, neither the leaders of this community nor its citizens have shown much enthusiasm for these pinkos. The soot-stained men who tumbled off the cars were sadly mistaken if they were expecting hot food and warm beds to be waiting. To say the reception was cool is an understatement. There'll be no tag days in this burg. All-in-all, it's the first happy news this reporter has sent your way in weeks.

By all appearances, the organizers are fit to be tied. Already trekkers have begun slipping away. Now and then one hears shouts and curses and turns to see men being dragged back and punished for trying to escape. Mutiny is in the air. Minutes ago, the order came down for every squad captain to keep his group in sight at all times.

Oh, yes, there's bravado, but eyes tell another story. When I asked a boy of no more than fifteen how he expected to survive the cinders and sulphurous smoke through the long, slow, seven-mile Connaught Tunnel, his puffed-up chest collapsed like a punctured tire. He'd been told it was a mere mile in length and there would be only one smoke-belching engine up front, not two. Before we separated, he asked me to write his name and address on a piece of paper for him. I did. He stuck it in a pocket. "If I don't make it through the tunnel, they'll at least know who I am and who to contact," he said.

For freedom-loving people, this is a happy morning. Go to church. Light your candles. Pray that Kamloops' reception will be Calgary's, Regina's, and Winnipeg's. God willing, this red wind will blow itself out before it crosses the Prairies. If it doesn't, gird your loins.

———————

June 4, 1935
Kamloops

"YOU OKAY?" TAUNO ASKED. He was on his feet, frowning down at Marty, who was sitting on the ground sheet they shared.

Marty sat back on his hands, studying the men as they lolled in the park assigned to them by a frosty Kamloops town council. Some attended to aches and bruises. Most were curled up, sometimes four to a blanket. Few talked. "Just pissed off that the advance team failed to organize the food," he replied, taking off his boots. "That's all."

Tauno stared at him. "From the look on your face, I'd say there's more'n that buggin' ya. We've gone hungry before."

Marty lay back, covering his eyes with his forearm. "There was a letter for me at general delivery yesterday. From Riva. Seems she's finally done it, booked passage for Russia. Know what that means?"

Tauno knelt on his side of the ground sheet. "Yeah, you'll never see her again. Russia, they let you in and throw away the key."

"Do you really think so, Tauno? I mean, cripes, in this day and age how could . . . maybe that's all just capitalist propaganda."

"Not according to my Finnish relatives." He shook out his poncho. "Look, it's none of my business, but that girl's had you wrapped around her finger half your life. Let her go. You've got Connie to consider now. Don't go getting yourself tied in knots over something you can't change."

"She's still a friend, Tauno, and I'm afraid for her and . . . there's something else, too . . . she doesn't know about Connie."

Tauno rolled his eyes. "You dumb bugger," he said. "You've got a habit of keeping things to yourself."

"I was afraid if I told her, she'd be off booking passage before she'd finished reading the letter."

Tauno sat down beside him. "So, why should that bother you now? You've got a better deal waiting in Vancouver." He pulled the poncho over both of them. "When's she leaving?"

"In two months, August 4, on the *S.S. Alexander Peshkov*, New York to Odessa."

"That's that, then."

"Know what I think I'll do?"

"I'm afraid to guess."

"Go to Montreal as soon as we're finished in Ottawa."

"I thought you were hightailing it right back to Vancouver."

"That way I can tell her about Connie in person. Maybe talk sense into her while I'm at it."

Tauno rolled onto his side. "If I were you, I wouldn't make too many plans until we see how this trek ends. This morning's reception may be a bad omen. With us coming down the tracks, the feds are capable of anything. If we don't starve first, they'll be scheming to get us all in the slammer."

———

June 18, 1935

Regina, Saskatchewan

REGINA—SHOWDOWN LOOMS, END NEAR
by D. Desjardins

If ever there was a place to take a stand against these panhandlers (now 1,800 strong with a reported thousand more waiting to join in Winnipeg), it has to be Regina, city in the middle of nowhere and national headquarters to the RCMP. To date, the missing ingredient has been government fortitude. That may be about to change.

After two weeks of reporting on friendly receptions in Golden, Calgary, Swift Current and Moose Jaw, there are finally signs that the tide may be turning against the trekkers. Oh, make no mistake, Regina, too, is falling over itself to welcome these shirkers, but the wind has shifted. It appears that the feds—yes, the same government that has been idling on the sidelines for months—is finally getting nervous. Doesn't it tell you something that, as the trek gets closer to Ontario, Ottawa should suddenly be taking note?

Does this mean our national government is about to spring into action? Colour this reporter skeptical. Nevertheless, by cancelling welfare and by blocking all access into and out of Regina, the strikers now find

*themselves caught between a rock and the proverbial
hard place. The noose tightens. As of today, by order of
law, all trains in transit through Regina must speed up
and any trespasser caught on railway property will be
jailed. Hallelujah, you say. But does this spell the coup-
de-grâce for the strikers? Perhaps, but only if Ottawa
has the resolve to spring the trap they've set. The jury
is out.*

*Still, with more RCMP pouring into town every
day, Slim Evans may just have blinked—he's agreed
to leave his men behind while he takes a small group
to Ottawa for talks with Prime Minister Bennett. Who
wouldn't love to be a fly on the wall for that meeting?
There are sure to be fireworks. Bennett, who calls this
trek an "attack on democracy," will be no pushover. For
his part, Evans makes no bones that there'll be blood in
the streets if the feds try to stop them. But Evans and his
band would do well to remember that barely four years
ago, and not far from this town, the Mounties shot and
killed three miners in a coal strike. So, as we await the
outcome, chew on these facts: the insurgents are closing
in on Ottawa; the feds have resorted to extreme force
in the past; the trap is set; Regina is the perfect place to
take a stand. Stay tuned.*

―――――――――

July 1, 1935
Regina, Saskatchewan

AS A PARK, REGINA'S MARKET SQUARE—a block in the downtown
core—was far from impressive. Small but functional might best describe it. That grass grew here at all was a minor miracle, considering
the tire ruts, tent peg holes, and beaten paths shortcutting the corners,
byproducts of weekly markets. As for the false-fronted buildings surrounding the square, they could have been from any of a hundred prairie villages. The businesses—a couple of bottle exchanges, a cigar store,
two warehouses, three cafés, sundry car accessories, and an inexpensive
hotel—were of little note. To add insult to the concept of park, a police
station and fire hall had been built on the southeast corner, further whit-
tling away at the footage. All in all, the square was a poor cousin to those

Marty was used to in Montreal. But it was what it was—a working park crowded on market day and abandoned the rest of the week, except for the odd circus and special event.

Today was July 1, Dominion Day, a time for celebration, although Marty and Tauno hadn't found much going on in the inner city. They'd walked in earlier from the Exhibition Grounds at the western edge of town, where the trekkers were quartered. Tauno was pining to get back for a ball game. The strikers were pitting their best sluggers against a local team—a welcome diversion from the pressure cooker they were living in—but Marty had talked him into staying until after the early evening speeches soon to get underway in Market Square. They'd chosen the Sunlight Café above the square for their evening meal, partly because it accepted trekker chits, but mostly because of the music—the radio was tuned to a hillbilly station Tauno liked. That evening, regulars like the Carter Family and the Delmore Brothers had been pushed aside by Huddie "Lead Belly" Ledbetter. He'd just sung "Irene, Good-night," and Marty couldn't shake it. It played over and over in his head as they circled the streets hemming the square—Halifax, Eleventh, Osler, Tenth—waiting for the On-to-Ottawa leaders to arrive and get on with the speeches.

"At least at the Exhibition Grounds there's a ball game to watch," Tauno grumbled. "We're just wasting our time here; all these hours pounding the pavement and still no speeches."

Marty's jaw tightened. "Haven't you had enough of those putrid stables?"

"We've slept in worse."

"Two weeks stepping over bodies, lining up to crap, and inhaling cow shit—it's inhuman."

"Yeah, but at the ball game we'd be outside."

Marty nodded to the young couple with the pram who'd been circulating the square in the opposite direction. "It's important to be here, Tauno," he replied. "Something's wrong. I can feel it. How come we haven't been told what really happened between Evans and Bennett in Ottawa? And why're our leaders working overtime to keep us occupied—choirs, ball games, church services?"

"Keeps the boys out of trouble, doesn't it?"

"It's as if there's something they don't have the guts to spill. Or don't they know how to get us out of this trap? Lots of questions, Tauno. No answers. I've got a feeling that tonight, with locals in the audience, they just might find the nerve to spit it out."

Tauno shook his head. "There you go, getting—what did you call it?—paranoid, again."

"Just putting two and two together, that's all. Notice how it's the feds making all the moves these days—declaring us illegal, locking us up in this town. What have we done to counter, except send Slim Evans and a committee to Ottawa for talks?"

"We're getting three squares a day, aren't we? Which is better than hanging onto trains, or fighting."

"Think of it. Evans has been back four days and hardly a word on where we go from here. The boys are getting fidgety. They've got no idea if it'll be On-to-Ottawa or back to the relief camps. Some are making weapons. Evans had better come up with a plan and fast."

A crowd began to form around the back of a two-ton truck near the southwest corner of the park, so Marty and Tauno stepped off the pavement onto the grass. Tauno cleared his throat. "I've said it before and I'll say it again, meal chits or not, it's time to heel-and-toe it outta here."

"How you figure going about that?" Marty asked. "What with the police roadblocks and all? Face it, Regina's a cage."

"Some guys make it through the lines," he said. "The locals hide them in cars and drop them off outside of town."

"Let's give it a few more days."

"You keep putting it off."

"I'm wavering, but I can't shake the idea I'd be running out on the boys. Something inside tells me they're going to need us."

"For what?"

"I dunno. With all these cops around and guys making weapons, anything's possible."

Tauno stared at a toad that somehow had escaped trampling. "And if that was to happen, just what would *you* do? You hardly top one-forty."

"It's first aid I had in mind."

"For crying out loud, Marty, don't tell me we're hanging around this powder keg so you can play Florence Nightingale. They do have hospitals here, you know."

"Question is, would they be allowed to treat our guys?"

"'Course they would, and stop fretting. The cops aren't stupid enough to start anything. Not with eighteen hundred of us in town and the local support and all."

"Supposing they were to manoeuvre us into separating?" He

scanned the square for fellow strikers. "Like right now, for instance. How big you figure this crowd?"

Tauno shrugged. "Dunno. Maybe two thousand."

"And how many do you see sporting wrinkled clothes and five-day beards?"

Tauno looked about. "I'd say a third." He fell still, as the significance of the numbers kicked in. His gaze flitted across the crowd and back to Marty. "What are you getting at?"

"Just a feeling, Tauno. Just a feeling. But then, I'm paranoid. Remember?"

A group of men climbed onto the back of the truck. The tall man with the dark hair parted in the middle was easy to recognize. It was Slim Evans, back from Ottawa where, rumour had it, the prime minister had informed him he "wasn't fit to lead a Hottentot village." At the sight of Slim, the crowd pressed forward and cheered.

"Shit!" Tauno muttered, as he watched his toad leap into the path of a hobnailed boot. The boot moved on, leaving behind a squashed mass of pinky flesh.

At the microphone, someone was announcing yet another collection for the strikers. "Now, folks," he joked, "gotta tell ya, word's come down that we won't be accepting any ten-dollar bills this evening." A titter made the rounds, cut short by an unexpected commotion at the back. Marty turned to see police officers with baseball bats racing in from three corners. Heads began jerking in all directions. It was only when astonishment finally gave way to comprehension that the crowd reacted. In a unified, almost choreographed movement, they leapt to their feet, fleeing west onto Osler Street. Marty and Tauno bobbed along helplessly in the current.

"Look!" Tauno yelled into Marty's ear. To the right, blue uniforms were dragging Evans and company off the platform toward a waiting van. A bystander, "On-to-Ottawa" scribbled on his jersey, lunged to the rescue to be felled by a baseball bat. The man disappeared, as whistles, screams, and curses pierced the air. Orders blared from speakers on a police van, instructing locals to "return home immediately." Police continued to push from behind, hemming in the crowd. A woman fainted into her husband's arms. He strained to keep her erect. Marty and Tauno tried to get to them, but the current was splitting, carrying them against the buildings, away from the couple. For several minutes, they bumped against the walls, until they were belched into an alley.

There, Marty attended to a woman with a twisted ankle, then attempted to console a man who had lost his wife and four-year-old in the retreat. Around him, trekkers soon found their tongues, swearing revenge, growing bolder with each curse. Locals wisely began drifting away as the trekkers gathered up rocks and sticks. Armed, the men peeked out from the alley to see police officers strutting around the nearly empty square. All of a sudden, a cry went up and men poured out from all alleys to form a united charge.

Marty's heart pounded, but to his surprise, he found himself ducking, weaving, picking targets. A full-fledged riot was in progress, yet he kept his head. When he saw that ammunition was nearly spent, he pulled the boys back into the alley. Around him, men limped and bled, but the doctor in him had vanished, so, instead of tending to wounds, he kicked slats off a fence and handed them around.

They charged again, screaming like banshees as tear-gas canisters rained down on them, turning the air foul. Marty and Tauno held their ground. Then, through tears, Marty strained to make out strange monstrous forms moving in the haze. "Mounted police," someone yelled. Instantly, the rag-tag army wheeled in retreat.

This time, the crush, fumes, horses, and flashing truncheons drove them past the sanctuary of the alley. Retreating west on Tenth, Marty caught a last glimpse of Market Square where a mustard haze rose like gas at Ypres. Projectiles—rocks, bricks, pipes, shovels, tools—littered the park. Downed combatants from both sides writhed on the ground or limped away. A body lay under a sheet.

"To the Exhibition Grounds," he yelled to Tauno. The throng continued westward, along Tenth to Broad, then south to Eleventh, where they turned west again. Behind them came the mounted policemen, cleansing the street of union vermin, pushing forward. Ahead of the Mounties, the men fled, checking over their shoulders as they half ran, half stumbled.

"Christ," Tauno exclaimed. "The locals. Do they take this for entertainment, or what?"

Marty glanced at the sidewalks, lined four deep with civilians, gawking as if it were fair day. But not all the locals were spectators. From the crowd, projectiles were handed out, and in minutes the trekkers found themselves rearmed. Marty began looking for a suitable site for a second stand just as City Hall came into view with an unidentified group huddled in front of it. Were they police or strikers? He checked over his shoulder. The horsemen continued to advance. If the men ahead turned out to be cops, Marty's cohort was boxed in. He selected a piece of broken concrete from the arsenal cradled in his left arm.

"Who's ahead?" someone near him shouted.

"Yours," the crowd replied. A cheer went up. The two groups rushed to join ranks. Together they dragged cars into the middle of the street and waited for the Mounties to come into range. Around them, spectators scurried in search of safer vantage points. The horses sped up. Missiles arced through the air. The police wavered, but kept coming, dislodging the strikers from their hastily constructed barricade.

The rout continued with the Mounties clubbing stragglers and passing them back to foot patrols following behind. Marty smarted as years of injustice boiled up. At every turn, authorities squelched fair play: quotas on Jews at McGill; doctors driven from internships; girls forced into sweat shops for pennies a day; young men locked up in relief camps.

"Justice!" he screamed. Others picked it up. The spectators, too. It became a chant. "Jus . . . tice! Jus . . . tice! Jus . . . tice." A strange, delicious sensation coursed through his veins as he looked at his comrades marching beside him.

As Scarth Street came up, Marty became nervous. "Something's wrong here," he announced. Ahead, a streetcar sat stalled in the middle of the intersection. The spectators seemed to sense something and stood silent, mouths agape. He suddenly remembered that RCMP town headquarters was just one block away. Instinctively, his hand went up to slow Tauno. To his amazement, the entire column halted. He looked around, realizing for the first time that they'd been mimicking his moves since the second charge back at the square. Swelling with new-found responsibility, he waved the others back, while he cautiously approached the streetcar. Behind it, everything was in shambles—broken windows, overturned vehicles, battered bodies, empty tear-gas canisters. A black dog with a polka-dot bandana sat next to a man who appeared to be in charge. It snarled.

"We gave 'em what for," the dog owner shouted. "Didn't we, boys?" A cheer echoed off the surrounding buildings.

Marty motioned his group forward, recognizing the man as the leader of another division. Tall with a square chin and thick cropped hair cut an inch above his ears, he oozed authority. Together, they peered around the end of the streetcar at the advancing Mounties.

"We tried running," the man said, "but they pick you off unless you turn on 'em. No need for all of us to go down, though. We'll buy youse guys time. Right, boys?" Heads bobbed around him. "You break through to the Exhibition Grounds and come back with reinforcements. Then, together, we'll whup their asses."

Marty reeled around to his unit, swooping his arms in large circles. "Keep moving," he shouted. They hesitated, eyes flitting from their comrades on the barricade to Marty. "We gotta go, guys. If the RCMP see us moving, they'll think there's no one here and walk into a trap. Look alive! Form up! On the right, quick march!"

It worked. Three abreast they marched away singing, "Hold the Fort." Behind them, the mounted police moved into single file to swing around the streetcar, only to be greeted by a hail of projectiles. For several minutes, the defenders gave a good account, but it wasn't enough, as the constables regrouped and charged anew. A few at the back of Marty's group returned to join the fray, but already the ambushers were being pursued into alleys and onto the rooftops.

Two blocks ahead they ran into a police barricade, so Marty wheeled his group south onto Lorne, hoping to break through to the west on Twelfth. That, too, was blocked; police squads had leapfrogged the trekkers to prevent them reaching the Exhibition Grounds. Reluctantly, he turned his column east and back toward the downtown. It was a dangerous gamble. At Scarf, they'd be only one block south of the stalled streetcar. But as they approached, prospects brightened. A pitched battle was in progress, with trekkers giving as good as they got. The late arrivals charged, tipping the scales. Marty took stock. From the rooftops, strikers showered the police with missiles. To protect themselves, the police had formed a scrum half a block away, looking like Custer's men at Little Big Horn.

Suddenly, gunfire ricocheted off the buildings. To Marty, it all seemed like a movie, but the cordite, panic, and screams were real. Outmatched, the strikers scrambled. "The Monaco Café," Marty yelled. "There's a back door." Abreast of the café, they leapt through the smashed plate-glass window. Others followed, including two trekkers dragging a friend with a blood-soaked pant leg. Marty glanced at the ashen face of the wounded man, too young to grow a beard.

"Leave me here!" the boy moaned.

It wasn't until he'd reached the back door that Marty had a change of heart. "That lad'll bleed to death," he yelled to Tauno. They turned and, together with the lad's friends, got him on the counter and pulled off his trousers.

"Holy shit," Marty said, pressing down with his thumbs above the hole in his inner thigh, "the bullet may have perforated the femoral artery. Get me a rope and a stick!" No one moved. "Get them!" he screamed. Tauno leapt toward the window, yanking cord from the curtains. A wooden spoon appeared. Marty fashioned a tourniquet. The pulsing geyser became a trickle.

A city corporal appeared on the sidewalk. "Out on the street, assholes," he shouted. No one budged. "You heard me? Move!" More constables in blue joined him, jumping through the window, billy sticks drawn.

Marty held his ground. "We've got a wounded man here," he protested.

"Don't give me that shit."

Two officers advanced to pull the wounded trekker off the counter and onto his feet. Four trekkers intercepted, while Marty raised his hands in a placating gesture. "He'll die if you move him," he said in his best hospital voice. "He needs a transfusion."

The corporal sneered. "Bullshit!" he shot back, signalling his men to continue. More policemen entered the café. The trekkers surrounded the wounded boy.

"Are you blind?" Marty yelled. "This man's unconscious. He needs an ambulance."

The corporal was the first to move. His truncheon arced upwards, but Tauno's boot caught him between the legs before it made its descent. At the same instant, the wounded boy's friends tackled their opposites before the sticks could hit home. A giant policeman, pistol drawn, leapt to confront Marty.

"Your move, four eyes," he said.

Marty, obsessed with the bluecoat about to yank the bleeding boy off the counter, ignored him. Instinctively, he lunged to protect his patient, smashing a sugar jar against the constable's head. He was turning to confront the pistol when the world went black.

It wasn't until the paddy wagon was pulling into the police station on Market Square that Marty came to. The wagon was packed. Tauno, cut and bleeding, was sitting on the floor with Marty's head on his lap. As they lurched to a halt, they heard the sound of heavy boots approaching the rear door. The corporal from the café stuck his head in. "Out!" he ordered.

Marty's head spun as he raised himself. "What happened to the boy?" he mumbled, as he was helped out.

"You're on our turf now, buddy," the corporal replied. "We ask the questions here."

"All I want to know is—"

"Shut your trap!"

"I was just—"

"You're in deep shit—rioting, destroying public property, resisting arrest, striking an officer. Maybe even a rope if it turns out you had anything to do with Charles Miller."

Marty looked at Tauno. "Charles Miller? Who the hell's that?"

"He's the cop you trekkers killed on the Square."

"Killed? We had nothing to—"

"There were photographers on the roof of the station. If it turns out you touched a hair on his head, you'll swing."

Marty's face went white. He looked at Tauno. "Vancouver," he stammered. "I've got to go to Vancouver."

"Vancouver?" the constable scoffed. "That's rich. If you're going anyplace, fella, it'll be up river, and when I'm finished testifying, for a long time."

PART SIX

Montreal, June 1939

Chapter Twelve

DOLLARD BLINKED AT HIS WATCH, surprised he'd been at it for hours—collar up, head down, eyes peeled, looking for familiar faces. Strolling old haunts was turning out to be a good idea. He was making progress, and about time; Father Latendresse couldn't look after him forever. Four months ago, trying to do this had sent him into panic. Even two months ago, the visit to the butcher shop had been a disaster. He was getting better. Soon he'd be able to face the Kellenbergers and make arrangements to see Connie.

Today had seen him zig-zag through Outremont, cross Laurier to the rag-trade district, and finally buck the teeming crowds on St. Laurent down to Ste. Catherine. Twice, seeing acquaintances from his old parish had forced him to avert his face, but he'd made it through undetected. His feet felt light, head, too, almost dizzy, as if he'd been dropping into the countless taverns lining his route. But if he felt drunk, it was from the excitement of pilgrimage. His discharge from Hôtel-Dieu into Father Latendresse's care had seen him slowly come down off the hyper-tension wire. Not that he agreed with the doctors who said that recovery would only be achieved if he acknowledged his alcohol problem. Even his mother had never gone that far and, God knows, she was the real alky in the family. Besides, only he knew what drove him to drink in the first place. Once or twice he'd almost confided in Father Latendresse, but something had always held him back. Even though he trusted the man, he didn't trust the Church. To bare his soul to Latendresse would have been like confiding in one's rapist. Not that Pierre, or thousands of priests like him, had lifted a finger to harm him or anyone else. It was the institution they subscribed to that Dollard had fallen out with. Some day he'd have to exorcise that demon, maybe even with Father Latendresse's help.

The walk down Shannon's street had been the toughest. Approaching her duplex, his step had quickened, lest a parent, or one of her innumerable siblings, or worse, Shannon herself, appeared on the sidewalk. Abreast of her front steps, his gaze trained straight ahead, he felt rather than saw movement at the curtains. His spirits took instant flight, but no door had opened and no voice had called out. The surge of relief was quickly overpowered by disappointment. Wouldn't catharsis come from a reunion, end the turmoil one way or another? He longed for Shannon,

but had he chosen to walk in his father's footsteps, shunning her for defi-
ciencies in the *pure laine* department? If only she knew how he'd changed.
But maybe there was someone new in her life. And if there wasn't? . . . he
scarcely dared hope. Glancing back at the duplex, a resolution formed in
his mind. When he straightened himself out, he'd go to her. Starting life
anew, even without her, called for absolution.

He smiled inwardly as he entered Woolworth's, unbuttoning Father
Latendresse's faded pullover as he headed for the lunch counter. Lately,
like a troublesome tune, his mother had been playing on his mind. Bizarre
that, at twenty-eight, he felt so little connection to the woman who'd borne
him. Until now, the only traits he'd admitted to having picked up from her
was cowardice in the face of his father and a propensity for bending the
elbow under stress. Unexpected guilt came as a surprise. Had he given her
a chance?

Straddling the lunch-counter stool, he dropped the jacket across his
legs and ordered a malt. Since an early age, he'd run to Cook with his woes
and, in the offing, written his mother off as inconsequential. What role had
he played in driving her to those bottles she squirrelled away at her end of
the Outremont mansion? It was a blow to discover that her weakness was
also his. Perhaps her real fault was sensitivity, and he'd been oblivious to it.

The waitress plunked his drink down on the counter. He took a long
swig, annoyed that a pent-up desire for the taste of malt, a fantasy that had
sustained him through Spain's blistering heat, should be interrupted by an
image of his mother. He blinked. The image refused to evaporate. The desire to speak to her intensified. Like her, he had shut himself off in a dark
corner. Ten months back in Canada, yet, aside from stumbling bleary-eyed
past the Outremont home in full darkness on a rainy night, he'd made no
effort to contact his family. As far as they knew, he was still MIA somewhere in Spain. Probably dead. Religious meddler or not, Latendresse was
forcing him to rethink his relationship with his parents. He'd returned determined to cut them off permanently. Now second thoughts were creeping in. Keep this up and he'd be feeling the same way about the Church.

An unsolicited plan for contacting his mother was worming its way
into his consciousness when he became aware of a man staring at him from
the end of Woolworth's u-shaped counter. Instinctively, Dollard hunched
over the half-finished malt before him. The sound of hard leather on ter-
razzo grew louder, then stopped behind him.

"Say, aren't you young Desjardins? Emmanuel's boy?"

Dollard sipped his malt, then, swiping at the chocolate moustache with the back of his hand, turned. "Bonjour, Monsieur Talbot. How goes the world of yellow journalism?"

Talbot smirked at the insult. "Bumped into your father last week at a St. Jean-Baptiste meeting. He mentioned nothing of your return. It's a relief to see you home and safe."

"You sure that was a St. Jean-Baptiste meeting and not La Patente?"

Talbot drew a deep breath as he shrugged, then, pushing his fedora back on his head with a middle finger, slid onto the stool to Dollard's right. On the other side, a man shoved a nickel under a saucer. The older man waited for him to leave before continuing in a hushed tone. "You of all people should know better than to utter that word in public."

"You'd rather I referred to it as the Ordre de Jacques Cartier?"

"I'd rather you not refer to it at all."

"Afraid the world might object to your secret little group and its plans to right society?"

"The world doesn't always know what's best for it."

"And La Patente does?"

"Our *group* takes a keen interest in the spiritual and moral purity of our people."

"Funny, I once read the same thing from an Alabama Grand Wizard."

"Perhaps you're still too young to understand."

Dollard stared straight ahead in silence. Talbot began rubbing his hands like a man with more pressing matters on his mind. "Those articles that Arcand brought over to us at *Le Devoir*," he said, "the ones you wrote up in Spain. We printed them word for word, you know. Pretty good stuff. Christ, priests were quoting you from the pulpit. Then you disappeared."

Dollard smirked. "What I'd write now wouldn't get repeated from any pulpit." He turned to the newspaper man. "By the way, I don't recall getting paid for any of that stuff."

"Wouldn't know about that," Talbot responded, waving his hand. "Call accounting. Right now, I'm more interested in what happened to you. Word we got was you'd been taken, probably shot by the Republicans. Then nothing, 'til today." He stroked his Errol Flynn moustache and placed his hat on the counter. "Do I smell a story here?"

Dollard's mind raced as he sipped his malt. "Teruel," he muttered.

Talbot's moustache curled up in a frown. "Who?"

"Teruel. It's a city in Spain. That's where I was captured."

"Jesus!" the journalist muttered, cracking his knuckles while he absorbed the news. "What did they do to you? How'd you get away?"

Dollard didn't answer. Talbot's face flushed with excitement as he turned his stool to face Dollard. "Two years, Desjardins. That's how long our readers have been left hanging. That's one hell of a void. But they won't have forgotten you. If you were to give us something now, they'd eat it up. *Câline*, we could drag it out for weeks. What do you say?"

"I haven't touched a pen since Teruel."

"Then it's time to climb back onto that horse, isn't it?" Dollard stiffened. The journalist frowned. "If it's money you're worried about," he said, adopting a conciliatory tone, "we'll pay. Name your price. And I'll make sure accounting makes good anything already owed you."

Dollard raised his glass and turned to the editor, a "no" forming on his lips. But in the split second between sip and swallow his situation flashed before him. Spain, and everything that had happened since, was more a burden than an obstacle. How long could he rely on Latendresse's good graces? The priest had taken him under his wing and provided room and board, not to mention a bit of spending money—albeit never enough to get wasted on drink. The results, Dollard had to admit, were encouraging. He was stronger; the pull of the bottle weaker.

"What if you didn't approve of what I wrote?"

"Nonsense! I've known your father for forty years. The name Desjardins is as solid as the Rock of Gibraltar."

"I'd have conditions."

"Shoot."

"Half up front and my own byline." Talbot nodded. Dollard stared hard into the journalist's eyes before continuing. "And I get to complete all the articles before the first is printed." Another nod. "Most important, you're not to breathe a word to anyone about my return to Montreal until the first article goes to print. No one's to know."

Talbot's face screwed up. "No one?"

"You got it. No one."

"I don't under—" Talbot straightened. "Mother of God! Your parents don't know you're back. Do they at least know you're alive?"

"No questions. That's my offer; take it or leave it."

Talbot's eyes flicked back and forth across Dollard's face as if seeing him for the first time. "Three years ago you came to me begging for a chance to write. 'Just give me journalist credentials and I won't let you down,' you said. Now you're dictating conditions."

"Times have changed."

"You've changed, Desjardins, and I'm not sure it's for the better."

Dollard nodded. "Maybe I'm just a wiser version of my old self." He caught the journalist taking in his mismatched clothes and laughed. "Don't be fooled by the duds, Monsieur Talbot."

"What's your father going to think?"

"He's got a lot of adjusting to do, but that's none of your business. Do we have a deal?"

"These articles better be good," Talbot said, proffering his hand.

"What's going on?" Father Latendresse asked. He'd come hurrying down the basement stairs to investigate all the noise and had stopped dead at the bottom.

Dollard got up and took a deep breath. In his excitement, even the mélange of cellar smells—coal dust, wet cement, laundry soap—had failed to rein in his industry. "I've had an offer of some work." He prayed the expression on the priest's face was one of surprise and not disappointment. It would be tragic to discover that Pierre preferred his charges weak and clingy.

"*Tante* Carmen said it was all right to fix up a place to work down here." He swept the room with his arm and bowed. Yesterday, the basement had been a jumble of broken furniture, wooden crates, and broken-down tools, over which an octopus-armed furnace reigned in the corner. A meagre pile of low-grade, bituminous coal lay next to it. While he understood the widow's need for frugality, he couldn't wait to see her reaction when the high-grade anthracite he'd ordered arrived—his first expenditure from Talbot's cheque. To Dollard's relief, a smile worked its way onto Pierre's face.

"Quite a transformation," he said, taking in the scrubbed floor, neat piles of discards, and an old door astride stacked crates that now served as a desk. Light from a naked bulb beamed onto a spanking new Underwood. Beside the typewriter sat a battered spectacles case.

Dollard watched Pierre's smile broaden. "Well?"

The priest approached. "Am I to believe that the basement is not the only transformation I'm witnessing?"

Dollard blushed. "Possibly, thanks to you."

Pierre pulled up a crate and sat down. "Wonderful, but take your time. You're only halfway home."

Dollard rolled a blank page into the Underwood, the click, click of the gears filling the space. Flexing his fingers, he rested them on the keyboard then began to type. Pierre stood, backed away and disappeared up the stairs.

PART SEVEN

1937–38

Chapter Thirteen

———

January 17, 1937
Montreal

SUNDAY, JANUARY 17, brought the heaviest snowstorm of the new year. Even so, the usual crew made it to the Desjardins household for dinner, and now the men were lighting up their Montecristos. For once, Dollard was not pining to be elsewhere. If he felt light-headed, it had nothing to do with the cognac in his snifter. A week earlier, l'abbé Groulx had come to him with a proposition for ending his misery. He'd returned from the ill-fated On-to-Ottawa Trek a minor celebrity. *Le Devoir* had run his articles to mild acclaim. Friends slapped him on the back and paid for drinks. Shannon paraded him up and down her neighbourhood like royalty. Intoxicating. Also short-lived. A year and a half had passed without a repeat. And now he found himself stuck in the printing shop and miserable. Then, just before Christmas, Groulx had dropped a present into his lap. The challenge, as usual, was to convince his father that it was indeed a gift and not a stab in the back.

Monsieur Desjardins had been circumspect about his son's fame. He'd played it down, underscoring what he thought were the low points of the western junket—smelly hoboes and greasy food. "Good to get it out of his system," he repeated for all who'd listen. "Now, maybe, we can get some real work out of him." But after eighteen months, Dollard still lusted for another such opportunity.

Shannon understood his problem, but not his refusal to remedy it. Talk of marriage had petered out. That she was a wonderful girl went without question, but doubts had set in, fanned by duty to his own set. He knew that going "outside" for a wife would create repercussions that wouldn't end at the altar. Dollard refused to admit that he was a jellyfish. But he was no Edward VIII, either. Shunning one's birthright came at a price, one that he wasn't sure he wanted to pay. Then there was the problem of her father's dismissal. She'd conceded that it was due to cutbacks and not Monsieur Desjardins' interference, but the mere suspicion had taken its toll on their relationship.

The four men settled into the chairs. L'abbé made eye contact with Monsieur Arcand, then cleared his throat. Dollard knew his role was to keep quiet and play the dutiful son. He rose to refill their glasses.

"Emmanuel," l'abbé began, in a casual tone, "any thoughts on Spain?"

Monsieur Desjardins looked up from the generous pouring of cognac his son had just served him. "What's not to like about Franco?" he frowned. "He's putting the atheists in their place, isn't he?"

"You're not concerned with the lack of balance in the reporting? One side getting all the coverage?" Groulx asked.

Monsieur Desjardins focused on his glass. "Where're you going with this?"

"It doesn't bother you that Republican sympathizers swoop into Montreal with their lies, take up collections, and return to Spain to kill more priests?"

Desjardins frowned. "Of course it concerns me when news agencies don't bother to cross-reference. And, yes, I'm aware that General Franco seldom gets to tell his story. And you know damn well what I think about those Republicans."

Arcand opened his mouth to speak, only to shut it again when Groulx made a barely perceptible shake of the head. "So, would you say people are confused on Spain?"

Monsieur Desjardins moistened his lips. "Worse. I'd say they were being misled. As much as it hurts to admit, for once the federal government's got it right with that new law they're talking about—the one that will prevent Canadians from volunteering to fight in foreign wars." He chuckled. " 'Course, I might have second thoughts about that if there were more Canadians joining Franco's side."

Goulx nodded. "So, I take it you wouldn't be averse to more balanced reporting? Bringing Quebecers around on Spain?"

"I'd say wonderful," Desjardins replied, then stiffened, before leaning forward and waving his finger. "You've got that tone, Lionel. The same one you used when you dropped the bombshell about my Yvette joining the Grey Nuns."

Groulx puffed on his cigar and moved the ashtray in closer, careful not to scrape it along the end table's ivory inlay. "A wonderful opportunity has presented itself," he said, "one that could provide greater insight into Franco's cause." Monsieur Desjardins waited. "It involves having a Quebecer moving with the Generalissimo's troops." He hesitated. "A reporter, not a soldier."

Monsieur Desjardins cast a quick look in Dollard's direction. "You after my money or my son?" he growled.

Groulx ignored the question. "Luis Bolín? Is that a name familiar to you?" Monsieur Desjardins shook his head. "He heads up Franco's press bureau in Salamanca, Spain. Bolín's launched an initiative to offset biased reporting in the Western press. His plan calls for bringing over Catholic reporters of good character to see for themselves and set the record straight. For a small fee, they're to be taken to repatriated territory for a first-hand glimpse at the barbarity of the anti-Christians. In return, they're to come home to spread the truth about what's really happening over there."

Dollard watched his father take a long puff on his cigar, then check the end. It had gone cold. "Commendable," he said. "Why am I suddenly feeling ill at ease?"

Groulx pressed the tips of his fingers together in his lap. "It can't be just any Catholic, Emmanuel. They prefer men of breeding with reporting experience."

Monsieur Desjardins rose from the wingback chair and slid behind his desk. He repositioned items around the perimeter of the large blotter—ink bottles, nibbed pens, stapler. "Forget it!" he replied at last. "Spain's a killing ground. My son will not be going."

"He wouldn't be in danger, Emmanuel. The journalists only get to the front after battles have been fought and won. Dollard's a perfect candidate—healthy, athletic, smart, experienced, and Catholic."

"His mother would never allow it."

"Emmanuel," Groulx said, drawing out the last vowels, "we can get him on at *Le Devoir*. A short-term assignment, of course, lasting only until he returns to you and the business. Right, Dollard?" Dollard nodded eagerly. "He'll be treated well. We'll send him off with letters of introduction from myself and the cardinal. Think about what an education it'd be—for him, for us, for all God-fearing Quebecers."

Dollard sat wide-eyed, not daring to speak. Monsieur Desjardins struck a match. For several seconds, he held his cigar in the flame before putting it to his mouth. He puffed. The air turned blue. "There's lots of cannon fodder available," he said. "Try Jeune-Canada."

Arcand spoke up for the first time. "But we know Dollard's capabilities."

Monsieur Desjardins stiffened. "I'm the head of this family and I'm not changing my mind. Get used to the idea that he's not going to—"

L'abbé held up his hand. "Dollard," he said, "leave us alone for a few minutes." Groulx waited for the heavy door to close behind the young man before resuming. "We're all family, here, Emmanuel, which is why we look out for each other. Right?" His host stared at the ornate letter opener on the desk, his slightly widened eyes the only sign of his true feelings. "Adrien is going to tell you something that might make a difference."

Arcand, his brow furrowed, glanced at the door, before speaking in a low voice. "That Irish girl. The one we thought we'd dealt with months ago. He still sees her."

"Damn!" Monsieur Desjardins responded, pounding the arm of his chair. "In spite of all our . . . efforts?"

L'abbé raised his chin to Arcand. "I've talked to her priest at St. Raphael. He speaks highly of her. Her wages keep the family going."

"*Maudit!* A girl with character. Why couldn't she just be *une petite salope?*"

Groulx cocked his head, choosing his words carefully. "We've got nothing against her personally. But think of the ramifications. Desjardins is an important name in this province. If people were to see your son marrying 'outside' they'd . . . well, personally, I'd hate to see that happen."

"And you think sending him to Spain will be the end of it?"

"Put it this way, Emmanuel. Dollard would be away for at least half a year. They're young with healthy appetites. Anything can happen in that time."

★

January 22, 1937
Montreal

DOLLARD TRIED TO MARSHAL HIS THOUGHTS as he made his way down Laurier to the Café Sans-Pareil. Used to taking the initiative, he was uncomfortable with Shannon's insistence on setting the time and place for this meeting. This was his neighbourhood, *Maman* had her hair done down the street, *Papa* bought his cigars at the smoke shop on the corner, and Cook's brother owned the clothing store on the next block. He was troubled, too, by her choice of wording. Meeting is what she'd called it, not rendezvous.

He couldn't remember his own mother ever questioning his father. Yet, lately, Shannon had been doing it often. Then, when he'd told her about Spain, she'd fallen sullen and asked to be taken home. Outside her place, she had sat silent in the car for several minutes. "We need to talk," she'd said as they parted. He'd been having similar thoughts, but hearing it from her had him tossing all night. By morning, he was determined to get their relationship back on track.

Now, en route to the café, he decided to be firm. Only then would they be able to talk this through. It didn't make sense that she insist he pass up Spain. Hadn't she encouraged him to go for journalism and branch out on his own? What could be more independent than getting away from the people she accused of "managing" his future? Best to take a tough stand now. For several steps, he was certain that this was the proper course, but with the café now in sight, his resolve began trickling away. He remembered her note. There was something unsettling about the tone.

Entering the café, he instinctively headed for the back booth. He'd only taken a few steps when he heard her call his name. He turned, annoyed that after years of discrete meetings, she'd chosen a table near the window. He forced a smile. It wasn't returned.

"We have to talk," she said, pushing away her untouched coffee.

"Want something to eat?" he responded.

She shook her head. "What I have to say isn't going to be—"

"The Café Sans-Pareil is famous for its Boston cream pie. *Maman* and *Papa* used to bring us 'ere after church on Sundays. They'd save the large table for us at the back and we'd all pile in and—"

"Dollard."

"We came so often, we each 'ad our favourite places. Yvette would sit at one end and me the other, like we were the parents and *Maman* and *Papa* the kids. Then when—"

"Dollard. Please. Listen to me." She put her hand over his. "I don't want you to misinterpret what I've got to say. This is not an ultimatum. The fact is, you've made a decision. Well, so have I. Yours is for Spain. Good for you, but I won't be here when you get back."

"But I 'ave not made that decision."

"Yes, you have. You just don't realize it yet."

"You can't . . ."

She held up her hand. He stopped. "Dad finally found a new job. A good one. Now he's insisting I follow my own path." She paused. "I've been accepted to nursing at a small hospital in Ontario."

The waitress arrived. He opened his mouth to speak, but, not trusting his voice, pointed instead to Shannon's cup. "Where?" he asked, in a squeak he didn't recognize.

She looked off for a second before replying. "I think it better you don't know."

He began sliding the sugar bowl back and forth. "Is all this because I did not write enough when I was in Vancouver?"

"That hurt, but no."

"I don't get it, Shannon. I thought we had an understanding."

She hesitated while the waitress set his coffee down. "We did, but we were dreaming. We thought we could forge a new path. Our faith was to be the bridge. Plainly, it isn't enough. I've been trying to tell you for months. Unfortunately, listening is not one of your strong points." She watched him pass the sugar bowl, back and forth, faster and faster.

"You encouraged me to get serious about journalism. Now that I am getting a break, a big one, you are upset. You knew reporting would mean long separations. We talked about it."

She leaned forward. "That's not it, Dollard. It's the terms under which you're leaving. You don't get it. The hold they have on you hasn't changed and never will. They're only letting you go to get you away from me."

He shook his head. "No, you don't get it. This time I got my way, in spite of my father."

She reached out, intercepting the sugar bowl with one hand and placing the other over his. "I know you believe that, Dollard, but that's not how I see it. You may have won a skirmish, but you haven't won independence. It's plain to me now. Language, culture, and Outremont are in your bones. You can't shake them. No matter how hard you try, you'll always be sucked back in. I know you've done your best to break free—for me—but you can't do it. And even if you could, it wouldn't work, because I'd just be holding you back and, in time, you'd come to resent me for it."

"I can make the break, Shannon. After Spain—"

"You said that about university and then Vancouver." She shook her head. "No, it's too late. I have my own future to consider." She withdrew her hand. "I leave in a week."

He sat back and swallowed. "I don't believe it. Just like that. Without even telling me where you're going."

"It's for the best, Dollard. With me gone, you'll be able to bloom in your own garden." She smiled. "You've got a great future. I see you as a prominent businessman, maybe even a politician. You'd be good at that."

She rose. He grabbed her hand. "Where in Ontario? At least tell me that. I want to be able to imagine you in a real place. I wouldn't follow you. Honest."

She glanced out the window then back at him. "Promise?" He nodded. "Stratford. It's a small town west of Toronto."

"I won't go back on my word," he said, "but if we did meet, say by accident . . .?"

She dropped his hand, her voice breaking. "Please don't, Dollard."

He watched her leave, cross the street, then disappear.

Chapter Fourteen

———

January 25, 1937
Toronto

TRUDGING THROUGH SNOW—collar up, ear lugs down—it wasn't surprising that Marty didn't hear the streetcar approaching from behind. Even so, he knew it was there. He'd sensed it in the vibrations oscillating along the frozen earth, up through the sidewalk, and into his gut. The streetcar passed, then stopped just ahead at the corner of Church and Queen. The accordion doors folded open. Neither Marty nor Tauno quickened their pace. It had been a long while since they'd been able to afford the five-cent fare.

For two weeks, they'd been making the morning trek from their lodgings on Pape along Queen to the Seaman's Union Hall on Spadina. Today was tougher than usual. A gale-force wind was blasting in off the frozen harbour. The shovellers were out, but worked at a relaxed pace. Marty and Tauno had experience on the snow-removal brigade. They understood the compulsion to stretch the job out—partly for the joy of being employed, but mostly to wring every possible penny from the city coffers. Standing with the other bundled-up pedestrians waiting for the light to turn, Marty eyed the cozy commuters behind the frosted windows of the streetcar. When the light turned green, they stepped off the curb, tucking in behind three men in fedoras and heavy overcoats who'd just turned off Church Street. The streetcar clanged as it passed. Neither man looked up. Tauno tightened the hood of his parka. "What do we do if the union turns us down on Spain?" he asked.

Marty lengthened his stride to match that of the man ahead of him. "You're fine," he answered. "It's me they're having trouble with. I'm the one without a union card. And what do you think my chances are of getting one, now that they've found out I was with management on that textile strike in Montreal?"

"You explained all that, Marty. They know you were really working for the union side."

"Sure! And did you see the guy's eyes when I told him?"

"They'll check it out. You'll be fine. Especially knowing you were on the On-to-Ottawa march and spent twenty months in jail." He reached down to scoop up a handful of snow and began packing it into a ball.

Marty's pulse quickened at the prospect of having his request denied by some ignoramus in a tie. "You know what it means if they turn me down, don't you?" he said. "No union card, no Spain."

Tauno's snowball was ready for firing. He glanced around for a target. "It'll come through, you'll see. Just don't lose your temper again with the union guys."

Marty shook his head. "Has to be soon. Your uncle can't afford to put both of us up much longer."

"What's so bad if they turn you down? You can do what you should have done when they let us out—go back to Connie and finish med school. Christ, you'd have your shingle up in no time. What's the matter with you, anyway?"

"We've been over that a hundred times."

"And I still don't get it."

"You know my reason. The fascists are taking over the world one country at a time. Now it's Spain's turn. We all have to do our bit to put a stop to it. If I went back to Vancouver now, I'd never leave. It's as simple as that. Connie understands."

"What Connie doesn't understand is how screwed up you've become. Ever since jail you've been boiling to get even. It's become personal and it's going to ruin you. You were more fun when you just rolled with the punches."

"Jail made me focus. There's a lot wrong with this world."

"Or is it that you're still trying to live up to Riva Lilovsky's class-struggle nonsense? She's been gone over a year, let her go."

Marty shot him a look. "You know, Jaakkola, you can be really disappointing. All we've been through and you still don't get it."

"Get what? Guys with money and power shit on guys with none. That's the way it's always been, and Marty Kelly throwing his life away is not going to put a stop to it."

"Jesus, Tauno! As long as people have that attitude, nothing will ever change. If people would stand together we could . . ."

Tauno raised his hands. "All right, all right, spare me. Just tell me what we do if there's to be no union card or clearance for Spain? We can't ride the rails in these temperatures."

Marty grabbed Tauno by the arm and stopped, causing traffic on the sidewalk to eddy around them. "Not *we*, Tauno! *You* have an option. *You* can go to Spain. *You* can still make a difference."

Tauno wrenched his arm free and resumed walking. "Bullshit! We agreed to stick together after Regina. No secrets, we said. We're a team."

"This is not just about you and me," Marty said, catching up. "You said yourself the Spanish need help and—"

"Yeah, yeah," Tauno interrupted, throwing his snowball into the air and catching it. Another streetcar passed.

"—you cursed Franco for revolting against education and land reform and free elections, didn't you? And agreed he's only interested in reinstating his wealthy cronies."

"I said I got it, didn't I?"

"But you're not committed. Even after all those radio broadcasts we've heard."

Tauno shrugged. "Sure, I think he's an asshole. Just not as much as you, that's all. For me, Spain's more about heat, excitement, and something to do." He threw his snowball at the disappearing streetcar, watching it arc through the air, falling short of its target. "Truth is, you're too hung up on those guys."

"What guys?"

"Franco, Mussolini, Hitler. None of them ever hurt us."

Marty took a deep breath. "Not yet, but they've got a schedule, and we're on it."

"Where do you come up with that stuff? Pathé Newsreels? No one holds with all that totalitarian shit on this side of the ocean."

"For Chrissakes, Tauno! Open your eyes! You don't think Richard-bloody-Bennett was playing the fascist when he gunned us down in Regina?"

"It got him kicked out of office, didn't it?"

"And Mackenzie King's any better?"

Tauno shrugged. "Dunno yet. Give him a chance."

"Look around! We've got our own homegrown Mussolinis, right here. And it's not just the Hepburns and Duplessis either, it's all those tycoons putting unions down. You don't find it strange that our prime minister thinks Herr Hitler—the man who robs and jails Jews—is doing a wonderful job in Germany?"

"Look, so they don't like Jews over there, and that's terrible. But from what I hear, the Jews are used to it."

"'The Jews are used to it?'" Marty mimicked. "You think you get used to beatings, evictions, and having your property confiscated? You've no idea what you're talking about."

Tauno threw his hands in the air. "Oh! And I suppose you do . . .

Martin Kelly."

Marty broke into a trot, his mind going a hundred miles and hour. What was the use? This whole argument was academic. Neither of them was going anywhere. Without a union card, there'd be no taking up arms against Franco for him. And if he wasn't going, Tauno didn't have the conviction to join up on his own.

Tauno caught up. "Look," he said, "your heart's in the right place and that's great. All I'm saying is, don't take it so damn personal."

"Maybe it is personal."

"Don't talk nonsense. My folks are from Finland and yours from Ireland. From where I sit, neither the Germans nor the Italians have done anything to hurt our relatives in the Old Country."

"God, this coffee's weak," Tauno complained.

Marty grinned. "It's free, isn't it?" His eyes roamed the Seaman's Union Hall, taking in the drab walls, the fifty-watt bulbs, the sixteen-foot ceilings, and the steel meshing that boxed in the dirty windows. The chairs had been placed in neat rows parallel to the stage, but as the unemployed ambled in, they rearranged them in little circles, each group huddled around its own make-believe campfire. Habits died hard. The stench of yesterday's boiled cabbage lingered in the air, mingling with the acrid mélange of unwashed bodies, musty hair, and sour, slept-in clothes. Marty searched for familiar faces from the hobo jungles and the On-to-Ottawa March; someone to vouch for him. No luck.

It was only ten after eight, but already the noise level was rising. With the cold and snow, there'd be a full house today. Although most had long since abandoned hope of ever finding work, they came here for the warmth and the soup and sandwiches served at noon. Marty could tell at a glance the financial state of each man; it showed in the look in their eyes, the state of their duds, and the length of their whiskers. The best-off had relatives to stay with, so got to shave. A few lucky ones in the hostels got a chance to clean up, too, but only if they were first in line, or there was enough hot water. No one, not even down-and-outers, had the balls to wash in the frothy-grey scum left by the twenty-odd men who'd gone before.

The best-groomed men in the hall by far were the union work-ers. Not that Marty resented them for it. He understood they had to be presentable for meetings with government and management. Still, he couldn't help but remember the threadbare clothes worn by rabbis back in Montreal and the respect that garnered from their flocks.

He blew on his coffee in the thick mug and examined his out-of-work comrades. Tired eyes pored over the leaflets and the few hastily scribbled notes plastered on the HELP WANTED board. It was like going to a dance and finding there were no women. Mostly, the notices were pleas for friends and relatives gone missing: "Looking for Nicko-las Rukavina, last seen in boxcar west of Belleville"; "Sam Hatch, come home, Mom has cancer"; "Lost dog, black with floppy ears and white patch over left eye, answers to Toby." The formal notices contained valuable information on soup kitchens, shelters, and instructions on keeping warm. There was what Marty saw as useless information, too, like advice on grooming for interviews and how to behave when apply-ing for work.

The wall surrounding the bulletin board was plastered with political posters—union, CCF, communist—featuring broad-shouldered, mus-cular labourers wielding mallets, axes, and picks. There was a stage at the front of the hall over which a banner announced a fundraising drive by the Committee to Aid Spanish Democracy. *Lousy timing*, Marty thought, *it's mid-January; don't they have the sense to wait for May Day when people might be in a festive mood and feeling generous?* He was about to comment on this to Tauno when three burly union officials in tweed jackets stomped onto the stage.

"What have we got here?" Marty mumbled.

Heads began to turn. "Brothers," MacTavish, the union president, shouted, banging the lectern with the flat of his hand. "Attention! Please!" As he waited for silence, his finger travelled over the raised-scar highway that connected his ear to his jaw.

"How was the walk in this morning, laddies?" The statement pro-voked frowns from those who had trouble with his thick Scottish accent and groans from those who understood. He chuckled. "Have ye heerd the forecast?" The groans intensified. "Aye, two more storms heading straight for Toronto."

"What's he driving at?" Tauno sneered.

"Well, brothers," MacTavish continued, "dark as they may be, there's a wee silver lining in those clouds." A hush filled the room. "It appears the city fathers are desperate for what all this snow might do to commerce. After all, capitalists can't rake in the dough if business comes to a halt, now can 'ey?" Smiles began to bud.

MacTavish tugged on his braces. "With the big dump, Toronto'll be needing more shovellers. Three hundred, to be exact." The men cheered, but the union president raised his arms for silence. "But this time, there'll be no getting *our* labour for nothing. Since four this morning, your leaders have been negotiatin', and it's my pleasure to announce that, through our untiring efforts, the city has agreed to pay each man . . ." he hesitated, teasing, "twelve . . . cents . . . an hour!"

The room erupted and people leapt to their feet, racing for the exits.

"Let's go," Tauno shouted, tugging at Marty. "They'll be stampeding City Hall from all over town. Three hundred's not that many when you think of it."

"Hang on," Marty cautioned, pulling his friend back and pointing to the panicky union officials, as they tried to stem the rush to the doors.

"What's with them?" Tauno asked.

"I'm guessing they'd planned to get our names and march us down in a solid block, but MacTavish got carried away and forgot to outline the process. Now the workers are off to City Hall on their own."

The words weren't out of his mouth when union workers began setting up army tables along the front of the stage. "Don't leave!" MacTavish repeated over and over. "You can sign up here."

Marty and Tauno hustled to join the lineup. "Union card," an official demanded when Marty's turn came.

Marty looked down at the man's identity badge. "Lost in a boxcar, Mr. Jordan. I'm awaiting a replacement."

Jordan shook his head. "Bullroar! No union card, no work. Next!"

Marty didn't budge. "You can't do that!"

"I just did! Now shove off!"

Marty raised a clenched fist. The heavy-set official rose to his feet and smiled down at him. Behind them, conversation ceased at the prospect of a dust-up. For several seconds, the two men glared at each other.

Tauno placed a hand on Marty's shoulder and whispered, "Temper. Spain." Marty turned and headed for the door. A murmur of disappointment swept through the line.

Jordan lowered himself onto his chair. "Next," he trumpeted.

Tauno handed over his card and leaned down. "Mr. Jordan," he began in a soft voice, "my name's Jaakkola, and the guy you just turned down is Martin Kelly, On-to-Ottawa vet. He travelled with Slim Evans and George Black. His reward was twenty months in jail. He's a good Joe. Deserves a break."

Jordan leaned around Tauno to get a better look at the small man in glasses fuming at the door. "He's a hothead."

Tauno nodded. "Yup, and just the kinda guy we brothers need to take down the parasites. Right?"

Jordan scratched his head. "Tell you what. A list of the trekkers just came in upstairs. If there's a Martin Kelly on it, he can join the shovel brigade. If not, he's out of luck."

Tauno waved Marty back from the door. "It's arrived," he yelled. "The list of trekkers they've been promising."

Marty shuffled back. "So what? These assholes still won't let me shovel."

Jordan returned with the papers and began scanning them, lips moving as he read. At last, he looked up. "I'll be damned. You're both on the list."

Tauno brightened. "So we get to shovel?"

"Not on your life," Jordan answered.

Marty threw his hands in the air. Around them, the men perked up, anxious to know if the fight was back on. "Screw these guys," he said. "Let's get out of here. If we hurry we can sign on at City Hall."

"Not so fast," Jordan interrupted, pointing upwards. "The president wants to see you in his office." Marty and Tauno looked at each other then bounded for the stairs.

"Where's them goin'?" the next man in line asked.

"Beats me how they swung it," Jordan replied, "but them two is goin' to Spain."

February 15, 1937
Toronto

MARTY WATCHED MACTAVISH'S FINGERS dance along the scar on his cheek. It had been three weeks since he and Tauno and a handful of other volunteers had been cleared for Spain. In that time, the union had arranged for passports and other sundry papers. Now, with the legal work out of the way, a grim-faced MacTavish had called them in to deliver bad news.

"There's nothing we can do about it," the president said. He was standing at the window, looking down onto Spadina Avenue. Eight dejected volunteers sat at the table along with representatives from each of the Communist party, the CCF, and the Committee to Aid Spanish Democracy.

Marty cleared his throat. "Are you're telling me that if this was last week, we'd be on our way, but today, just like that," he snapped his fingers, "it's all off?"

MacTavish turned from the window. "Sorry, son. Blame the politicians. First the League of Nations banned foreigners from volunteering for Spain, and now Mackenzie King's gone and done the same thing. It's the new law. If we ignore it and sponsor you anyway, they'll shut us down."

"Why would Mr. King want to do a dumb thing like that?" a broad-shouldered truck driver from Saskatchewan asked.

Marty shuddered at the feeble grasp some volunteers had of the big picture. MacTavish gave the questioner a fatherly look. "Guess he wants to keep the country neutral on Spain," he replied, "just like England, France, and the U.S.A. I suspect it also has something to do with his recent visit with Herr Hitler."

"What about Italy and Germany?" Marty asked. "Any chance of them doing the same?"

"Not bloody likely," MacTavish replied.

Marty drummed his fingers on the table. "Let me see if I've got this right," he said. "You say you can't legally sanction our departure?" MacTavish nodded. "And if the government were ever to prove it was the union who provided us with the papers, clothes, and money for Spain, you'd be punished?" The president's finger picked up speed as it travelled back and forth along his cheek. "But, so far, you haven't told us to hand in our tickets, passports, and other documents?"

MacTavish glanced at the other officials in the room as he returned to his chair. "Not yet, but official notification is in the mail," he shrugged. "Until it arrives, I guess the documents are still in your hands."

Marty and Tauno looked at each other and smiled. So did a couple of other volunteers. Broad Shoulders from Saskatchewan frowned. "What?"

MacTavish nodded reassuringly. "I'm sure your friends will explain it to you," he said.

Marty studied the faces of his new friends, soon to be comrades-in-arms. He wondered what skills each would bring to the struggle. Broad Shoulders would be a good man to have around. Ditto the butcher from Winnipeg. Even the two Jewish lads from Toronto might be all right. Marty made a note not to get too close to the last two, lest they detect his Montreal origins. He was under no illusion. They wouldn't all make it home. He felt a heavy responsibility for Tauno, who was still lukewarm on Spain. He resolved to take special care of his friend.

With handshakes over and the men about to exit, MacTavish spoke one last time. "This meeting never happened," he said. "And another thing; something you should consider. You can sneak out of the country, but getting back in may not be so easy. When your job is done, and it's time to come home, it's not clear the government will take you back. If any of you were born outside of Canada and have never been naturalized, you may want to reconsider."

Chapter Fifteen

April 21, 1937
St. Jean-de-Luz, France

DOLLARD CHECKED HIS WATCH. "Should be 'ere any second now," he said, cocking his ear, hoping to hear the sound of marching feet above the church bells. He was breakfasting at a sidewalk café on rue Gambetta in St. Jean-de-Luz, close to the Franco-controlled portion of the Spanish border. Across from him sat his new acquaintance, McCullagh, the veteran Irish reporter he'd been hoping to impress. The man spoke in a singsong brogue that reminded him of parishioners at Shannon's church.

For two weeks, Dollard had been trying in vain to get a hearing with the Conde de Ramblas, Franco's representative at the border — the man who would decide whether or not he was worthy of joining other Catholic journalists on the War Route of the North Tour. St. Jean-de-Luz was full of international journalists all pining for something called a *salvoconducto*, the magic safe-conduct visa that would enable them to ply their trade inside Franco's Spain. Before arriving, Dollard had never heard of the document, but, suddenly, the prospect of life without one had become unbearable. *Salvoconducto* or War Route Tour, either, both, or none, the Conde de Ramblas held the key. The difficulty was getting past his secretary. Like countless other journalists, Dollard spent his days waiting for an audience at the consulate and his nights rotting his liver in the local bistros. However, as Dollard saw it, there was one difference between him and the others. He had a plan that he thought was brilliant. McCullagh, though, wasn't impressed.

The Irishman's brow wrinkled as he picked up the approach of marching feet. "Begod," he muttered, shaking his head, "the man can't be that predictable."

Dollard's eyes held to his wristwatch. "It'll be the conde for sure, and bang on time. Ten more seconds and 'e'll be coming off Boulevard Thiers." He began the countdown: "Ten, nine, eight . . . the guy's a machine . . . six, five . . . attends mass at eight sharp every morning . . . three, two, one . . . never moves without his coterie of soldiers . . . zero." Both men held their breath. The sound of tramping feet on cobblestone intensified. Then, in an explosion of jackboots that ricocheted off the stone walls, the Spaniards blew onto Gambetta. Conversation halted in the café, as local Basques glared icily at the approaching foreigners. Dollard fixed his gaze on the broad shoulders of the conde, who towered over his red-bereted Carlist Requeté guards.

"For the life of me," Dollard said in a low voice, "I can't figure how a man of 'is importance would follow the same route to mass every morning. This town's crawling with Republicans. Wouldn't they just love to bump 'im off?"

The sound of tromping feet began to recede, and the locals returned to their espressos. McCullagh dragged on his Gauloise then spit out a piece of tobacco. "He's got enemies for sure," he said, "but St. Jean-de-Luz is France. The Republicans aren't stupid enough to kill him here. That would enrage the French something fierce and cause them to put a complete halt to the smuggling of arms at the Republican end of the border."

Dollard made a gun with his finger and pointed it at the conde's back. "A 'ead taller than 'is soldiers, and with that aristocratic swagger 'e'd be a 'ard target to miss."

"The height comes with the bloodlines, me boy," McCullagh said. "Aristocracy eat better. If you ever get into Spain, which in your case is highly unlikely, you'll learn that to see a tall Spaniard is to see ruling class."

"Then 'ow come the guards are so short? Aren't all Carlist Requetés upper-class?"

"Officers, yes, but rank and file are mostly commoners hankering for the monarchy and the good old days."

Dollard washed down a mouthful of croissant with the dregs of his coffee and stood to leave. "Mass beckons," he winked.

McCullagh smirked. "You're wasting your time with that church nonsense, I fear. Even if he takes note of it, it will only fan his suspicion."

"That man's my ticket to Spain," Dollard shrugged, reaching into his pocket for money to cover both their breakfasts. "What 'ave I got to lose? Beats spending the day blotto at the Bar Basque with your journalist cronies."

Unlike any other church Dollard had ever attended, the entrance to the Église Saint-Jean-Baptiste was midway along the length of the church. He pushed open the high wooden door, stepped down onto the worn twelfth-century floor, and stopped. The world went black, but like a mole at midday, his face tipped heavenward. For an instant, he was home, engulfed by burning incense, tinkling bells, and the inevitable coughing. By now, he calculated, the conde would be genuflecting and entering his pew in the second balcony. Dollard dipped two fingers into the holy water and crossed himself. He then turned toward the stairs that led to the five levels of galleries at the back and sides of the church. Far up the nave, beyond the second transept, a priest, flanked on both sides by white-clad altar boys, began to chant.

As expected, the conde was surrounded by his guard in his usual pew. The Carlist guardsmen, hair slicked down and reeking of eau-de-toilette, took mass seriously. They sat ramrod straight, like pins in a bowling alley, red berets tucked under starched epaulettes, chests swelling proudly under the Sacred Heart of Mary embroidered on their tunics.

Dollard selected a row ahead of the entourage. He genuflected, then positioned himself in Ramblas' sightline. The hope was that Ramblas would take note of the tall, fair-haired stranger who, like him, attended mass seven days a week. It was a long shot, but at this point Dollard was game for anything that might spare him the humility of returning to Quebec without ever having set foot on Spanish soil.

Not that attending mass didn't have its rewards. It eased his homesickness and provided material for his letters to l'abbé Groulx. Such as the fifteenth-century Basque ship suspended from the ceiling over the central aisle. Or the seating arrangement of the parishioners, which placed the men in the five storeys of balconies at the back and sides of the church, and the black-shawled women in the nave.

The church's history was interesting, too. In 1660, Louis XIV of France had been married here to l'Infante Marie-Thérèse of Spain. It had been an attempt to unite the two kingdoms, but if there was any love left for the Spaniards, it didn't show in the Basques. This puzzled Dollard. It was reasonable that they would resent their neighbours for pillaging their cities over the centuries, but those days were long past. Weren't they all Catholic? Wasn't Franco saving Mother Church from the rapacious Republicans? He recalled his surprise at the heavy turnout for mass on that first Sunday. Groulx had led him to believe that Catholics in France had been seduced away from the church by a left-leaning government. Wasn't it Prime Minister Blum who'd taken the crosses out of their schools and furthered the separation of church and state? That Groulx had been mistaken on this matter troubled Dollard, but his faith had been renewed with the realization that many of his fellow worshippers were sons of the French aristocracy—boys on their way to fight for Franco and strike a blow for the old order. He felt at home here.

Dollard arched his back. Couldn't Franco's government afford more comfortable seating for their consulates? He was spending a lot of time on these benches and had the sore backside to prove it. He glanced around. A dozen bored reporters sprawled about the stuffy, smoke-filled room, as they intermittently napped, read, wrote, smoked, and conversed in hushed tones. Overhead, the fans laboured to clear the air, but failed. A door opened and a Carlist soldier emerged carrying a piece of paper, causing conversation to cease. Dollard glanced at the clock on the wall—1:30. In a half hour, the consulate would close for siesta. Another wasted day. How much longer could he keep this up? If nothing happened soon, he'd have to do something drastic. McCullagh had suggested they visit Perpignan, on the Mediterranean side, and attempt crossing the Pyrenees on foot. But that would get him into Communist-Republican Spain. With all the killings over there, who could tell how Catholic reporters might be treated.

Hard-nosed, cynical, and humble of origin, McCullagh was okay. He was Catholic, after all. However, if his claim were true that the Irish had raised a battalion to fight for Franco, why was he having so much trouble getting a *salvoconducto*? Dollard wondered if McCullagh had secretly been covering the war from the Communist side, and Franco's people had gotten wind of it. If so, he should steer clear of him. On the other hand, he found comfort in the prospect of travelling with a seasoned reporter.

The Carlist soldier at the conde's door ran a finger down his list, "El Señor Desjardins," he shouted. A collective moan ran around the room and it took Dollard a moment to realize that it was his name that had been called.

Attempting to regain his composure, he rose, smoothed his clothes, and followed the guard. At the end of a long corridor, he was ushered to a desk where a middle-aged functionary in civilian dress sat shuffling paper. Dollard, shifting from foot to foot as he waited, stared first at a picture of Franco on a white horse, then down at the bureaucrat who held his future in his hands. The man's suit was too big, he noticed. Dollard wondered if it was a hand-me-down from the conde, which the functionary felt obliged to wear. But if Dollard felt an urge to chuckle, it was crushed by the certainty that it was this man, relegated to a desk in the hallway, and not the Conde de Ramblas, who would be handling his petition. He moaned inwardly; all those morning masses for nothing. A trickle of perspiration ran down his neck. He shifted his weight again.

"You are El Señor Desjardins?" the man asked at last, without looking up.

"*Si, Señor,*" Dollard answered, calling on his limited Spanish. "*Soy Dollard Desjardins de Canada.*"

The functionary seemed to wince at the word Canada. He closed the file, pressed his fingers together as if in prayer, and fixed Dollard with an icy stare. "*El Movimiento Nacional* have hatred for countries that stick nose in beesness of *España*," he announced in English. Dollard frowned, trying to grasp where the man was heading. "This *la guerra española*. We fight alone. Foreigners go home."

"But I'm not 'ere to meddle, *Señor*. I'm 'ere to—"

"From Canada come freemasons, communists, and Jews to fight *el cuadillo* Franco."

Tiny tributaries of sweat joined the main stream on Dollard's neck. "But it's against the law of Canada, *Señor*. Our government is trying to stop those people from joining the Republicans. I personally oppose anyone who—" A double door opened to the right. Dollard paused, as a Carlist soldier stepped into the hall, followed by the Conde de Ramblas. The conde mumbled something to the functionary about food. As he turned to leave, his eyes fell on Dollard and he rattled off something in Spanish.

"He want to know where he see you before?" the functionary translated.

Dollard felt his heels come together and his head tip. "*Soy Dollard Desjardins de Canada.*" He cursed himself for letting *de Canada* slip out again.

Ramblas snapped his fingers and spoke. The functionary turned to Dollard. "He see you in *iglesia*, but has *cuestión*. Are you honest *Católico* or make-believe *impóstor*?"

"No. Yes," Dollard replied.

The functionary frowned. "Wheech?"

"Honest *Católico*."

"You have proof?" With fumbling fingers, Dollard withdrew a rosary from his suit pocket and watched the conde blow air through his lips before speaking. "He says that ees no proof," the functionary translated. "Now times many infidel carry *el rosario* to save neck."

"But can they match the prayers to the beads?" Dollard asked as he began to recite.

Ramblas shook his head. "The conde says imposters also learn prayers." Ramblas turned to go.

"Wait!" Dollard shouted, loosening his tie in a quick movement and ripping open his shirt. When a button popped off, the functionary leapt to his feet and the Requeté guard drew his sidearm. Dollard froze.

Ramblas stiffened, then relaxed, as he took in the vestment pressed against Dollard's skin. He motioned to the guard to lower his pistol and for Dollard to continue. With the shirt gone, he circled Dollard slowly, examining the two fist-sized panels that lay glued by sweat to Dollard's chest and back. Finally, he traced a finger around the embroidered religious crest on the front panel.

"He wants to know where you steal *el escapulario*?"

The blood returned to Dollard's face at the sight of the Requeté's pistol dropping back into its holster. "The cardinal who gave it to me is an admirer of Franco," he replied. "And so am I. 'E has sent me 'ere to observe and to report on the resurrection of the church in Spain. With your permission, *señor*, I would like to show you a letter of introduction from Cardinal Villeneuve de Montréal. I 'ave also journalism credentials with *Le Devoir* de Montréal, Québec."

Ramblas waited for the translation before accepting the papers. When he was done examining them, he handed them back to the functionary and spoke. Dollard listened to the melodic hum of the Spanish tongue, praying he detected a softness in the tone.

The functionary nodded and turned to Dollard. "He says tell you he ees just doorman. He can get you on War Route of the North Tour, but no can geeve *salvoconducto*. For that, you must go to the Spanish Press Bureau at the Headquarters of Franco in Salamanca. If El Señor Luis Bolín no approves, you will leave *España pronto*. But he warns, Bolín ees tough man. He has no use for *extranjeros*, uh . . . foreigners. Do not cross heem. If you get a *salvoconducto*, which ees *no probable*, you must obey all rules. Report only on what ees permitted. Foreign newsmen who play games with Bolín go for walk."

Ramblas turned and headed down the hall. "Walk?" Dollard asked as he began buttoning his shirt.

The functionary's mouth exploded in a wide grin. "*Si*," he replied, "at night. Alone. To the wall. Eet ees one-way."

"Hell's fire," McCullagh repeated, as he examined Dollard's travel visa over his Pernod. "This proves it. Spain's in terrible trouble, sure. They give an entry permit to a wet-behind-the-ears neophyte and leave this seasoned vet banging on the door."

It was going on midnight in the noisy Bar Basque. Dollard and Mc-Cullagh were celebrating in a room packed with reporters, Spanish aristocrats, and employees from numerous consulates that had sprung up to do business with Franco's side of Spain. There was also a large contingent of swaggering young French aristos. Fists pounded on tables, patriotic songs rose and fell. Edith Piaf wailed from the radio.

Dollard slipped the visa back into the money belt under his shirt. With so many desperate journalists in St-Jean-de-Luz, it wasn't a good idea to flash it about. "Cheer up, McCullagh, you'll get in."

"Jaysus Christians, I can't wait much longer. I'm freelance. Gotta eat. There's no rich daddy handling my expenses."

"Hey! I'll be paying my own way soon."

"Not yet, young fella," McCullagh replied, looking at him over his drink. "Not until his majesty, Luis Bolín, sees fit to bless you with a journalist visa. Until then, you're just a tourist on a *franquista* propaganda junket."

"Orientation tour," Dollard corrected. On the radio, Piaf ceased warbling "Le Fanion de la Légion" and turned the microphone over to Maurice Chevalier. Dollard winced as Chevalier struck up with "I Can't Give You Anything But Love, Baby." L'abbé Groulx was right. With American culture taking over the world, how was tiny Quebec ever to survive?

"Orientation tour!" McCullagh sputtered. "Jesus, Mary, and the wee donkey. If I got you right, you'll be sightseeing in a car with a priest from Chicago, a high-order knight of Columbus from Dublin, and some mucky-muck from London with the Spanish Relief Fund for Sufferers from Red Atrocities." He sat back in his chair. "You're deluding yourself, sure, if you think travelling with such an *open-minded* coterie will be giving you a balanced perspective on the new Spain."

Dollard frowned at the poster of a toreador on the wall. "I'll be keeping an open mind," he said.

McCullagh smirked. "No offense, Dollard, but you don't have the experience for that. They'll be bombarding you with tales of the illustrious *Caudillo*, and how his glorious Whites are saving Iberia from those nun-raping, priest-murdering Reds. And you'll be doing exactly as you're told—regurgitating every word for the good folks back home."

"Whose side you on, McCullagh?"

"Don't get me wrong, boyo. Franco's got the high ground. I sincerely believe that the infidels have to be brought down. But, as a journalist, it's my duty to write about Nationalist Spain, warts and all." He drained the last of his Pernod and looked longingly at the waitress.

"What about Bolín's rules?" Dollard asked. "Unless you want to be 'taken for a walk,' you toe the line. All articles get censored before filing. Even I know that."

McCullagh sighed. "Sons of donkeys, you are a babe in the woods. They must love guys like you. Press a few buttons and you do what you're told. You've a lot to learn about circumventing the rules. Tell you what, do Uncle McCullagh the turn of buying him another Pernod and I'll give you a lesson. Come on, I'm good for it." Dollard looked at the poster again. "Do you doubt my word, you Thomas, you?"

"The more drinks I buy you, the more you dump on me."

"Fine, seeing that's the way you feel, I'll be providing the next round."

A smile worked its way onto Dollard's lip. "Right. With what?"

"With this," McCullagh said, tapping his temple. "It doesn't always take money." He gestured to the boisterous young men at the bar. "See those French toffs over there? Little Lord Fauntleroys all. They've all got rich fathers, just like you." Dollard ground his teeth. "Know why they're so anxious to join *la Bandera Juana de Arco* to fight for Franco?"

"Because they believe in the cause?"

"Because for them Spain's just a rehearsal, a training ground for the day they get to kick the shit out of their own socialists, communists, degenerates, and Jews. Their ultimate goal is to reinstate the French aristocracy to its rightful place. They're going to Spain because they hate Red France."

"What's that got to do with getting you another Pernod?"

"Those brats are about to get shipped out to where money won't save their *derrières*, so, why not spend a little of it on this grouchy old journalist and his young idealistic friend?"

"*Tabarnac*, McCullagh, 'ave you no—"

The radio trilled "Ar-rriba España!" and the room fell silent for the midnight news. Excited patrons held their breath as they drank in the latest exploits of *nuestros gloriosos soldados*. Apparently it had been another humiliating day for the Republicans. The announcer signed off, and the room leapt to its feet, arms outstretched in the fascist salute, to sing the Nationalist anthem. Dollard joined in with gusto. He noticed that some patrons remained seated, glumly staring at their drinks.

With the singing over, McCullagh winked at Dollard as he approached the young Frenchmen at the bar. He chatted and laughed with them for several minutes before his hand came up, waving his friend over.

Chapter Sixteen

April 24, 1937
Pyrenees Mountains, France

"EHBREEBOODY DOWN!" Alphonso shouted from the front of the bus. Immediately the nine passengers dropped to the floor. Marty and Tauno snickered as they landed on their backsides across the aisle from each other. Not that there was anything rib-tickling about their run through France to the Spanish border, but, like Boy Scouts off to camp, the volunteers were finding humour in ridiculous things and generally acting silly. For Marty and Tauno, it was their diminutive guide's accent that got them going. Granted, "everybody" is a tough word for a Spaniard, but from Alphonso's mouth it came out as if he were Enrico Caruso bursting into song. The first time he'd given the order, no one had understood, until he'd leapt to his feet at the front of the bus pumping his arms up and down in a double Hitler salute. That was many, many villages back. Still, with each visit to the floor, Marty and Tauno lost control.

Not that the driver helped to stem the giddiness. He and the bus were waging a war of their own. So far it had been a draw, although Tauno's money was on the bus. To the driver, the bus was an obstinate student in need of discipline: When it failed to respond on a mountain curve, he smacked the wheel with the flat of his hand; when the brakes went limp, he pummelled the pedal with his foot; when the gears refused to engage, he knocked the shift about with his fist. In the end, the bus would always submit, but in protest, as evidenced by the backfires and high whine from the drive shaft.

"Cook's would go broke running tours like this," Tauno joked.

"You have to pay for a Cook's tour," Marty responded. "This one's free."

"Yeah, but wouldn't it be nice to actually get to see some of the sights?"

"And be seen in turn, Tauno. Or have you forgotten that the French are on the lookout for guys like us? If we're caught heading for Spain, it's the hoosegow for our little guide up there and back to a jail in Canada for the likes of you and me."

"It'd still be nice to set eyes on a French face."

"You had that in Paris. Down here, you have to settle for the scenery."

"What scenery?" Tauno answered. "It's been drizzling all day, and we have to hide on the floor at the approach to every village."

Getting this far had been as exhilarating for Marty as those first few weeks riding the rails back in 1934. They'd lurched from one heart-pumping situation to the next—crossing the border at Niagara Falls, hiding in the hold of a freighter until it cleared New York City, lying to the French customs officers in Le Havre. The crossing had been long—two weeks—but memorable.

Until reaching international waters, Marty had believed their small band of brothers from Toronto to be the only illicit passengers on the steamer, until sixteen additional conscripts for Spain had emerged from their hidey-holes. They were an eclectic bunch—Americans, Cubans, Mexicans, Canadians—but with four guitars, a squeezebox, and a banjo, they'd gotten along famously. Even with Marty ready to puke if he heard the "Internationale" one more time, they'd come together. The mix of backgrounds was interesting, too. From the articles on the Spanish Civil War that had fuelled Marty's ardour, he'd concluded that most of the volunteers would be intellectuals. But the ones on this boat were mostly unemployed labourers. Only Barton, the fat philosophy professor from the University of Chicago, seemed to fit the academic mould, and for the life of him, Marty couldn't see what contribution he could possibly bring to the conflict. Then again, maybe others were thinking the same thing about the skinny Montrealer with the wire-rimmed glasses.

He'd expected to spend time during the crossing mentally preparing himself for the war against totalitarianism—resources needed, sacrifices to be made, how he might react under fire. But try as he might, those nebulous concepts were no competition for more immediate concerns—Tauno, his parents, and, most of all, Connie. It was a heavy load. Marty had hoped the other volunteers' commitment would rub off on Tauno. So far it hadn't. He was off to Spain for all the wrong reasons, in his opinion—adventure, employment, and, worst of all, loyalty to a friend. Volunteering on his own would never have entered his mind. Marty staggered under the weight of it all. As for his own parents, he hadn't seen them since leaving Montreal. Even so, he sensed their disillusionment in their letters. He'd been the apple of their eye before the disappointments had begun piling up. Risking his life in someone else's conflict and hiding his Jewishness to do it compounded the guilt he carried. Ditto Connie. He was stealing her best years by running off to a foreign war. Why did she stand for it? Did she really share his commitment? How long would she wait?

Then there was the problem of the other Jewish volunteers on board. Five in all. The number had been a surprise. He was as proud of them as he was ashamed for hiding his own background. To make matters worse, they often conversed in Yiddish. It was a struggle not to laugh at their jokes, or get angry when they made fun of the others, including the bespectacled Montrealer with the Irish name. In the cramped quarters, there was no way to avoid them. He felt spineless in their company.

The first test of the men's resolve had come minutes after tying up in France. Suitcases in hand, they'd assembled on the deck at the urging of the ship's captain where a man in a homburg hat and dark suit waited. "Police," Marty moaned, feeling his pulse quicken. He'd been warned that the French were taking steps to stem the flow of Republican supporters to Spain. His eyes wandered from the gangplank to the pier, then to the street beyond. Something was amiss. As far as he could see, there were no uniforms on the dock backing this man up.

Dark Suit spoke. "Gentlemen," he said in a Boston drawl, "my name is Hanson, and I'm the United States consul here in Le Havre. Hands up if you're American."

The volunteers shuffled to form a cohort. No one spoke. Marty noticed a New Yorker, squeezebox in one hand and suitcase in the other, slide in behind Big Shoulders. Dark Suit looked across to the next ship as if it offered more potential. He coughed into his fist and nodded. "All right, if that's the way you want to play it, I'll get to the point. You haven't come to take in the World Exhibition in Paris. I'm here to ask you not to embarrass your country. Spain's a worthless cause. Your government and the League of Nations see no reason for you getting involved. Whoever said you could help was lying. You'll only get yourselves killed. There are already too many American boys and . . ." his eyes fell on the short Cuban, "other foreign nationals, rotting in Spanish soil." Still no response. "Go home, boys. American or not, my government will pay your passage," his eyes roamed the deck, "and on a better ship than this rust bucket."

Marty scanned the faces of his fellow volunteers. Each had made his own pact to put a stop to fascism and had crossed an ocean to do it. Now some suit was telling them that theirs was a worthless cause. He was about to speak when Professor Barton broke the silence. "We're men of different flags, Mr. Hanson, but we've a clear purpose. The world is drifting off course. When did it become unpatriotic for Americans to stand up for what's right?"

For a moment, no one spoke. The men grew restless.

Barton picked up his bag. "I don't think you have any jurisdiction here, Mr. Hanson. So, if you'll step aside, we have a rendezvous with Franco."

Hanson shrugged. "Have it your way, boys. I've done my bit."

"And we intend to do ours," Barton replied.

On the dock, they were met by a couple of underground railway representatives who split them into two groups. "Mutt and Jeff," someone sniggered at the difference in their heights. "Jeff" spoke English. "Mutt" did not. Marty and Tauno drew Mutt. After handshakes and waves, Jeff marched his cohort, including the Cuban and the Mexican, away. "That's a mistake," the professor mumbled to Marty. "I'm the only one left with any Spanish and mine's rusty."

When they were gone, Mutt turned to his group. "*Quelqu'un parle français?*" he asked, hopefully.

Marty stepped forward, listened to instructions, then turned to the volunteers. "His name's Alphonso and he'll get us to Spain." The men smiled at Alphonso, who smiled back. Marty continued. "But it won't be easy. Once we clear customs at the end of the dock, it's off to the Bureau des Syndicats in Paris to await further instructions."

"Yippee!" someone blurted out. "Gay Paree."

"Not quite," Marty said, raising his hands for silence. "We're to keep a low profile."

"For God's sake," Tauno exclaimed, "they can't be thinking of locking us up?"

Marty shook his head. "He says we can go out, but in twos and threes; enough for protection, but not so many as to raise suspicion."

"How're we getting to Spain?" someone asked. "Train?"

Marty shrugged. "Alphonso doesn't know, yet. They keep changing arrangements to stay ahead of the police."

Paris was a gift. The men behaved. No one got too drunk or drew too much attention. For six days, while transit plans were being worked out, it was free Metro tickets and enough money for food and sightseeing.

Marty and Tauno roamed. They found the Paris Exhibition. As it hadn't officially opened, getting in was easy. They swooned over the modest Spanish pavilion and sat under the friezes of the Soviet pavilion, thumbing their noses at the massive swastika on Albert Speer's Third Reich tower. Tauno found roots at the Finnish exhibition designed by the great architect, Alvar Aalto. In the years they'd been together, Marty hadn't taken much note of his friend's Finnish origins, but watching him converse in his native tongue with employees who shared his high cheekbones and blue eyes was a revelation. On the seventh day, they were roused before daylight, fed, and trooped to Gare Montparnasse for the train to Toulouse—gateway to the Pyrenees. Alphonso wasn't happy about something, but Marty couldn't find out what.

If Toulouse was a beautiful city, the volunteers were not to know. For two days, they languished in a cheap hotel across from the railway station, under strict orders not to leave the building. Late on the first night, they pooled the remainder of their French francs and sneaked Marty out to buy wine. To a man, they got plastered. Alphonso was furious, but Marty knew the real source of his anger lay elsewhere. The next day, with each man nursing a hangover, there was no urge to defy orders.

Bouncing along on the rickety bus, with exhaust fumes seeping up through the floor, Marty vowed never to drink again. Professor Barton slipped into the seat beside him. "Know your geography?" he asked in a low voice. Marty shook his head. "We just turned south at Axat."

"Should I care?"

"The road we're on takes us into the mountains."

Marty stared at Barton, unsure where the man was headed. "Weren't we told there'd be a hike at the end of the line?" he asked cautiously.

"Right! Through the foothills near the Mediterranean, a few miles north of Portbou. But the route we're on takes us into the High Pyrenees. That's not a hike. That's an alpine climb."

"Might be interesting," Marty replied.

Barton wasn't smiling. "For Christ's sake, Kelly," he said, raising his voice. He looked around quickly, relieved that no one was paying attention. "It's mid-March," he continued more quietly. "Have you noticed what we're wearing? We could die up there."

Marty glanced at the nearest volunteer, dozing in his seat. He took in the canvas shoes, light trousers, and long-sleeved shirt, realizing that, like himself, and probably every other man on the bus, his friend possessed little more than a sweater and windbreaker to ward off the cold. They'd been advised to travel light, that uniforms were waiting across the border. "We've been having good weather," he said, "maybe it'll be spring up there, too."

Barton shook his head. "Not at a mile and a half above sea level. At that elevation, anything's possible—ice, snow, blizzard . . ." His voice trailed off.

Marty squirmed, longing for the next pee break. "I'm sure Alphonso will have warm clothes waiting for us." When Barton didn't respond, he wondered if it was because the professor feared the answer, or because he was fixated on the extreme elevation awaiting them. The prospect began to haunt him. How were a pudgy, pencil-pushing academic like the professor, or a scrawny Montreal doctor for that matter, to get themselves over the High Pyrenees? This time there were no giggles from Marty when Alphonso ordered, "Ehbreeboody on de floor." The Boy Scout adventure had come to an end.

The bus whined along in low gear for several minutes before Alphonso gave his "Okey-dokey" signal that they'd passed through the village. Marty wished he had a map. Since Barton's bombshell, the bus had been climbing and switch-backing steadily. He longed for a clear view, but whatever was out there was obscured by fog and condensation on the windows. He checked his watch: 6:20. Night was settling in. The men sat in silence, staring at the road ahead and praying that, with one headlight angled up into the pine trees and the other to a point ten feet in front of the bus, the driver would be nimble enough to avoid going over a cliff. Marty couldn't remember when they'd last met another vehicle. He began to sweat. Were there police barriers this close to the border? How would they get Barton over the top? Would this dilapidated bus ever make it to their destination? The bus groaned in protest, as the driver struggled with the gears. "Grind me a pound," some wit hollered. They passed through another village with an indecipherable Basque name. Alphonso came down the aisle, more nervous than he'd been all day. "Thirty meenutes," he announced.

The instant Marty stepped off the bus and into the light pouring out from the sheep herder's window, he began to laugh. Partly it was relief in discovering somebody waiting for them way up here in the clouds; mostly it was the sight of Tauno. "You should see yourself," he said, pointing to the exploding hair, the dazed expression, and awkward gait. "You look like a scarecrow."

"Find yourself a mirror, asshole," Tauno shot back, "and you'd be looking at that hunchback they told us about in Paris."

Marty tried to straighten, but even pressing a hand against his backbone and arching his spine couldn't quite return his torso to perpendicular. Around him, men were swinging arms to regain circulation and stepping about cautiously, like old duffers. Eleven hours on a bus with no springs had its price. Still, they were in good spirits. With sunny Spain a scant five kilometres away, albeit through the pea soup, their journey was practically over.

"Shit!" a voice shouted in a New England drawl.

Marty stiffened. "What?" Around him, movement stopped.

"Shit! Shit! Shit!" The man repeated, brushing his hands.

"WHAT?" Marty hollered.

"Sheep shit! It's everywhere."

Marty laughed with the others, but with the smell of cooking meat drifting out from the hut, his heart was at the table. Pressing matters concerning the hazards ahead could wait. Right now, food, a good night's sleep, and, with luck, a change in the weather were in order. Alphonso signalled for them to join him inside.

They ducked their heads passing through the low door to find themselves in a large room with an earthen floor and limestone walls. Open shelves, a counter on which sat a freshly severed sheep's head, a tiny table with four homemade chairs, and a huge fireplace completed the scene. A coal-oil lantern hung from a rafter, midpoint in the room. The men sat on the floor with their bowls in hand, waiting for the food. Marty leaned against a ladder that led to the loft. He wondered if there would be enough room up there for all the men to sleep. The mother and daughter attended to the cooking. Father kept his eyes on the men.

"Alphonso," one of the volunteers blurted out after they'd all eaten their fill, "when do we draw straws to see who sleeps with the farmer's daughter?"

The men howled. Marty cursed the wiseacre under his breath. Alphonso looked to him for translation. "He says to compliment the women on the food," Marty lied in French.

Alphonso rose, turned to the cooks, and began speaking slowly and deliberately. The father glared at the joker, who went white. "Jesus, Marty, what did you tell him?"

"That you'd pay to sleep with his daughter."

The joker brought his hands up in a protective pose as the mother approached, wooden spoon poised menacingly in her hand. Only at the last second did she smile. "*Merci, merci,*" she repeated in her best French, bowing and returning to her pot.

The men revelled in their comrade's discomfort, but kept quiet for fear of offending Mom and Dad. "Since the farmer's daughter appears to be unavailable," Tauno said, "I reckon some of you farm boys will be eyeing the sheep."

The chorus of baas that followed baffled the hosts, but was cut short by the squeal of hinges and an unexpected blast of cold air. A stranger, dressed in a sheepskin hat, matching leather jacket, scarf, and thick boots, filled the doorway. He stood stock still as he scrutinized the men. From his expression, or lack of it, Marty guessed they weren't measuring up. Alphonso approached the stranger nervously, addressing him in what must have been Basque. The conversation progressed from finger-wagging to shouts. When they moved outside, Marty stepped to the window, swiping at the condensation with the back of his hand. "Better get your things together," he advised the others.

Outside, the dispute had taken a dramatic turn. The stranger spat, then stomped off into the darkness toward the gate. Alphonso yelled something, then pulled an object from his pocket, which he pointed at the disappearing man. Marty swallowed, praying he wasn't about to hear gunshots. A flashlight came to life, shining on the object Alphonso held. It looked like a work sock. The stranger reappeared, snatched it from Alphonso, then extracted a wad of bills. More words were exchanged, this time of a softer nature. Alphonso returned to the house and motioned the volunteers into the yard.

"His name ees Xanti," Alphonso told Marty. "He ees to be your *guia*. He ees one tough *hombre*, but very good at getting people over the mountains alive. His family has run contraband across this border for centuries. You are to leave now."

"But we haven't slept!" Marty protested, "and he's a rumrunner, for God's sake, *un contrebandier*. I saw you paying him off."

Alphonso shrugged. "Dangerous times, *mon ami*. Guides get paid according to risk. They're no good to their families in jail or dead." His eyes wandered to the professor. "You will need to move fast to get off peaks by daybreak. Up there, Italian planes kill anything that moves. Xanti ees worried about the fat man; says you could all die because of heem."

Marty glanced at the others, who watched him with worried eyes. "How long does it take?"

"Ees never the same," Alphonso replied. "*Guias* keep changing the route to fool French border patrols."

"Is it far?"

Alphonso frowned. "In straight line, no; maybe four kilometres. But here," he pointed to the ground, "ees seventeen hundred metres. Up there ees twenty-five hundred metres."

Marty calculated in his head. "Eight hundred metres," he gulped, "that's twenty-five hundred feet, straight up."

Alphonso checked his watch. "Ees now 9:30. Important depart *immédiatement*." He took off his cap and coat, which he handed to Marty, then moved down the line shaking each volunteer's hand.

Alphonso's gesture reminded Marty of the last funeral he'd attended. He turned to the group. "Anybody for Spain?" he yelled, putting all the exuberance he could muster into it. The reply was timid. Marty spoke again. "It's not too late to back out." He was looking at the group, but speaking to Barton. Everyone picked up their suitcases and began shuffling toward the gate, Barton, too. Marty caught up to him. "You sure about this, Professor?"

The professor didn't break stride. "It'll take more than a little alpine ramble to hold me back," he replied.

They moved in silence behind Xanti, feeling alone as their ears tuned to the sound of crunching gears, squealing brakes, and whining drive shaft as the bus worked its way down the steep incline. That bus was their last connection to the outside world. They strained to hold onto it as the sound faded, rose, then faded again, like a short-wave radio broadcast from a far-off land. Finally, all was quiet.

"Spain, here we come," Marty muttered, stepping blindly into the night.

From what Marty could make out, their trail seemed to hug the mountain in a long, steep arc. Xanti moved like an alpine goat, with the recruits scrambling to keep up. Barton was having a tough time. About an hour into their walk, a stone hut popped up directly in their path. Following Xanti's signals, they tip-toed around it, one at a time. Shortly after, they were led off the beaten track toward what looked like a solid wall of rock. Marty feared they might be expected to climb it, but Xanti found a narrow passage through which he led them.

The rain was a mixed blessing. It deadened the sound of movement to any border guards, but it also greased the rocks. Leather soles became a nightmare. Marty hunched forward as he felt his way, suitcase slightly ahead, ready to buffer a tumble. Most times it worked, but the latches tended to catch and open, coughing up contents. The problem was endemic. Soon, a trail of personal items on rocks and shrubs marked their way. Marty picked a piece of clothing from a shrub and was using it to dab at his bleeding forearm, when he realized it was someone's underwear. Clean, he hoped. From the gasps and limps, he figured they were all hurting; especially Barton, who was bringing up the rear with Marty and Tauno taking turns propping him up.

Shortly past two a.m., the column halted on a small shelf. Marty and Tauno let go of Barton and flopped to the ground. Beside them, men sprawled and wheezed, while Xanti nibbled calmly on a biscuit. "*Viente minutos*," he announced.

Tauno cleared his throat and spat. "*Minutos* I get," he said, puffing. "I just hope to hell *viente* is a lot of 'em."

Marty closed his eyes, expecting to hear despair in the grunts and muted conversations around him. But something strange was taking hold. There were no complaints, no grumblings. Instead, he saw his comrades massaging backs, helping each other with cuts and blisters, and sharing apparel. A hand appeared before his face. It was Broad Shoulders, passing out beef jerky carted all the way from Moose Jaw. A pang of guilt shuddered through Marty. For hours, he'd been cursing the others for leaving him and Tauno at the rear, attending to Barton. Now he realized they were all in this together. He hadn't felt this camaraderie since the On-to-Ottawa Trek, years before. "Hold the fort for we are coming," he sang in a stage whisper. Others picked it up.

Xanti shot to his feet. "*Isildu! Arrabat, bat gehiago eta bertan behera uzten asitut hemen*," he hollered. The singing ceased. The men looked to Barton.

"Basque," he said between wheezes. "I think he wants you to shut up." Tauno passed the canteen to him. The professor swallowed, then spoke again. "*Mas despacio*," he mumbled. "Slower . . . make the guide go slower."

Marty handed him a piece of beef jerky and motioned Xanti over. "Necessary, *mas despacio*," he said, looking to the professor to see if he'd gotten it right.

Xanti shook his head. "*Arriskutsuegia. Dagoeneko atzean gaude.*"

"I think the answer's no," Tauno groaned.

It wasn't long after they'd resumed climbing that it became clear why Xanti had picked the flat shelf to rest on. They'd just fumbled their way through a cut in the rocks when the column halted again. Xanti pointed the way with his flashlight.

"Holy shee. . .it!" Tauno exclaimed, squinting through rain now turning to sleet. In front of them and to the left rose a cliff; to the right fell a cavern and oblivion. A narrow, upward-sloping ledge no more than three feet wide had been chiseled along the cliff face.

Xanti, speaking in encouraging tones, pointed to his eyes as he fastened one end of a rope to himself and the other to a dwarf tree. "*Egiten duden guztia nire entzera egize,*" he said, pulling on the rope to test it. He then stepped onto the ledge, fumbled for seemingly invisible handholds, and sidestepped out of sight. The men blinked, straining to hear sounds of his return. After several minutes, Broad Shoulders spat into the pit. "Son of a bitch better come back," he threatened. Others began to curse under their breath.

"Shut up, you guys," Marty said. "He's probably tying the rope on the other side." In the silence that followed, he listened. After several minutes of hearing nothing but his own beating heart, Xanti popped out of the blackness, crabbing his way sideways across the ledge, and firing off orders in rapid Basque.

"What the hell's he saying now?" someone asked.

Marty spoke up. "From his gestures, I'm guessing he wants us to cross one at a time. It can't be that hard. If you lose your balance, let your bags go and grab the rope with both hands."

For a second, no one spoke. "This hurts," a volunteer finally said, kissing his guitar case goodbye before flinging it into the abyss. Marty listened for an impact, which never came. Others donned second or third shirts and pairs of socks, then jettisoned all but the bare essentials. The Jewish lad from New York moved hesitantly to the cliff's edge, squeezebox in one hand, suitcase in the other. "Eenie, meenie, miney, moe," he said, swinging his arms back and forth. At last, the suitcase rose into the air and disappeared into the void. One by one, they crossed over, with Marty, Tauno, and Barton preparing to go last. From the darkness came words of encouragement, interspaced by Xanti's advice to "*presa zaitez,*" whatever that meant. Marty feared it was hurry up.

"Tauno goes first," Marty said to Barton when their turn came, "then you, then me. Leave your suitcase. I'll come back for it." He removed his belt, securing it to Barton's waist and wrapping the other end around his fist. On the other side, Tauno did the same.

Barton's eyes bulged as he hawked up phlegm. "Two leashes," he wheezed, "what a bad boy I must be."

Marty forced himself to laugh. "You hold the rope with both hands, Professor. We'll keep you steady. Easy now."

By six a.m., the sleet had stopped, but the winds had risen and the temperature continued to fall. A thin sliver of grey appeared on the horizon behind them. Not quite enough to see by, but enough to end the blind fumbling of the night hours. From the sound of cascading water, it was clear they'd been skirting a mountain stream for some time. Despite the exhaustion, leg cramps, and cuts, Marty and Tauno counted themselves fortunate; they had better footwear.

Spirits brightened with the light, but an hour of it revealed another hazard: the same sun that now lit their way was beginning to burn off the cloud cover. As it dissipated, Marty surveyed the path ahead. They were entering a snow field above which sat two barren peaks.

Xanti pointed to a spot between them. "*España*," he announced.

Marty called to the others. "Spain!" he shouted. "Up there."

"*Es zayt nisht oiss ahz eez azoy veit*," one of the Jewish boys quipped in Yiddish.

"You wish," Marty replied without thinking. "It's farther than it looks and distances are deceiving in the mountains." The words were out before he caught himself. The Jewish lads looked at him, but before he could say anything, Xanti was swinging his arm to keep moving.

It was Barton who brought the procession to a halt when he sank into the snow and refused to budge. The others gathered around and watched as he sucked air. For several minutes, they huddled together in the wind, waiting for him to come around. Xanti grew increasingly agitated and began jabbering instructions. In a flurry of hand signals, he pointed to the professor, his watch, and the air. "*Hegazkinak*!" he shouted. "Dug, dug, dug, ratta-tat-tat," his face a billboard of worry as he imitated an airplane strafing.

Tauno glared at the guide. "I think this Basque prick wants us to abandon the professor," he said.

"He's right," Barton whispered from the snow. "Without me . . . there's a chance of getting . . . over the top before the planes find you."

He began making hand signs to Xanti, who finally nodded. "You fellows keep going," Barton explained. "Xanti will take me back down to the rocks then catch up to you. He promises to come back for me tomorrow."

"You trust him?" Tauno asked.

Barton shrugged and raised a fist in the Republican salute.

Relieved of the professor, the volunteers found themselves reinvigorated. The prospect of enemy planes blasting over the mountain at any second also helped them pick up the pace. In his mind's eye, Marty could picture what they must look like from the air. He saw a long line of black silhouettes against a white background, like in the daguerreotypes of gold-rush miners struggling up the Chilkoot Pass. He forced his mind back to high-school geography class, trying to remember if the notch they were heading for was called a cirque or a col, but the puzzle quickly evaporated in the rarefied air and gale-force winds.

Xanti caught up and forged ahead for the protection offered by the rocks at the top. He'd be there long before the group, leaving them exposed in the open. Marty noticed that he'd reversed his poncho. The inside was white. The others saw it, too. They cursed him and made salacious suggestions about his mother's sexual preferences.

With the climb now very steep, Marty found his nose poised only inches from the feet of the person ahead of him. He stared in wonderment at the man's street shoes and thin socks. The snow had graduated from ankle-, to knee-, and now to waist-deep. The shorter men were having the hardest time. They would bottom out at the crotch and have to be rescued. But with the higher elevation and increasing cold came a change in the snow's consistency. The crust became a thin blade of ice that broke into jagged shards when punctured. It wasn't long before a red trail marked their passage in the snow. Once again, Marty blessed his boots. Then, halfway to the top, the snow mutated again. "Look!" he called to the others, "it's hard enough to support us."

No one answered. Just breathing at this altitude took energy, and they were saving theirs. Marty fell into a rhythm—ten steps followed by a breather. He knew he should also be keeping an eye out for planes, but the white patch spreading across Tauno's cheek had his attention. He'd just decided it would be a good idea to rub his friend's face to get the circulation going, when he heard a scream. All eyes shot to the sky, but no plane dotted the horizon. More screams directed them to look behind, to see Broad Shoulders tumbling down the glacier. The column watched helplessly as his body grew smaller, before it finally disappeared into a crevasse.

Marty turned away. "There's nothing we can do," he yelled. "Stay in line! Keep moving! Let Tauno and me go first. We've got boots. We can pound dents in the crust."

Arriving at the summit—and Spain—was an anticlimax. They smiled, hugged, and proffered frozen fingers for handshakes. But Broad Shoulders' death, the abandonment of Barton, and a hunger for safety cast a pall over the celebration.

"Be a cinch goin' down," someone suggested hopefully.

Marty knew better. He'd hiked the Selkirks in B.C. while healthy and knew that the same elements faced on the way up awaited their descent. Gravity would help, but it could kill, too. He looked around. Every man in this company was cut, frostbitten, famished, and ready to drop. Some ambled on limbs so frozen they moved like clowns on stilts. Yet the closeness of the moment was empowering. It was a welcome sign. Spain would be good to them. He could feel it in his bones.

Chapter Seventeen

———

April 25, 1937
Republican Spain

WALKING ACROSS THE DRAWBRIDGE at Castell de Sant Ferran de Figueres was a step back in time. Mouth agape, Marty's band explored the moats and five kilometres of pentagon-shaped, double-enclosed walls.

After spending the night in a herder's shack on the mountain, a truck had appeared. In it were twenty other foreign volunteers who had also come off the mountains. As introductions were made, Marty wondered how many men had met Broad Shoulders' fate, or had to turn back like Barton. He tried not to think about that as they bumped their way through the rugged, lush countryside of Catalonia. If there was a war on, he could see no evidence.

When it was built in the eighteenth century, Sant Ferran was the most advanced fortress in all of Europe. Situated on a hill outside Figueres, the vegetation and climate was excitingly Mediterranean, which soon meant nothing when the volunteers were shown their quarters in the subterranean horse stables. They groused at the stench of horse piss, rotten oats, and mildew. Marty ignored them, as he pulled together some straw, spread the blanket he'd been issued, and curled up.

Tauno hovered over him, frowning. "Up for a bit more exploring?"

"No," Marty replied without looking up.

Tauno frowned. "You all right?"

"Pain in my side. That truck. And those roads."

"Bah!" Tauno replied. "No worse than the ones in B.C. Remember that time we—"

He was interrupted by what sounded like military commands. The men looked at each other, unsure what to do, as a soldier marched into the stables. They'd seen enough movies to realize that snapping to attention might be appropriate, but weren't sure how. In their confusion, they froze. Marty laboured to his feet. "What's he speaking?" he whispered to Tauno.

"Dunno. Sure isn't Spanish."

Marty tipped an ear. "Cripes, it's English," he concluded. "The guy's Cockney, for crying out loud." The officer repeated himself three times before the message sank in. Marty translated for the others. "We're to assemble on the parade ground, pronto. And we're to bring our passports."

They hustled outside where they found other men babbling in a host of languages. Marty scanned the crowd for the other half of the group from Le Havre, but saw no sign of them. At the edge of the square, officers stood behind tables ready to process the newcomers. The setting sun had reached the ramparts, as Marty gazed across the yellowing grass to take in the grey stone walls, red-tiled roofs, and archways of the inner buildings. A sharp call from an officer brought him back to attention. In spite of the pain in his side, he snapped his heels together, happy to be getting instructions at last. Even the abdominal pain couldn't overpower the magic of the moment—journey's end, a new beginning, a rare opportunity to hit back.

The official welcome was delivered in German, Italian, French, Polish, and English—in that order. Marty, with his French and Yiddish, was able to pass the information along to his group even before the English officer had had his turn.

"It appears it's the Abraham Lincoln Battalion of the Fifteenth International Brigade for us," he announced. "See that table with the Stars and Stripes? That's where we're to go. Tomorrow, they take us to a town called Villaneuva de la Jara, near Albecite. We'll get basic training there. And, oh, yes, another thing. When we get to the table, we're to surrender our passports." He noticed Tauno blanch.

"Hold on a minute!" Tauno protested when his turn came at the table. "Why would I part with my passport?"

The recruiting officer rolled his eyes. "Don't get your knickers in a knot. We keep them under lock and key at regimental headquarters in Albecite. When the war's over, you get them back."

"What if I need it in the meantime?"

The officer grinned. "What for? There'll be no trips abroad. You belong to us now."

Tauno turned to Marty. "What if we have to get out of here?" he mouthed.

Marty shrugged and whispered back. "Then we'll leave the way we came in. Give it to him."

Tauno turned to the officer. "I don't like this," he said, dropping the passport on the table.

"You're better off without it," the officer replied. "The rebels don't take kindly to soldiers they catch with foreign passports."

Marty was next in line. He hesitated, staring from the passport to the forms on the table. With a stroke of a pen, he'd be surrendering freedom to a foreign army. It was the right thing to do, he was certain, or so he'd told himself a thousand times. A strange dryness seized his throat. He coughed. The pain in his side intensified.

The moment the train jerked forward, Marty acknowledged his stupidity. On the straw in the stable, he'd been fine, but the swaying car was agony. He understood now what was ailing him and the risk he was taking. There was a simple solution, but if he and Tauno were to separate now, how would they ever find each other? As he was responsible for Tauno being here, he resolved to hold out to Villaneuva de la Jara, then get done what had to be done.

Something else glued him to this train, too. It had begun with the march from the fortress through the town to the station in Figueres. The locals had gathered along the route cheering them like heroes, passing out oranges, sharing wineskins. The girls, too, showed their exuberance, waving and shouting, "*No pasarán*," their fists raised in the Republican salute. It had transformed the men. Years of idleness, rejection, and defeat fell away like skin off a snake. There was a job to be done, and they were up to it. The adulation in Figueres, and at every whistle stop along the way, became a wage advance for deeds yet to be done. They would hold with these people to the last breath.

"Holy shit!" Tauno said, returning to their compartment. He'd been hanging out a window in the passageway with the others, waving to workers in the fields. Marty had stayed behind, and was trying to keep from falling off the jerking wooden bench and passing out from the pain in his gut. "You're whiter than a polar bear."

The train lurched and Marty began to slide. His friend lunged for him, pulling him up by the waist. "Gotta get to a hospital," he moaned. "Appendicitis."

Tauno rushed into the passageway and came back with the Cockney officer. "How ya know it's appendix," he asked, "and not somethin' you ate?"

"He's almost a doctor," Tauno answered.

Cockney looked surprised. "He didn't put none o' that down on his papers."

"Because he came here to fight!"

Cockney held up his hands. "All right! Girona's comin' up in an hour. We'll get 'im off there. He can catch up with us when he's better. But you," he said, tapping Tauno on the chest, "have two months of basic ahead. You're going through to Villaneuva." He turned.

Tauno waited for him to disappear down the crowded passageway. "Screw him! We're not splitting now. I'll jump train after Girona. Had lots of practice at that."

Marty shook his head. "You crazy," he managed weakly. "It's not worth getting shot for. I'll be in Villaneuva in two weeks, tops. The Lincolns won't be hard to find."

April 28, 1937
Girona, Spain

"WHERE DID YOU LEARN THE LANGUAGE?" Marty asked, stretching his limbs and revelling in the feel of starched, white sheets after so long. He was surprised by his good fortune. Of all the hospital beds to recuperate in, he'd lucked into one next to a local who spoke English. He chided himself for not taking advantage of the opportunity to work on his Spanish—the day might come when his life would depend on it—but the stitches in his side hurt too much to make the effort. Besides, diminutive, balding, fifty-something Eduardo Ruez was good company.

"Me, I'm learning English in Palestine and America," Eduardo boomed, in a voice that echoed around the ward. "I'm a Jew, you know, like my grandparents—one American, one *Español*. They moved from Girona to Tel Aviv when I am still a baby."

Marty swallowed, wondering if the Spaniards in the beds around them understood the English word, *Jew*. "That would make you bilingual," he said.

"Multi," Eduardo scoffed. "English, French, Spanish, Catalonian, and Hebrew."

"Guess no Yiddish, though, eh?"

"Why you saying that?"

Marty shrugged. "Just a guess. As a Spaniard, I figure you for a Sephardim Jew. Yiddish is an Ashkenazim dialect, isn't it?"

Eduardo brightened. "Very good," he said, "for a Gentile. But are you knowing what Jews are speaking in Girona in the old days?"

Marty was sure he knew and was about to answer, but reconsidered. There was something disconcerting about the proud way this man announced his devotion to Judaism that caused him to hesitate. "No idea," he responded.

"Ladino, a kind of mix of Spanish and Hebrew."

Marty tried to show surprise. "Interesting," he said.

"With sadness, I say it ended in 1492. On that year, in only three months, the king, Ferdinand, and the queen, Isabella, were bringing to a shut a thousand years of history. They had just pushed the Moors back to Africa and were thinking, why not we should get rid of the Jews, too." He stopped. "Forgive me. I am boring you."

Marty stared at the ceiling and cleared his throat. "No, it's fascinating . . . really," he responded, embarrassed by the sudden lack of timbre in his voice. He cast about in his mind for ways to change the subject.

"My wife says, 'Eduardo, you talk too much.' You say when I talk too much, eh, my friend?" Marty nodded. Eduardo continued. "Before 1492, Girona was having three synagogues. Here, every Jew boy could read and write." He shook his head. "Today, since a long time, many children no can read. Today, my family are the only Jews in Girona." He sat up cranking his voice to cantor level. "Hear, O Israel: The Lord is our God, the Lord is one." He stopped and smiled at the perplexed expression on Marty's face. Around them in the ward, lips had begun to curl in puzzlement, suspicious of chatter in a foreign tongue.

"So the Jews cut and ran?" Marty asked, cursing himself for his flippancy. Eduardo frowned. Marty tried again. "Left the country, uh . . . disappeared?"

Eduardo threw up his arms. "*Si, si.* For nothing, they sold everything and went away — Africa, Europa. Run away or hide. Some choice, eh?"

Marty nodded, recalling his father's advice on the Rabinovitch Affair: *He who resists the wave is swept away,* he'd recited, *but he who bends before it abides.* He'd put it down to Old World foolishness; now here it was again. "Did your family hide? Is that how they survived?"

"Hide, yes. *Marranos* they became — Christian by day, Jew by night. Gave the young ones names like Jésus, José, and Maria. In secret, they observed the holy sacraments. Alas, alone and with no synagogue or rabbi, it went dead. Well, almost, until my grandmother, may her soul rest in peace, found old records that she got translated. From that she went to Palestine, married, and got the family back to the faith."

Marty lowered his voice as if the others in the ward could understand. "And you're fine with it? I mean, professing your Jewishness and all that? It hasn't . . . caused trouble? Set you back?"

Eduardo frowned. "In Catholic Spain? Of course. But to ignore my true heritage would make of Eduardo Ruez *un cobarde* . . . coward. How could I turn my back on my people and be a man? I have too much . . . too much . . . how you call that in English?"

Marty swallowed. "Pride," he whispered, "integrity." He felt the heaviness settle in around him as the words sank home. He'd experienced it before. This time there was no pushing it away.

Eduardo continued. "I am not for broadcasting my Jew faith in the old days, but today, with the Republic, it is much safe. Then here comes Franco with big, old idea—nobles, army, and Church must rule again, not the people—same idea as Ferdinand and Isabella. Know what that means for Jews?"

"Pogrom?"

"Big scale. Like in Germany. In Nationalist Spain, it has begun. Already my sister in Vallodolid and her husband have been liquidated. Many others, too. Nationalists! What barbarians." He lay back on his bed, looking up at the ceiling.

For a few minutes, Marty listened to Eduardo's heavy breathing, wishing the infection around his own stitches would flare up and mask the deeper pain growing in his breast. Eduardo had forced him to acknowledge his own integrity, or lack of it. The word swirled in his gut, like bile. "Can I ask you something, Eduardo?"

"Feel free, young man; Franco does not rule here already."

"You're past fifty, yet you still joined the army to save the Republic?"

Eduardo pushed himself up onto his elbows. "You find me too old to fight for freedom?"

Marty avoided the query with another question. "Do your officers know you're . . . Jewish?"

Eduardo turned to face Marty. "*Si*, they know. For me, does it make life easy? No, but I am sleeping good." Marty felt the tears coming and fought to hold them back. "You okay?" Eduardo asked. "The nurse I should call?"

"No," Marty replied, shaking his head. "Continue."

"Little more to say, except my wife, with needle and thread, has put a little red circle on my uniform; just like the one my ancestors were forced to wear in 1492. Most people are not knowing what it means, but for Eduardo Ruez, it is a badge of honour. I will never again—" He stopped. Marty had turned his back and curled into a ball. "Those stitches, they cause much pain, eh?" Eduardo said, soothingly.

"No . . . not the stitches . . . conscience. I'm one of your *cobardes*. My name's not really Kelly, it's Kellenberger. And I'm no Irishman. I'm a Jew, just like you."

Eduardo sank back on his pillow. "Poor boy," he said, after a long silence. "What will you do?"

"Don't know."

"My wife could bring you a red circle. You enough man to wear it?"

"Don't know that, either."

Chapter Eighteen

April 29, 1937
The Border, Nationalist Spain

DON'T LOOK BACK. DON'T LOOK BACK, Dollard repeated to himself.

It was McCullagh's last instruction, delivered with a finger wag. The red line at mid-bridge marking the border was coming up fast. Instinctively he slowed. In a few seconds, it would be too late to change his mind. The knot in his gut got tighter with every step. His head felt as misty as the early morning brume obscuring the Basque hills. The suitcase tugged at his arm. Ahead, Spanish customs officers eyed his approach from behind the barrier gate with growing suspicion. Behind, on the French side, McCullagh, along with an assortment of border officials and curiosity-seekers, watched his progress. Below lay the Bidosso River, calm now as it prepared to dump its sludge into the Bay of Biscay. He reached the line and hesitated, ruminating over McCullagh's counsel. "There are great terrible doings happening over there," he'd said. " 'Tis no game. Hundreds die every day. Journalists, the likes of you and me, too."

Dollard halted, forgetting instructions to approach in a resolute manner. "The Spanish border police are gods," he'd been warned. "Entry visa or not, they'll turn you away, or worse, drag you in on the slightest suspicion."

A car approached from behind. Dollard stepped aside and saw the Spanish barrier gate swing up and the car pass through. Even before the barrier had fallen, gun-carrying *guardia civil*, in their tricorne, patent-leather hats, were swarming it.

He saw the *aduaneros* go to work, then looked back over his shoulder. McCullagh was still there, waving him on, like a parent shooing a reluctant child up the path to the schoolhouse on opening day. The Irishman had accompanied him on the short hop from St. Jean-de-Luz to Hendaye on the French side across from Irún, peppering him all the way with last-minute instructions. Dollard waved back then stepped over the line, his eyes watering in the acrid fumes rising from the fetid waters below.

Dollard swallowed as the gate rose then slammed down behind him. Immediately, he was engulfed in a fanfare of Spanish, too rapid for his

228

limited grasp of the language to fathom. Orders were shouted, fingers pointed, directions given. No one smiled. For a second, he stood clutching his passport, his eyes darting from face to face as he remembered McCullagh's instructions to deal only with the *guardia civil* sporting the most stripes. Having made his selection, he handed the document over. The commotion ceased. The guard with the bars looked from Dollard to his photo. A smile forced its way onto his lips and, with a sweep of the arm that would do justice to a maitre d' on the Champs Elysées, he directed Dollard to the customs office. A narrow path opened in the milling crowd. Dollard took it, running the gauntlet of suspicious stares.

Inside sat a solitary *aduanero* and a woman he couldn't help but think had strayed in off a movie set. The *aduanero* rose as he entered, while the woman extended her hand, exposing more teeth than a Coca-Cola billboard. Blonde with blue eyes, she was at least ten years his senior and graceful in that Continental way so common to ladies of breeding.

"Welcome to Spain," she drawled. Dollard wondered if she'd taken a wrong turn at the Mason-Dixon Line. He wasn't certain whether to shake the hand or kiss it. "I'm Jane Anderson."

"You speak good English," Dollard replied, pumping her hand once.

"I would hope so. I'm from Atlanta. You're on my tour."

"Wonderful," Dollard said, working hard to control his voice. "I was warned there'd be a female journalist in the group. Daring of you to come." He looked around. "Where are the others? Weren't we supposed to be met by the tour leader?"

Miss Anderson squared her shoulders, the smile hardening. "I'm the Marquesa de Cienfuegos," she said, "and *I am* the tour leader. I hope you're not one of those men who have problems taking instructions from a woman?"

Dollard swallowed. "No! No, of course not."

"Because if you are, it's not too late to walk back across that bridge."

Dollard chilled at the iciness of her tone. "I'm sorry if—"

"Give me your passport," she commanded. He began patting pockets, not realizing he held it clutched in his hand. The marquesa sighed, snatched his passport, and plunked it on the *aduanero*'s desk. He stamped it and returned it to Dollard. She pointed to the door. They made their exit.

Outside, the occupants of the car that had passed him on the bridge weren't doing well. A shouting match had erupted over what appeared to be a vigorous search of their vehicle. Personal articles were strewn about—blouses, stockings, foundation garments. The driver went to the aid of the woman who was in a tug-of-war with a customs officer over a handbag. He was immediately cross-checked by another officer with a rifle. As Dollard took a step toward them, the marquesa grabbed his arm. "Walk," she ordered, frog-marching him toward a car and driver waiting in the parking lot across the road. "And don't look back."

Dollard pulled his eyes away, shuffling stiffly in front of the elegant marquesa. "They didn't even open my suitcase," he said. "'Ow come?"

"Because you're with *me*," she said, stopping to face him when they'd crossed the road. "Now look. You just about landed yourself in deep trouble back there. Spaniards have no time for do-gooders or busybodies. We're at war—*Civil War*."

"But didn't you see the way—"

"Listen to me! As long as you're my responsibility, you'll follow my rules." Her finger came up in the same gesture his father used when scolding him. "You're to mind your own business at all times. Understand? And never stray off on your own." Dollard nodded. "Our side's not perfect—yet. We're working on it. Meanwhile, we've no time for meddlers. My job's to show you the terrible, terrible things the Republicans have perpetrated on Catholic Spain. Your job is to listen, take notes, and go home to tell the truth about what's really happening over here. You've a role to play; there've been too many lies about Franco in the outside press."

The marquesa led him to a long, black Hispano-Suiza H6. Under normal circumstances, he might have swooned at the sight of the vehicle, sure to rouse the envy of André and the boys back home. There'd be no end to their jealousy if they could see him sliding into this Continental touring car with its whitewall tires, spoked wheels, oversized headlights hanging off the long nose, and twelve full cylinders under the bonnet. This was a vehicle right out of the Sunday afternoon movies. The type favoured by the gay set in Paris as they dashed their way down *les routes nationales* to the Riviera. And to think he would be touring Spain in such splendour.

But the moment had been ruined by the marquesa and her haughty reception. Did she see him as a childish colonial? Untested? Gun-shy? He'd prove to her that he had the right to be on this excursion. Hadn't he braved the adversity of a hospital strike in Montreal, union demonstrations in Vancouver, and rioting and death in Regina? Not quite wars, perhaps, but not church socials, either. He'd improvised, survived, and done well, *merci beaucoup*, and come home to the kudos of the same paper he was now representing in Spain.

The marquesa opened the front door for herself and motioned for Dollard to take the back seat. "This is Raul," she said, when they were seated. "He'll be our driver for the next few weeks." Dollard wondered why she seemed so anxious to sit up front with the chauffeur.

No one spoke as they exited the parking lot, moving slowly along the boulevard. Dollard sat back, arms crossed, struggling not to be the one to break silence. After a few minutes, he could stand it no more. "So, where are the others?" he asked at last.

"At the Maria Cristina Hotel in San Sebastián," the marquesa replied. "An hour's drive in good times, but at least three with the mess the Republicans have made of the roads."

"Oh!" he said. He hoped she'd elaborate, but gave up waiting and began concentrating instead on the passing scenery. Irún appeared to have been torched. Stumps, once noble plane trees, lined the streets. Sunken-eyed citizens stopped to watch them pick their way down the shell-pocked boulevard, as if it were an event to see motoring civilians. He thought of the grace and beauty of St. Jean-de-Luz, "Irún's twin city with a Spanish twist," as the tour book put it, and tried to imagine this town in its former glory. The marquesa began to hum. Dollard decided to put her in her place. She'd be Jane Anderson from now on and not the Marquesa de Cienfuegos. More blocks passed, continuous destruction. Irún ended abruptly. The countryside began.

Progress on the highway was scarcely faster than in town. Traffic was dense—all military—and road conditions abysmal. A plume of sooty, blue-black haze marked their route. Raul seemed impatient. Several times he pulled out to pass, only to swerve back so as to avoid colliding with military vehicles coming the other way. At last, he gunned the Hispano-Suiza past the oil tanker they'd been trailing and tucked in behind a truckload of soldiers. The faces on the troopers lit up with lusty smiles as they craned their necks for a peek at the blonde in the car. When they began making lewd gestures, Raul laughed. Jane, too. He made a comment in Spanish, and she slapped him on the thigh with the back of her hand. It was the first time Dollard had seen her smile.

Several minutes later they came to what was to be the first of many roadblocks, where the Hispano-Suiza was pulled over to the loud dismay of the soldiers in the truck.

"Let me do the talking," Jane ordered, rolling down the window. The officer approaching wore khaki breeches, a blue tunic that matched his knee socks, and a black wedge with a red tassel dangling over his forehead. Ammunition pouches and a bayonet hung from his belt. He cradled his carbine in his arms while he talked to the marquesa, the barrel pointed halfway between the front and rear seats. Dollard noted that his finger never strayed from the trigger. Young and seemingly nervous soldiers took up position around the car. Dollard slid to the middle of the seat.

"*Falangista*," Raul said, in a barely audible voice that suggested caution. Dollard couldn't decide if there was respect or disgust in his tone.

For what seemed like an interminable time, the officer shuffled their documents and inspected the car, all the while scowling. Jane drummed her fingers on the dashboard before finally machine-gunning him with a burst of Spanish. Raul blanched, but Jane continued her tirade, pointing to her watch and repeating the name, Luis Bolín, several times. With a click of his heels, the officer returned their documents, and the guards lowered their rifles as they were waved on.

When they were underway, the duo in the front broke into laughter. Dollard joined in, more from relief, praying they hadn't sensed his panic. Looking over her shoulder, the marquesa offered him her best smile. "You did just fine," she said.

Dollard counted them. Four words, that was all. But they were words of praise, and she had directed them at him. He settled back, stretching an arm across the top of the seat, his hand stroking the plush velvet, as if sensing it for the first time. No, she was the one who'd done just fine; more than fine, magnificent. She'd sized up the situation, seen her advantage, and taken the initiative. He wondered what scrapes lay ahead. Would the time come when he would be the one to save the day, maybe even extricate the marquesa from a tight situation?

After three roadblocks, two detours, and a long wait while a convoy of war vehicles crossed a makeshift bridge, they finally left the army behind. Traffic grew light. Dollard wondered if the battle lines were close by and listened for sounds of war. Nothing. The world seemed at peace. With the knot in his throat easing and tension in the car evaporating, he began to focus on the rolling countryside with its plump sheep, green grass, and neglected fields scattered amongst rocky outcrops. The mixture of coniferous and deciduous trees separating the wooden cottages on the hillsides reminded him of trips to his uncle's summer home on Lac Massawippi. Occasionally, the marquesa would reach over and blow the horn at dark-clad peasants on the road. Apparently this was funny, because Raul chuckled each time. Dollard joined in, though he wasn't sure why. The marquesa blessed him with another smile.

He began to study the people alongside the road. The men wore floppy berets and dark wool coats; the women, black dresses to the knees and matching shawls that covered their heads. Collectively, they gave off an aura of weariness, expected from a region so recently rescued from the communist yoke. There were no young men in evidence. He wondered how many had taken up with Franco, how many with the Republicans, and how many had opted for the hills? This would be a good question for the marquesa, but he feared destroying their new-found comradeship with the suggestion that perhaps not every Spaniard was enthralled with el Caudillo.

"Will we see any fighting in our travels?" he ventured.

The marquesa placed an arm on the back of the seat to face him. "Not unless the Republicans surprise us. My instructions are to take you to recaptured areas and show you enemy devastation and the repairs we're making." She said something in Spanish to Raul as she turned back to the road. They both laughed. "Don't look so worried," she said, "we'll keep you away from the front—and safe."

The marquesa closed her eyes, and Dollard watched her head bob against the side of the car as she dozed. He wondered how anyone could sleep with all the braking, lurching, and banging that was part and parcel of driving on the cratered roadbed. Maybe she wasn't asleep at all, just trying to avoid conversation. It puzzled him that she hadn't asked one question about his experience or expectations, but then she seemed comfortable in the company of Raul the driver. Dollard wondered about her husband. What role was he playing in the resurrection of Spain?

San Sebastián was a pleasant surprise. That a war was in progress was evident in the absence of private cars, the abundance of horses, the predominance of pushcarts, the lineups at shops, and the damaged buildings. But the city didn't have Irún's bombed-out appearance. On the contrary, the *avenida* on which they entered appeared regal to the young Quebecer. With the first bridge closed, they detoured to the Puente Maria Cristina, with its ornate towers and numerous sculptures. If there was disappointment, it was in the expression on the faces of the civilians, which reflected the same sullenness he'd detected in Irún. He wondered if this was a Spanish trait, something he'd get used to.

Marching soldiers sang their way down the Paseo de Franco alongside the river, where they joined the lineup for the railway station.

"What regiment are we looking at now?" Dollard asked. With the marquesa's help, he'd been doing his best to identify the armies by their uniforms. There was something about this group of strutting soldiers that appealed to him. In their kelly-green pants, light green shirts open at the neck, and dark green wedges, they swaggered more than marched.

"*Legionario*," the marquesa replied, "Spanish Foreign Legion. The best."

Dollard nodded. "Like the French one?"

She shook her head. "Better." She saluted through the window to a bearded *capo* who was scolding his men. He blew her a kiss. She blew it back. The Hispano-Suiza pulled away.

At the Maria Cristina Hotel, they were met by a gaggle of elderly porters in operatic uniforms falling over each other as they reached for the car doors. Dollard stepped out and stretched, entranced by the scent of the sea, the crash of waves against the breakwater nearby, and the rustle of palm leaves in the late morning breeze. As if in welcome, a medley of church bells began to echo off the buildings. "Catholic Spain," he said aloud, pinching himself, "I made it." He inhaled deeply then noted the pockmarks around the windows of the hotel. "War-ravaged Spain," he reminded himself.

A pod of snappily dressed officers flowed around their car, hurrying toward the front steps. None of them made eye contact, but Dollard heard the word *extranjeros* as they passed. His chin fell. He hadn't come to be a foreigner. He wanted to be one of them, a defender of the true word. The marquesa ignored the slight as they followed the officers into the hotel.

The lobby reminded Dollard of the Château Frontenac. The scale was familiar, but the Maria Cristina seemed to possess a greater dollop of *la belle époche*—marble pillars, chandeliers, intricate patterns on the tiled floor, Persian rugs, French doors to the patio. He trembled inside. This was a country to fall in love with.

The marquesa approached the front desk and nodded as the clerk pointed to the dining room. She turned, looking at her watch. "The others are having a bite," she said. "We'll join them. If we get away by noon we can still make Burgos by nightfall. Wouldn't want to be caught on the highway after sundown."

Dollard nodded with a polite smile, but was troubled. Why the aversion to travelling at night? Could the road be worse than the one they'd just travelled on, or was it something else?

The consensus in the car was that the trip to Burgos was exhausting. Dollard disagreed. With his face tipped to the cobalt blue sky and blazing sun, he revelled at the changing landscape. For several hours, they had driven through luxuriant fields and forests, then, having traversed a range of mountains, they had dropped onto the yellow interior plateau of Castile. If he didn't know better, he could have been back in Saskatchewan, looking out the train window en route to Regina. When conversation lagged, he resorted to impressing the others with his newly acquired ability to identify regiments at roadblocks. No one asked him how he'd come upon such knowledge, which pleased him. He hoped they'd assume it was from first-hand experience and not newspapers while cooling his heels in St. Jean-de-Luz, or the marquesa's tutelage. As for the marquesa, she spent her time charming the others with romantic tales of glory. This began to annoy Dollard, but didn't seem to bother his companions, who scribbled down every word, like first-year university students. Their pens stopped only when ordered, which was usually because the object in question was classified and not to be reported—like the long train loaded with tanks and Italian soldiers. Why such information should be a no-go subject was beyond Dollard. Wasn't it comforting to have Mussolini on their side, and Hitler, too?

His fellow passengers on Franco's "tourist trail"—one male, one female—were an obsequious lot. They laughed uproariously at the marquesa's anti-communist, anti-anarchist, anti-socialist jibes, sighed on cue, and agreed that the only good Republican was a dead Republican. Dollard had heard the line before, in those westerns l'abbé Groulx disapproved of so vehemently.

The woman, a Miss Swanson—hair of lip, mole of chin—was in her forties and physically and socially the marquesa's opposite. She wrote for the *London Sunday Dispatch*, a paper quoted occasionally by Arcand. The man, McGonegal, turned out to be a Dublin priest with the Passionate Fathers who'd been assigned to the *Catholic Cross Weekly*. On the advice of his bishop, he travelled in civvies to avoid a possible ignominious end at the hands of Republican demons—sodomization, torture, death. He talked in glowing terms of the great contribution made by the *Bandera Irlandesa*, the Irish 15th Battalion, and its illustrious leader, Colonel O'Duffy, in Spain to rescue the True Faith from ignominy.

"How many volunteers 'ave they raised?" Dollard asked.

Father McGonegal leaned over Miss Swanson, who was sitting in the middle, to answer. "T'ousands, they say."

Dollard nodded solemnly at the information, puzzled that McCullagh had never mentioned his countrymen. "'Ave they been tested, yet?" he asked, pleased with his wording. "Tested" was a term that spoke of sound journalism to him, in as much as it suggested a withholding of judgment until proven. He'd picked up the expression from McCullagh, who claimed to believe only what he had triple-sourced, or witnessed with his own eyes. It was a rule Dollard would like to apply, although, under the circumstances, the marquesa's explanations were proving to be thorough, albeit on the preachy side.

"Not sure," McGonegal replied. "Would you happen to know the answer, Marquesa?"

She shook her head and exchanged glances with Raul. "Ask O'Duffy yourself. We'll be at the Gran Hotel in Salamanca in a few weeks. He seems to be a fixture in the bar there."

McGonegal sat back, letting the matter drop.

But Dollard's imagination was racing. What a wonderful project for Adrien Arcand. Instead of stomping around Quebec with his National Socialist Christian Blueshirts, why not raise a battalion to join Franco? It would certainly counterbalance those misinformed Canadian volunteers rushing to the Red side. He longed to learn more about this Irish Brigade, especially in view of the marquesa's reticence. He made a mental note to ask around.

"'Ave other national groups enlisted in the cause?" Dollard asked.

Again Jane and Raul exchanged looks. "I'll tell you this, off the record," she answered. "Not to be reported." The back seat nodded in unison. "Portuguese, Italians, Germans, Romanians, French, White Russians—they're all here."

"And the Irish," Father McGonegal added.

"So, why the 'ush-'ush?" Dollard asked.

She turned to face the tourists square on. "Because, and this you can report, unlike the Republicans, we don't need foreigners to solve our problems. We could do it alone, but the restoration of the Church has international significance, so it's only natural that others should want to be involved. Think of it as a crusade. As for the Spaniards, you can report that they long for the restoration of Church and monarchy. True, some have been confused by foreign atheists with their ideas on free land, voting rights for the uneducated masses, and new roles for women." Pens flashed in the back seat. "But, ask yourself, what does it gain a country to have ignorant *campesinos* choosing a government?"

Not recognizing her question as rhetorical, McGonegal attempted to answer. "Chaos," he snapped, "and the Republicans are proof of it with their—"

The marquesa glared at him and ploughed on. "The Reds will stop at nothing. Take the sex card, for instance." Miss Swanson's hand went to her throat. Father McGonegal looked solemn. "It's free love for the troops with the *milicianas*, those young peasant girls who've been forced to abandon home and family for army life. And when they get pregnant, it's off to the abortion factories in Barcelona and Valencia." She turned abruptly to face the front. "Write about that if you want to expose the influence of foreigners on Spain."

Dollard locked onto the back of her head, as if he could somehow read her thoughts. She had so many faces—coquette, femme fatale, diplomat, superintendent, mastermind. He wished he could find the formula for guessing which she'd be next. He couldn't make up his mind about her, but one thought was constant: he was here to prove to himself and to his father that journalism was a respectable profession and that he had the talent to succeed. Whether he was allowed to stay past this three-week tour would depend on El Señor Bolín. The marquesa worked for him, was his friend. Staying in her good graces was essential. So far, her explanations were convincing, if a little pat. For now, he'd write them up and file them. They'd be a hit with *Le Devoir* back home. He thought of McCullagh. His advice about cross-referencing was sound, but sometimes instinct trumped caution. Sometimes, you had to trust what you were hearing. He had that feeling now.

"'Ow far to Burgos?" Dollard asked. He could feel the tension in the front seat, now that darkness was settling in. Raul had done his best to make up time, but had been forced to drive cautiously as they headed into the setting sun. Now it had dropped, the temperature dropping, too.

The marquesa shrugged. "Thirty minutes, maybe." Father McGonegal began rolling up his window. "Leave the windows down and stay quiet," she ordered.

"Why?" the priest asked.

"So we can hear."

"Hear what?"

"Airplanes! The Republicans come out at night looking for lights on the roads." Dollard swallowed. "And keep an eye out for our own soldiers. Our boys can be trigger-happy in the dark."

May 23, 1937
Salamanca, Spain

"ANOTHER LETTER HOME?" the marquesa asked, as he approached. She had watched his progress from the front desk where she was making arrangements to extend their stay at Salamanca's Gran Hotel. Dollard had come off the elevator, past the life-sized portraits of Hitler, Mussolini, and Franco, and was approaching the ornate mailbox at the end of the counter.

"Think it'll make it out of the country?" he asked, dropping the letter through the slot.

"'Course it will," she replied, "unless you've been foolish enough to stray onto forbidden topics."

He dropped his head to look at her. "That censor's list is a mighty long one," he chuckled. She turned back to her business.

Dollard held his breath, conscious that staring at such close range was considered extremely gauche. He studied her porcelain skin, delicate profile, and impeccable grooming. She was wearing her trademark bolero jacket and, although born American, he saw in her the epitome of everything he imagined a Spanish woman should be. Once again he calculated her reaction should he knock on her door some night, but dismissed the idea for what it was—tempting, but dumb. Their journey over the past three weeks had been long, dusty, and tiring. Yet, each morning, she emerged fresh with every hair in place. Despite his earlier vow to see her as plain Jane Anderson, she was unequivocally *la marquesa*. Passion drove her—passion for Spain, passion for *la causa*, passion for her own pleasures, but not, he suspected, for the man whose name she bore. Did she ever communicate with *el conde*? If so, how? With so much of the country's telephone grid still controlled by the Republicans, she would have to rely on the mail, yet he'd never seen her post a letter. Maybe she didn't relish sharing intimate thoughts with the censors, or, perhaps, with so many taboo subjects, there wasn't much left to say. And what role was the chauffeur playing? Dollard could swear he'd heard his voice coming from her room at more than one hotel. Or was she just attracted to dashing men? If so . . . ? He pushed the idea from his mind.

She was bang-on about the forbidden list. Letter-writing was a minefield. Say the wrong thing and they'd come for you. Not that he'd found many negative things to say. Of course, there was hardship and terrible, terrible damage, but you could hardly pin that on the Nationalists. To be safe, Dollard had heeded the advice of a popular American song and taken to "accentuate the positive." He'd also admitted in a letter to his father, and quite honestly, too, that the eight pounds sterling spent on the Marquesa de Cienfuegos' War Tour of the North was the best investment ever made on his behalf. He was here for information and was getting it in large dollops. That their vehicle, hotels, and food were superb was a bonus. Most important, he'd been polishing his journalistic skills and hoped it showed in the commentaries now appearing in *Le Devoir*.

If he was reading things correctly, his plan to win *la marquesa's* confidence was working, although it would be unwise to mention that in letters. She'd warmed to him when he'd asked her to proof his first article. After that, they fell into a routine. Each morning before setting out, they'd sit at the breakfast table at whatever sumptuous hotel they were staying in — Londres y Norte Hotel in Burgos, the Majestic in Seville, the Don Curro in Malaga — and she'd critique what he'd written the night before. After several days of this, she allowed he had flair, showed promise. She began abbreviating his name to D, and didn't object when he dared to call her Jane. He fantasized that they might get at it a little earlier each morning, say in her room, but so far that hadn't happened. Probably for the better.

The trip had been an eye-opener. One by one, irrefutable facts had been unveiled. The Republicans were living up to the "monster" billing. If he could just get his hands on a permanent *salvoconducto* and be allowed to stay on, he'd set the record straight for doubters back home. More than ever, it was clear that without strong leaders, Europe would be going down like dominoes to the Reds, Freemasons, and Jews. He boiled at the thought of bleeding hearts like Dr. Bethune and that French author, André Malraux, both of whom had visited Montreal to stump for the anti-Christians. God bless Jeune-Canada for disrupting their speeches and driving them out of Quebec.

Even though Jane had not been able to get them to the front lines to see action, it was exciting to realize that not far away — Asturia to the north, Aragon to the southeast — fierce battles were raging. Occasionally, he would be awakened by small-arms fire in the night, but had the good sense not to investigate, or ask what it might all have been about. Even when they'd stood on the platform outside Madrid, looking through telescopes across the destroyed grounds of the university to the Republican line, no angry shots had been exchanged. Nevertheless, his heart had pounded at the enemy's proximity. In every liberated town—San Sebastián, Toledo, Malaga—Jane proved to be a goldmine, always drawing attention to Republican atrocities and the wonders of the new order at work—churches reopened, crosses back on school walls, civil marriage outlawed, abortion clinics closed, seditious literature burned, dress codes enforced, land returned to rightful owners, respect for authority renewed, dignity restored.

"You're up early," Jane remarked, finishing her work at the counter.

"Join me for a walk?" he asked.

She seemed to hesitate, and his heart sank with the sound of approaching footsteps and the realization that she was looking over his shoulder. Turning, he found himself facing the syrupy grin of the white-suited, black-booted Italian general she'd dined with the night before. She held out her hand. The general kissed it. Two Italian colonels saluted as they passed. The general ignored them.

"Generale Phamphilii, allow me to present Dollard Desjardins. He's the young Canadian journalist I was telling you about."

Dollard felt his pulse quicken. Had she really talked about him to a *general*? This was progress, but she'd referred to him as young, which was not. "Quebec journalist," he corrected.

The general clicked his heals, tipping his nose upwards in a Mussolini pose. "And how does your country feel about our leetle conflict?" he asked.

"Desperate for facts," Dollard replied, "which is why we need more reporters on the ground."

Dollard felt Jane's hand on his shoulder. She crushed him with a motherly smile. "He's hoping they'll let him stay on full time. We're waiting for a meeting with the Spanish Press Bureau."

"Ah!" the general said, "El Señor Bolín." He wagged a finger. "Watch your step with that one."

A shiver wound its way up Dollard's spine. Jane's hand came off his shoulder. "He's not that bad," she said with a laugh.

Three German aviators, necks red from the Iberian sun, came down the marble staircase and headed for the dining room. One nodded to the general. *"Maledeetto sauerkrauts,"* he mumbled, watching them cross under the chandelier and approach the French doors. "Seence they took over the top floor, they think they own the Gran. They keep pestering the chefs for more bratwurst and cabbage. Imagine the stench." His shoulders quivered in disgust. Dollard nodded, understanding why the general might be miffed; not only about the food, but about the German officers in general. There was something aggressive in the way they occupied space that grated, as if other nationals, including the Spanish who owned the war, were somehow unworthy.

Across the lobby, an overweight Portuguese major had nestled his backside into a leather divan. He nodded to the Germans as they passed. Dollard smiled at the rainbow of uniforms hustling to and fro—brilliantly sashed servicemen, the black-and-red-robed clerics, government officials in their sober morning suits. With Madrid yet to be liberated, Salamanca had become Franco's temporary headquarters. History was in the making here, and, sensing it, each player yearned to leave his mark. Dollard longed to interview all of these men: the Italian tank commanders slapping each other on the back; the German pilots huddled around a comrade who was flying two hands above his head and making rat-a-tat-tat sounds; the Irish colonel strategizing with the Romanian officers; the Spanish generals scowling at the foreigners.

The general turned back to Jane. "Do me the honour of joining me for breakfast, Marquesa?" he asked. "Oh, and you, too, young man."

"Another time," Dollard replied. "I need a little air."

Jane tipped her head elegantly. "Thank you, Generale, but I've already promised Dollard a stroll around the Plaza."

They exited the hotel to a symphony of church bells. Of all the plazas in Spain the marquesa had taken them to—Segovia's, Avila's, Toledo's, Seville's—none had touched Dollard as profoundly as Salamanca's Plaza Mayor. The baroque façade over the north portal, the balconies rising three stories over archways, and the cameos of past monarchs in bas relief, all bound the present to the past. Puzzling how Republicans would want to throw it all away, like some shallow circus. There was stability here, culture, and a tradition to hang on to.

He inhaled the crisp morning air, wishing she'd take his arm, but contented when, after a full tour of the plaza, she was up for more. Making their way down the Rua Mayor, the kinetic energy of Franco's Spain hit him in waves—mothers in black mantillas herding scrubbed children to mass, Nationalist flags flapping from balconies, Art-Deco posters plastered on walls. The clothes were coarser than the long gowns, tiaras, and lacy mantillas he was used to in the hotel, but they were obviously cared for. Dollard took in the modest attire and, in spite of himself, found comfort in the absence of décolleté dresses and bare legs. Not that skin wasn't available—he'd learned from the officers at the hotels where to find it and agreed that, just like at home, it was best confined to appropriate places and times.

Jane took his arm. Dollard beamed at the soldiers who glared at them in jealousy from the packed sidewalk cafés. One group around a long table had locked arms and was singing the popular military song, "Los Voluntarios."

"Do you know the words?" she asked.

"Every verse," he replied. "A *voluntario* is what I've decided to become if the *salvoconducto* fails to materialize." He felt the squeeze of her arm as his eye fell on evidence of past foes vanquished over the centuries—the Jews, in a weathered Star of David over a stone archway; the Moors, in keyhole-shaped doorways and geometrically patterned façades.

Jane lifted her head. The bells of the Catedral Nueva were in competition with those of the Universidad Pontificia and the Iglesia de la Santisima Trinidad. "I'd forgotten it was Sunday," she said.

Dollard didn't reply. His mind was still on the Moroccan troops. "Know what puzzles me?" he said.

"What's that, D?"

"There are no fezzes or baggy-kneed trousers about. We never see Moorish soldiers on the streets on Sundays. 'Ow come?"

"Maybe they find it wise to keep a low profile on the Lord's Day."

"Ironic, though, no?" he chuckled. "Five 'undred years it took the Christians to drive the Muslims out of Spain, yet, 'ere they are, back at Franco's invitation to rescue the Church from the atheists." He felt her stiffen at his side.

"Best you learn to keep such thoughts to yourself."

"Oh, I do," he added hastily. "It's just that there are some things I need answers to, and I feel safe asking you."

They ambled past the house of shells, a refuge for pilgrims. "I see," she responded. "Dare I ask what else is floating around that little head of yours?"

He hesitated, wondering how far to go. They passed a bookstore across from the Catedral Veijo. Signs in the window read, "*Deutsch gesprochen hier*," and "*Viva il Duce*." "*Bien*, I look around and I see the kind of devoted people I 'oped to find. What I don't get is, 'ow so many Spaniards could possibly 'ave been duped by the Republicans in the first place."

She shook her head. "God, isn't it clear from what I've been telling you these past weeks?" Dollard straightened at the iciness in her tone. "We're not dealing with educated people here."

"No, I guess we're not."

"Ignorant masses are easily fooled," she continued. "Imagine yourself a peasant and some smart mouth comes along with ideas about how well off the priests and gentry are and how workers should have a say in running the factories. Suddenly, you see yourself as entitled, so you form up in gangs and take over. Then, when you've murdered and plundered, you sit back and wait for the money to roll in. Only it never does, because with no one working and no one with the intelligence and education to take charge, there's neither produce nor profit, and the country goes down the tubes."

"I see your point, Marquesa," he responded, cursing himself for venturing a second question.

She stopped and faced him square on. "I hope so, Dollard. This tour's an experiment. If the authorities think it's not working, it'll be cancelled. And another thing. You've an important meeting coming up with Bolín. If he has any doubts about your convictions . . ." She left the sentence hanging as she began heading back to the Gran. Chastened, he continued toward the Puente Romano, the bridge that had once trembled to the cadence of Roman legions in full march.

May 26, 1937
Salamanca, Spain

"STOP PACING AND SIT," the marquesa drawled, patting the chair beside her. "Luis is not going to eat you."

Dollard plopped down and slouched. Then, realizing bad posture would do little to advance his cause, pulled his legs in, forcing his torso upright. " 'E's got my future in 'is hands. I 'ave a bad feeling."

"I'll be putting in a good word," she soothed.

He turned toward her, wondering if she had as much influence on the director of the Spanish Press Bureau as she let on. Doubts had begun to set in the moment he laid eyes on her at breakfast. She'd come down dressed to the nines. Worse, El Señor's Legionnaire secretary had announced their arrival almost an hour ago and they were still waiting.

"I'll be needing it," he said.

The words were hardly out when the telephone rang on the desk. Dollard jumped. "El Señor Director will see you now," the secretary said, rising to his feet and rushing to hold the door.

The marquesa led. Dollard followed. "Luis," she cooed, oozing southern charm as she seemingly floated across the thick carpet to the marble desk behind which the director stood.

Flashing a perfect smile, he hurried around to kiss the proffered hand. "Marquesa," he replied in an exaggerated tone. "Forgive me, *por favor*, but as you can see . . ." He shrugged, waving an arm in the direction of the paper mound on his desk.

She fanned a hand in the air. "Nothing to forgive, Luis. I'm flattered that in spite of grave responsibilities you would take time to see me."

His tipped his head. "Marquesa, always I have time for you. Now tell me about this initiative with the foreign reporters. The potential fascinates me. Is it working well enough to expand? Would it be feasible to bring them in by the busload?"

"I'm dying to bring you up to date, Luis. But first allow me to introduce Dollard Desjardins, a brilliant young journalist from Canada. He's here this morning as testimony to the success of our project."

Bolín extended a hand for shaking and Dollard leapt across the rug to close the gap that separated them. He'd expected the Foreign Legion uniform—high boots and jodhpurs—but questioned the need for the Sam Browne belt and revolver. Tall and erect, Bolín exuded a confidence reminiscent of l'abbé Groulx back home. Both men were used to getting what they wanted. But there was an arrogance about Bolín that had Dollard digging his nails into his palms. The director's eyes bore into his.

"Alien newsmen seldom impress me, Señor Desjardins. Years as a journalist in England have not warmed me to my foreign colleagues. I find them deceitful—accepting our hospitality then going home to print lies." His eyes hardened. "Should I expect better of you?"

Dollard attempted to swallow, but found his mouth dry. He glanced at Jane who urged with her eyes for him to say something. "My newspaper prints only the truth, señor. It speaks for French-Canadians. We're a small nation of Catholics struggling to hold true to faith and culture in a degenerate America."

The director's eyebrows lifted as he turned and walked back behind his desk. "Fine words," he said, looking at Jane. "Are we to believe him,

Marquesa?"

Jane hesitated, cocking her head. Dollard's mouth sagged. "I'd say . . . yes," she announced finally. "He's the kind of idealistic young man I'd hoped to attract on our tours, and his reports do justice to our cause. He'd stay on to do more if he was granted a *salvoconducto*." She motioned with her hand for Dollard to present his credentials.

Dollard fumbled in his portfolio for the letters of introduction from Cardinal Villeneuve and *Le Devoir*. "I'm sorry, señor, but they're in French. Shall I translate?"

Bolín stiffened. "I am not an illiterate," he snapped, without bothering to look up. Dollard tried again to swallow, remembering the one-way, nighttime walks this man reputedly prescribed for those failing expectations. When Bolín had finished, he scribbled on a piece of paper and handed it to Dollard. "You're not getting a *salvoconducto*," he announced, "yet. But I will extend your visa while we check on your newspaper, as well as this cardinal who speaks so highly of you. If you measure up, we'll call. If you don't . . . well, we'll still call," he grinned.

Jane Anderson, Marquesa de Cienfuegos, walked out of Dollard's life soon after the meeting with Bolín. His instructions were to sit and wait for the director's decision. She was off to introduce a new group of reporters to the wonders of Franco's Spain. It irked him to think their relationship was nothing more than business, but he reconciled himself to her absence with the realization that he was having the time of his life.

Unlike Burgos and other centres he'd found so dismal with their nightly blackouts and wailing sirens, Salamanca was a city of lights and merrymaking. He was born for this life. At the Gran Hotel, officials strutted their finery. And, yes, while Spanish and German officers treated him coldly, Mussolini's men took him out to bars and bragged about their 30,000 countrymen here to save Spain. They scorned the efforts of the Portuguese, all 40,000 of them, and played down the effectiveness of Germany's measly 17,000-strong Condor Legion. Dollard would nod in agreement, but as the days and nights passed, he began to suspect that Franco's campaign would have died in its infancy if not for all the foreigners, including the Moorish troops, who'd been brought over from Spanish Morocco in the opening days of the conflict.

Yet, after nearly three weeks, with still no word from Bolín, even Salamanca began to pale. Dollard waited nervously as time ran down on his visa.

These worries, as well as his mounting liquor bill, were on his mind as he headed into the Gritti Lounge for an evening nightcap. "Hey! Frenchy," a voice called out in English from somewhere down the bar. "What's the news?"

"McCullagh! You old dog," he yelled back. "Still scrounging drinks?" The Irish reporter emerged from a crowd of Italians, and the two men punched each other in the arm.

"Thought they'd have packed you away to Canada by now, boyo."

Dollard raised two hands with crossed fingers. "Still waiting for that *conducto*," he replied. "If it doesn't come in three days, I'm toast."

"Mine came the day after you left. Bastards were holding out on me because I'm Irish. Apparently that idiot O'Duffy and his blue-shirted volunteers shamed seed and breed. They packed him off in disgrace. Put a stain on us all. Anyway, here I am, healthy and as busy as they'll allow me to be."

Dollard leaned in closer. "'Ave you met Bolín, yet? There's a piece of work."

McCullagh nodded. "Genuine asshole," he said in a whisper. "Evil things befall those who fail to follow his rules—especially if they're foreign."

The Germans next to them began loudly toasting a comrade. The two friends moved to another table to escape the heel-clicking. Dollard finished his cocktail and signalled to the waiter for another. "If I ever get my 'ands on that *conducto*," he said, "it'll be bye-bye Bolín for me."

"I used to think that, too," McCullagh said, lowering his voice, "'til I learned better. No matter where you are in this country, you don't shit without his permission." The waiter approached. When he'd deposited the drinks, McCullagh leaned forward. "Here's how it works: They tell you where you can go, when, and for how long. You provide your own car, but have to travel in convoy with other reporters and government supervisors."

"They can't be watching you every minute of the day?"

"Just about. They censor your reports before you file. And don't ever try talking to a soldier in the field. There's more, Dollard, but you get the gist."

"You advised me once to, 'ow you say . . . fuzz the text to get out a message."

McCullagh took a long drink then looked around. "Forget that. Don't even think of using obscure references or double entendres.

Bolín's censors are as fluent in French as they are in English. These guys aren't playing Monopoly; they're living it. And it's no Go Directly to Jail card they hand you, either. Those black squads we've heard about? The ones who take you for walks in the night? They're for real." He nodded, letting his words sink in. "Still want to be a reporter in this country?" Dollard smiled. "Good boy," McCullagh said, leaning over and slapping him on the shoulder.

"But I 'ave neither *conducto* nor car."

"You get the papers," McCullagh replied, "and I'll get the transport. I'm sharing a car with Kim Philby of the *London Times* and Virginia Cowles of *Hearst Universal News*. They'll be only too happy to split expenses one more way."

Chapter Nineteen

October 10, 1937
Zaragoza, Spain, near the Aragon Front

DOLLARD PUT HIS PEN DOWN and signalled for another *vino*. Coffee would be preferable, but that was as much a luxury in Zaragoza as in the rest of Nationalist Spain. He was sitting at an outdoor café on the Plaza del Pilar, trying to describe the basilica across the square in a letter to l'abbé Groulx. So far he'd only managed the date and a few unconnected descriptors—baroque, majestic, gargantuan. In the laid-back, holiday atmosphere that surrounded him, composing had become a chore. He'd been with McCullagh since receiving his *conducto* in August. Two months had passed, and they were still holed up at the Oriente Hotel in the old section of Zaragoza. They weren't alone; several carloads of journalists languished here, too, hungry for action. By now, he knew the city inside out. He could walk blindfolded through the maze of streets, from Caesar Augustus's wall to the Palacio de la Aljaferia. Their original arrival had been one of excitement—at last Bolín was letting him see the war. But as August became September, and then October, the only battles he'd witnessed comprised drunken donnybrooks between Spanish and Italian troops. Just as often the brawling was Spaniard on Spaniard—legionnaires, who claimed to be doing Franco's heavy lifting, versus aristocratic, Carlist noblesse-obligers, or political opportunists like the Falangists.

Dollard's wine arrived. "*Cerveza por favor*," a voice called from behind. He looked over his shoulder to see McCullagh hurrying toward him, all smiles. "I've got the *craic*, boy."

"What?"

"The news," McCullagh said, pulling up a chair and rubbing his hands. "Something big's up. It could be the front for us at last."

Dollard took a long swallow. "*Nom de Dieu!*" he replied. "We've been down that road before."

"Got it from a Carlist officer. Cost me a whole pack of English fags, too, or, in your currency, about what you'd pay for a girl." Dollard ignored the wisecrack. McCullagh drummed his fingers on the table. "According to my source, August and September were bad months for Franco, both in Madrid and here on the Aragon front."

"The Republicans, they are advancing?"

"Not quite. Do you mind that town we visited just east of here? Fuentes de Ebro?" Dollard's face screwed up. "The one with the rebel fortress atop the high ridge?"

"Do you 'ave to keep referring to the Nationalists as rebels?" Dollard replied, shaking his head.

The Irishman wagged a finger as the waiter set down his beer. "A spade is a goddamn shovel, Dollard. Time you learned that."

"It cheapens Franco."

"The guy took up arms against an elected government, didn't he? In my books, that makes him a rebel."

"But if 'e 'adn't—"

McCullagh raised a hand. "Drop it! I'm trying to tell you something." Dollard crossed his arms. "When Bolín sent us up here from Burgos—"

"I 'ated that place."

The older man rolled his eyes, "—the Republicans had just started their move against fortified Nationalist centres along the Aragon front."

"Burgos. Gloomiest city I ever set foot in."

"Will you shut up! What we were supposed to see was Franco's finest repelling the attack in a glorious counteroffensive. It didn't happen. They failed miserably at Belchite."

"Which they didn't want us to see, so they left us cooling our 'eels back 'ere in Zaragoza."

McCullagh leaned forward. "Correct. But word is the Republicans are on the move again. This time against Fuentes. If it's true, they're in for a shock. According to my source, the rebels are lying in wait."

Dollard caught the waiter's eye and pointed to their empty glasses. "Think they'll actually let us do some front-line reporting?"

"Dunno, but Franco's been having a terrible bloody time of it and could use some favourable publicity. If Bolín thinks a victory's in the bag, he'll want it splashed across the foreign press."

"So it 'inges on whether or not they think they can win?"

"Which is looking good, Dollard. My tipster claims the Germans helped plan the fortifications. And Franco's got good troops up there, too—the 150th Division and the 15th, not to mention Moors and Legionnaires. If they can't do it, who can?"

"Any idea who they might be facing?"

"My source hopes it's the International Brigades. He has a score to settle with those bastards after Belchite." He raised his glass. "So, my friend, keep your bags packed and your fingers crossed."

October 11, 1937
Republican Line, Fuentes de Ebro

MARTY HAD COME TO LOATHE a lot of things about Spain. Lately, it was those troop-transport trucks with the red stars painted on the tailgates. In his mind's eye, they were harbingers of doom. Just the sight of them set him into a funk. Now they were back and once again in pitch blackness. This time the troops were off to some obscure place called Fuentes de Ebro. A candy walk, they'd been assured. They'd heard that before.

After he'd been discharged from the hospital, he'd shown up in Villaneuva de la Jara healed, chastened, and back to Kellenberger. Reaction to the name change was mixed.

"Damnation," Comrade Captain ranted, "have you any idea the paperwork this makes for me? And, Kellenberger, or whoever you are, as long as I'm running this outfit, you are not going to wear that red circle thing on your sleeve."

Tauno claimed he suspected all along. "This is my Jewish friend Kellenberger," he shouted in the mess hall, practising the new name on his lips, "and he's going to tell us all about his first Catholic Christmas in Vancouver." The Yiddish-speaking lads who'd crossed the Atlantic with them sneered. The rest of the men shrugged—understandable considering the melting pot of languages and political affiliations in the Abraham Lincoln Battalion. In the end, no one stopped calling him Kelly and, in spite of the mismatched, ill-fitting uniforms that had them looking more like college freshmen than soldiers, they all got busy at learning the art of war.

The weeks in Villaneuva were happy ones. The barracks turned out to be a monastery, with the church across the street transformed into a mess hall. As for the food, they'd been fed a steady diet of barley, chickpeas, boiled rice, onions fried in olive oil, and what the cooks insisted was coffee. The training weapons comprised a hodgepodge of leftovers from a dozen Great War armies; however, with ammunition scarce, there was a lot of pretend shooting, which wasn't necessarily a bad thing, considering the frequency of explosions from mismatched bullets. The marching was a waste of time, but instructions on mapping, scouting, and signalling were bang-on. Ditto the lessons on explosives, fortifications, and how to manoeuvre and infiltrate as a unit.

During off hours, there were wine, cards, baseball, and radio broadcasts from Madrid. The lucky ones, courtesy of trusting townsfolk, even got to walk out with their daughters on Sunday afternoons. Marty wrote letters daily to Connie. For many of the volunteers, it was a respite from the unemployment back home and, in spite of diarrhea and other ailments, almost the summer camp they'd never had. Except for some political infighting that Marty had begun to notice, it was a united world — internationals, Spanish soldiers, local citizens. They locked arms, cursed the Nationalists, or Whites as they called them, and when harvest rolled around, spent off-hours helping the peasants bring in the crops. Of course it couldn't last.

Marty had finished basic training full of enthusiasm, but Belchite soon knocked that out of him. Yes, you could argue they'd won that battle, but at best it was a pyrrhic victory. He was no military tactician, but even he could see that men, materials, and precious time had been squandered trying to take a town that could just as easily have been bypassed and contained. The thirteen days wasted at Belchite gave the Nationalists just the right amount of time to regroup and halt the Republican offensive. As close as Marty could figure out, the senseless deaths of so many of his new friends in the Lincolns had come about because of jealousy, infighting, and political intrigue at the top. He might have sounded off about it, too, if not for the reputation of the battalion political-commissar who saw to it that dissenters, doubters, and criticizers met with severe punishment.

In the end, Marty and Tauno kept their mouths shut on Belchite, opting instead to transfer to the newly formed Mackenzie-Papineau Battalion. It wasn't really as all-Canadian as he'd hoped, but his countrymen formed the backbone, and it was comforting to hear chatter about towns and cities he'd once glimpsed from boxcar doors. He hoped the new leaders, Captain Smith and Comrade Political-Commissar Wellman, would be able to shield them from the stupidity of the high command, but he doubted it. In the meantime, he resolved to jump only when told and look after his own backside. Tauno's, too, of course.

"If you ask me, they'll screw this offensive up, too," Tauno moaned.

Marty checked to see if anyone in the crowded truck might be listening. No one was. To a man they seemed numb, lost in their own worlds. "Probably," he replied quickly. "How could the same army get

Quinto so right and Belchite so wrong?"

"Incompetence," Tauno sneered. "My guess is the air, artillery, and ground coordination that worked so well at Quinto was a fluke."

Marty raised the collar on the German aviator jacket he'd won in a card game, thankful for the extra protection from the cold. October nights on the high plains of Aragon were brutal. He leaned into Tauno. "Another blunder like Belchite might just get me reconsidering my future in this war."

Tauno stared at him, his body swaying with the motion of the truck. "We wouldn't get far without passports. And you've seen what happens to deserters."

Marty studied the exhausted men around him; half of them were plagued by pleurisy and dysentery and too sick to fight. Still, when the machine guns opened, they'd come to life. He felt Tauno press in tighter, his thin tunic providing little warmth. They'd laughed about their clothing. With Marty in possession of the best jacket and Tauno the best boots, they'd agreed that should either of them "buy the farm," the other would inherit the coveted apparel. Marty glanced up at the breaking sky over the hills to the east. "Daybreak soon," he said as the convoy lurched to a stop. Whistles screamed, while stiff, half-frozen Mac-Paps dismounted, some falling on impact with the ground and needing help to stand up.

"Ten jeezly freezing hours on an open truck," Tauno grumbled, staring at the food in his pannikin, "and they feed us cold slop. How can you fight on this?" The man beside him coughed up phlegm. Tauno's elbow came up to shield himself from the spray.

Around them, there was little conversation. What there was died as the new day revealed their first glimpse of the mile-long slope up the ridge to Fuentes de Ebro, the town they were expected to take.

Swallowing his gruel, Marty was about to comment on their objective when he noticed Comrade Commissar Wellman coming down the line, barking orders, and pointing. "In a few minutes, we move into the forward trenches," he shouted. "The attack begins at 0700 hours. As soon as the bombers drop their loads, tanks will come up from behind. You're to follow them in. Stick close. They've been instructed to move slowly. This is a big one, men. Clean out Fuentes and the road to Zaragoza lies open."

As soon as Wellman was out of earshot, Marty signalled for the new recruits in his platoon to move in close. "Listen up," he said. "Drink water 'til you piss, then drink some more. You may be freezing now, but it'll be a scorcher when the sun goes to work. There are no fountains where we're going." He gestured to the hill with his chin. "And keep watch when the tanks come through. They're half-blind in those tin cans and scared shitless. Just like us. You didn't come this far to get crushed. And another thing. You new guys are not to throw any grenades. Understand? Those Mills bombs can be tricky." He began smearing mud on his helmet and face. The recruits followed suit.

A whistle blew. They rushed for the shallow trenches, where they huddled in the damp cold, watching the sun crest over the horizon in the east and straining for sounds of motors overhead that would signal the start of the attack. Roosters and donkeys brayed in the distance. Four heart-pumping hours passed, but nothing happened. At 1000 hours, two Republican batteries lobbed a few shells at the enemy. Still nothing. Two hours later, tiny specks became visible in the cloudless sky, and a cheer went up for the bombers. Marty shook his head in disgust. "Too few and too high," he whispered to Tauno as they covered their ears. Minutes later, Fuentes disappeared in a cloud of dust. Blood up, they readied themselves anew, restless to get at it, anxious for the tanks to arrive. Again nothing. The grousing resumed. Another hour and a half passed under a merciless sun. A boy down the line wept.

"So much for mounting a co ordinated attack," Marty mumbled.

Tauno uncorked his canteen. "God help us," he replied as he drank greedily.

<hr />

October 12, 1937
Nationalist Line, Fuentes de Ebro

DOLLARD AWAKENED TO BANGING and shouts in the hall. Pulling the chain on the bed lamp, he checked his watch: four o'clock. Across the room, McCullagh sat up, burped, scratched the stubble on his chin, and staggered to the sink. Dollard cocked an ear nervously for air raid sirens before rushing to the door. In the hallway, Aguilera, Bolín's press czar in Zaragoza, was rounding up the journalists. "Fuentes de Ebro," he recited in his nasal, railway-conductor voice. "Motorcade leaves, *veinte minutos.*"

"Twenty minutes," Dollard protested. "What about breakfast?" He made eating motions to Aguilera with his fingers. "*Desayuno?*"

Aguilera looked disgusted. "You want eat, eat," he replied in his thick accent. "You want see Republican army get ass wiped, be at car in *veinte minutos*."

McCullagh shrieked from behind his towel. "That's ass-kicked, you benighted sod," he laughed.

By 4:20, Dollard, McCullagh, Philby, and Cowles stood by their car in absolute darkness, stomachs growling. Aguilera was nowhere in sight. Fifteen minutes later he showed up, pomaded and patting his lips with a serviette. The journalists cursed, but tempered their remarks when hotel employees appeared with thermoses, buns, and a picnic hamper. It was Outremont all over again, Dollard observed, with the servants preparing provisions for a weekend in the Laurentians.

The cavalcade set off in the prescribed order—number one government-escort vehicle in front, number two government-escort vehicle in the rear, reporters' cars sandwiched in between. As usual, Aguilera had opted for the safety of the rear. Manoeuvring the still dark streets with headlights half-painted out in blue made for slow going, but even that came to a full stop when they reached the highway to Fuentes. Before them, a stream of military vehicles filled both lanes, while here and there, provosts waved flashlights in wide swoops to keep the convoy moving. The journalists waited for a break in the traffic as one minute became five, then ten, then fifteen, with the army drivers refusing to let them in.

"Do something," Philby ordered their driver.

"*Pero, señor*," Manuel shrugged, in that age-old Spanish manner suggesting there was nothing he could do.

"Oh, for God's sake," Philby snapped as he reached over Manuel's shoulder and pushed hard on the horn. The other cars followed suit.

Out of the darkness, a provost screamed to a stop on his motorcycle, flashlight ablaze, to find Aguilera waving papers in a perfect parody of the Generalissimo himself. It worked. Traffic was halted, and the five-car cavalcade of spectators tucked into the current to continue its way to the show.

"These guys 'ave got to be invincible," Dollard remarked. "I mean, 'ave you ever seen so much ordnance on the go at one time?" Beside him, Philby blew air in disgust.

"We'll see," McCullagh replied. "At least it's beginning to look like they might actually put on a show for us."

A motorcycle passed them on the inside, lights flickering at intervals. In the glare, Dollard took in the crates packed haphazardly on the truck ahead. "'Ope they're not 'igh explosives," he said. The others stared, but no one responded.

Cowles glanced at her watch then closed her eyes. "Wake me if anything worth reporting turns up," she said.

Dollard bounced in his seat, wiping condensation from the window and straining to see in the darkness. He was amazed by the hodgepodge of humanity on the move: soldiers in rubber ponchos marching with their heads down; an old lady in a black shawl selling sweets from a cart; a priest on a side road blessing a column of tanks; civilians scurrying in the opposite direction, loaded down with prized items — animals, beds, rolled-up rugs, clocks, sewing machines.

It was still dark as the car approached Fuentes. Dollard opened the window. The cold air drifted in.

"What the hell you doing?" Philby grumbled.

"I want to 'ear if it's started."

"You'd hear! Now shut the damned window. It's cold."

A checkpoint on the edge of town popped out of the darkness. The vehicles ahead kept moving, but the cavalcade of journalists was shunted aside and forced to halt, where a puzzled legionnaire examined Aguilera's papers. There was a heated discussion, after which Aguilera began waving his arms. "Out! Out!" he told the reporters. "Walk, walk." The reporters scrunched around the press chief while he went through a litany of warnings. "Don't get in soldiers' way," he lectured. "*No hablo Ingles. Ingles* is enemy. Soldiers shoot. *Entiende*?" They nodded, fully aware of the army's suspicion of foreign tongues.

By dawn, the reporters had found a vantage point at the church. From there, they could see down the long, sloping hill to the Republican lines a mile off and, beyond that, the Ebro River. To Dollard's eye, the Nationalist fortifications were formidable. Above them on the heights, heavy German 88mm guns pointed down the valley. Just below the town, a series of trenches teeming with soldiers ran parallel to the highway. Connecting ditches from the town allowed them to enter or leave without exposing themselves.

By ten o'clock, Dollard began to relax. Cowles was right; another false alarm. Yet again, Montreal readers would be denied a first-hand report from the lines. McCullagh unscrewed his thermos, allowing himself a mouthful of coffee. "Got to make it last," he advised. "Those assholes at the hotel forgot to include water in the provisions." Dollard looked around. Some of the reporters were dozing with their backs to the church wall, while Philby was sucking on his pipe and trying to convince someone to fetch the picnic hamper from the car.

At 10:15, Dollard and McCullagh abandoned the others for a closer look at the fortifications. The Irishman was pointing out the advantages of the parapet on the forward trench when he was interrupted by a faint sound. To Dollard, it reminded him of a motor boat. They turned. The noise grew louder.

"*Aviones*," soldiers shouted as they scrambled for cover. Immediately, troops in the forward trenches began sprinting toward town, diving into cellars.

"Back to the church," McCullagh ordered. They were still running for cover when black shadows appeared in the sky and the earth began to shake. Panting hard, they rounded a corner and were in sight of their objective when a cellar door flew open, blocking their path. A wide-eyed legionnaire burst out, his carbine up, pointing at the foreigners. Dollard gasped. "*Viva la muerte*," he stammered, raising his arms and praying he'd put the correct intonation on the Foreign Legion's slogan.

"*Viva la muerte*," the surprised cabo responded, motioning Dollard and McCullagh down the stairs to shelter.

They'd scarcely reached the bottom when the first bomb hit. Dollard closed his eyes and began asking the Lord's forgiveness for past transgressions. A second bomb hit, then a third. Still the Lord made no move to take him. Then, as the drone overhead grew faint, officers on the street above began barking instructions amidst the shriek of whistles. In the cellar, all eyes were on the cabo. Slowly, as if this had just been a training exercise, he rose, issued a terse command, and marched his men up the stairs. McCullagh and Dollard followed.

Out on the street, soldiers had covered their faces with rags as they clambered over rubble and around obstacles. Despite the seeming chaos, there was no panic. Dollard coughed, a sudden fear seizing him as he reached for his handkerchief. "*Sacrement*!" he blurted. "Gas!"

"Dust," McCullagh shot back, in disgust. "It'll settle."

They waited in the doorway watching soldiers scurrying back to their posts. "What's to 'appen now?" Dollard asked, when the street had cleared.

"Fireworks," McCullagh replied. "Let's go. The Republicans will be out of their trenches and halfway up the hill by now. Our boys have to get back into position, fast." He paused. "Strange, though, there's been no shooting." They struck out for the vantage point at the church.

On arrival, the enemy was nowhere in sight. An hour passed, then two. Dollard made a trip to the car and returned with the picnic basket. Cowles handed out bread and olives, and shooed the flies away. As conversation lagged, Dollard pulled out his notepad. The day hadn't been a complete loss. He'd survived an air raid, giving him something, finally, to write about.

Around 1:30, the sound of racing motors and clanking metal echoed up from the valley floor. Dollard jumped to his feet to see columns of Russian tanks charging up the slope at breakneck speed. Atop each machine, figures squirmed and bucked as they tried to hang on. Behind them, far behind, foot soldiers struggled to keep up.

"'Ow far away you put them?" Dollard called out to McCullagh in a worried voice.

"About three-quarters of a mile," he replied.

Dollard's pulse shot up again. "That'll put them on us pretty soon, then, eh?"

"Only if they make it." McCullagh replied calmly. His expression suggested he'd seen this before.

Then, from above the town, shells whined overhead, exploding in puffs amidst the tanks below. Men and machines kept moving, larger now, but fewer in number. They must have reached some predetermined mark, because suddenly Fuentes came alive with Nationalist small-arms fire. Soldiers on the tanks were raked off, like leaves in autumn. Few got up. Dollard inhaled the smoke coming up from the burning tanks, wondering if it was the acrid smell or unbearable noise that provoked the high-pitched battle cry from the Moors. Their ululating drifted into the valley and mingled with the screams of the wounded.

A few Republicans were drawing closer, but most were either dead, or frantically scooping at the baked earth with bayonets and helmets. From the town, snipers pointed at targets and picked them off one by one, cheering and slapping backs as their victims bucked from the impact of high-expansive bullets.

Dollard focused on a particular tank with a four-leaf clover painted on the side. By some miracle, the machine had reached an advanced point and was only seconds from entering the streets. He cringed as the explosions around it intensified, anticipating the horror-cum-exhilaration of a kill at close range. But the four-leaf clover was proving true to its billing; the machine came on, only to disappear behind a house. Seconds later it was clattering over the cobblestone street leading to the church.

"Holy shit!" Dollard said, as they scrambled to safety. "'Ow can that thing manoeuvre these narrow streets?"

The tank fired, taking out a pillbox below the church. Instinct screamed at Dollard to take flight, but he found himself mesmerized by the advancing mechanical monster.

"*Tanquista! Tanquista!*" legionnaires shouted from the rooftops, followed by a loud "kaboom."

Dollard opened his eyes to see the tank aflame. He held his breath, wondering why the legionnaires hadn't budged. Then the turret popped open, followed by a soldier wearing goggles and a Red Grange helmet. He positioned his arms on the top of the hatch as if ready to spring from the tank, but one glance at the rooftops told him it was futile. Instead he threw his fist upwards in the Republican salute and shouted.

"Hell's fire!" McCullagh sputtered. "That's Gallic. That man's a countryman."

Several shots rang out and the soldier slumped over, blood pouring down the side of the tank. The body had barely gone limp when the Moors were on him, plucking at his carcass, until a sergeant approached and barked an order. The men stood to, displaying their booty. The officer pulled something from a pair of hands, then ordered them back to work.

Dollard gaped at the hole in the Irishman's head. The olives Cowles had fed him tried to exit. He swallowed hard, turning to McCullagh. "What'd he say?"

"Incredible! He was shouting, 'Home Rule,' as if he were a Sinn Feiner and this was Dublin 1916. Poor deluded bugger. Makes no sense 't all."

October 12, 1937
Republican Line, Fuentes de Ebro

"LOOK SHARP," MARTY SCREAMED, jumping clear. Russian T-26 tanks loaded with foot soldiers were charging at them from the rear. The Mac-Paps leapt up cursing and dodging as the machines passed through the lines. Some of the frightened Spaniards on the clanking mammoths mistook them for the enemy and began shooting. In the panic, a few of the men fired back. The boy from Stratford leapt clear of one tank and into the path of another. He scrambled frantically, but not fast enough, as the tank rolled over his foot leaving him screaming, his lower leg a mangled mess.

"Lucky bastard," Tauno mouthed. They were on their feet now, racing, trying to keep up with the tanks. Useless. After a hundred yards, they slowed to catch their breath, while ahead of them tanks began exploding. At some point, enfilading fire from Fuentes found its range and dum-dum bullets hissed by their ears, to explode on impact with the ground. Those still on their feet bent forward in an attempt to create a smaller target. Some raced in silence. Others screamed against the deafening roar. A few flopped to the ground for cover behind the bodies of the *carabineros* who'd been raked off the tanks.

Marty lay flat on the earth, raising his head as he tried to locate their sergeant. With no sign of him, he unleashed a stream of orders to those newcomers who'd flopped near him. "For Chrissakes, stop bunching up. You make too big a target. Thin on the ground. What you were taught in basic."

The fresh recruits just blinked. Marty shook his head in disgust. Like it or not, they were his charges now. "When you shoot blind, use your Spanish cartridges. Save the Mexican ones for targets you can see."

An overwhelming urge to lie still and wait it out surged through him. That's what the recruits would want. Tauno, too. He also knew that when a soldier went to ground, the hardest thing in the world was to jump up and renew the charge.

He took a deep breath, choking on the cordite. "See that crippled T-26 ahead?" he screamed. "That's were we're going." Should be safe there, he thought. He hoped the recruits were too terrified to notice that only a few of the machines were still mobile, while the rest were either afire or sitting useless with their lugs blown off.

"Go!" he yelled, banging two recruits on the head and tugging a third forward. To his surprise, they rose with him. Machine-gun fire intensified. "Hands and knees," he screamed. "Crawl!" Bodies flopped to the ground. The boy between him and Tauno tried to bury his face in the hard earth. Together, they yanked him to his knees, ignoring the tears and snot that covered his face.

For the next few minutes, Marty concentrated on getting them to the protection of the tank, but others had had the same idea, and the machine couldn't shield them all. To complicate the situation, the T-26 had been crippled, but not entirely disabled. It began to fire, attracting attention. Marty signalled for his group to push on.

"No," screamed the boy clutching the tank.

"I said move," Marty ordered. "The tank's a magnet. Artillery'll get us all if we stay here." Still, the boy refused to budge. Marty and Tauno exchanged shrugs and moved off. Where the hell was the goddamned sergeant?

Fifty yards up the slope, they went to ground to catch their breath and pluck pebbles from their shins. "*Morteros nacionales*," someone screamed. Shells exploded behind them, followed by screams from the tank they just left. "Don't look back," Marty ordered.

Reaching the part of the *barranca* where the climb began to get steeper was like emerging from a rain shower. One second they were under a hail of machine-gun bullets, the next it was behind them. But the respite was brief, as the riflemen in the forward trenches were about to have their day. Marty could picture them pointing out targets and laying bets.

"This is horseshit!" Tauno yelled between gasps. "We'll never make it."

Marty's eyes swept the terrain for cover. There was nothing but smooth, cement-hard earth from here up to the town. A small knoll ahead was a possibility, but he could see sprinters up front going down in their attempt.

"Screw it!" he yelled to his men. "Get down and start digging." In unison, they flopped to the ground and began scratching at the earth like gophers. Those with bayonets used them, others resorted to the tin mess-plates strapped to their belts. To raise yourself for leverage was an invitation to die, forcing them to lie prone with their arms stretched out front, cutting away at the baked soil.

"Cock-up!" Tauno hollered to no one and every one, scraping furiously. "Another goddamned cock-up."

Marty did a quick count. The corporal and sergeant were missing. Of the twenty men in the squad, seven were with him, counting himself and Tauno. Four others he'd seen go down—two Canadians, one American, one Spaniard. The rest had disappeared into the shell bursts and yellow powder that drifted and swirled like mustard gas across no man's land. He blinked, trying to make sense of it all.

With the sprint for Fuentes stalled, the defenders halted shelling to let the dust settle so the sharpshooters on the ridge could share in the fun. Marty calculated that it was only a matter of time before they were in for it. As visibility improved, he spied a slight dip in the terrain a few yards to the right. "Over there," he hissed. "Better protection. Kitten-crawl. All together. Go!"

"No!" the boy to Marty's right objected. "That'll draw attention."

Except for the boy, the group moved. Marty rolled over to him, punching and pushing, and when he refused to budge tried to drag him. The boy fought back, raising himself to take a swing. Bam. Like a pumpkin, the boy's head exploded. Body parts splattered across Marty and the battlefield. Marty dropped the arm he'd been holding and rolled to the others.

The new position was marginally better. They grabbed their knives, plates, and helmets and went back to work. Once satisfied with their shallow depressions, they lay still, panting. "That's a piss-poor hole for a coal miner," Marty said to the Cape Bretoner to his left.

"My dad's the miner, not me," the man replied.

"Who's got water?" the man to Marty's right called out, raising his head to look around. Instantly, bullets began ricocheting off the baked earth around him.

"For Chrissakes, don't budge," Marty screamed, grabbing his canteen by the strap and flinging it to the soldier. As the lad reached for it, the soil bubbled up with bullets, destroying the canteen along with the hand. Marty pulled in his arm and the empty strap.

"Sweet Jesus!" the man screamed. "My hand! It's gone!"

Marty could see blood arcing in the air with each wild pump of the man's heart. "Don't panic," he yelled. "Put a tourniquet on it . . . just like they taught you in basic." The youngster lay there, staring at his life draining away.

"He needs help," Tauno shouted.

"No!" Marty replied. "Stay put."

"But he's from Regina."

"So?"

"Are you forgetting how they backed us in the riots?"

"What you got in mind?"

"We throw grenades. Create some dust. Then I'll pull him over here."

"We'll blow up our own men."

"There's nobody alive up there. We're the friggin' vanguard, for Chrissake—posthumous medal material."

"Worth a try." They readied hand bombs. "On three," Marty yelled.

The canisters flew in the air and the Mac-Paps counted together, timing their movement to the explosions. When the grenades went off, Marty and the others lifted their rifles over their heads and began firing, while Tauno rolled to Regina. Dum-dums came bouncing down the hard slope searching for soft targets. Then Marty heard the sickening pop that would stay with him the rest of his days. The force blew Tauno back to the perimeter of Marty's shallow hole. Marty rolled onto his back, pulling him in.

"The boots," Tauno gasped, "the boots." His body went limp.

Marty stared at his dead friend, listening to the screech of shells, the bursts of machine fire, and the whine of bullets. Above, the sun had barely passed its zenith. He licked his cracked lips and considered raising his head. Six inches was all it would take. Why not go down with Tauno? His life had been a succession of screw-ups. He thought of Connie, patiently waiting for him to prove himself and grow up. Flies found their way to the blood and shit around Tauno's exposed bowels. Marty swiped at them.

"I think the tourniquet's working," Regina called out in a weak voice.

"Shut your fucking gob," Marty moaned.

October 26, 1937
Republican Trenches, Fuentes de Ebro

MARTY TOSSED AND TURNED on the shelf he'd carved out of the back wall of the trench. It had become his personal refuge. It wasn't the Ritz, but between the rotting canvas that covered the entrance and the sputtering candles, it was amazing how much more comfortable it was than out in the open. Lately, he'd been spending all his off-duty time in here. Not that he got much sleep. With sporadic shell bursts and machine-gun fire, not to mention the cold, rats, and lice, an hour or two was the most he could ever count on at a time. Tonight, as usual, he was wide awake on his back and thinking of Tauno when a hand pulled aside the soggy tarp.

"Comrade Captain wants to talk to you, Kelly."

Marty didn't recognize the voice. "What about?" There was no answer, only the sound of boots splashing off through the slop. Sighing, he swung his feet down and turned up his collar. Then, checking to see that he had left nothing of value behind, he set off. His route took him past troopers doing their best to survive: bodies curled up on homemade beds fashioned from rope, sticks, and boards; soldiers on guard duty, shivering under rubber ponchos and staring trance-like into the night; and groups hanging around open fires torching lice in their clothes with lighted cigarettes. Just before he reached the exit closest to the captain's dugout, he listened for machine-gun chatter. Hearing none, he climbed out of the trench. That he didn't hurry had as much to do with disregard for his own safety as lack of interest in what Smith might have to say. He moved cautiously through the smoky haze to avoid the refuse behind the trenches—jagged tin cans, broken bottles, rusted-out bed springs, buggy seats, shards of glass, discarded food, rat carcasses, human excrement. *The real smell of war*, he thought, *trench war*.

Marty had been expecting this summons. Two weeks had passed since Fuentes de Ebro and his funk hadn't lifted. Captain Smith had expressed his concern. So had the younger guys who'd latched onto him. As for Marty, he no longer gave a rat's ass. From here on, all that mattered was returning to Canada and Connie.

He cast his mind back to the hours after Tauno's death. No one could move until darkness fell, at which time he pulled off his friend's boots, before leading the others to safety. Commissar Wellman forbade him from returning for Tauno's body. "The place will be swarming with White scavengers," he said. "We can't afford losing any more men." Boiling inside, Marty sneaked back on his own, working his way through the Nationalist patrols. On finding Tauno, he saw that his prized items—water bottle, knife, flashlight—were already gone. Disgusted, he dragged his friend back for burial.

Next day, at dawn, he found himself in a new trench, a scant few metres ahead of the old one. In front of him, up the slope to Fuentes, the fields were littered with burned-out tanks, rotting corpses, and abandoned arms. Above that, the hilltop fortress they'd been assigned to take basked in the morning sun, untouched except for a few bomb craters. His mind went to Belchite. Two senseless slaughters in a row. Why?

During the fortnight since Tauno's death, he'd whiled away the hours, boiling by day, freezing by night, stewing over what he'd experienced. Although the rain had added to his gloom, it was all clear now. The glorious cause had turned to shit, its principles exposed as will-o'-the-wisps, undermined by incompetence and infighting. There had been thousands of lives lost with nothing to show for them. He and Tauno had come to fight the Fascists, only to find the Republicans engaged in a war within a war—liberals, socialists, anarchists, communists, Trotskyites, Stalinists, and anti-Stalinists, all in a life-and-death struggle for control.

By all appearances, the Comintern in Moscow was now in charge. They'd gotten there by murdering 4,000 Barcelonian fighters and anyone else who didn't subscribe to Stalin's brand of politics. Then, adding insult to injury, they ensured that communist battalions got the best equipment—tanks, artillery, rifles, maps, and field glasses, everything right down to trench periscopes and wire cutters. It didn't help that the Catalonians, Basques, and Asturians showed more interest in fighting for their own regional independence than preserving democracy. His head spun. He'd dragged Tauno into this. Now his friend was dead.

"Sit down, Kelly," Smith said, pointing to an empty ammunition crate to the left of Commissar Wellman.

From the jumble of maps and documents on the desk, it appeared the two men had been reviewing orders. Marty didn't like the smell of it. "Kellenberger," he corrected.

Wellman stiffened. The captain ignored Marty's impudence, holding out a package of Gaulois. "Smoke?" Marty accepted and leaned into the candle. "Comrade Commissar and I have something to discuss with you."

"Really?" Marty responded, spitting out a piece of tobacco. "Guess you'd be wanting my take on the screw-up at Fuentes?"

"Watch your language, Private," Smith replied, turning over a map that he must have decided was not for Marty's eyes. Marty glared at his superior officer, defying him to order disciplinary action. Smith was obviously having a similar internal debate. A few minutes passed before Smith spoke again. "The way you handled those recruits at Fuentes didn't go unnoticed." He stopped to let the compliment sink in, but Marty didn't bite. "We have a proposal," Smith continued.

"Four of those recruits died, Captain."

"But six came home better soldiers, thanks to you." He raised a hand to stop further rebuttal. "In spite of your . . . current attitude, the recruits in your unit have been looking to you for leadership. We'd like to make it official. Promote you all the way to sergeant. What do you say?"

Marty looked at his boots—Tauno's boots. Wellman crossed his arms. "Well?" Smith asked at last.

Marty looked up. "Tell the truth, Captain, right now that's the last bloody thing—"

"Take a few days," Smith interrupted. "They're pulling us back to Mas de las Matras for some R and R. My guess is we won't be seeing action again until spring." Marty looked for permission to leave. "Kellenberger," Smith continued, "you're a natural leader, and you've got battle smarts. You can make a difference. Ask yourself what your friend Tauno would want you to do."

"Is all this supposed to buck me up?"

Smith shook his head. "We noticed long ago that both of you were officer material. It was always a toss-up on who we'd go with first."

"Just what do you see as my capabilities?"

Smith threw a pencil onto the desk. "Well, you're quick at seeing developments unfold and reacting appropriately."

"And Tauno?"

"He followed orders. An important quality in a field officer."

Marty nodded, a smirk forming on his lips. "Figures you'd put blind obedience on a par with vision. Christ! No wonder we're losing."

Wellman stiffened. Smith shook his head at him. "A sergeant is not a field marshal, Kellenberger. Sometimes *smart* soldiers see too far ahead for their own good. They fancy themselves chess masters and withdraw because they foresee a trap six moves ahead."

"That's bad?"

Smith stared into the candle. "War is full of surprises. Ever hear of snatching victory from the jaws of defeat?"

Marty's lip curled. "You really think this army's smart enough for that?"

Wellman rose to his feet. "Careful, Kellenberger," he said.

True to his word, Smith had the Mac-Paps on trucks the next day and heading for Mas de las Matras. It turned out to be a peaceful country town, halfway between Fuentes and the Mediterranean. Noting the date, Marty was shocked that after the battles at Quinto, Belchite, Fuentes de Ebro, and two freezing, wet weeks in the trenches, it was still only November. Winter had yet to arrive. If sunny Spain could be this cold now, what would winter have in store? The weary Spanish troops they'd left behind at Fuentes had watched the International Brigades pull out with scorn in their eyes. Marty had looked away, ashamed of the joy he felt in leaving.

Captain Smith had promised two things: R and R and exemption from a winter campaign. So far he'd been true to his word on the first. Whether he could deliver on the second was anyone's guess.

Chapter Twenty

———

Christmas Day, 1937
Mas de las Matras, Spain

THE NEW LADS HAD COME A LONG WAY since Marty had accepted the rank of sergeant. He'd stopped calling them rookies. Still, they had a lot to learn, and he was doing his best. Not that they were always receptive. Plus, after two months at Mas de las Matras, they were bored. It was Christmas and homesickness was rampant, so he doubled the drills and promised them a piss-up come the twenty-fifth. That had put a bounce in their step.

So had Smith's conviction that winter combat was unlikely, although Marty wasn't sure. As a field officer, the captain was hardly privy to the overall strategy. Marty had given up altogether trying to predict what the Republican high command might have them do. These days he just kept his mind on his job, or at least his interpretation of it—get the war over with and go home. Even so, he wasn't immune to scuttlebutt, and what he heard was troubling.

On December 15, the army had thrown 100,000 men at the Nationalist line near a place called Teruel. This was to be an all-Spanish affair—no International Brigade involvement—so as to blunt the perception that non-Spaniards were now running the Republican show. Early gains at Teruel had been impressive, but rumour had it that the offensive had since bogged down. Franco was throwing everything he had into the fray, from Italian Black Flames troopers to the Luftwaffe. Marty tried not to think about it; especially, not tonight, Christmas Eve.

He and his men were enjoying themselves in a smoky *taberna* when he saw Wellman enter. In the far corner, Marty ducked down and kept on singing. With his mind on Connie and her father's generous offer, he'd been trying to recapture the spirit of that other Christmas in Vancouver. Around him, German, Polish, and Canadian International Brigaders were belting out carols in a fusion of languages. Missing from the chorus were the French, who huddled around the only pool table in town, and the English, who were caught up in the age-old British custom of bitching and moaning. Marty groaned inwardly as he saw Wellman approach him.

"You're a disgrace, Kellenberger," Wellman shouted over the racket.

Marty blinked in an effort to focus. "Got something against Jews singing Christmas carols?"

"You're drunk! Again. So are your men."

Marty dragged on his cigarette. "Did anyone . . . ever tell you, *Comrade Commissar*," he slurred, "that, even for a Jew, you've got an awfully tight ass." He closed his eyes in seeming delight as he drew the smoke deep into his lungs. The IBers beside him blanched.

Wellman puffed himself up. Marty could see his lips moving, but, with the carollers straining to get up and over "Sleep in heavenly peace," couldn't make out what he was saying. He cupped an ear. "Come again, sir," he hollered.

Wellman's response came just as the carollers finished the verse. "There's a truck outside," he boomed. "Have your men on it in five minutes."

The *taberna* went silent. "It's Christmas, for Pete's sake, sir," Marty responded.

"Which gives you no right to be drunk and disorderly in a public place. We've had complaints. With lunkheads like you loose on the streets, women are afraid to come out to the taverns or go to church."

Marty swayed then scratched his head in mock puzzlement. "People go to church in communist Spain, Comrade Commissar?"

The men roared. Wellman stiffened. "We're in the backwaters here, Kellenberger. Superstition dies hard. Now, get your men moving."

"Yes, sir, Commissar, we're going. Right, lads?" The men groaned. "Just promise not to send us to that jeezly Teruel. They say it's twenty below up there."

Laughter died. "Be on that truck in five minutes," Wellman repeated, as he headed for the door.

New Year's Eve saw Marty's squad heading north. The convoy switchbacked its way up the passes, bucking snowdrifts and struggling to keep from skidding off the road. Not all succeeded; especially those at the back of the line trying to negotiate the ice created by the spinning wheels of the vehicles ahead. A few disappeared over the bluffs, yet the convoy kept moving, leaving it up to the sweepers coming along behind to salvage what they could of men and materiel. Marty's boys pressed together under their truck's canvas, praying for hot food and shelter at the end of the line. "Crappy way to spend New Year's Eve," Marty muttered more to himself than anyone else. The truck came to a stop and the men had started to gather up their gear, when the back flap snapped open.

"Stay where you are, men," ordered Wellman. "They're just clearing the road ahead. Be on our way in a few minutes."

"Where to?" Marty asked.

Wellman hesitated. "Teruel," he replied, dropping the flap.

———

January 17, 1938

Zaragoza, Nationalist Spain

MCCULLAGH CAME FLYING INTO THE BAR and stopped. When he spied his friend, he cut through a circle of Falangist soldiers engaged in animated talk. "Ignorant foreigner," one of them mumbled. Across the room, Dollard saw him coming and automatically raised his hand to the waiter. McCullagh shook his head.

"Turning down a drink? You sick?"

McCullagh checked his watch. "Great doin's afoot. Aguilera's taking us to the front again. We've got twenty minutes."

Dollard slapped money on the table and leapt to his feet. "Wish the bugger'd give us more time."

"He did. I've been to half the bars in Zaragoza looking for you."

"The others coming?" McCullagh nodded. Dollard's shoulders sagged. "Philby, too?"

"Don't start that again, Desjardins."

"The guy gives me the creeps."

McCullagh shook his head. "He pays his share of the car. Just like you."

"Where we going?"

"Teruel. It just fell to the Nationalists. We're to be there in time for the glorious entry in the morning. Franco doesn't want the world to miss his latest victory."

"Teruel fell? You sure?"

"When have they shown us anything but a *fait accompli*? Aguilera's pretty anxious for us to get moving. My guess is the order came from Bolín himself."

As they hurried up Avenida Cesar Augusto, they saw the diminutive Aguilera pacing on the sidewalk. A cavalcade of cars sat waiting in front of the hotel, engines running. As Dollard turned to go into the hotel, McCullagh grabbed his arm. "No time," he said.

"Teruel's freezing," Dollard objected.

"I threw in some of your clothes. Your teeth will have to go unbrushed for a day."

"Think we'll be back that soon?" Dollard asked, climbing into the car and frowning. Philby was in his usual place. By some obscure fiat, he'd inherited the back-right spot—the one closest to the ditch in case of air attack.

"Positive," McCullagh replied. "Aguilera would never let us linger at the front lest we start poking around, or actually engage a soldier in conversation." He turned to their companion. "What's your take on it, Philby?"

"Twenty-four hours, tops. I figure, afternoon to get there, night spent in some ghastly *pensión*, and morning listening to lies from the generals. Manuel will have us back here in time for dinner tomorrow night." Manuel nodded. As a driver he was erratic and nervous, but his good command of English more than compensated for those failings.

"Wake up, Desjardins," McCullagh said, poking him in the ribs. "We're almost there."

Dollard opened his eyes, realizing he'd fallen asleep with his head on Philby's shoulder. A wave of disgust coursed its way up his spine. "I don't see any town," he mumbled. What had been light snow an hour earlier had become a blizzard. He could see nothing but a white wall.

Philby sighed in disgust. "Even in good conditions, one doesn't *see* Teruel from the plain. One climbs up onto it. It's on a high mesa. Like the ones in those Western movies you Americans are so fond of. Don't they teach geography where you come from?"

"*Baise mon cul*, Philby."

The Englishman chuckled. "Oh, my, such vulgarity, but then what is one to expect from a colonial who—"

Manuel braked suddenly, sending the car into a skid. McCullagh stiffened then pointed to tire tracks leading off on the left. "That could have been the road up to the city," he said.

"Don't think so," Philby replied. "No guards."

Dollard looked at Manuel, sensing the driver's terror. Ahead, Aguilera's car had extinguished its lights and was speeding up, soon disappearing in the snow. Manuel did the opposite. He took his foot off the gas, letting the car coast down the long incline. Dollard strained his eyes for signs of life. A long, multi-storeyed building that reminded him of the monastery back home at Oka loomed up on the left.

"Kill the fucking lights," McCullagh screamed.

A vehicle shot out of the blackness, trailing a plume of snow in its wake as it headed in the opposite direction. "That's Aguilera," Dollard shouted, turning to see the car disappear. Manuel braked to a halt, while behind them, the other cars in the cavalcade were manoeuvring to turn.

"It's all right, Manuel," McCullagh said in a steady, controlled voice. "Just turn the car around and take us back to Zaragoza." The sound of an explosion rocked the car to the right. Manuel moaned, but stayed frozen behind the wheel.

"Jaysus Christians," McCullagh shouted, as he jumped out, yanked open the driver's door, and tugged on Manuel. But Manuel's hands had locked onto the steering wheel. Dollard reached over the seat and began pounding his fingers. He heard Philby jump out, then saw him race for the car behind that was manoeuvring to turn. A door opened, swallowing him up. The car sped up and disappeared. A machine gun came to life, shredding the hood in front of Dollard's eyes and killing the engine. Manuel's moan became a wail.

"Get out!" McCullagh yelled, racing to the second car behind, which was already changing from first to second gear. Hands reached for McCullagh from an open door.

"Desjardins," he screamed, diving in, as the car sped up. Another round of machine-gun fire filled the night. Dollard ran like never before, but stumbled and fell. He raised himself to see the car disappear, then rolled into the ditch, burrowing his body in the snow. He gulped for air, willing the blood pounding in his ears to cease so that he could hear who or what was out there. Then, from the road, came the sound of snow crunching under feet, followed by the click of a weapon.

"On your feet, asshole," a voice from the American Midwest drawled.

―――

January 18, 1938
Teruel, Spain

TO MARTY, KEEPING HIS BOYS SAFE went beyond sharpening basic soldiering skills and into the realm of shirking, pilfering, and staking out the best positions. Which was why he was feeling in relatively good spirits as they dug in on the northern outskirts of Teruel. If Fuentes had taught him anything, it was that the shovel equalled the rifle in winning wars—or at least surviving them.

The battalion had positioned itself on little hillocks situated between two high cliffs. This permitted them to focus attention on the Navarrese, who'd soon be coming back down the valley. If he'd had a choice, he would have preferred the cliff behind, or the bluff two miles across where the German Internationals, the Thaelmanns, had set up, or even the long, sloping hill farther back claimed by the English Attlees. But this was not the time for wishful thinking. His immediate problem was how hard to work the men in strengthening their position. Certainly, digging, scraping, and piling improved their fortifications, as well as kept them warm. But in their weakened, half-starved state, pushing them too hard also sapped their strength for the coming battle.

He was directing last-minute improvements when an acquaintance from the Lincolns showed up with a message. "Johnson," he said to the man, extending an arm, "shake the hand that shook the world."

"You shred it, wheat," Johnson replied. For a few minutes, they chatted. Johnson had heard about Tauno, and so expressed condolences. He had turned to leave when he said, "Say, aren't you from Montreal?" Marty nodded. "Some of our boys brought in a guy from there last night. Caught him driving into Teruel, bold as brass, headlights blazing. There was a whole pack of them, apparently. Reporters, he claims, but nobody's buying that. The others got away. Dumb buggers actually thought the Whites had taken Teruel. Guess their communications are as screwed up as ours, eh?" They laughed.

"They pry anything valuable from him?" Marty asked.

"Apparently not. A few troop locations, stuff like that."

"What's his future?"

Johnson shook his head. "Not great, I'd say. Right now, he's sitting behind barbed wire shitting bricks and babbling away in French."

"He's still alive, then?"

"Far as I know. But that'll have to change, soon as the shooting starts up again. Can't get him to a prison camp in this weather and can't spare the guards when things heat up."

Marty looked off. "Cripes," he said, more to himself than Johnson, "guy from my own hometown. Wonder what part?"

Johnson shrugged and left. Food arrived. Marty ate while he read. He was to attend a briefing at Captain Smith's headquarters in the railway tunnel at 1600 hours.

The warmth at HQ was overwhelming. Marty had hardly plunked himself down on the bench when he felt his eyes grow heavy. Around him, soldiers griped as they waited for the briefing to start. In the background, clerks, cartographers, and signalmen went about their work. Finally, Smith arrived, and Wellman began the meeting with his usual lecture on the irrefutable joys of communism. Marty marvelled at the weight given to indoctrination. With the situation precarious and the troops poorly clad, underfed, out-manned, out-gunned, battle-weary, and mentally fatigued, the political commissar was still allowed his usual go.

At last, Smith took over to deliver the meat of the meeting. He was brief. They were in for it, but the bluffs had been refortified, along with the higher points on the valley floor. They could repel frontal attacks, but artillery and air bombardment were taking their toll. With the snow and poor roads, they were to conserve munitions.

After the briefing, Marty approached Smith. "The Lincolns took a prisoner last night," he said. "A reporter."

Smith nodded as he gathered up his notes. "So?"

"Supposedly he's from my hometown. I'd like permission to see him."

Smith's brow knit in a deep furrow. "General Aranda's up there," he pointed in the direction of the Nationalist lines, "with 100,000 battle-savvy troopers, 700 cannon, and the whole goddamned German air force, and you come to me with a case of the homesicks? Get outta here, Kellenberger."

"What's the harm?"

"The harm is that it's distracting and the Lincolns will palm him off on you rather than get rid of him themselves. Then he becomes our problem. Let it go, Sergeant. There's no time for this. For all we know, he's not even Canadian. And if he is, he's probably one of those Quebec fascists, over here learning a few tricks to use back home."

"All I want is a chance to talk to him," he said. "Suppose he really is a reporter? If he's executed, how'll that read in the press back home?" Noticing the captain pause, he pressed. "Imagine the headlines: 'Internationals Murder Canadian Reporter in Snows of Teruel.' Hell, it could become the biggest blunder since—"

"All right, all right," Smith replied, as he leaned over the briefing table and scribbled a note. "You go to Stores and finish your business there. I'll have this sent over to the Lincolns." He straightened up, note in hand. "This requests them to let you 'borrow' the prisoner for interrogation, but only if they're done with him. Give him a good look in the eye. If you see the slightest hint of Nazi in there, return him 'toot sweet.' If you don't, and the Nationalists renew the attack, he becomes your problem."

"Meaning?"

"Do I have to spell it out?"

"So, worst comes to worst, I'm to…?"

"I think you understand," Smith replied.

Wrestling supplies from the meagre stocks at Stores took longer than expected. Every platoon leader in the 15th IB was there arguing his case for more and better. By the time Marty had had his turn, it was getting dark; too late and too dangerous to get over to the Lincolns. It would have to wait until morning, by which time the Montrealer would likely be dead. However, when he finally made it through the checkpoints back to his men, he found that the prisoner had been delivered. That could mean but one thing—the Lincolns had washed their hands of him and were turning him over to the Mac-Paps for disposal.

His men had placed him on an empty ammunition crate next to the firepit and were gawking at him. Some circled, like he was a horse in need of assessment. Others stood with fixed grins, delighted for the diversion. Marty cursed his own stupidity. He should have listened to Smith. His first instinct was to push the men aside and return the prisoner to the Lincolns, in spite of the late hour. Instead he hung back and listened to the corporal as he rattled off questions.

"Gi' me your name, Frenchy," the corporal demanded.

"Dollard Desjardins," came the reply in a weak voice. Marty heard the name and frowned, struggling to locate it in his exhausted brain. "And just what is it you do for Franco?" the corporal continued. The response came in a mumble. Marty strained to hear. "Speak up!"

"I work for a newspaper in Montreal. *Le Devoir.*"

"Bullshit! You came to Teruel to scout. Admit it."

"I already answered this. Let me sleep." One of the soldiers kicked the crate. Desjardins straightened up, while some of the men laughed.

"Know why you're still alive, Frenchy?" No response. "Because the Lincolns are cheap with their bullets." Dollard's head dropped. "Want to hear what I think?" No answer. "You're not Canadian at all, just another piece of French-fascist shit wanting to turn France into little Germany. You better convince us otherwise and fast." The corporal stopped, noticing Marty at the back. Marty motioned him to continue.

"I told you. I'm Québécois. From Montreal."

"Oh, yeah? Who won the Stanley Cup last year?" one of the boys asked.

The prisoner turned. "Detroit; took New York three games to two. In 1936, Detroit again over Toronto. In 1935, it was the Montreal Maroons, and in—"

"Shut your gob!" the corporal yelled.

The men looked at each other then back to the prisoner. Marty rose to his feet, speaking for the first time. "And this paper," he began, "*Le Devoir*, I suppose you're all in favour of the racist garbage they print? That why they sent you here? So you could spread lies about Franco?"

The men turned to their sergeant, while the prisoner continued to stare into the fire. "They sent me because I was available and they liked my stuff."

"So, you've covered other wars, then?"

The prisoner shook his head. "Not wars. Strikes."

"What kind of strikes?"

"Textiles, mines, a couple of pulp mills."

"And maybe a labour camp strike that ended in Regina?" The prisoner stirred, his eyes coming off the fire. "Don't turn around," Marty ordered, looking over at Shevchuk who'd been with him on the On-to-Ottawa Trek. "So, just what did you say about the strikers in these reports?"

"I told the truth as I saw it."

"Which was?"

"They were hungry and out of work. But they could be unreasonable, too."

"And do you work for other papers?"

"Only one, *Le Miroir*, a small publication that reports on—"

Marty picked up an empty bottle and hurled it against the parapet. It exploded in a hollow pop. The prisoner startled. "He's Canadian, all right," Marty interrupted, "but a friggin' fascist one."

Dollard craned his neck to see who in the back was making the accusations against him. "'Ooever you are," he protested, "you're dead wrong."

Marty tried to control his voice, as he worked his way around to face him. "Listen, asshole. Half these guys are Canadian, and two of us were on that trek to Ottawa you reported on. As for me, I'm both Montrealer and Jew, and I'm saying those papers you work for are anti-Semitic rags."

Dollard's face collapsed as Marty pushed his way into the glow of the firelight. "You," Dollard mumbled, dropping his head into his hands after seeing Marty's face for the first time. The men looked on, bewildered.

Marty stood directly in front of him. "Look at me," he commanded. For a moment, the two men stared at each other. "Is it coming back?" Marty snapped. "Do you remember? Throwing me out of le Gesù? Kicking the shit out of those Jewish boys? Spreading lies about our trek to Ottawa?"

"You misunderstood from the start, jumped to conclusions. And my reports on the labour camp strike . . . they got exaggerated in the English press . . . poor translation."

Marty felt his fists tightening into balls. "*Caliss de ciboulette! Pas idiot, moi. J'suis capable de me faire comprendre. J'ai passé trois ans à l'université de Montréal avant de me faire foutre dehors. KICKED OUT parce que je suis Juif. J'aurai dû être docteur si ce n'était pour le racisme et le Jeune-Canada.*"

He turned to the men. "Koradi and Hosfeld," he ordered, "tie this excuse for a human being to the tree. And throw a tarp over him. I don't want to have to look at his face. If he as much as twitches, shoot the son of a bitch. The rest of you get busy shoring up the parapet before the bombardment resumes."

The wind came up and it began to snow. Hours passed. From time to time, as he went about his work, Marty glanced toward the prisoner. Snow covered the canvas, making it look like just another hillock, but beneath it was a man with whom he'd shared streets, a university, and goodness knows what else. How could they have become such enemies? His mind travelled to familiar haunts from home—Fletcher's Field, Mount Royal, Ste. Catherine Street on a spring evening. He went to his stash of rations and approached the mound, motioning the guard to remove the canvas and untie the prisoner. Marty used his foot to scrape out a place to squat in the snow and handed over a plate. Side-by-side they sat cross-legged on the ground.

"What's going to 'appen to me?" Dollard finally asked, playing with his food.

"Don't know yet," Marty replied, munching on a hard biscuit.

An artillery shell exploded in the distance. Dollard jumped. They'd been coming in more frequently, which was par for the time of night.

"Relax," Marty said, "they're just probing."

"When will it start for real?"

"Around midnight," Marty replied, helping himself to Dollard's untouched food. When he finished, he removed his glasses and rubbed his eyes. "You any idea how tough fascists like you make it for minorities in Montreal, Desjardins?"

"I'm not a fascist."

"Take us Jews. The English have their quotas and keep us out of their better clubs and schools. Then zealots like you print nonsense about how we're conspiring to take over the world."

"I 'ave never written stuff like that."

"Those editorials, about how it's not the Jews in beards and caftans you have to worry about, but the ones who take local names and pass themselves off as Gentiles—you really believe that stuff?" Dollard stared into the snow. Marty sighed and began carefully placing the wire stems of his glasses back over his ears. "What part of Montreal you from?"

Dollard rolled onto his knees and, using the tree for support, pushed himself to his feet. He began banging a foot against the trunk. Marty watched him, seeing his *zayde* in the slow deliberate movements. He could understand that the prisoner might be freezing, but something about the way he moved suggested the man's mind was racing—as if deciding whether a lie or the truth would best get him out of the mess he was in. "Outremont," he said, at last.

Marty's face screwed up. "Christ! Outremont, up there on the mountain, looking down at us poor *shmucks* trying to make a go of it off the Main. I suppose you're going to tell me you're not a xenophobe and you've never heard of the likes of l'abbé Groulx or Adrien Arcand."

Dollard began banging the other foot against the tree. After a few kicks, he slid back down into the snow and looked up at Marty. "From the time I was a boy, they 'ave been regular guests in my father's house."

Marty nodded. "And Jeune-Canada? What kind of nonsense did you get up to with them?"

"As little as possible. I never liked those guys. I admit, though, when André Malraux came to Montreal to raise funds for the Spanish Republicans, I 'elped bust up the rally. But I never trolled Boulevard St. Laurent looking for people to beat up like you think."

"So, now you've graduated to fighting for Franco?"

"I'm not *fighting* for Franco. I'm reporting on the war."

"And spinning pro-Nationalist propaganda in the process." Dollard hunched his shoulders. "If you're doing that you're fighting for him."

"*D'accord*," Dollard replied, "maybe I could 'ave been a little more . . . objective. But, it's not as if they give reporters a free 'and. Most times, they keep you back from the front. They feed you information you can't verify, so you wind up regurgitating it. I regret that, but if you don't file, they send you 'ome, or worse."

Another shell exploded. Several feet away, a soldier threw pieces of a broken crate onto the fire. In the sudden flare-up, Marty took in the prisoner's shallow breathing and wide eyes. He began to dread what fate was forcing on him. For an instant, he saw Desjardins streaking down the ice at the university, the crowd on their feet. A pang of sympathy worked its way into his consciousness—a welcome visitor to his mad world.

"Not as eager as when you arrived, eh?" he said. The prisoner shook his head. Marty leaned back against the rocks his men had so painstakingly piled and slapped his mitted hands together several times. "Me either."

"My old man used to give me 'ell for rushing into things blindly," Dollard said.

Marty chuckled. "Mine, too."

"Sitting 'ere for 'ours got me thinking. Mostly, about 'ow I got into this mess." He looked at his captor and saw him nodding. "You, too?"

Marty gazed over the parapet into the falling snow. "I figured that democracy was going to survive or perish in Spain, so I joined. But our side's been hijacked and the new masters are not what I'd call democratic. What's worse, they're making a mess of it. I feel cheated."

Dollard pulled his knees in close to his chest. He glanced at Marty several times as if making a decision. "Can I ask you something, Sergeant?" Marty nodded. "Why go on?"

It was a question a friend might ask a friend if the mood and setting were right, but not one to put to a man who held the power of life and death over you. Marty turned toward him, noting with shock how the interrogation had become a conversation. He wasn't alone. From the look on the prisoner's face, Desjardins must have recognized the recklessness of the question. Marty pulled off his woollen hat and frowned.

"Sorry," Desjardins blurted out, "I should never 'ave—"

Marty raised his hand. "It's complicated. I came here to strike a blow for the little guy. Somehow that seems to have been lost. But I still have my responsibilities."

A sound resembling a Victoria Day whiz-bang filled the air followed by an explosion fifty yards behind their position. Marty dropped to the ground. Pieces of rock and snow fell on them. "That was close, wasn't it?" Dollard said.

"You bet! Let's get outta here." They stood and headed for the trench, Marty helping Dollard get his legs going. More shells fell, before Marty realized that it was the Thaelmann Battalion on the ridge across the valley taking the pounding.

With the artillery barrage intensifying, Dollard took to counting his life expectancy in minutes. Even if he survived the shelling, what then? He cursed his luck. His one chance for winning the sergeant over lay in nurturing the connection they had been forging during their brief exchange. But the attack had put paid to that. As soon as the Moors, Navarrese, and Galicians came swooping down the valley, the sergeant would have no choice but to dispatch him.

Between shells, his spirits ping-ponged from hope to despair as he mulled over his interrogation. Kelly, as the men called him, had confined his questions to Montreal. That, surely, was the mark of a man above executing a countryman in cold blood. On the other hand, dead prisoners don't stab you in the back or eat up precious rations. Still, there was solace in the fact that Kelly had opted for a hundred pounds of shrapnel, which he'd tied to his leg, over seven grams of lead in the head. Ironic that the longer the bombardment continued, the longer he would live.

The barrage stopped with the first hint of morning light. An uncanny silence descended. Dollard opened his eyes to a world of white. The snow on the ground had been lifted heavenward by the explosions, then carried by the wind to swirl and settle on men and equipment.

With the cessation, weapons were brushed off, sights calibrated, and ammunition crates opened. Dollard tucked himself into a cranny in the trench, expecting to be turned on at any minute. It didn't happen. For the first time in twenty-four hours, he wasn't on the verge of panic. He began to survey the scene. It was hard to imagine men functioning under such conditions, yet the Internationals went about their business like labourers on a construction site, preparing for the next phase. They knew what to expect, and when it came he was stunned by the ferocity of it. First the bombers, then the fighter planes, strafing the ground, followed by renewed artillery fire.

Dollard was surprised by this second shelling, but caught on quickly. This was the much-vaunted Nationalist rolling barrage, which lifted as the attacking troops progressed toward the enemy. Their boldness astounded him, especially when he calculated the possibilities for killing their own troops. The Republican Army, of course, read the process perfectly and went to ground until the barrage moved past them. Afterwards, they emerged from their holes to clean off their equipment once again and greet the advancing army.

Dollard, along with the shrapnel attached to his leg, dragged himself to a vantage point so that he could take it all in. It was Fuentes all over again, only in reverse and much worse. Surrounded by bluffs on three sides, the Nationalists fell in their thousands. Like Indians in a Western, they simply went down. But unlike the stunt men in the flickers, no one would be dusting themselves off and going home for dinner. Dollard found himself conflicted — his heart with the Nationalists, his skin with the Republicans.

Day five saw Dollard's confidence in tatters. Admiration mixed with disgust, fascination with loathing, right with wrong. Haggard, unkempt, and dropping with fatigue, he'd become indistinguishable from his captors. Worse, a begrudging respect for them had set in. When they heard the bugles sound and Monasterio's 1st Cavalry Division came pounding over the snows, with banners flying, Dollard stood with them and gawked. "Crazy bastards," someone mumbled. But when the horsemen overran the German volunteers and were pounding a path directly at the Mac-Paps, they came to their senses. So did the British machine-gunners on the hill behind them. Horses and riders went down like wheat in a prairie hailstorm. Through it all, Sergeant Kellenberger issued a steady stream of orders, as if he'd been a soldier all his life. Yet, at one point, the maverick in him shone through, when he started screaming poetry at the top of his lungs. Dollard didn't recognize the poem, but in cadence and sentiment it was stirring. It concerned 600 men riding through shot and shell to certain death with no thought of disobeying an order. Inspirational, if not dumb.

It wasn't all going in the Republicans' favour, however. Franco's generals eventually began concentrating planes and artillery on the higher positions above the valley, and one by one they fell. Nationalist foot soldiers began closing in. Casualties mounted, and Sergeant Kellenberger was no longer reciting poetry. Dollard did his best to help, but was frustrated by the shrapnel tied to his leg.

"Kellenberger," he yelled out, when the men had collapsed after beating back another frontal attack, "'Osfeld's bleeding to death. Remove this *maudit* piece of iron and I'll bandage 'im." When all he got was a blank stare, he persisted. "*Tabarnac*, where could I go? Anyone and everyone out there will use me for target practice. Like it or not, I'm safe only with you."

As a student, Dollard had read books about military valour. All glorious. But nothing in print, celluloid, or even what he'd witnessed at Fuentes had prepared him for Teruel. He'd come to know the soldiers and he ached for them as they dropped from fatigue, frost, hunger, and Nationalist fire. So, with the shackles off, he went to work. At first, the men eyed him with suspicion, but quickly came to rely on him: "Doll, fetch me ammunition"; "Doll, help me shore up this barricade"; "Doll, hold him down while I pull the shell splinters out of his leg."

Active at last, he quickly regained his strength. In the excitement and commotion, his range of movement expanded. Although several avenues for escape opened, as he was no longer certain which way to go, or even where he belonged, he rejected the temptation. In the end, the Mac-Paps were ordered out of the line along with the other Internationals. If they were going to turn on him, now was the time. He walked alongside them, wondering when it would come.

Their destination turned out to be the railway line, twelve miles south of Teruel through the snow. Once there, they were immediately ordered to make for a point seventy-five miles northeast. Their assignment? Hit the fascists from the rear and stall their drive to Teruel.

Bundled in bloodied clothes taken off a dead soldier, Dollard slogged through snow and sleet with his captors, or were they now his comrades? He had no idea what was happening, only that they were constantly moving, and the Republicans were losing.

After two weeks, their platoon stumbled into another railway junction. Dollard took stock. He'd emerged looking the same as everyone else—filthy, frozen, exhausted, starving, and bent with chilblains. Even the lice had found him. He hobbled about, pushing their wounded onto a boxcar. When they were loaded, he looked up, suspecting it might be the end of the line for him. Instantly, hands shot down and he felt a slap on the back as they pulled him in. A cigarette was pressed on him. Someone called him comrade.

Chapter Twenty-one

February 19, 1938
The Mediterranean

THE OLD WOOD-BURNER PUFFING them to Valencia and the Mediterranean pulled and jerked its way up the long inclines. A cow could have plodded past them. Dollard stared at the men around him, some asleep, others sprawled in a daze, and a few laughing hysterically. He noticed Sergeant Kellenberger crawling over to him, at the same time reaching into an inner pocket for his spectacles. When he'd first noticed the metal case, Dollard had wondered how it got to be so battered. Now he understood. Without his glasses, the sergeant was helpless. So, each artillery barrage found them stored away, not to come out until the all clear.

"I can get you out of here," Marty whispered.

Dollard wouldn't have believed a smile could be so painful. He wanted desperately to show his pleasure, but his bleeding lips and frost-scarred cheeks made it impossible. "Thought you were going to check my credentials," he replied, "then choose between a bullet and a POW camp."

Marty examined his chapped hands. The sun had come up over the hills and was slanting in through cracks in the boxcar. He shifted to face its healing rays. "Whatever it is you're really all about," he said at last, "the guys will want to see you off safe."

"What if I want to 'ang around a bit?" Dollard asked.

Marty turned to focus on him. "You crazy? Why would you do that?"

"Curiosity, maybe."

"For what?"

"Well, for starters, where were all those *milicianas* I've been told about?" Marty frowned. "You know, the young Republican girls in uniform who move from trench to trench shagging the men?"

Marty coughed. The soldier next to them slapped a knee, starting a chain reaction of men shrieking, then clutching their shrunken bellies, as tears flowed down their cheeks.

Dollard listened to the laughter rise and fall like in a recording outside the fun house at the circus. "Looks like that one 'as been answered," he said, a blush visible despite the frost patches on his face, "but I've 'undreds more."

Marty studied him for a second. "You really are a reporter, aren't you?"

"I was not lying, Sergeant."

"Stop calling me 'Sergeant.' The name's Marty."

"Not Kelly?"

"Kelly, if you want."

When Dollard awoke he realized something had changed. The train still lurched like a drunkard, but it was no longer labouring up the divide. Rather, it seemed to be braking its way down a series of long inclines. As he looked at the sleeping men, he realized that something else was also new — he could no longer see his breath. They must be nearing the Mediterranean, he thought. He wondered if he'd get to see it or if marauding planes would find them first. He weighed the odds, surprised by the lack of panic in his reasoning. "You asleep, Marty?"

"Too much going on in my head."

"Look at the guys." Marty opened his eyes. "They've got this air of abandonment about them."

Marty nodded. "Happens after every battle. They've survived, so they feel invincible. It won't last. In two days' time, they'll be diving at the pop of a champagne cork." He turned to Dollard. "You should write down what you want to say about Teruel before the shakes find you."

"Know what you said back there, about getting me out of Spain?" Dollard asked. "'Ow would a guy go about arranging something like that?"

Marty checked the bucking heads around them then leaned closer. "There are people in Valencia who make good passports."

"'Ow come you know about something like that?"

"Call it self-preservation. Our passports are filed in Albacete. When . . . if, that city falls to Franco, we're screwed."

"Ah, so you'd like an extra one. For backup."

"Shh!" He looked around. "Wouldn't want anyone getting the wrong idea. As for the passport, it wasn't for me. I had plans for getting a friend out. That's all changed."

"Why?"

"He's dead, killed, kaput. When it happened, I considered getting out of here myself, but Smith and Wellman — the brass — read my mind. They sicced responsibility on me. Strange beast, that. It takes hold of you." He pointed his chin in the direction of the men. "Right now, their asses are more important to me than my own. I always figured on sneaking away if they all got killed, but they keep replacing them."

Dollard fingered the growth on his chin. "They'd do anything for you," he said. "You know that, don't you?"

"Wish they hated me."

"This war can't last forever."

"No, but probably longer than me. After Belchite, Fuentes, and now Teruel, I figure I've about used up my nine lives. I never thought . . . what's the matter?"

"You . . . were at Fuentes?" Marty nodded. "Me, too . . . as a reporter," he hastened to add.

The boxcar swayed. Marty stared at his feet. "I suppose you wrote up a glowing report for *Le Devoir*?" he said at last.

The train must have been negotiating a long bend because the sun peeping through the slats began flickering from body to body, reminding Dollard of a newsreel. He took in the bandages, blood-caked tunics, gaunt faces, and gnarled feet. "Nothing I'm proud of," he replied. "'Ope you never get to read any of it."

Marty sneered. "I might as well get used to it. The victors write the history books. And your side's winning."

"What makes it my side?"

"*Feh*! Desjardins. Lie to me if you have to, but not to yourself. You're a product of Outremont. Everything you stand for reeks of Franco. And don't tell me you picked the Nationalist side because you thought they were getting short shrift in the press. Your history is with the fascists."

"Fine. So a lot of people back 'ome think a little tightening up wouldn't 'urt."

Marty bucked like he'd been elbowed in the ribs. "*A little tightening up*," he mimicked in a squeaky voice. "That how you rationalize going after minorities and taking away their rights? 'Yep, time to pull them kikes up by the ears a smidge,'" he mimicked. "'Shut down their businesses and drive 'em out of town. And, say, them fellas, Hitler and Franco, seem to be doing a swell job over there in Europe. How 'bout gettin' behind them for a bit.' Christ, Desjardins, I bet you're a big fan of Cardinal O'Connell? He's the reason we're losing this war. With so many Americans signing that petition of his, President Roosevelt had no choice but to back out on helping us. Then you wonder why Spanish Republicans hate the Church so much."

The train was descending another long grade, the car rattling as it picked up speed. Some of the men began to stir. Dollard waited for them to settle before replying. "What you're saying, is that what all these guys think?"

"Sort of. But they don't talk politics, except to bitch. They used to, right up to when the first gun went off. After that, it was how to keep from getting their balls shot off, or whether or not the canteen was going to show up with chow."

"But you still do?"

"Yeah, well, maybe I think too much."

Dollard listened to the wheels clacking on the rails. He noticed that many of the men had shed their tunics. It definitely was getting warmer. He smelled the air. This time he was sure it was the Mediterranean. "Marty?"

"What?"

"If we're still together when we get to Valencia, 'ow about finding some *taberna* and getting ossified?"

Marty leaned over, extending his hand. "Wonder of wonders," he said, "Outremont inviting the Main for a brew. What would the folks say back home?"

<hr>

February 20, 1938
Near Valencia

"THERE'LL BE OFFICERS," Marty whispered, as the train slowed. "If they ask questions, shake your head and shout that a shell took out your hearing. I've already talked to the men. They'll back the story."

Dollard swallowed. The braking train sent the boxcars slamming into each other. Passengers lurched about and moaned. When it came to a full halt, they rose, crowding the doorway. Hands reached to help the wounded and get them to the ambulances idling nearby. Officers in fresh uniforms barked orders and pointed the rest of the men to a line of trucks. "I thought we were going to Valencia," Dollard whispered.

Marty groaned as he looked around. "We're just north of the city. They don't want civilians seeing us in this state. Afraid they might get the right idea about how badly the war is going."

"This truck's a Dodge," Dollard remarked, as they climbed on. "Captured booty, or are the Americans selling to both sides?"

Marty shrugged. "Probably raided from a showroom after the war broke out."

The trip was bumpy, but short. Twenty minutes over side roads brought them to a monastery at the end of a long lane lined with plane trees. Dollard climbed down onto the cobblestone courtyard and looked around. They were surrounded by a burned-out church, a four-storey stone building with tiny windows, and a long structure that he took for a barn. Through the open doors, he could see machinery that appeared to be presses of some kind. At the far end of the courtyard, a group of women laboured over cauldrons suspended above a roaring fire. Men from the other trucks swarmed toward them. It had been two days since they'd last eaten.

"They're not serving yet," Marty said, holding his boys back. "If we don't claim a place to sleep in the monastery fast, we'll wind up in the barn." The men moaned, but followed him up the stairs to the third floor, where they found a vacant room. It was large, with eight narrow beds and two windows looking out over an orange grove. Fruit hung from the trees, begging to be picked.

"Wonder who'll be harvesting the oranges?" Dollard said, more to himself.

"Won't be the priests," Marty answered. "They're either dead, in hiding, or blessing tanks for the other side." He threw his kit on a cot and removed a tin plate and spoon. Those last into the room—with promises that food would be delivered—were ordered to stand guard, while the others trooped downstairs to battle their way through the lineup to the cauldrons.

By five in the afternoon of the first day, the men had eaten their fill and fallen into a sleep that lasted sixteen hours. They rose only to relieve themselves in the honey bucket, and when that filled, there was the window. Two men with diarrhea gave up early and moved outside to be close to the latrines. When they finally came to, they drifted back to the courtyard where they were fed, stripped, deloused, shorn bald, and escorted to the showers. Ablutions over, they strolled about naked, smoking Picadura Popular cigarettes while they waited for their clothes to be pulled from the boiling vats and dried.

Just as Marty had predicted, the soldiers began sliding into a post-combat mode that lasted several days. Some stared off, rocking like Muslims at prayer, while others babbled incoherently, or clutched playing cards in trembling hands. It wasn't unusual to hear whimpering in the night. Marty said it wouldn't last.

As the days wore on, Dollard continued to steer clear of officers, but with Major Smith away at briefings and Commissar Wellman in hospital, there was no one of rank to challenge him. Still, he felt more comfortable in the seclusion of the orchard. Marty seemed to enjoy it away from the men, too, and it wasn't long before he was sharing bits of his letters from Connie and his family. In between, they argued about anything and everything—sports, politicians, the university, restaurants, food, girls.

Day ten brought the word they'd been waiting for—leave. Five days of it. One of the men produced a bottle of eau de cologne. Dollard winced, as the others slapped it on and went outside to wait for the trucks to take them into Valencia. "Come for a walk," Marty said, "there's something I've got to tell you." They headed for the orchard.

"Don't want to miss the trucks," Dollard replied, looking back.

"Don't worry. We'll hear them." As they walked in silence, Dollard could tell from his friend's furrowed brow that something was up. A few feet inside the orchard they stopped under a tree laden with fruit. Marty reached up to pluck an orange. "Don't take this personally," he said, "but when we get to Valencia, you're to keep going."

Dollard stared at him. "What are you talking about?"

"You getting the hell out of here while there's still a chance. You've got something to go home to. For Chrissakes, don't throw it away. Stick around here and you'll only catch a bullet. You've got a passport. Use it."

"My passport has 'Endaye stamped in it. What do you think the Republican border guards would 'ave to say about that? They'd know I came in on the Nationalist side. It would be the proverbial walk for me."

Marty examined the orange in his hand. "That was last year. My guess is they've started seeing the cause as hopeless and are thinking about themselves these days. Your family has money. Grease some palms."

"What if I just want to 'ang around 'ere a bit longer? Get some answers."

"After Teruel, I'd have thought you'd seen enough."

Dollard stared across the orchard toward the burned-out church. "Not enough to get to the root of the 'atred. I mean, *sacrement*, torch a church if you 'ave to, but killing priests and raping nuns?"

Marty looked away. "That was in the early days of the war. I've seen none of that."

They resumed walking. For several minutes, neither spoke. "What you said a few minutes ago," Dollard finally asked, "about Republicans seeing the war as lost? You really believe that?"

Marty aimed the orange at a tree and let it fly. It hit with a hollow smack and fell broken and bleeding to the ground. "I should know better than to spout off to a reporter."

They stopped and faced each other. "*Voyons*, Marty. Never would I print anything that might get you into trouble. You must know that by now."

Marty looked at the ground and nodded. "Sorry," he replied. "You're right. I'm turning into a suspicious SOB." He extended a hand. The two men shook and continued their walk.

"I'm not kidding when I say I'd like to get to the bottom of the *animosité*," Dollard said, "but it's not just for a good story. Truth is, it's got me kind of mixed up."

"You're not alone there."

"My preconceptions, they don't jive with the facts. I don't want to be a millstone around your neck, but I'd sure like more time to get things straight in my 'ead."

"Impossible. You don't have reporter credentials on this side."

"But as long as I'm with you, nobody checks my credentials; they think I'm just another IBer."

"Smith and Wellman will know, and when they get back, they'd never go for it."

"Can we at least think about it while we're in Valencia?"

Marty kicked at a patch of dirt and shook his head. "Afraid not. Truth is, I'm not staying in Valencia. Soon as we get there, it's off to the station for a ticket to Tarragona for me."

"Where?"

"Don't get me wrong. I'm not deserting these guys, but they're wide-eyed, small-town boys who won't give me a moment's peace. It's my leave, too. No way am I playing nursemaid to their shenanigans, hangovers, and squabbles for five days. I get enough Mother Goose on duty."

"I see," Dollard said frowning.

Marty smiled. "Don't look so downhearted. You can come with me if you like. Tarragona gets you closer to the border. Maybe there I can talk some sense into you."

A cheer went up at the monastery, and they turned to see billows of dust rising above the laneway. The trucks had arrived.

March 4, 1938
Tarragona, Spain

TARRAGONA TURNED OUT TO BE SMALLER than Dollard had anticipated, but it didn't disappoint. They found themselves a room in a *pensión* over a small *taberna* on the Plaza de la Font, next to the old city and close to the Amfiteatre Romà. The first day, they lay in the tub until their skin threatened to peel off. Then they headed downstairs to the *taberna* to get roaring drunk. Day two saw them venturing out for better food, civilian clothes, and, with luck, girls—nice ones, Marty insisted. By nightfall, they'd managed only the clothes—the restaurants, it appeared, were all victims to the same rationing, and "nice girls" spotted them for lice-infested soldiers so kept their distance.

"What say we find ourselves a couple of *putas*?" Dollard suggested.

Marty gave him a long look. "You crazy? You any idea what gonorrhea and syphilis do to a fellow?" Dollard shrugged. "If I had my medical text here I'd show you some pictures."

"Okay. Fine. Just a suggestion."

On day three, they played tourist. Dollard got to use his Classics education at last. "This region is full of 'istory," he announced. "The Carthaginians and Romans fought over Barcelona. And did you know that Tarragona was once 'ome to Julius Caesar, and that Zaragoza is really just a bastardization of the name of its founder, Caesar Augusta?" Marty was impressed.

That night they discovered a cellar cave that served black-market food. The prices were astronomical, but with the future so uncertain, what the hell. They left tipsy and happy.

"I can't 'old out much longer," Dollard announced, when they were back out on the sidewalk. "If the choice is *putas* or nothing, I opt for *putas*. You go back to the *taberna* if you like."

"I'll go with you as far as the door," Marty sighed, "but only to see you don't get into any trouble."

Finding the right place wasn't difficult. Dollard knocked, and a burly bouncer welcomed them in. A dark-eyed girl noticed Marty holding back and grabbed his hand, pulling him over the doorstep. Dollard smiled.

"You know what this will do to me, don't you?" Marty asked. "I'll be examining myself for months."

Each passing day saw the removal of yet another layer separating them. Outremont and Main, conservative and liberal, Nationalist and Republican—none of that mattered anymore. Day four saw them analyzing perspectives with nuance and depth—a healthy, sobering exercise. By early evening, as they were exiting a cinema on the Rambla Vella, they were feeling comfortable and relaxed. In *The Plainsman*, Gary Cooper had been at his laconic "yup" and "nope" best as Wild Bill Hickok. Jean Arthur had been a ravishing Calamity Jane.

"Tell me something, Dollard. Having seen both sides of Spain, how do they stack up?"

Dollard squinted and looked off, as if the answer lay somewhere up the street. "I've given this a lot of thought," he replied. "There's a great article in it. Of course, I'd 'ave to get myself back in a position to file."

"When you leave this country, which should be soon, you'll be able to file whatever comes into your head."

Dollard frowned and raised his hands in front of him, like an artist preparing to mould clay. "Reports back 'ome tend to be slanted in favour of the Republic, so I'd want to take a neutral point of view—analytical, but factual. I'd never be able to face my friend McCullagh if I did it any other way." They turned onto Via de L'Imperi Romà, heading for the Passeig Arqueològic and the walkway along the ancient ramparts. Somehow, strolling the ramparts had become their favourite evening pastime, especially with the unseasonably warm March weather and the great number of ladies taking advantage of it.

"So, this article," Marty pressed, "how'd you go about setting it up?"

"Visual similarities first—you know, lineups, uniforms, black-shawled housewives, craters, rubble, blackouts, flags everywhere, anti-aircraft guns on roofs, sandbags at intersections—that kind of stuff. Then I'd zero in on sounds—wailing sirens, boots pounding on cobblestones, martial music on the radio, singing in the bars. And I'd play up the smell factor, too—'orse shit, blue exhaust, rice and beans in fryers, olive oil burning in lamps."

"I'll be damned! It's like that on the other side, too?"

Dollard nodded. "Believe me, arrive blindfolded in Spain, and with those your only clues, you'd be 'ard-pressed to know which side you'd landed on." He stopped talking as two striking young ladies hove into view. Marty doffed his beret. The girls sniggered. To Dollard's embarrassment, the glances were for him and not his myopic friend.

Marty must have caught the look on his face. "Don't worry," he said. "I'm used to it."

Hurriedly, Dollard ploughed on with his outline. "It's only with closer examination that subtle differences begin to show themselves. That's where I'd 'ead next."

"Keep going."

"Take uniforms, for instance. On the Republican side, there's a make-do air about them, as if everyone had stitched their own. You 'ave to strain to distinguish regiments, or even tell who's an officer and who's not. Over on the other side, they wear them with pride. Walk down the street and you see Requetés strutting about in jodhpurs, or Falangists in black wedges, or Legionarios in green serge and combat boots. *Comprends-tu*?"

"Boots," Marty groaned, glancing at his feet. "We get ours from the dead, otherwise it's those rope-soled sandals they call *alpargatas*. There's no mystery to why half our guys fall to frostbite on the Aragonian front."

Dollard was on a roll, his hands moving as he spoke. "But it's the different way citizens 'ave been affected that is fascinating. Take the folks strolling this wall, *par exemple*." He pointed to the Tarragonians flowing past as if they were Exhibit A. "They're animated. They call to each other and clown about, like they don't 'ave to behave. And they actually touch in public." As if to prove his point, a young couple sauntered into view, the boy's arm around the girl's waist, her head on his shoulder.

Marty frowned. "You don't see that in Burgos or Salamanca?"

" 'Ell no! Try it and some Falangist priest, or Guardia Civil would be busting you for immorality."

Marty chuckled. "Maybe your article could use a separate paragraph for women."

"Paragraph? *Câline*, that would take a whole article. The Nationalists patronize them, but keep them locked up. Home, *niños*, and the spiritual needs of the family, that's their territory. Even the few women who get involved in service organizations, like the Auxilio Social, have to be exemplars of the role of the wife—piety, obedience, humility."

"But girls get an education, don't they?"

"Some, but mostly to learn domestic skills, and only for so long. And education is segregated. None of this co-ed nonsense, like over 'ere. To 'ear it from Franco's ministers, Republican women have been turned into *putas rojas* in Mono overalls."

"If that's the case, how come we keep striking out?"

"Maybe we're too ugly."

"Speak for yourself, blondie."

"Don't get me wrong, Marty. I understand where the Nationalists are coming from. And it's not all bad." He looked off. "Kinda like 'ome in many ways." Marty frowned. Dollard pressed. "No, really, think about it. They want to preserve their culture and hold onto the customs that give them meaning. Not like on this side. 'Ere, everything's up for grabs—tradition out the window."

"Right, and high time."

Dollard hesitated before continuing. "Something 'it me yesterday. We've been walking these streets for four days, but it was only then I realized what was missing—the bells are gone. When they burned the churches, they killed the bells. It's not just vestments and little old ladies with rosaries who've evaporated, it's the *angelus*, too. The magic's disappeared." He looked at his Jewish friend. "I don't care what you claim the Church 'as done, *that* I miss."

"Maybe, I do, too," Marty replied, looking up. "There're bound to be casualties. But don't be duped. That tradition you talk about keeps the peasants in their place. All that nonsense about Franco fighting to preserve the purity of Spanish culture is a smokescreen. His real aim is to restore the old order—aristocrats and clergy in power, *campesinos* at the bottom. Wouldn't want the twentieth century creeping into Spain, now, would we?"

"Come on, Marty! You keep saying that, but surely even you can see that some of the old ways are worth preserving."

"What's that supposed to mean? 'Even I can see?' You think Jews have no sense of tradition? Come on!"

"That's not what I'm saying. You're putting the wrong—"

"Take those institutions you seem so proud of—the upper class and the church. What's the first thing they do when they get power? Squash ideas and burn books." He paused to glance at Dollard. "But I guess that all sounds pretty normal to you, eh?"

"Meaning?"

"Figure it out, Monsieur Catholique Outremont."

"For Chrissake, Kellenberger, will you quit shitting on Outremont."

For several minutes, they picked their way down the darkened street in silence. Finally Marty swallowed. "Sorry," he said. "Our leave's up tomorrow. Guess I'm not thinking rationally."

"Forget it. Me with my privileged upbringing, must be 'ard to see where I'm coming from. But I'm 'aving trouble, too. To me, society needs dignity, a sense of continuance, and if it's classless, isn't it doomed to mediocrity?"

"Why should it be, Dollard? Why can't people advance on their merits? The cream rises if you give it a chance. That's what was beginning to happen here until Franco put a halt to it."

"Is that really why people 'ate the Church so much?"

"You bet it is! The clergy stabbed them in the back. After centuries, the peasants finally got a chance to advance, only to have the institution they were closest to—the church—line up with the aristocracy and army."

They came to a wall outside a *taberna* and stopped. Two men and a girl were putting up posters. "Same old message," Dollard said. They resumed walking.

"In this article you're composing in your head, guess you'd be talking about those propaganda posters, eh? I take it they're just as prevalent on your side, too."

"Jesus, Marty! Will you stop calling it 'my side.' "

"All right, all right."

Dollard took a deep breath. "Both sides use them. Same broad-shouldered, Charles-Atlas types, shaking fists at airplanes and charging enemy fortifications. I think they come from the same store. They're interesting, actually, in a neo-classical way. You probably love 'em, too, eh? I mean, the way they show change and speak of modernism and all?"

"They give me the creeps, actually. They're all about super humans. As if we commoners aren't good enough and have to be moulded to fit the new order. We're to become supermen fighting a great cause—theirs, of course. Nationalist or Republican, they're out to eradicate something. On one side, it's degenerates—Gypsies, Jews, Freemasons, Niggers, and homosexuals; on the other, it's the bourgeoisie." He shook his head. "The forms on the posters aren't really people, they're gods."

Dollard cocked his head. "You might be onto something."

"The message is always hidden, but it's there—put your faith in Father Figure, bust a gut to do his bidding, but ask no questions."

Dollard nodded. "Simple message for simple folk, eh? Which is probably why there's 'ardly ever any captions on the posters."

"There are few captions only because people are illiterate. But that doesn't make them stupid. They just haven't had a chance."

They were off the ramparts now, navigating the windy streets of the Old Town and heading for their *pensión*. Darkness had long since set in. Away from the ambient light from restaurants and *tabernas*, walking was dangerous; stray dogs and craters in the roadway made sure of that. They picked their way in silence and were almost home when Dollard began to chuckle.

"What?" Marty asked.

"Something funny just 'it me. Here we are, two sapheads a million miles from 'ome, stumbling about in the dark. I mean, does that define us or what?"

"Makes you wonder what the hell we're doing here, doesn't it?"

"Do you think we've been sold a bill of goods, Marty?"

"I think by now you know my answer to that one," Marty replied.

Their mood was sombre on day five of their leave. They breakfasted quietly on bread and what passed for coffee, along with the local patrons in the *pensión taberna*. The regulars knew the Internationales were leaving and tried to cheer them up, even the bartender who stood them each to a glass of harsh cognac. All raised their fists in salute and mumbled a *"no pasarán,"* as Marty and Dollard left to go pack. But their hearts weren't in it; enthusiasm for the war was waning—Nationalist Spain was growing, Republican Spain shrinking.

"They know they're done, don't they?" Dollard remarked.

Marty nodded. "Deep down, yes, but they're not admitting it. It's beyond their control, so they just keep plodding on, sending their sons, and anyone else who'll join, back into a doomed cause."

On the way down from the town to the station located on the coastal plain below, Dollard could tell Marty had something on his mind. He suspected it had to do with his getting out of Spain. If so, his argument was ready—he'd go, but only if they went together.

"This is where we separate," Marty said at the station platform, pulling a ticket from his pocket. "This will take you through Barcelona to the French border at Portbou." Dollard opened his mouth to protest, but Marty spoke over him. "Even with a bit of a rest," he continued, "our brigade is too shot up to be put back in the line for months. They'll be sending us to Villaneuva de la Jara for more training. You wouldn't fit in, and there's no way they'd let you stay. Chances are you'd wind up in jail."

"I could sign up," Dollard said.

"Don't be stupid."

"If it's so stupid, why are you going back?"

"You know why."

"Use your 'ead, Marty. Those guys you're so 'ell-bent on saving are going to wind up dead, no matter what you do."

"In that case, why would you want to join them?"

Dollard looked out at the Mediterranean. "It's complicated, but you and I get along, we understand each other. *Câlise*, in three months I've told you more about myself than anybody else, ever."

"Right, and you're an okay guy, so do me a favour. Go to France."

"You make it sound like a nice little train ride, and out I go. We both know I've got the wrong entry stamp in my passport. They'd pick me off for sure."

"Maybe so, but it's safer than the alternative."

"I feel safe with you. Is that a problem?"

Marty crossed his arms as he stared down at Tauno's boots. "Yes, that's a problem. I've been down this road before. Tauno stuck with me out of friendship and what did it get him? An unmarked grave at Fuentes de Ebro. It's too much responsibility." He thrust the ticket at his friend. "Take it! Please."

Dollard stepped backward, arms raised. "But you wouldn't 'ave to worry about me, because I wouldn't be in any danger. I'd just be the reporter travelling with the troops, the kind that runs for the rear when the firing starts. Just like 'Emingway."

"Major Smith would never go for it."

"So why not let 'im make that decision?"

"Goddamn you," Marty replied, pocketing the ticket. Dollard took a step toward him and held out a hand. They shook. "If Smith says no, promise you'll take the ticket and get outta here."

In Valencia, they paid a market-gardener to deliver them to the monastery. Coming down the lane, they were surprised by the jammed-up line of trucks and commotion and Smith barking out orders. "Where the hell have you been?" he yelled. "We've rounded up all your platoon, except for you."

"What's going on?"

"The Nationalists have broken out and are driving into the Ebro Basin."

Marty looked at the men's long faces as the major stormed off. He ran to catch up. "Jesus, Smith, they can't be sending these guys back in."

"Think I don't know that?" the major replied, without breaking stride. "We've got orders. If not stopped, the Nationalists will push through to the Mediterranean and cut Republican Spain in two. If they manage that, it's all over." He was signalling for the men to mount up when he noticed Dollard. "Who the hell's that?"

"The Montreal reporter."

"What the Sam Hill's he doing here? You were supposed to get rid of him."

Dollard cut in before his friend had a chance to speak. "All I want is a chance to tag along with the troops."

"Get out of here before I put you under arrest."

"He really is a reporter, Major," Marty interrupted. "He's got the papers to prove it. Show him, Dollard."

Dollard shoved his credentials at Smith. The major pushed them away. "Shit! Just what I need, a wannabe Robert Capa on my hands." He turned to Marty. "You sure about this, Kellenberger?" Marty nodded. "Then he's your responsibility. Just make sure his paper doesn't come crying to me if he gets his ass shot off."

Chapter Twenty-two

DOLLARD LAY ON HIS BACK squinting up at the noonday sky. Deep blue in all directions. He tried to see the blacks, purples, and yellows his mother swore were there, in happier days, when he was a boy and she was more into oil-painting than gin. An idea crossed his mind, a humourous one. He intended to merely guffaw—at the nonsense that there was anything but blue in the sky, at the pickle they were in, at the date he suddenly remembered—but with the rush of air shooting up from his diaphragm it got away on him, morphing to a cackle that tumbled off the rocks and descended to the *barranca* below. "Know what day it is?" he asked.

No response. Marty had his eyes trained on the activity in the valley. The remnants of the Internationals, once a proud army, were in full flight. For several minutes, there'd be no movement, then, like ants pouring out from a under a disturbed rock, pockets of men would appear, limping, dragging wounded, clutching firearms, or, ominously, carrying no weapons at all. Occasionally, there'd be trucks and those do-it-yourself, boiler-plated vehicles constructed in the dockyards in Valencia; the ones that reminded Dollard of beached submarines. They'd shoot up from behind the *carabineros*, honking, waving frantically to clear the way, scattering infantry to the ditches. From the valley floor came shouts that the Nationalists were close behind. As if reminding was needed. Over the past few weeks, Dollard had witnessed the wrath of the Nationalists up close; theirs was an army replete with every modern weapon that money could buy from the killing factories of Stuttgart and Turin. Meanwhile, Marty's beggars' army was at the mercy of the British blockade and the mood of their Russian suppliers.

Around Dollard, the men tensed. More soldiers had appeared on the road. Nothing new there, but these troopers moved cautiously, with no hint of panic. Nationalists. The Internationals opened fire and bodies began dropping. Some lay still, while others writhed and screamed. The rest scattered behind rocks or retreated from whence they'd come. The firing stopped.

Marty's men, along with others, had been assigned to slow up the advance. However, down to rifles, a few machine guns, and a handful of tank bombs, it wouldn't take much for Franco's troops to push them off this cliffside. At Teruel, three months earlier, there'd been twenty soldiers in Marty's section. Twelve had survived. Today his flock numbered six, counting himself and Dollard. For almost two weeks, they'd been in retreat, fighting, stalling, and falling back to new lines of defence. They'd been separated from the rest of the Mac-Paps for days. The lines had become such a jumble that no one knew who was where.

"You don't know, do you?" Dollard repeated to Marty.

Marty turned, his face screwed up under the floppy beret picked up in Tarragona. "Don't know what?"

"What day it is. It's April first—*poisson d'avril.*" The Maxim a few yards to the right came to life. As a machine gun it was superb at its job, but it wouldn't be leaving with them when they cleared off this hill. Designed to be pulled by horses across the steppes of Russia, it was too heavy to carry. A mule had brought it up this high before being hit by shrapnel. The animal had still been writhing and braying when the men fell on it, like hyenas over a downed wildebeest, hacking off strips of flesh. Dollard wasn't shocked. During the retreat, he'd noticed the disappearance of animals—cats, pigeons, even those skinny dogs that ran the streets of every village.

Marty pointed to a car-sized boulder to the left of their position on the ridge. "Over there!" he called to the remnants of his platoon. "Let's go." They rose, hugging the ground as they ran.

"What was that all about?" Dollard asked, when they'd reached their objective, scarcely ninety metres away. "We spent two hours digging 'oles back there. And that machine gun was a real comfort."

"Premonition," Marty responded. "We've been beating off foot soldiers all morning. They'll have their artillery in place any time now, and when they do, that machine gun's a magnet. Those Dombrowski Brigade guys knew what they were doing when they dug in beside this huge rock. Soon's I saw them vacate, I figured we'd best beat the other sections to it. Besides, the Poles didn't take their foxholes with them, did they?"

It didn't surprise Dollard to see the Dombrowskis go. It'd been happening all day; small groups coming up to help, then rejoining the flight for the Ebro River at Mora. No one wanted to get caught on the west side of the river when the last bridge was blown. What had been an orderly withdrawal had become a rout. He turned to Marty. "Why are we still 'anging around?" A squadron of Fiats roared into the valley strafing the road, wagging their wings in victory. Cocky aviators from Italy and Germany controlled the air.

Marty waited for them to disappear before replying. "Soon as the artillery starts in earnest. But we're not going down." He jerked a thumb at the cliff behind. "It's up and over for us."

Dollard stared at the highway below that led to the last community they'd fought their way through hours earlier—Gandesa. It had been a gamble to go through it rather than around it, but the decision had saved time. They would have been closing in on the Ebro by now if not for the order to play rearguard on this cliffside. He flopped onto his back in the foxhole he shared with Marty. "'Ow long you going to put up with this shit?"

"Just told you. When the artillery starts in earnest we'll—"

"That's not what I'm talking about and you know it."

Marty stared down into the *barranca* as if searching for a target. "Don't start that nonsense again, Desjardins."

"This army's beaten, *fini*. You gave it your best, Marty. Why not go 'ome and get ready for the next war you've been predicting? Maybe you'll get more support for that one."

"And maybe, right now, help's just around the corner. What with Hitler moving into Austria and Mussolini falling on his face over Ethiopia and Albania, maybe the world is finally seeing the light. If so, all we have to do is hang on a bit more. Just long enough to give Roosevelt and Chamberlain time to come to their senses. The Ebro River's close. Across it sits the bulk of the Republican Army. My job right now is to get these guys over that river and join them. This is not the time for quitting."

"What about living to fight another day?"

"Drop it, Desjardins!" Marty said, scratching at the lice in his pants. "I got to work out a way to get us over the Ebro."

Marty was right about the rebels taking the hillside seriously, but wrong that it would be *los morteros nacionales* who'd do it. Sometime close to 0330 hours, Stuka dive-bombers came heading straight for them. Cries of "Planes! Take cover!" reverberated across the cliffs in a plethora of languages. All day, squadrons of Heinkels, ME-109s, and Fiat fighters had been circling the area in giant pinwheels, swooping down in turn to strafe the roads, then climbing back up into formation. For a student of war, it was an amazing sight. But this time, the screaming Stukas were coming at them.

Dollard watched a soldier raise his rifle to fire, only to see Marty reach out and bang the barrel with the flat of his hand. "Don't waste ammunition!" he commanded. The man dropped back into his hole.

A few seasoned veterans stared up at the planes, fascinated by their murderous howl, rival only to the explosion that would come at the bottom of a dive. Eight bombs were dropped, each creating a fountain of shrapnel, rock splinters, and yellow powder. Through it, the drone of engines began to fade, replaced by cries of, "Help!" *Socorro!*" and "*Au secours*," mingled with the sound of men scrambling for the road below. By the time the dust cleared, most had gone.

Two of Marty's charges, the ginger-headed miner from Timmins and the stevedore from Vancouver, lay dead. His command now numbered four.

Marty bent over the bodies, removing valuables, identity papers, and letters. Hastily, they then laid them in a depression created by one of the bombs and scraped dirt over top. Dollard placed pebbles in the shape of a cross on the mound and, together, they mumbled a few words. It was over in five minutes. "Grab your weapons," Marty said, "we're going up."

Progress to the top was slow. A Heinkel 51 spotter plane glided unchallenged back and forth over the valley looking for signs of movement. Dollard could picture the pilot, radio strapped to his head, excitedly radioing information to attack aircraft in the pinwheel formation higher up. The climb was difficult; moving across broken terrain, necks craned to the sky, made it doubly so.

The greatest danger came not from the aircraft they could see, but from those that might, unexpectedly, shoot over the summit from the neighbouring valley. Several times they were forced to freeze, the ground vibrating as the piston-driven engines roared over. More than once, planes banked and screamed back for a second look, but so far, they'd left without firing their cannons.

To Dollard's surprise, there were bushes, but few trees on the way up. He put this down to overgrazing and population increases that had forced the locals ever farther up the hillsides in search of fuel. While olive orchards on the shallower slopes provided some cover, not to mention the odd pine and broad-leafed tree, frequently they were forced to sprint across clearings and scramble up goat paths, fully exposed. Dollard caught the expression on Marty's face each time his charges dashed across open spaces. It was the look of a vigilant parent. He wondered if they'd erred in not opting for the valley roads, but now was not the time to add to Marty's burden by questioning his judgment.

"At the top we go to ground until midnight," Marty announced after another close call. "It'll be slow moving in the dark, but at least the moon's still got a few nights to it."

They hustled after that, reaching the plateau and taking shelter in a small cave under a pine tree, where others had obviously squatted before them. They'd been soldiers, not shepherds, judging from the cigarette butts and miscellaneous refuse.

"Ours or theirs?" Dollard asked, toeing an empty can.

"Probably both," Marty replied, opening his haversack and pulling out a mildewy potato and a liberated wine skin. The others followed suit and they pooled their cache. He stared at the meagre pickings—a can of chick peas, a handful of unripe olives, a hunk of stale bread, a small bag of lentils, and several strips of raw meat hacked from the dead mule.

They chewed in silence, stopping every once in a while to listen for sounds of danger—voices, footsteps, changes of pitch in the engines above. "'Ow far you figure to the bridge at Mora?" Dollard asked.

Marty shrugged. "Twelve miles, tops. Not far the way the bullet flies, but at the rate we're going, I'd say four to five days."

The skinny lad sat up. "But the bridge'll still be there, eh, Sergeant?"

Dollard studied the last two recruits. Marty had schooled them as best he could, and so far they'd listened, copied, and survived. Others who hadn't were either dead or wandering somewhere on the road between Gandesa and Mora de Ebro.

"Don't fret," Marty replied. "If the bridge has been blown, we'll swim. Piece of cake."

The boy sucked air like he was about to convulse. "They say the water comes from the glaciers in the Pyrenees," he blurted out. "And now that the rebels have opened the dams near Zaragoza, the current's supposed to be terrible swift."

Marty stopped chewing. "Where you from?" he asked.

"Ranch. Near Graysville. Manitoba."

He put a hand on the farmboy's shoulder. "Guess there aren't many swimming holes out your way, eh?" The lad shook his head. "We'll get you home safe," Marty soothed. "If the bridge is gone, we'll steal a boat, or make a raft if we have to."

Dollard burped. "That's it for the chickpeas," he announced, tossing the tin over his shoulder. It sailed out, pinballing into the canyon below.

The soldiers tensed. Marty grabbed his rifle, flopping to the ground near the opening, the two recruits following suit. "For God's sake, Desjardins," he said in a barely audible voice, after a few minutes, "have you lost your bloody mind? Why do you think we've been talking in whispers? Had there been a rebel patrol out there, we'd be toes up by now; each with a bullet right here." He tapped his forehead with a finger.

"I didn't mean to—"

"And don't be thinking you'd be a spectator, either. No way is some Moor going to care that you're a reporter taken prisoner. They'll drill you just as fast as the rest of us."

"I'm sorry, I . . . wasn't thinking."

"Get some sleep! All of you!" Marty ordered.

Dollard waited for the recruits to nod off before joining his friend at the opening. The sun was long down, but a firefight had erupted high on the other side of the valley. For several minutes, they lay side by side, peering out and listening. "We've got to think smart," Marty said. "Down to four rifles and with maybe fifty rounds of ammunition, we can't put up much resistance. And we're toast if the rebels show up with flame-throwers." He chuckled at the unintended pun.

Dollard tried his best to laugh with him. "'Ave you really got a plan?" he asked.

Marty glanced over at the others before answering. "Kinda, but I won't bullshit you; it's a long shot. We're in what they call the Sierra de Cavalls mountains. They're a series of rock islands, just like the one we're on, each separated by a valley. If I knew how many there were between here and the river, I'd be able to make a good guess. As long as we're on the high ground, we're relatively safe. It's crossing the valleys that'll be the killer."

They passed what Dollard guessed must have been an hour without speaking, listening for footsteps, but hearing only the trees creaking in the wind. The stars came out. "Crazy, eh?" Dollard said, at last. "All that bad blood back home; each of us in our own little ghetto."

Marty nodded. "Takes a shock to get your priorities straight. Riding the rails, jail, and this war did it for me. Now I know where I'm heading; I've got someone to go home to. The miracle is that after three years she still cares."

"You could 'ave been a doctor with a wife by now."

Marty propped his head up with his arm. "Want to hear something stupid?" he said. "Sure, I've been robbed. Who hasn't? But I've learned things about myself I'd have never known. Turns out, I'm stronger than anyone ever gave me credit for, myself included. People go through their whole lives wondering about stuff like that. Now I can go home and get on with my future."

"You've got a good 'andle on life. Maybe you should go into politics."

"Whoa! That's for the likes of you, Dollard. They'd never elect me."

"Who says? It's not as if you're a communist or anything."

Marty smiled. "I tried to be, first for Riva and then for the guys, but it wouldn't stick. Know what my problem was? The communists were for the poor sods at the bottom of the ladder, but that's not how I saw myself. I was going to be a doctor, rising above the ghetto, and getting through life on my own. No help needed, thank you."

"You wouldn't be the first Jew to run for office. There was a Jewish guy in the National Assembly when I left Quebec."

"I know, but he was squeaky clean. Nobody'd vote for a *schmuck* with my record. But you, you'd be great at it—tall, blond, good looking, athletic, bilingual."

"But you're the real leader."

Marty sat up. "I could work on your campaign. Bring in the Jewish vote and maybe some of those textile workers I got to know, too. Dolly would help. She's that union girl I told you about. Riva might have been crazy, but she taught me a lot about bringing people around. She had smarts that way."

"Did you ever find out what 'appened to 'er?" Shooting flared up across the valley, then just as quickly died out. More comrades gone, Dollard thought, wondering if they were Internationals, Mac-Paps perhaps.

Marty shook his head. "She got swallowed up in Russia. Last letter came while I was in prison in Saskatchewan. I used to figure that somewhere, somehow, she'd turn up. But I've talked to reporters who've been to the Soviet Union and I know better now. They all say the same thing: to survive there you keep your mouth shut. Unfortunately, that's not Riva. She'd never make it." He strained to see across the valley as if she might be over there, letting the fascists have it.

Dollard lay on his stomach, breathing in the scent of pine needles and picking at the ground with a stick. "So, you'll be going back to Connie when you get 'ome?"

"Fast as I can. 'Course, I'll have lots of explaining to do with the Mc-Meekins. They're generous people, even if they are Catholic and Irish." He shot Dollard a smile and got a punch on the shoulder in return. "But I shortchanged them by hiding my Jewishness."

"From what I've been 'earing, I think they'll overlook it."

"Wouldn't fault them if they didn't. What about you?"

Dollard shifted to his side with his head on his arm. "My Irish-Catholic girl's long gone," he said, looking off into the night. "I traded her in for Spain."

"She wouldn't wait?"

"She made me choose, but it wasn't really between 'er and Spain. She knew the real reason I was leaving, and she was right. I'm not proud of myself."

"Maybe she'll be there when you get back; women can be—"

Dollard's hand shot out to silence him. They cocked their guns as a strange sound came drifting over the trees from the far side of the valley. They strained to make it out, baffled by its origin—male voices in song. It grew louder, bolder. Marty raised his head. The tune was familiar. He began mouthing the words. "Hold the fort for we are coming," the voices sang, "Union men be strong. Fierce and long the battle rages, But we will not fear, Help will come whene'er it's needed, Cheer, my comrades, cheer." It carried across the hills, rising and falling in a slow, deliberate cadence. Here and there new voices joined in.

Marty clutched Dollard's arm. "We're not dead yet, my friend," he said.

You didn't have to be a genius to see that time was not on their side. By the third night, enemy patrols were so thick progress had slowed to a crawl. During the day, they lay on their backs counting birds and three-engined Savoia S79s on bombing runs from Zaragoza to Barcelona. Minutes ticked into days, with gunfire from the valley progressively diminishing. At first, Dollard took this for a sign that they were pulling away from the rebels. The harried expression on Marty's face told another story—the Nationalists were gaining, leap-frogging along the roads, cleaning out pockets in the low areas, and isolating stragglers on the hillsides. Valley crossings grew progressively perilous. The young recruits had been more or less mute since day four. That was the day the ground had trembled and a cloud of dust and smoke had risen in the east. It meant one thing—Republican *dinamiteros* in Moro had done their job—the last bridge over the Ebro River was no more.

"There it is," Marty said on the sixth day. He was pointing from a crag to the black line on the horizon a mile to the east. "It's the Ebro. One more valley and we're home free. We'll move down after sunset." Dollard saw the river, but his eyes were fixed on the glut of war machines in the valley, all with Nationalist markings.

The Graysville boy's chin trembled. "The river. It'll be swollen, won't it? What are the chances of us getting to the other side, Sergeant?"

"Cut it out!" Marty snapped. "I said I'd get you across, didn't I? Now get some rest."

Dollard tried to tell himself that this final descent was no different from the others. Certainly, the procedure was the same—take a few steps, stop, listen, move on, give wide berth to voices and movement. Tonight, though, something definitely had changed. A chill shot up his spine as it hit him: The Nationalists in the lowlands made no secret of their presence, as they called to each other, belted out regimental songs, and added fuel to their open fires.

They'd just worked their way onto the valley floor when Marty motioned them down. Hearing voices was common, but these were uncomfortably close. "Are they in front of us or behind?" he signalled. There was a communal shrug before they resumed their trek.

After several yards, Marty's hand went up again. The muffled hum of conversation had grown louder. Dollard swallowed. Not because of the fire nearby, but because of the smell of the food cooking over it. He felt his stomach leap and pressed on it with a fist to cut the rumbling. Lamb. He was sure of it, but, then again, in his starved state, it could have been dog or horse and the reaction would have been the same. He strained to make out the language, praying for English even as he detected a Latin cadence. He looked to Marty who was shaking his head and pointing to the line they were to follow. They pushed forward. Light from the fire flickered through the bushes. The lad from Sydney stumbled, but recovered. They halted and listened, fingers poised over their triggers.

They'd only taken a few steps when Dollard heard the click of weapons followed by a voice from the shadows. "Comrades," it said, "we've got chow."

Dollard jumped.

"Lincolns," Marty whispered, "that's a Brooklyn accent."

In unison, they lowered their rifles and approached. Brooklyn stepped from the shadows, motioning them down an alleyway of junipers. Smiling soldiers stepped out of the bushes, gesturing to the fire crackling just beyond a stone shed. They didn't need encouragement. The flame and the contents on the grill over it were siren enough. A barrel-chested officer sat next to the fire in a broken chair, cradling a machine pistol in his lap.

Dollard sniffed the air. "*Les oignons*," he exclaimed, too exhausted to realize he was talking in French. *"Merci, mon Dieu."* He raised his arms heavenward and turned to Marty who seemed preoccupied with something other than food.

"You take that off a dead German?" he asked, gesturing with his chin to the machine pistol. The officer chose not to reply, glancing instead at Brooklyn.

"He doesn't speak English," Brooklyn said.

Dollard saw Marty's reaction and tensed. He watched Marty's finger inch to the safety latch of his gun and might have done the same had it not been for Graysville and Sydney, who'd already propped their rifles against a log and were warming themselves by the fire. "Lived in the Empire State long have we?" Marty asked in a controlled voice.

Brooklyn's response was equally calm. "I've cousins in the States."

"Then you're not . . . from New York . . . yourself?"

Brooklyn smirked and said something in Italian. "Palermo," he answered. Machine Pistol raised his weapon. At the same instant, more guns appeared from the shadows. All pointing at the Mac-Paps. They raised their hands.

Marty's chin sank to his chest. "Shit! Shit! Shit!" he mumbled. "Italian Black Flames."

Dollard felt a crushing weariness descend on him, like he was passing out. The next few minutes became Kafkaesque, happening but not happening, his brain sensing, but refusing to process. Soldiers surrounding them, taunting as they frisked for weapons and valuables. Machine Pistol barking an order. Brooklyn ordering them to empty their pockets as he held out his forage cap, like a parishioner taking up the offering in church. Brooklyn sorting through the confiscated items, setting some aside for further inspection and tossing the rest in the fire. Flames licking at the edges of Marty's snapshots of Connie and Riva, the girls curling up and turning to ash.

Dollard came out of his trance with Brooklyn screaming in his face. "Are you the one from Man-i-to-ba?" he demanded, holding out a card. Graysville moaned. Brooklyn turned an icy stare on him. "This here's a union membership," he proclaimed, shaking his head in fake sorrow. "You're a goddamned communist, aren't you?" Brooklyn and officer exchanged words in Italian. The conference ended abruptly with Machine Pistol's chin jerking in the direction of the stone shed.

A soldier swung his rifle at Graysville, catching him in the plexus, dropping him like a steer in an abattoir. Two men dragged him to the shed, where they tried several times to prop him up against the wall. Finally, in disgust, they stepped back, pointed their guns at him as he lay with outstretched arms and fired. One soldier cursed at the blood that splattered his pants. The others cackled at their colleague's misfortune.

Dollard convulsed with the sudden disconnect between mind and body—thoughts careening backward to happier times, even while bowels and bladder were beginning to fail.

The Italians slapped their knees, held their noses, and pointed to the wet stream soaking his pants. A high-pitched wail rang through the air. It baffled Dollard, but drew his attention away from his own state. The source was from deep down in the man beside him—Sydney. It grew louder, like a revving engine, until Sydney's legs kicked in, sending him leaping across the fire and zig-zagging for the darkness. Excited soldiers shrieked for joy as they fired, but when they failed to find a mark, it was left to Machine Pistol. He rose from his chair and squeezed off a burst from the hip. The fleeing man went down. Machine Pistol smirked. Dollard flicked his eyes from Grayville's limp body to Sydney's bleeding remains, then back to the fire. There was comfort there. A screen went up in his mind. Thoughts of the Laurentians filled his head. He saw smiling faces, wieners on a stick, marshmallows turning golden in the flame.

A soldier sauntered over to Sydney's jerking body, rifle raised. The *coup de grâce* echoed through the trees, while Brooklyn went on with his work, holding up a passport. "Which one of you is the Frenchman?" he demanded impatiently. Dollard's arm lifted itself, his eyes never straying from the blaze. "Says here you're a reporter. That true?" Dollard's head rose and fell on its own. Brooklyn shrugged, conversed with Machine Pistol in rapid-fire Italian, then turned back. "My captain says Western reporters spread lies about our glorious troops in Spain. It makes him sick."

The captain nodded, as if he understood the translation, and jerked his thumb to the stone shed. Soldiers encircled Dollard, nudging and prodding him toward the wall. He moved in baby steps, a curious cross between a small boy heading for bed and an old man suffering from dementia.

Halfway to the wall, Marty came to life. "Kill him and you kill one of your own," he shouted. "He's my prisoner. Check his passport. You'll find a visa from Nationalist Spain. He's here at the invitation of General Franco. Executing him will really piss off *El Caudillo*."

Brooklyn raised his hand. The procession to the wall came to a halt while he read aloud the entry points in the passport: "Rock Island, Vermont; Le Havre, France; Irún, Spain." He looked up impatiently, expecting further explanation.

"Go ahead, Desjardins. Tell him why you came to Spain. How you were captured."

Dollard blinked. He knew they were talking about him, but he couldn't make sense of it.

"And show him that Catholic thing you wear around your neck. The one your cardinal friend gave you."

The fire popped, sending a spray of sparks into the night. Dollard smiled at the unexpected glimpse from the past that blazed through his head. He saw an ember landing on a silk blouse and a hand, his hand, patting it to put it out. The hand lingers . . . boy and girl exchange glances, she smiles. Good things follow.

"For Chrissakes, Desjardins, snap out of it!"

The edge to Marty's voice annoyed him. Why the need to shout?

Marty turned back to Brooklyn, talking fast. "He was invited to Spain to work for El Señor Bolín's press agency out of Salamanca. A convoy of foreign reporters came to Teruel to witness a Nationalist victory. Only we were still there, and he became our prisoner. Check it out. It's true."

Brooklyn stroked his chin. "Teruel was months ago."

"I was supposed to get rid of him. But I kept putting it off. Made him do stuff for us. He became our slave."

"You turned him against us?"

"No! He's too stupid for that. Bugger's still a believer—Franco, church, nobles, all that shit. I even caught him on his knees with a rosary and fingering that holey-moley thing around his neck." He turned. "Didn't I, Desjardins? Admit it, asshole!"

Brooklyn spoke to the soldiers holding Dollard. One of them ripped open his shirt and stepped back, extending a reverent hand to touch the scapula. Brooklyn conferred with Machine Pistol who rang his hands like Pontius Pilot. Eyes swung back to Marty. "My captain says we'll verify his story, but not because we give a damn about pissing off Franco. We're Italians, not bumbling Spaniards."

The trance that had seized Dollard began to lift. One second he was heading for the wall and the next rifles were prodding him away from it. As his head cleared he became aware of two things, the sticky stench from his groin and the shift of attention from him to Marty.

"So, now we come to you, Mr. Big Mouth," he heard Brooklyn say. "You've got no papers, no identification, no nothing. Know what that tells me? You've got something to hide. What are you? Freemason? Communist? Atheist? Jew?"

Marty shook his head. "I've never knowingly met a Freemason in my life," he replied in a barely audible voice, "and I don't think much of communism."

"That leaves atheist and Jew," Brooklyn shot back.

Marty hesitated. Machine Pistol rattled off a sentence in Italian and jerked his head to the wall. The soldiers lunged for Marty, but he shook them off, moving on his own. When he reached the stone structure, he turned to face his friend, resignation in his voice. "Don't watch, Dollard! Turn away!"

Dollard felt his mouth open and close, but his lips refused to move. Every muscle in his body was shutting down. Even his eyes were failing to work. He couldn't pull them away.

Marty tipped his head back. "Connie! *Oy gevalt*! Connie!" he wailed to the sky, "I'm sorry. I'm sorry. I'm sorry." The soldiers stepped back several steps and raised their rifles. "My Kaddish?" he moaned, "who will say Kaddish for Martin Kellenberger?"

The soldiers cocked their rifles. Marty straightened, placed his glasses in their metal case, and raised his voice: "Hear O Israel, the Lord is one God, the Lord is One. Blessed be the name of the glory of His kingdom, forever and—"

The volley echoed in the night. Marty's body flew against the wall and slumped to the ground. The soldiers closed in for a final frisk. A belt, a flashlight, and a good-luck charm were produced. The tallest came up with a watch, which he rushed to the firelight for closer examination.

Dollard's voice came to life as they jostled for the biggest prize of all—Marty's boots. "Please don't do that," he begged softly. No one heard, or listened, or cared. They were busy. One had Marty by the armpits. Another had a foot to his groin as he tugged at the footwear. They'd just gotten them off when Brooklyn shouted a command. Sullenly, the boots were handed over to Machine Pistol, who examined them carefully, a scowl spreading across his face. He screamed something in Italian. Brooklyn turned on Marty's body, as if expecting a response.

"He thinks this leather is Italian. He calls you a son of a bitch for stealing them from a dead countryman." Machine Pistol pointed his weapon at Marty and fired several rounds. Soldiers scattered, while Marty's body jerked under the impact, and the glasses case flew from his hand. Dollard covered his head with his arms and fell to the ground. Brooklyn sneered.

PART EIGHT
Montreal, September 1939

Chapter Twenty-three

September 24, 1939
Montreal

"INCREDIBLE!" FATHER LATENDRESSE SAID, sitting back on the park bench and pressing his fingertips together. "The way you tell it, this man sacrificed his life for yours. What a magnificent image to hold onto." He stopped and looked off for an instant before resuming. "Not to take away from it, Dollard, but is it possible, considering the trauma of the event and all, that maybe you're reading too much into it?"

At the other end of the bench, Dollard sat hunched over with his elbows on his knees, a finger plunging in and out of the hole in the battered glasses case he cradled in his hands. His head jerked up, like he'd been hit with cold water. Served him right for confiding in an old priest whose window on life had never opened on more than the darkened confines of the confessional. How could such a man begin to understand the depth of his shame? He felt doubly cheated. It had taken months to overcome his pain and succumb to the cleric's coaxing to "get it off his chest." All morning he'd been spilling his guts. Now, at the point of maximum exposure, the priest was dismissing his nightmare as the result of an overactive imagination. The weariness he'd shed began to fall back on him. He moved to bolt, and would have, if not for the old woman with the canes blocking his way. By the time she'd hobbled by, the urge to flee had begun to dissipate. Instead, the two men rose together and headed for the park exit.

"Forgive my clumsiness," Latendresse said as they walked. "I can be a bumbling old fool." He smiled. "You know, something just occurred to me. This friend of yours . . . he wasn't the first Jew to sacrifice his life for others."

Dollard caught the analogy and dropped his head. "So, we know who that makes me, don't we?" he stammered, his hands tightening around the glasses case. "Maybe I didn't collect thirty pieces of silver for my betrayal, but I stood by and let it happen. Those bullets were meant for me."

"And what would protesting have accomplished? Got you both killed, I'd say. It strikes me your friend would never have wanted that."

Dollard's eyes held to the ground, as if searching for a hole to claim him. There was comfort in the thought. At least his hole would be marked for family and friends, infinitely better than what Marty, Sydney, and Graysville had been given.

When the killing had stopped that night, he'd been forced to drag their bodies to a ditch and dig out shallow graves. Then, sometime in the small hours, wild dogs had arrived scratching away at the earth. He'd lain on the ground, hands over his ears, blocking out the growls and snarls. But the images seized his mind, becoming the foundation for the mental torture now so easily triggered—a grey stone wall, a Bronx accent, a barking dog, a campfire.

"By the rules of the Spanish War, Father, he could have executed me at Teruel. Instead, he took a chance. In no time, he'd opened my eyes, to things over there and back home, too."

Father Latendresse clasped his hands behind his back as they moved. "Good! Good!" he nodded.

"Through him, I came to loathe zealots. Spain was full of them—both sides. They were the law and they answered to themselves. Betraying, confiscating for gain, executing at the slightest pretext—a strange dialect, the smell of gunpowder on a man's fingers. God help us should it ever happen here."

"Surely, you're not suggesting that—"

"Strong men come to power, Father. Laws get passed. Things escalate. Take our new premier with his Padlock Law. Wasn't it enacted to suppress petty irritants—labour unions? Communists? Jehovah's Witnesses? Any group that doesn't fit the mould? That's how it gets started, with small, seemingly innocent laws. Next thing you know you've got a *caudillo* on your hands."

Latendresse placed a hand on Dollard's shoulder. "That worries me, too," he said.

"How do we stop men like that from taking root, Father?"

Latendresse shrugged. "That's for your generation to solve, my son. My question is this: do you have what it takes to see that it doesn't happen? Show leadership?"

Dollard frowned. "Look at me, Father. What do you see? A depressed alcoholic. Does that strike you as leadership material?"

A woman approached pushing a pram, so the men stepped off the path to let her pass. "You sell yourself short," Latendresse replied. "To hear you tell it, you took from your friend and gave nothing in return. I can't accept that. Friendship is a *quid pro quo*. I dare say he also profited from your relationship."

Dollard turned the glasses case over and over in his pocket as they walked. "And just what might he have gained from me? How to recognize superior wine? How to mark a poker deck? How to get laid in a whorehouse? Some *quid pro quo!* I shortchanged him, then watched as he took my place at the wall. How do I live with that, Father?"

Latendresse spoke in a low voice. "By carrying on his work and correcting society's ills. You're young, but you've seen more of the world than most. In all my days, the farthest I have ever strayed from Quebec was to an ecclesiastical conference in Chicago, in 1921; hardly an eye-opener. But I've tried not to be blind to human nature. Last week I dug up the newspaper articles you filed from Spain and compared them to the ones you're about to submit to *Le Devoir. Mon Dieu,* how you've matured. You've come home with a global outlook. You're needed here, Dollard."

"Surely, you don't really believe *Le Devoir* will print those latest submissions of mine?"

"There are other papers. Start your own if you have to. This province is hungry for people with your perspective. Somebody has to nudge us into the modern world. Get busy. Surmount your demons. Be a credit to your friend's memory."

Dollard angled his head up a few degrees. "I want to, Father, desperately. But after all these months, I'm still scampering up and down those mountains in Spain and listening to the wild dogs. Will I never get to the river?"

Father Latendresse swung open the park gate to the street and gestured for Dollard to exit. "You're closer, my son. Maybe this is where God intends for you to travel. Listen to Him. Take up His challenge."

"What if, deep down, I'm just a coward? Since coming home, I've had opportunities, but have done nothing. I could have raised my voice against the government for refusing to repatriate those Mac-Paps not born in this country. Many of them were Jews, you know, forced back to Germany. What'll happen to them? Or I could have written articles condemning the shunning volunteers got when they returned. Instead, I watched them drag their broken bodies off the ships in silence. Just like the rest of the country."

"You weren't ready then."

"I was drunk."

They were on Hochelaga now, a young man and a priest, shuffling along with brows furrowed. People smiled at what could easily be mistaken for a nephew concerned for an aging uncle at his side.

It was an oppressively hot day for September. The sewers reeked. A panel truck draped in blue bunting turned onto the street, blaring a political message on behalf of the election campaign just getting underway. Kids rushed out from alleyways. Adults stopped to listen as the speakers crackled out the merits of one Maurice Duplessis and his Union Nationale. Dollard and Pierre watched from a distance, taking in the crowd and the banners hanging from the lampposts—blue for Duplessis, red for his Liberal rival.

"Your friend in Spain," Latendresse began, "you said he—"

"He has a name, Pierre. Use it. Please. It's Marty."

Latendresse cleared his throat. "You said that just before the end, you and . . . Marty . . . talked about improving things when you got home." Dollard nodded. "Isn't it time to get busy?"

"I wouldn't know where to begin."

"Start by looking around. You'll find a lot of people worse off than you." Dollard accepted the criticism with a sigh. The priest continued. "Take that old woman with the canes back in the park. I know her story. She could tell you a thing or two; like how her husband was chopped to death in a factory because of unsafe machines, leaving her to raise eleven kids alone. With no money, there was no schooling. Now they've grown up with families of their own, but, with no education, their prospects are poor. Who's to help her in her old age?"

Dollard's hand tightened around the glasses case. "The government should set up a—"

"She'd vote for any government promising to bring in reforms. But, of course, she won't be doing that because women in this province don't have the vote."

Dollard turned to him. "These reforms you seem to be pushing for, do they include education?"

"Of course."

"Aren't you out of step? You're a cleric, and your Church controls the schools, doesn't it?"

"It's *our* Church, Dollard," Latendresse corrected, "yours and mine, and it's messing up education. We've got to stop schooling everyone to be priests, doctors, and lawyers, and nothing else. We need managers and engineers."

"Does the bishop know of these ideas of yours?"

Pierre waved his hand in dismissal. "People like Duplessis hold us back."

"Seems to me you're a lone voice on this, Father. Aren't priests telling parishioners that voting *bleu* gets them into heaven and *rouge* into hell?"

"Stop seeing things in black and white, Dollard. You've written the Church off, just like you have your family. There's a new breed of priest coming along that wants our people to progress. The seminaries are full of them. What they need are skills like yours to explain things to the public. Get involved. I just wish I could be around when it happens."

Dollard frowned. "You sick or something?"

Pierre smiled. "Just old. People my age have no illusions about immortality. The hardest part is knowing you won't be around to see change come about."

For several minutes, Dollard and Pierre watched the crowd that had gathered for the political show. When it was over, a group of young men set to defacing a Liberal poster. What had been *"Votez pour Godbout"* had become *"Votez pour Godboutski"* with a hammer and sickle added. Dollard shuddered, his mind skipping back to his days with Jeune-Canada.

"Ignorant fools," Latendresse mumbled, as they resumed their walk. "They vilify what they don't understand."

Dollard looked at him. "You like this guy, Godbout, don't you, Father."

Latendresse sighed. "Unfortunately, he's ahead of his time. I fear we're still too conservative for him. Those young goons speak for a lot of people."

"I belonged to a group like that in university," Dollard said.

Latendresse looked at him. "If it's the group I'm thinking of, all I can say is some of them have grown up and have had a change of heart. Just like you."

"What's so special about Godbout?"

"That my, young friend, is for you to find out."

Dollard smiled. "You want me to start reading his literature, I suppose?"

"It wouldn't hurt, but I have something better in mind. Would you agree to talk to some young friends of mine?" Dollard shrugged. Pierre tipped his head and smiled. "No, make that one friend. I think it's time. There's a person I'm dying to have you meet."

"You make it sound mysterious."

"Let's just say I've been holding back."

<hr>

September 30, 1939
Eastern Townships, Quebec

THE EXPEDITION TO GODBOUT'S FARM in the Eastern Townships was Father Latendresse's idea. Dollard wasn't expecting much, but had agreed to go out of respect for the priest. The trip was for reporters, something Dollard hoped to call himself once again. The drinks en route were free, meaning that within half an hour, the bus was rocking with backslaps, shouts, and feigned insults. Dollard kept to himself. He suspected this junket to be some new form of grassroots politicking—bring reporters to your home turf to show them what a good fellow you were. Whatever the motive, he was just going along, for the time being. After Spain, a politician would have to walk on water to impress him. Still, Pierre had seen this as an opening for him, and he was probably right.

With *Le Devoir* no longer interested in his talents, getting here hadn't been easy. While his articles on Spain had sold papers, they ran contrary to the light *Le Devoir* wished to flash on that troubled land. In the eyes of the editors, D. Desjardins, erstwhile defender of the faith and classic provincial values, had become D. Desjardins, agnostic on all fronts. Ergo, the paper was no longer interested in his services. However, the competition, *La Presse* in particular, didn't see it that way. They'd heard the cash registers ringing and were considering giving him a go. In the meantime, they were prepared to consider any freelance articles he sent their way.

Of all the political shindigs underway, he wasn't sure why Father Latendresse had been so insistent that he attend this one. Regardless, whatever his motive, Pierre had worked hard to get Dollard's name on the invitation list.

Although Godbout was to address them on the front lawn as soon as they'd toured the farm, halfway through, Dollard had seen all the cows and milking devices he could take, so broke away from the group. Leaning against a fencepost and staring across the field at more cows, his thoughts involuntarily strayed to those brave Spanish peasants he'd seen struggling in the midst of war, when he was interrupted by a female voice.

"Do you know your animals?" she asked.

He turned and straightened immediately. From the confident tone, he expected a middle-aged woman, not a green-eyed Helen of Troy his own age and near his height. Squaring his shoulders, he calculated her to have a good eight inches on the average woman. He hoped she might be a fellow reporter, but the badge on her lapel announced her as a worker for Adélard Godbout. His hand shot forward. "Dollard Desjardins," he said hurriedly.

"Délorèse Laplante," she replied, shaking his hand with a firm grip.

He felt awkward, proffering a silly grin while his mind scrambled for something meaningful to add. Finally, he remembered that she'd asked a question. "Know my animals? Not really, aside from the fact that I'm looking at a herd of cows. Never been around animals much. My mother loves cats and I guess, recently, I've seen a lot of sheep and donkeys, not that I've learned a great deal about them, well nothing actually, they were just there . . . around . . . kind of." He stopped, feeling ridiculous for babbling, doubly so, because she was grinning. "What?" he asked.

"Those aren't cows, Monsieur Desjardins. Cows are what we saw in the barn."

Dollard blinked. "They're not?"

"They're steers."

"There's a difference?"

"Cows are for milking. These boys will wind up on the table." She leaned in closer. "They've been fixed, you see. Neutered."

"Ouch!" he responded. "Why would they do that?"

She chuckled. "Makes them grow faster. They get fat and lazy and better to eat."

His head bobbed up and down, as if she'd just shed light on a puzzle that had been keeping him awake nights. "Is that what they do to donkeys to turn them into mules?"

She threw her head back in a laugh so genuine he couldn't help but join in. It didn't matter that he'd said something foolish, he wanted her to go on laughing—the joyous face, the sparkling eyes, the Grecian nose. When had he last experienced genuine mirth? Not that he could tell the what or the why of it, but he didn't want it to end. A tingling sensation worked its way down his limbs. It was a feeling he'd forgotten.

When she got hold of herself, she put a hand on his arm and swallowed. "Oh, Monsieur Desjardins, I'm sorry, that was rude of me. I grew up on a farm in La Beauce. Sometimes I forget that city people aren't, shall we say, conversant with animal husbandry."

Dollard beamed at her. "Not too many cows in Outremont. Or donkeys, either."

"So I've noticed."

"You live here on Monsieur Godbout's farm?"

She shook her head. "Montreal. Not that I could ever completely forsake agriculture; especially the kind that Mr. Godbout advocates. But the sons get the farm, and, at sixteen, I wasn't ready to marry the boy next door."

"Glad you didn't," he blurted before he could stop himself. He hoped he hadn't sounded forward.

"Like half the girls in Montreal, I wound up working in a textile factory. That was an education. I got mixed up in a strike and lost my job. Fortunately, the Union needed people with inside experience and hired me. I'm still with them. Believe in them, too. Just like I believe in Adélard Godbout. That's why I volunteer for him."

A curly-headed red steer with a white face sauntered over to the fence and nuzzled Dollard's arm. He jumped back. "Those things bite?" he asked.

She smiled, extending her hand over the railing. He watched the steer sniff then lick it. Her hand disappeared in the animal's mouth. Dollard's jaw dropped.

"Don't worry," she said, "he's not about to devour it. Cattle have a craving for salt. He'll just suck on my hand for a bit. They have no upper teeth, you see. Can't bite." She extracted her hand and wiped it on her handkerchief. "You mentioned that you've seen a lot of sheep and donkeys lately," she said, smiling. "Where might that have been?"

The steer ambled away, his tail swishing at flies. Dollard leaned on the fence. He noticed that the herd was staring at him, as if daring him to answer honestly. "Spain," he said, without hesitation. The ease with which Spain fell from his lips surprised him. It had taken Father Latendresse months to extract that word without his having to fondle the glasses case in his pocket.

She stepped in closer, relaxing against the fence, and sighing, as if she'd just made a discovery. "Oh, you're that Desjardins, the one who wrote those articles on the Spanish War." She clasped her hands, exposing a hint of nervousness. "Those accounts meant a great deal to me—cleared up my confusion. I'm a Catholic girl at heart, but working for a union, yet leaning toward the Republicans, kind of put me offside.

Then along came those latest articles of yours and it all made sense. You were hard on the Church, but I got the feeling not quite prepared to abandon it."

"Why the interest in Spain?" Dollard asked. "Why not Germany, now that we've just declared war on them?"

She turned to face him. "I have a friend who went there, but hasn't returned. I've met every ship that docks, but no sign. A few people had heard of him, and one soldier had last seen him at some place called Gandesa. He was Jewish, you see, studying to be a doctor when he got caught up in . . . other stuff. I visit his parents. They're frantic. It's not healthy to be a Jew in Europe these days."

Dollard felt an electric shock course its way through him, forcing him back from the fence. "What kind of other stuff?"

"A strike at my factory. The one that got me fired. He sided with the workers. Unfortunately, the boss was his uncle and . . ." She stopped. "What's wrong, Monsieur Desjardins?" Dollard's eyes welled up. "Forgive me," she said. "I've hit a nerve."

Something must have gotten to the cattle, because they were now moving off in a long procession, down a well-worn path. Dollard stared at them vacantly, trying to hold himself together. At last, he faced her. "This man, was his name Marty?" He swallowed as he watched the blood drain from her face. "Marty was my friend, too," he said in a thin voice.

She touched his arm. "Is he . . . alive?" she asked. Dollard shook his head. "Are you sure?" He nodded. From his pocket came the glasses case he'd pulled from Marty's hand the night he'd buried him. She shuddered and turned away.

Dollard had no idea what happened to the time. Only when he heard a honking horn did he realize that the bus was about to leave and he'd missed Godbout's speech. The two of them had wandered off to the shade of a tree on a little hillock and for two hours had been talking. Somewhere along the line, Monsieur Desjardins had become Dollard and Mlle. Laplante, Dolly. He hadn't held back. She smiled through the good parts, laughing occasionally, weeping often. He told of his aborted visit to the Kellenbergers' shop; how he'd intended to return Marty's glasses, but had lost courage and fled. They agreed this was something he had to do alone, but she offered to arrange an introduction. He also told her of his drinking problem and Father Latendresse's untiring efforts to get him back on his feet. It turned out she knew the priest well. In fact, he'd checked with her several times to make sure she would be here today. They both laughed at this, but fell solemn when he explained how Marty had cried out for Connie in his last moments and how, with the money from his articles on Spain, he could at last afford a ticket to British Columbia to visit her and her family.

The horn sounded a second time. "I'm going to miss my bus," he said, making no effort to move.

"Let them go," she answered. "There's room for one more in Monsieur Godbout's car. It'll be a chance for you to get to know him."

"You don't think he'd mind?"

She shook her head. "He'll like you, Dollard. You've got a lot in common."

"You think a great deal of this guy, don't you?"

"He's got big plans—roads, electrification of the farms, the vote for women." She stopped. "Why are you smiling?"

Dollard raised his hands in mock self-defence. "I'm not laughing at you. Honest. I'm just . . . loving what you're telling me. If he's half of what you say, he's got my vote. Maybe I'd even work for him. That is, if—"

"What?"

"If he'd take me on."

"Why wouldn't he?"

"Well, I hear he's a bit of a churchman. And I wasn't very kind to politicians in my articles, either."

"Monsieur Godbout'll support any man who speaks out against society's ills."

"I have no idea what you do for him, but might it be possible for me to . . . maybe give you a hand? Sort of learn the ropes."

"Don't know about that," she smiled. "It would depend on Monsieur Godbout, now, wouldn't it?"

"Yes, but couldn't you . . . put in a good word?"

"Perhaps," she teased, "but then I don't know much about you, do I."

They heard the bus pull away and watched it go in a cloud of dust that drifted over the fence and across the fields. It might have reminded him of the dust trails the trucks made as they left the monastery at Valencia for the front, or vehicles scooting from Gandesa for the last bridge at Mora d'Ebre. But the thought never entered his mind.

Dollard stood, reaching down to help Dolly up. She took his hand, and he began to sing a toe-tapping Bolduc tune: "*Madamoiselle, voulez-vous danser, la bastringue, la bastringue.*"

"*Oui, oui, Monsieur,*" she sang in reply, "*je viens danser, la bastringue va commencer.*"

Hand in hand they jigged along the fence toward the farmhouse, tossing verses back and forth, until they came to the end. For a while, neither spoke. Dollard sensed the sudden change in the world around him, as if some clever Hollywood director had magically transformed the scene from black and white to technicolour. He was alive and Dolly was real. So was the world they were walking through—cedar fences, stubbled fields, black butterflies, bees, and asters, the last flower of the season. Was it too late for him? Yesterday, he would have said yes. Today, he found himself adjusting his stride to match that of the woman beside him.

Spanish Civil War: Chronology of Events

Prelude to War

1930: King Alfonso abdicates and is exiled.

1931: Republican government comes to power in a free, general election.

1936 (February): Republicans overwhelmingly returned to power; right wing unrest follows.

1936

July: Right-wing *coup d'état* sets off civil war; General Franco leaves the Canary Islands to join insurgents.

July: Hitler's pilots and planes transport the Spanish Foreign Legion from Spanish Morocco to the mainland.

October 1: Franco emerges as supreme commander and is named Chief of the Spanish State.

November 7: Franco begins offensive against Madrid, but is repelled by citizen army.

November 15: Hitler's Condor Legion airplanes begin air raids on Republican-held Spanish territory.

December 22: Mussolini sends Italian units and planes to assist Franco's insurgents.

1937

February 5–24: Battle of Jarama—Nationalist forces rebuffed trying to encircle Madrid.

March 8–18: Battle of Guadalajara—Italian forces routed by Republican Popular Army.

April 26: Condor Legion bombs Guernica on market day; 300 civilians die.

July 1: Mackenzie-Papineau Battalion formed, anchored by Canadian volunteers.

July 6–26: Battle of Brunete; Republicans capture Brunete, then quickly lose it.

August 24: Republicans victorious at Battle of Quinto on the Aragon Front.

September 1–14: Battle of Belchite on the Aragon Front; a pyrrhic victory for the Republicans.

October 12: Battle of Fuentes de Ebro on the Aragon Front; disaster for the Republicans.

December 15: Republican Army launches offensive on Teruel in spite of −18°C temperatures.

1938

February 3: International Brigades withdraw from Teruel.

February 22: Nationalists recapture Teruel; 100,000 casualties in total (one-quarter due to frostbite).

March 9: Nationalist Army breaks out of Aragon front and drives for the Ebro Basin.

March 10: Republican "Retreats" begin through Gandesa to the Ebro River.

April 15: Republican territory cut in two as Franco reaches the Mediterranean at Vinaroz.

July 24: Republican Army launches 80,000 men across the Ebro River in a last-ditch attempt to halt Franco's Nationalist insurgents; advancees forty kilometres then falters.

October 28: International volunteers leave Spain after farewell parade in Barcelona.

1939

January 15: Tarragona captured.

January 26: Barcelona falls.

February 15: Mass exodus begins across border into France.

April 1: Franco declares end of war.

Spanish Civil War: Miscellaneous Details

Battle Scenes in Story:

Fuentes de Ebro, October 12, 1937

Teruel, December 14, 1937–February 22, 1938

The Retreats, March 9, 1938–April 2, 1938

Role Played by Outside Countries:

The League of Nations' call for non-intervention is ignored by Germany, Italy, and Portugal. The British, French, U.S., and Canadian governments respect the League's plea, thus starving the elected Republican government of the materials needed to rebuff the Nationalist insurrection. The U.S.S.R. was the only large power to come to the aid of Republican Spain.

Statistics:

> 500,000+ deaths (150,000 by execution)
>
> 50,000 foreign volunteers joined the Republican cause
>
> 1,600+ Canadians fought in Spain; some 400 died. So divisive was this conflict that, to this day, Spaniards have difficulty speaking of it.

War Route Tours: April 1938–44:

The purpose was to raise money for Franco's cash-starved government and to give international legitimacy to the Nationalist insurgents. The tours highlighted Republican atrocities and depicted the Nationalist insurgency as a Holy Crusade against the forces tearing Spain apart—godlessness, communism, regional nationalisms.

15th International Brigades:

Freedom-loving people around the world saw in Spain an opportunity to halt the spread of fascism. Volunteers from dozens of countries defied governments to join the cause. The bulk of the International volunteers wound up in one of the following brigades: 11th Brigade (Thaelmann Battalion; primarily Germans opposed to Hitler); 12th Brigade (Garabaldi Battalion; Italians opposed to Mussolini); 13th Brigade (Dombrowski Battalion; East Europeans); 14th Brigade (French and Belgian); 15th Brigade (volunteers from English-speaking countries—Abraham Lincoln Battalion [Americans and Canadians], George Washington Battalion [Americans], Attlee Battalion [British], Mackenzie-Papineau Battalion [Canadians]).

Madrid:

Although attacked in the early stages of the war and subjected to air and artillery bombardment for three years, Madrid was never taken by force of arms, so became a symbol of anti-fascism. Only when the Republican Popular Army was finally vanquished in Aragon and Catalonia, in 1939, did the defenders of the city lay down their weapons.

Index of Historical Names
Occurring in the Story

Anderson, Jane (1888–1972)

American; married a Spanish aristocrat and became the Marquesa de Cienfuegos. An ardent fascist and Franco supporter, she led War Tours in Spain, beginning in 1938. During World War II, she was dubbed Lady Haw-Haw, for her pro-Hitler broadcasts from Germany.

Arcand, Adrien (1899–1967)

Published several small newspapers from 1929–39; Quebec nationalist, anti-foreigner, anti-Semitic, and pro-fascist. In 1934, he founded the National Socialist Christian Party of Quebec and dubbed himself the Canadian Führer. Although few in numbers, his adherents wore blue shirts, swastika armbands, and attended fascist rallies. Arcand was interned by the Canadian government during World War II.

Bennett, Richard Bedford (1870–1947)

Prime Minister of Canada, 1931–35; came to power when unemployment was at an all-time high of 26.6 percent. In spite of his reform initiatives—unemployment insurance, minimum wages, Prairie Farm Rehabilitation Act, Canadian Wheat Board Act—his name became synonymous with hard times. He took a firm stand with the On-to-Ottawa Trekkers in 1935, resulting in the Regina Riot.

Bethune, Norman, Dr. (1890–1939)

Socialist, communist, humanist, his achievements included: pioneer work in the treatment of tuberculosis in Montreal; organization of ambulant blood banks to treat wounded Republicans during the Spanish Civil War; doctor to Mao Tse Tung's soldiers during the Long March. Bethune died from an infected cut incurred while operating in China. To this day, he is considered a hero by the Chinese people.

Black, George (n.d.)

Union organizer and second-in-command to Slim Evans on the On-to-Ottawa Trek. Along with Evans, arrested from the speaker's platform in Regina's Market Square on July 1, 1935. This act, along with brutal treatment by the police, resulted in the Regina Riot.

Blum, Léon (1872–1950)
Prime Minister of France, 1936–37; first Jew to hold this office; jailed in France during World War II for anti-fascist leanings.

Bolín, Luis (1897–1969)
Headed foreign press services for Franco's Nationalist government in Spain.

Caballero, Francisco Largo (1869–1946)
Reformer and Socialist premier of the Spanish Republic at the outbreak of the war; forced out of office by the Communist Russian Central Committee, May 1937; replaced by Juan Négrin.

Cagney, James (1899–1986)
American film actor, famous for tough-guy roles.

Caruso, Enrico (1873–1921)
World-famous Italian tenor; made more than 290 recordings.

Cecil-Smith, Edward (n.d.)
Led the Mackenzie-Papineau Battalion; highest-ranking Canadian in Spain. Competent military commander, but strict and aloof with his men.

Clark, Paraskeva (1898–1986)
Russian-born Canadian painter (Montreal); friend of Norman Bethune; active member of Committee to Aid Spanish Democracy. Her art can be found in: National Gallery of Canada, Art Gallery of Greater Victoria, Dalhousie University Art Gallery, University of Lethbridge Art Gallery, and Virtual Museum of Canada.

Colbert, Claudette (1903–96)
Popular American film actress of the 1930s and '40s; won an Academy Award for best actress in the 1934 movie *It Happened One Night.*

Cowles, Virginia (1910–83)
American journalist with Hearst Universal News; reported from Nationalist Spain during the Civil War; spent time in St. Jean-de-Luz, France, on the Spanish border, waiting for a *salvoconducto* (travel pass) from the Conde de Ramblas; published *Looking for Trouble*, 1941.

Dempsey, Jack (1895–1983)
World heavyweight boxing champ, 1919–26.

Duplessis, Maurice (1890–1959)
Ultra-conservative Quebec politician who formed the Union Nationale. Served as premier, 1936–39 and 1944–59; ruled with the blessing and close co-operation of the Catholic Church; kept such a tight lid on social

and economic development that his reign became known as *La grande noirceur* (the great darkness).

Edward VIII (1894–1972)
King of Great Britain and uncle to Queen Elizabeth II; renounced his throne in 1936 to marry American socialite and divorcee Wallis Simpson.

Evans, Arthur (Slim) (1890–1944)
Relief Camp Workers' Union organizer; principal leader of the On-to-Ottawa Trek; led delegation of RCWU representatives from Regina to Ottawa for talks with Prime Minister Bennett.

Franco, General Francisco (1892–1975)
Senior officer in the Spanish Army in 1936. Referred to as an *Africanista* due to his years in Spanish Morocco; extremely popular with his troops in the African wars; demoted and sent to the Canary Islands by the Republican government, who feared his anti-Republican intentions; joined the insurgent generals in 1936 and quickly took charge of the Nationalist side. Authoritarian ruler of Spain, 1939–75.

Godbout, Adélard (1892–1956)
Agronomist and reformer, premier of Quebec, 1939–44. Created Hydro Quebec, brought electricity to farms, gave the vote to women, and rescinded repressive Duplessis laws against labour; encouraged Quebecers to join the World War II war effort, promising there would be no conscription; betrayed by federal Liberals in 1944 with enactment of conscription.

Groulx, Lionel (*l'abbé*) (1878–1967)
Historian, priest, and editor of French-nationalist newspapers such as *L'Action Française*. Struggled for the purity of Catholicism and French Quebec; advocated against outside influences—Hollywood movies, "racy" magazines, Anglicisms, intermarriage, the influx of foreigners. An ardent nationalist favoured by René Lévesque and Claude Ryan, who called him the "spiritual father of modern Quebec."

Hemingway, Ernest (1899–1961)
American author and reporter, 1925–55. Supported the Republican cause in the Spanish Civil War by raising money in the U.S. and visiting troops at the front.

Kaiser Wilhelm (1859–1941)
Last emperor of Germany (1888–1918). Although related to the British Royal Family, he competed vigorously with England in the realms of trade, economic development, and foreign aggrandizement; engaged

England and France in an arms race that developed into World War I; forced to abdicate in 1918, and was exiled to the Netherlands.

King, William Lyon Mackenzie (1874–1950)

Prime Minister of Canada, 1921–30 and 1935–48. Abolished Bennett's work camps; enacted the Foreign Enlistment Act to prohibit Canadians from volunteering for Spain.

Laurendeau, André (1912–68)

Influential Quebecer and Canadian who, along with Pierre Dansereau and Gilbert Manseau, was a founding member of Jeune-Canada. Nationalist, anti-Semitic, and pro-Catholic in his youth, he adopted liberal views during his years in France. In 1936, he publicly condemned Franco and the Nationalist insurrection in Spain; in later years he recanted earlier comments about Jews and worked to preserve Canadian federation.

Malraux, André (1901–76)

Famous French writer and aviator. Became a senior officer in the Spanish Republican Air Force; toured Europe, Canada, and the U.S. to raise money to buy warplanes for the war effort.

McCullagh, Francis (1874–1956)

Irish freelance war correspondent and Franco supporter. Published *In Franco's Spain: Being the Experiences of an Irish War-Correspondent during the Great Civil War Which Began in 1936* (London: Burns, Oates & Washbourne, 1937).

Négrin, Juan (1892–1956)

Socialist member of the Republican government who was forced to accede to the communists as the Spanish Civil War progressed; became prime minister in 1938.

O'Duffy, Eoin (1892–1944)

Organized and led the 15th Bandera, an Irish brigade of 670 volunteers for Franco. The brigade disgraced itself with its unruliness, drinking, and failure to obey orders under fire and were asked to leave by Franco. On return to Dublin, they marched through the streets to silence.

Philby, Harold (Kim) (1912–88)

While a student at Cambridge University in the 1930s, Philby was recruited by the Russians as a sleeper spy. In 1936, his handlers got him on as a correspondent for the *London Times* and sent him to Spain. His mission was to get close to the Nationalist leaders with a view to organizing the assassination of Franco. In short order, he become friendly with German generals in Salamanca and won the praises of Luis Bolín. Philby was a passenger in a car that was shelled by the Republicans during the final days of the Battle of Teruel; he was the only survivor. Three fellow correspondents from *Newsweek*, the Associated Press, and Reuters died. Franco personally awarded him the Red Cross of Military Merit for his head wound. In 1939, he joined the British secret service. From that date until 1962, when he was uncovered as a Russian spy, he passed on British and American secrets to his Russian handlers. He spent his last twenty-five years in Moscow growing increasingly disillusioned with communism.

Rabinovitch, Samuel (1909–2010).

A Jewish doctor who studied at the Université de Montréal, where he was top of his class. In June 1934, he was assigned to intern at Notre-Dame Hospital in Montreal. Almost immediately, doctors walked out in protest, refusing to work with a Jew. In total, doctors from five Montreal hospitals joined the strike. Rabinovitch resigned and moved to the United States, where he set up practice. After several years, he returned to Montreal, where he became a popular and talented doctor.

Rockwell, Norman (1894–1978)

Popular twentieth-century American painter. His illustrations of everyday American life made the cover of the *Saturday Evening Post* several times a year over four decades.

Rose, Fred (1907–83)

Polish immigrant; Jewish, communist, trade union organizer and orator; friend to Norman Bethune, enemy to Premier Duplessis, whom he accused of having close relations with Hitler and Mussolini; jailed in the 1930s; elected to the House of Commons in 1943 and 1945; jailed in 1947 on a vague charge of violating the Official Secrets Act; deported to Poland.

Roosevelt, Franklin D. (1882–1945)

Four-term President of the United States, 1933–45; guided the U.S. through the Great Depression and World War II.

Salazar, António de Oliveira (1889–1970)

Prime Minister of Portugal, 1932–68; opposed liberalism, socialism, trade unionism, and communism; championed the role of clergy in all aspects of Portuguese life. With the assistance of the secret police, he repressed civil liberties and social freedoms; an inspiration to ultraconservatives in the western world.

Schmeling, Max (1905–2005)
German boxer and world heavyweight champ, 1930–32; became a symbol for Hitler's Germany after defeating black American boxer Joe Louis in 1936. In a rematch in 1938, Louis demolished him in the first round. Served with the German paratroopers in World War II.

Schweitzer, Albert, Dr. (1875–1965)
World-famous German musician, philanthropist, theologian, and medical doctor. Left Europe and a brilliant career to open and maintain a hospital in Gabon, Africa. Recipient of the Nobel Peace Prize in 1952.

Stalin, Joseph (1879–1953)
Russian communist leader who seized control of the government after Lenin's death in 1924. Ruthlessly implemented reforms in agriculture and industry resulting in millions of deaths; led his country to victory over Hitler's invading armies.

Glossary of Terms and Organizations

Abraham Lincolns
Battalion of the 15th Brigade of the Republican International Volunteer Army; made up primarily of North American volunteers.

Achat chez nous
Program sponsored by French-Canadian nationalists in the 1930s to encourage their people to patronize French-owned enterprises.

Alpargatas
Cheap, rope-soled sandals issued to Republican soldiers during the Spanish Civil War.

Attlees
Battalion of the 15th Brigade of the Republican International Volunteer Army; made up largely of volunteers from the British Isles.

Bandera Irlandesa
The 15th Battalion in the Nationalist Legionario Army; made up of 670 Irish volunteers for Franco. See entry for Eoin O'Duffy for more detail.

Black Flames
Italian army division sent to Spain by Mussolini to assist Franco. The Black Flames were formed from volunteer militia from the Fascist party (Mussolini's Blackshirts) and from regular soldiers.

Carlist
Political movement in Spain before and during the Civil War; advocated a return to the monarchy and the re-establishment of the Roman Catholic Church in affairs of state; raised a fanatical army of devout Catholics—the Requetés—to fight alongside Franco.

CCF
Co-operative Commonwealth Federation, a socialist political party formed in Canada in 1932. In the late 1950s, the name was changed to New Democratic Party.

Chilkoot Pass
A mountain pass used to get from the Pacific coast to the Klondike gold fields in the Yukon, 1897–98; steep and dangerous.

Comintern
Short for the Communist International, an organization founded in

Russia in 1919 and disbanded in 1943. Controlled from Moscow, its objective was to spread revolt and communism to the world using whatever means necessary — persuasion, infiltration, armed force. In the 1930s, it worked its way into many Canadian unions.

Condor Legion

Collective name given to the German units fighting for Franco and fascism during the Spanish Civil War; used by Hitler to train troops, test weaponry, and experiment with such tactics as carpet bombing and ground-air coordination (a dress rehearsal for World War II). An estimated 19,000 German airmen and ground troops gained combat experience in Spain with the Condor Legion.

Cook's Tours

A tour company founded by Thomas Cook in the eighteenth century to provide Grand Tours of the European continent.

Corporatism

A philosophy by which elected officials, business, labour, and clergy share in the decision-making process for the greater benefit of all society. In theory, this was to achieve harmony in all sectors; in practice, strong elements from the government, corporations, and clergy tended to make decisions detrimental to workers.

Dombrowski

The 13th Brigade of the Republican International Volunteer Army; predominantly Slavic volunteers.

Falangista (Falange)

A fascist party founded in Spain in 1933 to counter the politics of the Republican socialist government. During the Civil War, it raised more than 250,000 soldiers for Franco. In 1937, Franco co-opted the party and blended it with the Carlists to form an authoritarian body that would govern Spain, under his leadership, until his death in 1975.

Garibaldi

The 12th Brigade of the Republican International Volunteer Army; Italian volunteers opposed to Mussolini and fascism.

George Washington

Battalion of the 15th Brigade of the Republican International Volunteer Army; predominantly American with some Canadian and Spanish volunteers.

Guardia Civil

Spanish rural police force famous for their tricorne patent-leather hats.

Organized in the nineteenth century to deal with bandits in the country-side, they were brought into urban areas on occasion to suppress various movements. By 1936, they had become a well-organized and unpopular paramilitary organization.

Internationale

Anthem of international socialism as promoted by the U.S.S.R.,1922–44. For years, it was the U.S.S.R.'s de facto anthem. The lyrics appeal to the downtrodden: "Stand up damned of the earth, Stand up prisoners of hunger, Of the past let us make a clean slate, Enslaved masses stand up, The world is about to change."

Labour Camps

Established by R.B. Bennett in 1932 as a solution to the problem of large numbers of unemployed men during the Great Depression. Run and operated by the Canadian Army, the camps were established in remote areas, where the men were paid twenty cents a day, plus food, clothing, and shelter, for menial, often meaningless, work. In them, radicals abounded, and socialism and communism were rampant. In total, 20,000 men joined the camps. They were abolished by Mackenzie King in 1936.

La Patente

Colloquial name for the Order of Jacques Cartier, a secret organization of influential Roman Catholics. Members were selected to join; their mission was to promote language and faith and to assist in keeping people and society on the correct moral path.

La Sagrada Familia

Roman Catholic basilica in Barcelona, Spain, designed by Antoni Gaudi. Construction began in 1882 and continues to this day, interrupted only by the Spanish Civil War.

League of Nations

Formed after World War I to maintain peace among nations; failed in the 1930s to halt foreign invasions — Italians in Ethiopia, Japanese in China, Germans in Poland. Reconstituted as the United Nations after World War II.

Legionario

Soldier of the Spanish Foreign Legion (in reality, few foreign nationals joined). (See Spanish Foreign Legion.)

Mackenzie-Papineau Battalion

A battalion in the 15th International Brigade of the Republican Army, formed July 1, 1937. Named after two Canadian freedom fighters of the nineteenth century, due to the large number of Canadians in its ranks.

Moors

Muslim troops from Spanish-controlled Spanish Morocco. Trained alongside the Foreign Legion in the Spanish-Moroccan wars of the 1920s, they proved invaluable to Franco.

No pasaran

Republican rallying cry coined by popular anti-fascist politician, Dolores Ibárruri (also known as La Pasionaria). An inspirational orator, she harangued the troops with slogans such as "better to die on your feet than live on your knees."

Pathé News

A company that provided newsreels in movie theatres before the advent of television.

Pure laine

Term for French Canadians who can trace their ancestry to New France.

Requeté

See Carlists above.

Schmata trade

The clothing industry; from the Yiddish word, *shmat*, meaning old piece of cloth.

Spanish Foreign Legion

Formed in the 1920s to put down rebellions in Spanish Morocco. It worked closely with local Moorish units in those conflicts and, under Franco's leadership, became a highly professional army in the process. Shortly after the right-wing insurgents had risen up to overthrow the Republican government in 1936, Franco made arrangements with Hitler to have the Foreign Legion, plus Moorish troops, flown to southern Spain. As the Civil War spread, they became his elite military spearhead.

Teruel

Major battle and turning point for Franco's Nationalists during the Spanish Civil War, where temperatures reached −20°C. Of the 100,000 casualties over two months, one-quarter were due to severe frostbite.

Thaelmann

The 11th Brigade of the Republican International Volunteer Army; volunteers were predominantly German citizens opposed to Hitler.

YMHA

Young Men's Hebrew Association.

Select Bibliography

SPANISH CIVIL WAR

Beeching, William. *Canadian Volunteers: Spain 1936–1939*. Regina: Canadian Plains Research Center, 1989.

Beevor, Anthony. *The Battle for Spain: The Spanish Civil War 1936–1939*. London: Penguin Books, 2006.

Borkenau, Franz. *The Spanish Cockpit: An Eye Witness Account of the Political and Social Conflicts of the Spanish Civil War*. London: Faber and Faber, 1937.

Cowles, Virginia. *Looking for Trouble*. New York: Harper, c1941.

Davis, Frances. *A Fearful Innocence*. Kent, Ohio: Kent State University Press, ca. 1981.

Fraser, Ronald. *Blood of Spain: An Oral History of the Spanish Civil War*. New York: Penguin Books, 1981.

Gurney, Jason. *Crusade in Spain*. Newton Abbot: Readers Union, 1974.

Howard, Victor. *The Mackenzie-Papineau Battalion: Canadian Participation in the Spanish Civil War*. Toronto: Copp Clark, 1969.

Keene, Judith. *Fighting for Franco: International Volunteers in Nationalist Spain during the Spanish Civil War, 1936–39*. London: Leicester University Press, 2001.

Landis, Arthur. *Death in the Olive Groves: American Volunteers in the Spanish Civil War*. Paragon House, 1989.

Martin, Russell. *Picasso's War: The Destruction of Guernica and the Masterpiece that Changed the World*. Penguin Group, 2002.

McGarry, Fearghal. *Irish Politics and the Spanish Civil War*. Cork University Press, 1999.

Nash, Mary. *Spanish Women in Nationalist Spain*. Denver, CO: Arden Press, ca. 1995.

Orwell, George. *Homage to Catalonia*. 1938. Reprint, New York: Harvest/HBJ Books, 1980.

Pawel, Rebecca C. *Death of a Nationalist*. Soho Press, 2003.

Petrou, Michael. *Renegades: Canadians in the Spanish Civil War.* Vancouver: University of British Columbia Press, 2008.

Preston, Paul. *Franco: A Biography.* London: HarperCollins, 1993.

Thomas, Hugh. *The Spanish Civil War*. London: Penguin Books, 1977.

Wyden, Peter. *The Passionate War: The Narrative History of the Spanish Civil War, 1936–39*. New York: Simon and Schuster, 1983.

Zuehlke, Mark. *The Gallant Cause: Canadians in the Spanish Civil War*. Vancouver: Whitecap Books, 1996.

QUEBEC AND MONTREAL

Anctil, Pierre. *Le rendez-vous manqué: Les Juifs de Montréal face au Québec de l'entre-deux guerres.* Québec: Institut Québécois de recherché, 1988.

Betcherman, Lita-Rose. *The Swastika and the Maple Leaf: Fascist Movements in Canada in the Thirties.* Fitzhenry & Whiteside, 1975.

Brisson, M., and S. Coté-Gauthier. *Montréal de vive memoire.* Triptyque, 1994.

Burns, Patricia. *The Shamrock and the Shield: An Oral History of Montreal.* Montreal: Véhicule Press, 1998.

Cook, Ramsay. *Canada, Quebec and the Uses of Nationalism.* Toronto: McClelland & Stewart, 1995.

Davies, Alan, ed. *Antisemitism in Canada.* Waterloo, ON: Wilfrid Laurier University Press, 1992.

Délisle, Esther. *The Traitor and the Jew: Anti-Semitism and the Delirium of Extremist Right-Wing Nationalism in French Canada from 1929 to 1939.* Montreal: R. Davies Publishing, distributed by Stewart House, 1993.

Dumas, Evelyn. *The Bitter Thirties in Quebec.* Montreal: Black Rose Books, 1975.

Horton, Donald J. *André Laurendeau: French Canadian Nationalist.* Oxford University Press, 1992.

Kinsella, Warren. *Web of Hate.* HarperCollins, 1994.

Layton, Irving. *Waiting for the Messiah.* Toronto: McClelland & Stewart, 1985.

Lowe, Mick. *One Woman Army: The Life and Times of Claire Culhaine.* Toronto: Macmillan Canada, ca. 1992.

Marelli, Nancy. *Stepping Out: The Golden Age of Montreal Night Clubs.* Montreal: Véhicule Press, 2004.

McLeod, Wendell. *Bethune: The Montreal Years.* Toronto: J. Lorimer, 1978.

Medresh, Israël. *Le Montréal Juif entre les deux guerres.* Sillery, Que: Septentrion, 2001.

Nulman, Stuart. *Beyond the Mountain: True Tales about Montreal.* Callawind, 2002.

Oliver, Michael. *The Passionate Debate.* Montreal: Véhicule Press, 1991.

Richler, Mordecai. *Oh Canada! Oh Quebec: Requiem for a Divided Country.* New York: Viking, 1992.

Robinson, Ira, and Mervin Butovsky, eds. *Renewing Our Days: Montreal Jews in the Twentieth Century.* Montreal: Vehicle Press, 1995.

Viau, Roger. *Au milieu, la montagne.* Montreal: Éditions Beauchemin, 1951.

Weintraub, William. *City Unique.* Toronto: McClelland & Stewart, 1996.

Young, Robert. *The Struggle for Quebec.* McGill-Queen's University Press, 1999.

LABOUR / RIDING THE RAILS / ON-TO-OTTAWA TREK

Algren, Nelson. *Someone in Boots.* Reprint, New York: Thunder Mouth's Press, 1987.

Baird, Irene. *Waste Heritage.* 1939. Reprint, Toronto: Macmillan Company of Canada, 1974.

Brown, Lorne. *When Freedom Was Lost.* Montreal: Black Rose Books, 1987.

Caragota, Warren. *Alberta Labour: A Heritage Untold.* Toronto: J. Lorimer, 1979.

Grayson, Linda M., and Michael Bliss. *The Wretched of Canada.* Toronto: University of Toronto Press, 1971.

Horn, Michiel. *Years of Despair, 1929–39.* Toronto: Grolier, 1986.

Howard, Victor. *We Were the Salt of the Earth.* Regina: Canadian

Plains Research Center, University of Regina, 1985.

Liversedge, Ronald. *Recollections of the On-to-Ottawa Trek*. Toronto: McClelland & Stewart, 1973.

Neatby, Blair. *The Politics of Chaos: Canada in the Thirties*. Golden Dog Press, 2003.

Purdy, A.W. *The Iron Road*. Purdy Papers. University of Saskatchewan, Regina. (Purdy's personal notes of his experiences riding the rails in the Depression; available on-line.)

Scotton, Clifford A. *Canadian Labour and Politics*. Canadian Labour Congress, 1979.

Waiser, Bill. *All Hell Can't Stop Us*. Calgary: Fifth House Ltd., 2003.

About the Author

TERRENCE RUNDLE WEST was raised in Hearst, Northern Ontario, and studied at Carleton University and the University of British Columbia. His second book, *Run of the Town* (GSPH), won the 2007 Northern "Lit" Award. A former teacher and school administrator, he lives in Ottawa with his wife, Peggy.

TO ORDER MORE COPIES:

GENERAL STORE PUBLISHING HOUSE
499 O'Brien Road, Box 415, Renfrew, Ontario, Canada K7V 4A6
Tel 1.800.465.6072 • Fax 1.613.432.7184
www.gsph.com